D0815970

WILD SUN

Explore more of the Wild Sun universe:
TheWildSun.com

Follow the authors;
Facebook.com/TheAhmadBros
Twitter.com/TheAhmadBros

For more great science fiction and fantasy novels:
UproarBooks.com

Follow the publisher:
Facebook.com/UproarBooks
Twitter.com/UproarBooks

THE WILD SUN SERIES | BOOK ONE

WILD SUN

EHSAN AHMAD AND SHAKIL AHMAD

Uproar
Books

5232 ALMADALE CIRCLE, NASHVILLE, TN 37027
UPROARBOOKS.COM

WILD SUN

Published by Uproar Books, LLC.

Cover illustration by Kirill Pashkov.

Printed in the United States of America.

ISBN 978-1-949671-00-1

First paperback edition.

To Jd'A

1

Cerrin had waited a long time for the river lilies.

Early in the season they were too soft and she'd never have reached the far bank. But having watched for the last month she knew they would be rigid now, the dark green skin hard to the touch. Even the smallest lily was eight feet across; they formed an unbroken carpet across the water, flowing past at quite a speed.

Cerrin was moving a lot faster. She charged down the slope, heart pounding in her ears, grass thrashing at her legs.

Twenty-five, twenty-six...

That's how long the siren had been going; she guessed someone had spotted her climbing over the wall. The Vitaari on patrol duty would be ready, but Cerrin knew they couldn't get to the river in under eighty seconds; it took them that long to power up and launch.

Thirty-one, thirty-two...

She had to reach the thick forest on the other side. The guards couldn't see through the thick canopy from the air, and on foot they were slow. If she got across, she could get away.

Cerrin altered direction slightly to make sure she was heading for the island. It was small and covered with trees, but she would move quicker across solid ground and there was only forty feet of water between it and the far bank.

Her last step was inches from the edge. She launched herself into the air, clearing the closest lily easily, landing in the middle of the next one. Water had collected on the surface. She skidded but did not fall, used her impetus to keep her body moving.

Forty-one, forty-two...

She leapt onto the next one, disturbing a flock of yellow-beaked hyatha on the island. They flapped away into the still-dark sky.

This lily was weak. The middle of it folded, her foot almost tearing through the base. But she dragged herself clear, reached the edge, leapt once more.

More surface water. Both feet went at the same time, and she came down on her backside. It seemed to take an age for her to get back on her feet and go again. She was close to the island when she heard the hyatha squawking. That meant they were coming.

Already? Don't look back.

She jumped onto the slick, grassy bank. As she tried to throw her weight forward, her right foot slipped. She clutched a handful of branches from the nearest tree and hauled herself up.

Ikala, god of battle–hear me, see me, help me.

The engine screamed as a guard swooped down. Sounded like just the one. Cerrin heard the combat shell's jets strike the water as she charged on, dodging through the narrow trees. The Vitaari wouldn't actually fire on her, she knew that—they never had before. Then again, with the help of their cursed machines they wouldn't need to.

Don't look back!

Judging by the noise, the guard had landed and was simply smashing his way across the island. Cerrin stumbled through a thorn bush and glimpsed the water ahead. A slender tree trunk came flying over her right shoulder and struck another, showering her with berries and twigs. She looked up as the trunk plummeted toward her. She dropped low, threw her hands up to cover her head.

But no impact came; the trunk had lodged itself in the branches. She set off again.

The guard bellowed something in his own language. As a clear path opened up ahead, Cerrin stole a backwards glance. He was blundering through the trees, the bulky metallic suit tangled in vines and branches. Cerrin might have felt happier had she not known they usually operated in pairs.

Picking her spot carefully, she jumped out onto another solid lily. She caught her first sight of the red-leaved scorra bushes on the far bank.

Not far now. I can make it.

Suddenly she was in a patch of smaller lilies. She landed hard, and her foot went straight through. Fingers scraping at green fibers, she pulled her herself out of the water and leapt again.

Two steps, jump, land. Two steps, jump, land. Her legs were aching, her throat tight. The lilies ahead looked wide and strong. Five more, maybe four.

Now she could hear the howl of a second engine, and it came at her quicker than the first, blocking out every other noise.

Three more lilies. Beyond the last of them was a thick patch of scorra. She would dive straight in, scramble through, stay low.

She threw her arms out as she landed, ran on, leapt again.

Two more.

Water blown up by the jets blasted at her back. She could hear something beeping.

One long step took her across the lily. She leapt, landed well. The bank was only feet away. She could almost touch the leaves. She ran, jumped—

Something big and impossibly strong gripped her right ankle and lifted her. She screamed as her momentum was stopped in an instant. She fell forward, then hung there, blood dripping from her ankle and rushing to her head. She felt a bone splinter in her leg, pierce her flesh.

Cold water hit her face. The pitch of the engine altered as she was lifted higher.

Ikala, god of battle, strike with me.

She pulled the tiny dagger from her belt, pivoted upward and spied the giant white fingers gripping her leg. She stabbed at one of the silvery knuckle joints, but the blade broke.

She screamed again. The hand moved, turning her toward the Vitaari guard. The combat shell boosted his height to twelve feet; the bulbous metal limbs magnifying his already huge bulk. Through the transparent helmet she could see the leering stare. He was known as Stripe because of the blue streaks tattooed across his face.

He was grinning.

They gave her thirty days in the cage. It was a rusty old thing hung from a solitary tree next to the mine path. A few of the other workers risked a nod as they trudged past, but none of them said anything. Most of them had been in Mine Fourteen for many years. Cerrin had been there only two, one of the newest arrivals. She was proud of that.

For the first week she had to sit; the ankle was too weak and painful to stand on. The Vitaari surgeon who fixed her up at the infirmary had told her she was lucky. The hands of the combat shell could easily crush a human, but Stripe had not snapped her ankle, only fractured it. The surgeon said that wasn't the only reason she was lucky: after three escape attempts, anyone else would have been eliminated. But the governor of Fourteen had been told that the building of a new mine in the Great Forest was going ahead. A scout ship would be dispatched there soon, and she would be on it.

No one else in Fourteen understood the terrain and the creatures of the Great Forest like Cerrin. She knew it; the Vitaari knew it. She helped them because it got her out of the camp and back to where she wanted to be, even if only for a day or so. Some of the other prisoners hated her because of it, but she hated them too; they had given up.

At the end of the second week, Governor Yeterris came to visit her. Even amongst the invaders he was tall, nine feet at least, with a lean, powerful frame that belied his age. He was wearing his usual outfit of flowing white robes with a golden chain around his neck. The translator was attached to his collar. It used what was known as trade or Corvosian—an unsophisticated but widely spoken language that enabled the disparate tribes of the planet to communicate. The Vitaari had insisted that only trade be spoken by their captives; Cerrin had known only a few words when she arrived but was now fluent.

The translator got most words and meanings right, but it used only the one impassive voice and caused an awkward delay.

When Yeterris arrived beneath the cage at dusk, the last of the returning day shift gave him a wide berth. He clearly felt no need for either a weapon or a bodyguard. The dying rays of the sun lit his silvery skin as he looked up at her.

"They are feeding you well, I trust?"

Cerrin had learned how to handle him—with grudging cooperation. She alone in Fourteen had an alternative to absolute, unquestioning subservience.

"They are."

The food was in a sack at the back of the cage. She'd had to ration it carefully, but there was enough. She had plenty of water too and had even managed a shower during a rainstorm.

"Fifteen days left?"

"Yes, governor." She stood up straight for him, even though her ankle hurt.

"I do like your hair, girl. It's as dark as my daughter's."

Yeterris had complimented her before but only when they were alone. At six feet, Cerrin was one of the tallest natives at the mine, male or female. The guards often told her that with some "proper" clothes and some skin coloring she could pass for one of them.

"Can I trust you to behave yourself from now on?" Yeterris continued. "There will be other senior officers joining us on the next scouting mission."

"If I gave you a promise, you wouldn't believe me."

The governor paced around, hands clasped behind him. "If you try anything like this again, the consequences will be most unpleasant. Three attempts? *Three*, Cerrin? It simply cannot be tolerated. I will not allow you to disrupt the smooth running of this installation in such a way. So, I ask again—will you behave yourself?"

Cerrin wished she had her old bow in her hands. She would launch an arrow straight into that veiny neck and watch the black blood flow. With a hundred more like her and the favor of Ikala, they could take

Mine Fourteen: slay this brutal bastard and every last one of his men. But there were no hundred warriors. There weren't even ten.

"Yes, governor."

Sonus knew what was coming. He leaned his drill against the cavern wall, removed his gloves and took a long drink from his water flask. Tanus arrived out of breath, face smeared with dust from his morning's work. There wasn't much chance of being noticed down here, but he would have only minutes to spare.

He was a large man with thinning hair and a blunt nose. Like Sonus, his overalls had been gray to begin with but were now almost as black as the terodite they drilled out of the mountain. He cast a brief glance at the impressive haul Sonus had cut that morning.

"What you said about the dump—the parts in there. Do you still think you can—"

"I should not have mentioned that."

"How long? How long to make something we can use?"

Sonus sighed.

"How much damage would it do?" Tanus took a step closer, shadowing Sonus's face. "Listen, Rinus isn't up to it. He doesn't know what he's doing. But you..."

"I shouldn't have said anything. Yes, the materials are there to create some sort of crude device, but it would be hard to locate them and almost impossible to put them together. And what's the point? One weapon?"

"It's a start."

Sonus held up his hands. "I'm sorry. I can't help you."

"Can't? Or won't?"

"What difference does it make?"

Tanus shook his head. "I saw you—trying to avoid me yesterday. I saw you, with them. Like some little pet, fixing their machines in return for light shifts and better rations. You make me sick, Sonus. You would rather help them than help us?"

Sonus said nothing until Tanus turned and walked away. "I've made some calculations."

The big man stopped. "What?"

"Based on what I've picked up from the guards. Did you know there are no more than six thousand of us left in the mines? Maybe less."

"And?"

"The Vitaari are only constructing one more new mine. The reserves of terodite and aronium will be gone within two years, the malkus within three. They will leave. We must do what we can to preserve those of us that remain."

"You think you're the only one that listens, Sonus? I listen too, and I know what they did to the people of the other worlds they conquered. Has anything you've seen of them suggested to you that they are stupid enough to leave us alive—so that we can rebuild and one day take our revenge?"

"They are not all the same."

"The others said you wouldn't listen. Have you no honor?"

"I believe so. And more sense than some."

Tanus muttered an oath and left.

Sonus leaned back against the chilly rock. From the shaft and all the others connected to it came the endless, familiar buzz of the drills.

For fifteen years he had labored here. At first, they had been working just twenty yards beneath the surface. Now he was half a mile down, and what he coughed up in the morning had gone from gray to brown to black. The pain in his lungs was getting worse too, though it had been partly eased by the medicine he'd requested instead of extra rations. Tanus wouldn't care that he'd given most of it to his neighbor for his ailing son. Nor would he care that it was Sonus who had persuaded the governor to allow the workers to take pure air canisters down to breathe during their breaks. Or that his pleas had saved the life of a man who'd dared insult a guard.

Because Tanus listened only to his heart. Sonus knew it would be easy to do the same. Every last man and woman left alive on Corvos had the same collection of sad tales, the same burning desire to be free. Tanus was now left without a single member of his family since his daughter had perished the previous year.

Sonus *could* create a weapon, perhaps even kill one or two Vitaari before they killed him. But men had tried before, and all they had achieved was to endanger those closest to them and make life harder for everyone else. Sonus listened to his head.

He had his gloves back on and was about to recover his drill when the com-cell pinned to his sleeve beeped. The Vitaari needed him.

It took him half an hour to reach the surface: twenty-five minutes of walking, then five in the elevator. The colossal main shaft was almost empty; everyone was working below. Sonus trudged slowly toward the light, giving his eyes time to adjust.

The guard on duty was sitting on a metal pallet, bulky rifle laid out beside him. He was shorter than average but very broad. The dot tattoos across his face were red; most of the others were blue or green. His fellow guards called him "Faraway" because he came from some remote, isolated region of their home world. Sonus had seen them laughing at him and playing practical jokes. And because he often seemed to take his frustrations out on the workers, Sonus kept his distance and waited for his permission to pass. Without looking up, Faraway waved one huge hand toward the light.

The compound was almost as quiet as the main shaft. Eyes still narrowed, Sonus drank in the sweet first breath of air. He hurried on, walking alongside the conveyor that took the largest and hardest chunks of ore to the warehouse. He passed the guard barracks, the infirmary, and the armory. The only sign of activity was two cleaning drones scrubbing the wheels of a trailer.

The tower loomed over all else, bulbous head blinking with red and orange lights. At the bottom were two guards on sentry duty, rifles cradled across their chests. They wore identical plain black fatigues with wide belts and enormous boots. Two administrators were also there, clad in their gray robes, both poring over a data-pad. One of them was Kadessis, the Vitaari who gave Sonus his assignments.

"Ah, there you are."

Sonus nodded cordially and looked up at him. "Sir."

Like all the invaders, Kadessis had protruding bones in his cheeks that seemed to be pushing at the glittering skin. When he was anxious—as he was today—they twitched and looked as if they might burst through. Sonus found Kadessis more even-tempered and approachable than most of them and respected his intellect; the Vitaari had picked up trade in a matter of months.

"Another problem with a drill motivator. It's over in the maintenance yard. The drones aren't getting anywhere, and all the engineers are occupied. Have a look, would you? I've assigned a team of four to help you with the labor."

"Yes, sir."

On his way to the yard, Sonus passed two women. They were carrying trays loaded with steaming food, probably for the staff in the tower. Sonus knew them both by name and greeted them. One replied coldly; the other said nothing. He had become accustomed to such treatment.

There was only a single guard on duty at the yard, and he ignored Sonus as he approached the heavy drill. The big machines usually ran well enough, but occasionally the motivators got clogged up with aronium dust. It was usually a case of removing the affected parts, then cleaning and replacing them; a task that seemed beyond the drones. Two of these white cubic devices hovered, dormant, close to the rear of the drill.

Also present was the work crew. All four were from Sonus's shift; men he had worked and lived with for years. He was delighted to find that one of them was Karas. Sonus smiled, but his old friend barely looked at him. The others seemed happy to escape their usual work in the mine.

"Let's get the cover off."

Karas hung back as the other four began work.

Sonus gave some instructions, then walked over to him. "Are you all right?"

Karas could usually be relied upon for a story or a joke. Sonus had always admired his ability to raise the spirits of others. But he still hadn't spoken.

"Is it Qari?" he asked. "I thought she was feeling better."

Karas gripped his arm, fingers trembling. He whispered, "Sonus, she is with child."

Sonus held onto his friend, but now he could find no words. It was hard to believe there had been a time when such news was greeted with joy.

2

Troop Captain Erasmer Vellerik had his hand on the small container's handle when the wall-screen flickered into life. The voice came a moment later.

"Sir? Captain Vellerik?"

"Accept."

Leaving the container, he plucked his sleeping tunic from the bed and pulled it on, then wandered in front of the screen. Officer Kereslaa looked as annoyingly fresh and eager as ever. Could it really be that another three days had passed? It was so hard to keep track of time aboard the ship.

"Yes?" Vellerik wiped his sore eyes.

"The update, sir." Kerreslaa examined his superior's clothing, or rather the lack of it. "Should I call back?"

"No. Go ahead."

"We've just finished the cycle. There are five issues worthy of discussion."

Vellerik nodded wearily and wished he'd stayed in bed and turned off coms.

"Firstly, an incident at Mine Two. A worker claimed illness, but the infirmary confirmed he was suffering only from a minor ailment. He returned to work, but a small group of others protested. The duty officer ordered two jolts for each. Production was not affected."

"Two? Was that really necessary?"

Kerreslaa paused. "Clearly the duty officer thought so, sir."

Vellerik had never heard of jolt-rods before he'd been assigned to Corvos. He had now seen the punishment delivered numerous times. The Planetary Administrator claimed the permanent damage was minimal, but the smoke that rose from the natives' skulls suggested otherwise. Vellerik was amazed that any of the poor little bastards ever dared put a foot wrong.

"Perhaps you might suggest to Governor Varrata that one jolt is probably sufficient."

"Yes, sir."

They both knew it wouldn't make any difference. Technically speaking, all such matters came under the jurisdiction of the Administration. Vellerik—who led the small but well equipped Colonial Guard detachment—was kept informed of anything related to security but usually only required to mobilize his force in the event of a significant uprising. There hadn't been one for months—a brief, bloody affair at Mine Six—and he hoped it stayed that way. There was, however, a price to be paid for this peace. His twelve-strong team were almost as bored and depressed as he was; there were only so many drills you could run in a cargo bay.

"Secondly, Mine Ten reports more sightings of primitives."

Vellerik peered at the footage now running in one corner of the screen. It showed around ten barefoot natives in rudimentary clothing. One man was shaking a spear, having presumably noticed the observation drone.

Vellerik almost laughed. "Is Governor Sekithis worried?"

"They did damage those water pipes last month, sir."

Theoretically also a member of the Colonial Guard, Kerreslaa acted as a liaison between Vellerik and the Administration. But he spent most of his time on the planet and consequently saw things from the governors' point of view.

"When Sekithis sent out a squad, they gathered in significant force before eventually retreating," the officer added.

Vellerik sighed. It was all so pathetic. The natives had barely advanced beyond bow and arrow. His unit, when fully armed, could muster enough firepower to conduct a small war.

"Tell him I'll bring the troop down to scare them off. It'll do them good to get some fresh air."

"Very well, sir. Thirdly…"

And so it went on. The next three issues were even less interesting, and Vellerik was glad when it was over. Afterwards, he gave serious thought to returning to bed. Instead, he changed the wall-screen to a mirror and looked at himself.

His skin was pale and dull, his eyes lined with yellow; all sure signs that he was in poor condition. He tried to tense his body and was unimpressed with the results. Much of his tall, broad frame now lacked definition, and his hair, which had stayed so black for so long, was at last showing signs of gray. Vellerik shrugged. A man of one hundred and nine was permitted a bit of gray.

He glanced over at the container, which had remained buried under some spare uniforms since he'd arrived all those months ago. He'd tried to keep himself busy—the drills, exercise, games with the troop, more drills, more exercise. He'd even made an ill-fated attempt to learn the local language. But, like a prisoner, he was marking time. His chosen one—Seevarta—was on the other side of the quadrant, and he wouldn't see her until he completed his seventieth (and last) year of service.

He'd heard a rumor that the ship was due to receive an important visitor in the next few days. But until he was called upon, Vellerik had nothing to do.

He walked back to the container, typed in the code, and watched the lid ease open. At the bottom was a transparent cube strewn with fake greenery. Vellerik was relieved to see that the status light was on, which meant that the insect was still alive. Also still functioning was the small but essential device that regulated the air and provided sustenance. The Almana soarer was a rather beautiful creature, its narrow body dwarfed by the broad, delicate wings. Vellerik reckoned the poor thing must miss flying; it had been in the cube since he'd bought it from a dealer on Deskalon V.

He picked up the cube, checked his door was locked, then sat on the bed. Refusing to allow himself second thoughts, he clicked one of the capsules in a row attached to the side of the box. It would take about a minute for it to fill itself with the substance known as Almana's Breath.

Vellerik lay down beside the box, hand on the capsule. The trick was to concentrate solely on the visions you wanted the narcotic to augment. The effects varied, but some of his best sessions had seemed more real than the most convincing dream. He closed his eyes and thought of Seevarta.

The capsule beeped, which meant it was full. He detached it from the box, removed the cover, and put it in his mouth.

An hour later, Vellerik rose slowly from the bed, mind still awash with her. Wondering why he hadn't indulged sooner, he replaced the cube in the container and hid it. He would limit himself to one session every few days.

Vellerik washed his face, then put on his uniform. He knew now that he would never get used to the dark blue of the Colonial Guard, having worn the black of the Imperial Legions for most of his career. He left his decoration bar on his bedside table; it was so heavy now with rings of various colored metals that he found it uncomfortable. There had been a time when he wouldn't leave his room without it.

"Captain Vellerik."

This time it was Deputy Administrator Rasikaar.

"Accept."

Rasikaar did not look happy. Behind him, others were rushing around.

"Count Talazeer is already here."

"What? I thought—"

"So did we. Just prepare yourself and your troop. I have already notified your second-in-command. Ceremonial dress. All personnel will assemble when the count is ready for us."

"Very well. What—"

Rasikaar had already gone.

It took Vellerik a while to find the glossy red band used for such occasions. He hung it from his right shoulder to his left hip, then clicked his sidearm onto his belt. Still feeling slightly dizzy, he threw water on his face again and checked himself a final time in the mirror before leaving.

As the door slid shut behind him, he marched away along the corridor. To his right was a long, narrow viewport; outside, the endless oblivion of deep space. The *Galtaryax* was on the far side of Corvos from its star; there was only the single planet and its two moons orbiting what the natives called the "Wild Sun." He rather liked the name, though he had no idea of its origin.

Two elevators and another long walk took him to the loading bay allocated to his unit. The men were lined up outside and snapped to attention when Troop Lieutenant Triantaa gave a shout.

"Morning all," said Vellerik quietly, walking down the line. Triantaa was a good man; conscientious and well organized. Consequently, Vellerik could find no fault in the troop's appearance. He could have invented an imaginary stain on a boot or blemish on a uniform, but what was the point?

"Excellent. How's the arm, Vaterann?"

The trooper's combat shell had malfunctioned five days previous, throwing him into an airlock door. The surgeon had already done his work, but this was the soldier's first day back on his feet.

Vaterann's mouth opened, but nothing came out. He was looking over his superior's shoulder toward the elevator. Vellerik turned and saw Deputy Administrator Rasikaar approaching. He was a small man—barely two-and-a-half meters—but immaculately attired, red sash vivid against his gray robes.

Vellerik assumed he had come down to fetch them. "Are we late?"

"No, captain. It appears there is to be no formal ceremony. His Excellency has decided he wants to begin work immediately. He is currently meeting with the Administrator."

"Ah."

Vellerik turned. "Well, men, I suggest you get changed and prepare yourselves for another maneuvering drill."

Noting that Rasikaar hadn't left, he spun around again, rather too quickly in fact. He had to put his hands out to steady himself and hoped no one had noticed. "Was there something else?"

"Yes, captain. Count Talazeer would like to see you too."

Administrator Danysaan was standing outside his own office, staring blankly out of the viewport. He didn't hear Vellerik approach.

"Administrator."

Danysaan looked like a man who had received some rather unpleasant news. "Captain. The—His Excellency—said you can go straight in."

"Are you all right?" Vellerik couldn't have cared less; he just wondered if he might get some warning of what was to come.

"Yes, of course." The Administrator looked out at Corvos. As was often the case, most of the surface was obscured by swathes of white and gray cloud. A solitary shuttle was approaching the *Galtaryax*, navigation lights flashing.

Vellerik approached the office, thankful that the walk seemed to have cleared his head. The doors parted and he strode in. The sight that greeted him sent his hand toward his gun.

The man smiled, his slit of a mouth showing small, jagged teeth. But it wasn't really a smile, and he certainly wasn't a man.

He was a Drellen, one of a handful of survivors from a planet the Vitaari called Kan Arle's World. Most had been wiped out by the Legions during the five decades it had taken to subjugate them. Their tough reptilian skin and remarkable resistance to pain made them a formidable foe. Though they hadn't advanced beyond basic firearms, their devotion to bladed weapons had served them well. Masters of stealth and ambush, they had slaughtered so many soldiers that The Domain had been forced to bring in conscription for the first time in ten generations. The Drellens' preference for skinning the invaders alive had not helped with recruitment.

Vellerik had always felt grateful that they'd been defeated before he left the academy. He'd seen a few here and there but—like most of his people—he harbored a deep distrust and fear of the breed they called—

"Skinner," said the Drellen, his voice an oily hiss. "The captain is thinking—what's a skinner doing here?" His head was a smooth green dome, his eyes dead yellow globes.

Vellerik's hand was still on his gun. He only removed it when the count appeared from an anteroom. He wore a military uniform not unlike Vellerik's, apart from the fact that the red sash was woven into the lustrous material. At the shoulders were the golden stripes that marked him as nobleman, a member of one of the twelve families that ruled The Domain.

"Ah, captain. I hope Marl didn't alarm you."

"Not at all."

"He has been my bodyguard for several years now. It seemed a wise move, once my posts took me out to the colonies."

Vellerik thought it more likely that—like many of his class—the count considered an exotic, imposing bodyguard a status symbol. It certainly made an impression.

Talazeer added, "What he lacks in manners, he makes up for in other areas."

The Drellen scratched his teeth together, then withdrew to the wall, wrapping his black cloak around his freakishly slender frame.

Vellerik strode forward and bowed. "Excellency. It is an honor to meet you. Welcome."

"The honor is mine, captain. I was quite thrilled when I heard that you led the Colonial Guard detachment here. Thrilled—and a little surprised."

"Sir?"

"Come, let us sit."

Beside a triangular viewport were two couches and a table. As he followed the count, Vellerik noted a stack of cargo containers in the anteroom.

"Would you like wine?"

Talazeer gestured to a jug. Judging by the smell, it wasn't particularly strong, but Vellerik was in no need of further intoxication.

"No, thank you, sir."

Talazeer poured some into a glass for himself. "Space travel disagrees with me. I hope it will help me sleep."

Vellerik was surprised he didn't have an attendant or two. The last time he had seen him, Talazeer had been little more than a boy, watching a victory parade with the rest of his family. Now he was a muscular and rather striking young man, though the perfectly symmetrical features of his face suggested surgery. A lot of the younger nobles went in for such things.

Talazeer glanced at Vellerik's uniform as they sat down. "Your decorations, captain?"

"I don't often wear them, sir."

"You? The hero of Akaari Prime? I remember asking my father to recite tales of the Fourth Legion until I knew them by heart. The defense of the High Ridge? The assault on the Skartan capital?"

"All a very long time ago, Excellency."

"'Sir' will suffice. 'Excellency' is such a mouthful." The count sipped his wine. "Why Corvos, Vellerik? What chance of glory out here at the edge of it all? Someone in the general staff must have it in for you."

"To be honest, sir, actually I called in a few favors. I wanted something... quiet."

"Seeing out your final months in peace, eh? Well, understandable, I suppose—for one who has given so much." Talazeer adjusted the shimmering bangle on his wrist. "But I should warn you—this is no flying visit. I am here to stay."

Unlike Danysaan and most of the others aboard the *Galtaryax*, Vellerik hadn't been particularly concerned about the prospect of the count's arrival—until now. He had assumed it would be the usual token visit to improve morale.

Talazeer put down his wine and leaned forward. "I have not shared this information even with Administrator Danysaan. A civilian's word is of little worth when it comes to matters of state. But we are both military men. I know I can trust you."

"Of course, sir."

Both military men?

Vellerik doubted if the count had ever shot at anything that wasn't small, slow, and guaranteed not to fight back.

"You have heard of the Red Regent?"

"Only the name. And that she is believed to be immortal."

"Intelligence-gathering is proving difficult, but we know now that her forces were behind two attacks on our ships in the last year. Intercepts suggest that, while not particularly advanced, her vessels number in the thousands. My father has been ordered to construct a new run of class IV destroyers to reinforce the Third Fleet."

Vellerik knew that Lord Talazeer was second-in-command of the Imperial Navy. He was old, and his was a hereditary position that would be passed to one of his sons. The count was the youngest of the three, and the other two had made names for themselves in the political sphere. He had been known in his youth as an irresponsible rogue; why had he now acquired such obvious ambition?

"How is Lord Talazeer?"

"Ailing, sadly."

So that was it: a bold, if belated, move to impress his father might allow the young nobleman to see off his brothers and secure one of the most prestigious posts in The Domain.

Talazeer continued: "The construction of the new ships means we need more materials than ever, particularly terodite and aronium. Corvos is not producing enough. I aim to increase our contribution by a quarter."

Even with the little he knew about the mining operation, Vellerik imagined this would be difficult, if not impossible.

"There can be no half-measures, captain," continued the count. "I was able to secure a few additional mining drones, but our laborers must be pushed like never before. All must give their absolute maximum; the females, any child of sufficient age. And I was disturbed to hear that acts of revolt continue, even now?"

"Hardly worth bothering with, sir. They are a broken people."

"I don't see how that can be true, captain. A broken people could not—would not—resist. I think it likely that your troops will be seeing a good deal more action over the next few months. I can rely on you, of course?"

You greedy, arrogant, ruthless little bastard.

"Captain?"

"Of course."

3

Cerrin was already counting the days. The governor hadn't told her exactly when she would be needed, but she longed to be out of the mine: free, if only for a few hours.

Along with about a dozen other women, she was working inside a dank, moldy cavern close to the main shaft. They were standing in a line beside a slow-moving conveyor, their job to remove patches of unwanted fungus stuck to the precious terodite. Cerrin picked up a hand-sized chunk of rock and cut away the growth with her chisel, letting it fall at her feet. She then chucked the rock back into the container, the clanging impact eliciting yet another head shake from the woman standing next to her.

They had been working for three hours, so no one was speaking. But no one had spoken to Cerrin anyway, even though she'd been out of the cage for a week. Some of the women were Echobe—forest folk, like her—but they weren't about to associate with a known troublemaker, even though the guards only checked on them every hour or so.

It was Stripe who looked in on them next, and the hulking Vitaari had to bend his head to avoid the bar lights hanging from chains above the conveyor. He walked along the other side of the rumbling machine, pretending to be interested in the passing lumps of rock. Cerrin was close to the middle of the line, and he stopped opposite her, the misty yellow light making his tattoos seem more green than blue. Cerrin hacked at another bit of fungus.

"Morning, Longlegs," said Stripe, who had his translator turned up loud. "How's the ankle?"

She said nothing, kept working.

Despite the noise of the conveyor, she could feel the tension gripping the other women. They had mastered the art of working with their heads down and doing absolutely nothing to draw attention to themselves.

Stripe tapped a colossal gloved hand against each container as it passed. "You know there were a few wagers made. On how long it will be before you try and get away again—and what the governor will have to do to you next time. We have some of our own ideas for punishments. I came up with quite a few—very imaginative, even if I do say so myself."

Had it been just the two of them, Cerrin might have replied; she'd traded insults with him and the other guards before. But the truth was she didn't want to make herself even more unpopular. She would be out in the forest again soon. Until then, she had to avoid trouble as best she could.

"Not talking today?" added Stripe. "Makes a change."

Cerrin pulled away another handful of fungus and dropped it.

The Vitaari picked up a lump of rock. "Maybe you've finally caught up with these others. Accepted how things are. Accepted who's in charge."

She lowered the chisel, looked across at him.

His head was cocked to one side, dark eyes unblinking. "I've served all over, me. Fought the Dal Karaar, the Black Ghosts, every bloody creature the Jedna threw at us. They all lost in the end. But even when they should know they're beaten, there's always the odd one who just doesn't get it. Who just doesn't know when to give up. They never last long."

Stripe threw the rock into the container passing Cerrin, showering her with black dust.

She grabbed it, pulled her arm back ready to throw.

One of the women cried out as she and the rest of them scattered. Stripe, who didn't appear to be armed, leered at Cerrin.

She put the rock down.

"That wager," he said. "I bet you would last another forty days. But you know, I don't think I'll see any of that back. I doubt you'll make another twenty. See you around, Longlegs."

With that, Stripe sauntered out of the cavern, heavy boots crunching on the rocky floor. The women didn't need telling to keep at it; they were already back at the conveyor.

Cerrin felt her hands shake, her teeth grind. She would have loved nothing more than to jam her chisel into that freakish, glistening face. She tried to breathe deeply, let out the anger as her father had taught her. He'd always told her she needed to be calmer: more thoughtful, less impulsive. It was a lesson he had never quite managed to teach her, and it was far too late now.

Returning to her work, Cerrin forced herself to think only of the forest: the wind in the branches, the softness of moss underfoot, the cool, clean water of the Crystal Lake.

"Excuse me."

Cerrin moved aside. The young girl came along every few minutes to collect the fungus and place it in sacks. The women looked after her: giving her some of their food, warning her to stay clear of the conveyor. Cerrin looked down as the girl expertly gathered the detritus with a sweep of her arm, then stuffed it into the sack. She didn't look more than twelve or so, though it was hard to judge these days: there were so few children around and they didn't grow as they had before. The girl stood, then looked up at Cerrin, eyes bright in her grimy face.

One of the women stepped out of the line. "Come away, Yarni."

Yarni grabbed the sack but didn't take her eyes off Cerrin. "I thought you were going to throw that rock."

The closest woman grabbed the girl's shoulder and turned her around. "On you go, girl."

Yarni did as she was told but walked backwards, watching Cerrin every step of the way.

• • •

At dusk they were ordered to the landing strip. Wincing at the pain from her ankle but determined not to limp, Cerrin joined the scores of others from the day shift marching past high stacks of bright blue barrels. She was surprised to see the night shift already lined up on the strip; she couldn't remember the last time the governor had gathered the entire workforce.

A grunt and an extended arm from a guard directed her and the rest of the women into the sixth and last line. Cerrin inspected the gun hanging from his shoulder and thought of the first time she had seen one used. The tongue of fire had arrowed right past her, scorching a vine and burning a hole in an Echobe warrior's chest.

As the women shuffled to a stop, Cerrin glanced over at the wall. Even though she knew better, she sometimes felt as if there could be nothing beyond it. But to the south was the Great Forest, to the north the Empty Lands. The sun—now a brilliant orange disc—had almost disappeared from view. She mouthed the prayer of farewell and wondered how many of the other Echobe still bothered to do the same. Noting movement to her right, she saw Yarni peer at her, then straighten up and face the front.

Governor Yeterris stepped onto a cargo pallet and examined the workers. Cerrin wasn't sure why he needed the stage; he was at least three feet taller than all of those he was addressing. She heard a snatch of the invader language before the translator cut in.

"An announcement. You would be wise to listen and listen well. These are the words of Excellency Count Derzitt Kan Talazeer, who is now in charge of our operation here. Greetings, loyal subjects of Corvos. Be assured that The Domain remains appreciative of your hard work and peaceful conduct. Due to urgent need, it is essential that we increase production within all installations. That will mean a reduction in breaks and an improved yield from every single one of you. We are confident that you will work alongside your supervisors to achieve this improvement."

Reduction in breaks? Cerrin wasn't sure even the Vitaari would manage that. Both shifts worked for twelve hours straight with only half an hour for a midday meal and two water breaks. There was barely enough time to get the food or drink down before a siren sounded or some guard shoved you back to where you were supposed to be.

Cerrin had picked up the odd bit of information while working outside the mine with the invaders, but she had never heard of this Count Talazeer. In fact, she didn't even know what a count was, not that it really mattered. He would be just like all the rest of them.

The governor offered his own words. "I share Count Talazeer's confidence in you. I am proud of the productive, peaceful record I have established here at Mine Fourteen. With the exception of a few… isolated cases, you have all done well for me. I do not wish to hear complaints or see malingerers at the infirmary. You will work quietly, and you will work well, and we shall all benefit. Now, we are wasting time. The night shift will leave first."

With a gesture toward his chief guard, the governor stepped down off the pallet and strode away, accompanied by several administrators.

Block A was an enormous cargo container—a hundred feet long and thirty high. Large though it was, it never felt that way with so many inside. Divided into two levels, the forty compartments housed the entire day shift.

Cerrin waited patiently for the queue to clear, then took a last breath of vaguely fresh air and went inside. It took a while for her to reach her ladder, during which time she watched the weary workers cast off their filthy clothes and lie on the rusting metal beds with their thin, holed mattresses. She looked on as a mother and father helped their exhausted son out of his clothes. Cerrin had seen him around; the Vitaari used him to retrieve bits of fungus that got caught in machinery. The lad could barely lift his arms. Considering his work, Cerrin reckoned he was lucky to still have both of them.

Trying to ignore the blisters on her fingers, she gripped the rungs of the narrow metal ladder and climbed up. She shared her compartment with two sisters: Palanians, from the hill country to the far north—a people who seemed convinced that they were somehow better than every other tribe on Corvos. The sisters had long since learned to keep such opinions to themselves and had only made one ill-fated attempt at admonishing Cerrin for encroaching on their half of the cramped space.

They were already under their covers and talking quietly when she crawled to her bed. Once her boots and overalls were off, she pulled her blanket over her and sat back against the wall, just grateful to be still. After a while she summoned the energy to look out the window she'd made by pulling out a long-dead ventilation unit. It had been a wonderful moment when she realized she could just see over the wall. Some nights she saw moonlight glittering on the river, but tonight there was too much cloud. Only by craning her head could she see the edge of the forest: the endless dark mass that symbolized everything for her: past and future, loss and hope.

The lights inside the block would only be on for a few more minutes. Cerrin reached into the pocket of her overalls and took out the cutting of creeper she had found just outside the mine. She needed something of the earth around her and had cultivated a few plants in little pots filled with soil. She chose only hardy things that could survive without much sunlight. The creeper was the hardiest of them all and needed only a little water. It wasn't much to look at, but it would grow quickly and she liked the hard, diamond-shaped leaves. Once the cutting was in the pot, she placed it carefully in a corner with the others.

Cerrin then poured herself some water from the yellowing plastic barrel she shared with the sisters. Grimacing at the sour taste, she looked down at her pathetic selection of belongings. Everything she'd had with her when she'd been captured had been taken by the Vitaari and burned. The jacket, boots, and two sets of overalls were standard issue, as were the hygiene kits handed out every month.

(One set of overalls had been given to her at the infirmary—to replace those torn and soaked in blood when Stripe had grabbed her). The latrine was in a separate building and—like every man, woman, and child in Fourteen—she was expected to shower on every third day (in under ten minutes). Cerrin closed her eyes and thought again of the Crystal Lake; she would give anything just to see it again.

Somebody rapped on the ladder, and a bald head appeared. "Dukas, for Cerrin."

"What is it?" she said, though she had a good idea what he would say. Dukas came up another rung so she could see his broad, stupid-looking face. He clearly thought himself some sort of leader, but to Cerrin the Palanian was a weak-minded fool. He would never have been respected by her people. His idea of leadership was telling everyone how best to avoid antagonizing the Vitaari.

"You heard the speech?"

She even hated his accent.

"This Count Talazeer," continued Dukas. "They say he is bad as any of them. He visited Mine Eight yesterday and overheard a worker say his name. The man was given three jolts—to the head."

"You better hope there are no informers around then."

Dukas leant into the compartment. "There are no informers here because the Vitaari know they don't need them. I would like us to try and keep it that way."

"Sorry, I can't understand what you're saying," she lied. "Your accent."

The sisters were whispering again.

Dukas sighed. "Trying to escape is futile. And now is certainly not the time. You endanger us all."

She leant back against the wall. "Sorry, didn't get that either."

Just as Dukas shook his head, the lights went out.

It sounded as if he were leaving, but he halted. "At Eight. It wasn't just the one man given the jolts. They took one in ten from his shift and one in ten from his block. Men and women."

The sisters went quiet.

"You know that I speak for most here," added Dukas. "Please, Cerrin. Just think of the rest of us for once."

She almost always slept well. It didn't seem to matter what happened in the day; night always brought her relief and rest.

She had slept on the first night news reached her village—talk of lights in the sky and shattering cracks louder than thunder. She had slept on the night her father left to join the warband taking on the invaders and the night when she'd heard he would not be coming back. She had slept the night her mother died, her heart giving out as they were pursued through the forest by the Vitaari and their machines. The only night she had not slept was the one before the final battle, when the invaders had cornered the last of the Echobe. Even though they had prayed to the god of battle for hours, made endless offerings, she had feared even Ikala would not be able to help them. She had not slept then because she had known it would be her last night in the forest.

Cerrin turned over and looked up at the faint rectangle of light coming from the makeshift window. Every day since the river she had thought of ending it. No one would be surprised, least of all the Vitaari; it was rare for a month to pass without someone throwing themselves down one of the deep shafts. But she couldn't do that. She had broken enough promises to her mother, especially after her father died.

Live, girl. You must go on. For me, for the ancients, and for all our people.

Cerrin felt the familiar warm surge of hope that somehow always saved her.

4

There were no walls at Mine Three. The buildings and the landing strip had been constructed upon a natural platform that jutted out from the side of Mount Origo. Other than a narrow ridge along which several fatal escape attempts had been made, there was no other hospitable terrain and no usable route down to the ground three thousand feet below. Origo and the lesser peaks that flanked it were freezing in winter and cold for much of the rest of the year. On the rare occasions when the heat of the sun could be felt, even the Vitaari would stop to enjoy it. Sonus had grown up hearing of the mountains in tales of ancient adventurers hunting huge, soaring birds. He had never seen a bird near the place; he occasionally wondered if they had been driven away or had never existed at all. To the Echobe—and some Palanians—the mountain was a sacred place. Origo held no spiritual significance for Sonus; it was just another part of Corvos the Vitaari had defiled for their own gain.

The platform of rock sloped downward and tapered at the bottom. Here the Vitaari had mined out a series of caverns in which to house the workers. Accessed by a rusting stairway that had claimed several lives in the icy months, the caverns were never warm. Though the Vitaari refused to provide the natives with fuel for fires, they had given them hundreds of oversized blankets that just about did the job. Sonus wasn't sure what the strange material was, but it had a remarkable capacity for insulation.

Marching through the caverns, he saw scores of people sitting wrapped in them or lying under them. As usual, his services were in high demand, and he felt guilty about telling two men that he would have to attend to their portable lights another time. The Vitaari had provided these too, and though they were durable and effective, everyone wanted the adjustment that only Sonus could effect: varying power.

He was in a hurry because he wanted to catch Karas before he and Qari settled down for the night. She wouldn't suspect anything out of the ordinary; he called on them regularly. Nodding to a familiar face, Sonus then saw another and hid behind some boxes stacked outside a cavern. Only when Tanus was well past did Sonus continue on his way. The last thing he needed was another confrontation with the man.

Karas's cavern was one of the farthest from the outside, which meant there was less wind but more of the numbing chill that seemed to radiate out from the bowels of the mountain. Mumbling a greeting to the older couple who occupied the cavern next door, Sonus saw Qari bending over a tub, washing clothes. Karas was sitting on their bed, watching her. He didn't look particularly pleased to see Sonus.

Qari offered her usual welcoming smile. "Hello."

They were still a handsome couple—Karas tall and even-featured, Qari red-haired and slender—but there was a weariness in every action and a sadness etched into their faces.

"Evening." Sonus patted down his thick, brown hair and hovered uneasily near the gap in the barrels that formed the entrance to their dwelling.

"You hungry?" asked Qari.

"No, thank you."

Karas got off the bed and ran a hand across Qari's back as he walked up to the barrels. "You all right?"

"Yes. Can I borrow you for ten minutes? Another light needs fixing, and I could do with a pair of steady hands."

Karas waited for an approving nod from Qari, then followed Sonus back along the passageway. Walking side by side, they watched a family with a boy of about eight arrive at their cavern. Sonus led the way between two dwellings into a narrow fissure where they could talk without being overheard.

Karas stood there in silence, rubbing his brow with a finger. "Those children, are there any younger?"

"Boras's boy. He's six. It wasn't long after he was born that they—"

"I know."

Sonus felt his stomach turn over as he recalled how the situation had worsened. To begin with, the Vitaari had showed little interest in pregnant women or babies. An early ruling stated that the women could be given lighter duties during the last quarter of the pregnancy and three days with no work on either side of the birth. Other than the governor suggesting that couples try to avoid the situation entirely if possible, the invaders had not interfered.

That was until someone discovered what a Corvosian infant would fetch back on the home world. Aside from fashionable Vitaari families interested in unusual-looking slaves, there were scientific institutes eager to pay well for healthy subjects—for experimentation.

When the next baby was born, the medical officer invited the mother to the infirmary, then took the child and sent it off with the next shipment of aronium. The rumor was that he had done extremely well out of the transaction. The hysterical mother had been killed by guards while trying to get the baby back. No one seemed to know who the father was.

That medical officer had long since been replaced, but there were several more such incidents before the governor acted—encouraging the use of a medicinal root employed in many parts of Corvos as a contraceptive. He made it very clear that this was done to reduce disruption and maintain discipline, not to benefit the workers. If prepared and administered correctly, the concoction was effective. But not entirely reliable.

"We were so careful," said Karas. "We always did precisely as we were supposed to."

"She is sure?"

Karas nodded. "Four months. She gets more tired every day. Soon she will show."

"Has she tried taking more of the root?"

"Of course. Old Marla says that there are chemicals she could drink—to stop it. You could get them for us."

"That's been tried before. Remember Seri? She burned half of her stomach out."

Karas stepped toward him. "What then? You always have an answer for everything, Sonus. Tell me what I must do."

"What does Qari want?"

"She thinks we must try to escape. The three of us."

"You know that's impossible."

"Better to die together than…"

"Karas." Sonus put a hand on his arm.

Though they did not speak of it, they both knew what had happened after the last time a pregnancy had been discovered. The governor had ordered that the unborn child be terminated and the mother be put back to work the following day. She worked on the night shift and—although Sonus couldn't remember her name—he knew she hadn't uttered a single word to anyone since.

"We both know what they'll do," whispered Karas. "And you heard about this one that's coming tomorrow. They're saying he's worse than any of them."

"I will do all I can to help."

"Thank you, my friend. But it seems the Maker has ignored our prayers. I fear we are beyond help already."

Sonus did not enter the mountain at all the following day. He was plucked out of the line by Kadessis and sent immediately to the maintenance yard. The cleaning drones were all needed urgently, and Sonus was put to work on a malfunctioning pair with the same navigation problem. He was close to the yard entrance, working unsupervised, and able to observe what was going on. The Vitaari—administrators and guards alike—had seemed unsettled ever since the news of their new leader, but the prospect of a personal visit had even more of an effect.

Every one of them was up and working, including the governor, who seemed intent on inspecting every last corner of the installation. He had already been into the tower when he passed the yard, barking orders at a trio of subordinates. Kadessis was trailing along behind them and glanced briefly at Sonus as he hurried past.

Sometimes they would talk. Kadessis liked to practice speaking trade and was interested to hear Sonus speak of his past. The administrator had been surprised to learn that he was not from this region, that he was a Palanian, from the most advanced of the planet's peoples. Sonus had been an engineer, working alongside other innovative thinkers on using water and steam to power machines. It had been a glorious period for the Palanians, a time of progress and achievement. During his life, women had been allowed to cast their votes in elections for the first time and inventors and academics seemed to offer something new almost every week. Then the Vitaari came.

Though nothing so overt was ever said, Sonus could tell that Kadessis did not entirely approve of what had been done to his people. Unlike most of the others, this Vitaari was open and curious, a thoughtful individual. Sonus had learned that he was required to complete several years of service for The Domain before embarking on his preferred career. Kadessis wished to be a historian when he returned to the home world.

Sonus was so lost in thought that he now found himself staring blankly at the ground. Shaking his head, he re-focused on the green status screen in front of him. He was kneeling beside the egg-shaped drone, one hand holding up the access hatch because they had a habit of closing without warning. He tried to absorb and process this particular combination of error messages. But though he knew enough Vitaari to understand exactly what they meant, he couldn't arrive at a solution.

He had parted from Karas and Qari at the top of the walkway that morning. She was out of breath, and Karas had to help her up the last section. Sonus could not forget the look on his friend's face as he watched his wife move into a separate line and walk away.

Sonus tried to apply some logic to the situation. He'd thought they might have a few weeks, but given Qari's condition it might not even be that long. The Vitaari were never slow to spot anyone not pulling their weight, especially at the moment. If she were sent to the infirmary…

No. That could not happen. Until they could come up with something close to a solution, they needed to buy some time.

Qari had been assigned to the secondary shaft for several months. She worked there with a clearance team, removing debris that might clog up the drills. It was hard, hot work. If she could be put on a lighter duty, she would at least be spared the strain and the greater likelihood of her condition being discovered.

Kadessis had some sway over work assignments. Twice he had been able to arrange rest days for Sonus when his coughing fits had been at their worst. There were lighter assignments available for the older, weaker females—cleaners and cooks for the tower and the Vitaari accommodation block. Sonus had done endless favors for the administrator—helped him with his equipment, tweaked the heating within his quarters. He felt that he knew him, understood him even. But could he trust him?

Hearing a shout, Sonus looked up. A detachment of twenty guards—about half the total force—had just come to a halt in front of the tower. The Vitaari stood with their arms by their sides, weapons across their chests, as an officer inspected them. The sky was clear, and the sunlight danced off the gleaming weapons and metallic trim upon their dark green uniforms. The officer stopped several times, pointing out deficiencies here and there. Close to the end of the line, he ran his finger along the barrel of one of the guns and showed it to the soldier holding it. The man hung his head in shame.

Sonus glanced up at the sun. Three hours beyond dawn at least and the visitor was expected around midday. He had to get this drone working; he could not afford to displease Kadessis. He rubbed his eyes and looked again at the screen.

The *Galtaryax* was an old ship: forty-one years old, apparently. There were dark stains across the curved expanses of the gray hull, even the odd dent. The red lettering of the name was patchy and mottled. Inside a nearby vent, an errant piece of cabling stuck up at an unlikely angle.

Turning toward the door, Vellerik was dismayed to see that there was still no sign of Talazeer and his party. Troop Lieutenant Triantaa and the other two soldiers were standing in a line, as quiet and as bored as Vellerik. Administrator Danysaan and Kerreslaa were also waiting in the shuttle attached to the *Galtaryax*'s side, but nobody dared say anything.

Vellerik kept his hands behind his back and paced along beside the viewport, relieved that at least Talazeer's tour of the mines was almost over. They had taken in eight installations on the first day, eight on the second; thankfully there were only six left for today. Presumably the count felt he had to show his face to his underlings and the natives, but he didn't seem to grasp the irony of disrupting mining operations while simultaneously demanding an increase in production. At least there hadn't been any more problems after the incident at Eight. Vellerik had expected the punishment but not that Talazeer would extend it randomly to individuals the offender happened to work and live with. Still, at least he hadn't killed any of them and the message would undoubtedly spread; it might even prevent further suffering in future. The count had certainly made an impression.

Vellerik just wanted to get it over with. He didn't want to see the natives. Not the females and certainly not the children. All he could ever think of was what Seevarta would say. She said young ones were always sweet. Even animals. Even primitives.

He heard footsteps behind him. Military boots but a light step. Kerreslaa.

"Captain."

Vellerik stopped but barely turned, making the liaison officer walk around to address him.

"Mine Ten. I know things were quiet when we visited, but this problem with the natives remains. His Excellency is keen to remove any threat to the water supply, and another pipe was attacked only a few days ago. I think the time has definitely come to—"

"I am old, Kerreslaa, but my memory still functions fairly well. You mentioned this matter yesterday. Twice."

"Yes, captain, but Governor Sekithis is reluctant to risk his troops that far outside the installation. This is precisely the type of operation that the Colonial Guard is—"

"I suggest you concentrate on your own decision-making rather than mine. For example, the decision not to leave your quarters without removing that unsightly stain from your uniform." Vellerik nodded at Kerreslaa's chest.

Aghast, the young liaison officer stared down and pulled the material out to check it.

Vellerik was already on his way by the time Kerreslaa realized there was nothing there. He walked past his men and over to Administrator Danysaan. Though he had little cause to celebrate Talazeer's arrival, Vellerik had observed with some amusement Danysaan's response to being rendered virtually redundant.

"Morning, captain."

Vellerik nodded. He didn't particularly like the man, but his regime had at least been consistent; Danysaan had allowed each governor to run his operation as he saw fit. Unless there was a significant fall in production, he seldom intervened. And though he insisted on being notified of every sanction, to Vellerik's knowledge he had never actually been present to observe a punishment being delivered.

When the guard at Mine Eight had jabbed his jolt-rod into the unfortunate local, the worker had fallen, vomited noisily, then undergone spasms that had lasted for a long time. Danysaan had watched; Vellerik had watched him.

"Hopefully there will be no... unpleasantness today," said the administrator.

"Hopefully not."

5

Sonus was the last to join the line. Having repaired the second cleaning drone, he'd then been instructed by another administrator to fix a landing light. Breathing hard, he took his place not far from the low wall that ran along the edge of the platform. Beyond it was a sheer drop into a deep gully perpetually shrouded by mist and shadow. The workers had been assembled in front of the gaping entrance to the main shaft.

The landing strip was needed for the shuttle and—though he had now seen flying craft hundreds of times—Sonus always experienced the same sense of wonder that such heavy vehicles could be propelled into the air and across space. Though he now grasped the basic principles of how the vessels were controlled, the specifics of the engineering remained a mystery, largely because none of the Vitaari he spoke to seemed to know much about the subject. He was just as curious about the combat shells, and their weapons, and their communication technology. But they only ever wanted him to help out with basic maintenance, nothing more.

Now familiar with the flight path, Sonus saw the shuttle before anyone else. It dropped out of the cloudless sky above the plain, then disappeared behind the tower. When it reappeared a minute later—easing in gently over the top of the generator station—the Vitaari all looked up. They were gathered at the side of the strip: the governor, his staff, and half of the guards. The other half had surrounded the workers, but they were watching the shuttle too.

Sonus had only seen this vessel a few times before, usually when the Administrator himself or some other dignitary was visiting. It was sleeker and smaller than the bulkier freighters that brought in supplies and collected the minerals. The shuttle hovered, executed a turn, then descended, white plumes shooting out from under its four short wings. Sonus wondered if the pilots were Lovirr. The diminutive easterners had been the first tribe to surrender to the Vitaari and were sufficiently intelligent and dexterous to control the ships. Sonus knew from occasional discussions with them that they also possessed little knowledge about the internal workings of the craft. Kadessis had explained to him that the Vitaari directorate that ran the Corvos operation were always looking to cut costs but considered only the Lovirr both trustworthy and unthreatening enough to be given such responsibility. Unlike the other tribes, they had little history of resistance.

The shuttle's landing struts splayed outward as it touched down. The access ramp descended a minute later, and the first figure to reach the ground was a soldier, clad not in the usual green but in blue. Sonus had also seen these men only a handful of times; they belonged to something called the Colonial Guard.

Vellerik approached the governor, faintly embarrassed by the jangle of his decoration bar (Talazeer had insisted he wear it). They shook forearms, then turned as the count marched down the ramp, his Drellen bodyguard two paces behind him. Boots gleaming, uniform shining, Talazeer fixed the governor with an earnest stare and waited for the bow before offering his hand.

"Good day, governor."

"Excellency, my staff and I welcome you to our installation."

Talazeer breathed in deeply. "Ah, fine air up here." He turned around slowly, taking in the tower, the barracks, and the mine before glancing up at the snow-capped peak of the mountain. "How high is it?"

The governor's eyes widened. "Er…"

One of his men volunteered the answer. "Eleven thousand two hundred meters, Excellency. The temperature up there is minus sixty-five at this time of year, and the winds can reach three hundred kilometers an hour."

"Is that so? I might take a look later."

Danysaan, Kerreslaa, and Vellerik's men stopped a respectful distance behind the count.

"I must commend you and your staff on recent yields, governor," said Talazeer, patting down some strands of hair that had blown out of place.

"Thank you, Excellency."

"You will continue to improve, of course."

"We will try our hardest, sir, though there are limited…"

The expression on the count's face dissuaded the governor from continuing.

"Er, what would you like to see first, sir?"

Talazeer was now looking at the workers. "Them. After I've inspected your guards."

The chief officer stepped forward, a bulky individual with his hair cut short. Vellerik wasn't sure if he'd ever spoken to the man. He didn't deal much with the guards, nor did he particularly respect them; they were generally drawn from inferior regiments and received commensurate training and pay. No ambitious soldier would be satisfied with such a posting.

"Troop Sergeant Kalitarr. He has worked here for many years."

"Sergeant."

"Excellency," said Kalitarr with a low bow. "Please allow me to introduce my men."

Knowing he was expected to follow, Vellerik fell in behind Talazeer and found himself walking along next to the bodyguard. The Drellen's black cloak covered his entire body except for the green, hairless head. Vellerik examined the scaly skin.

"What pretty colors," hissed Marl, peering at his decorations.

"What are you mourning?" asked Vellerik, nodding at his cloak. "Your people? Or your personality?"

The Drellen's only reply was a guttural grunt. He had barely spoken to Vellerik, but when he did, it was usually some form of insult. Vellerik wondered why—was it because he had fought for the force that had defeated Marl's people or simply because Talazeer treated Vellerik with more respect than anyone else, the Drellen included? Abruptly realizing he couldn't care less, Vellerik listened in as Talazeer questioned Chief Kalitarr.

"Any trouble?"

"No, Excellency. We haven't had any major problems for years."

"Minor problems?"

"No, sir."

"That is why there are so few of you here."

"Yes, sir. Some of our men were re-distributed to other installations where there are more… significant security issues."

Talazeer waved Administrator Danysaan over and lowered his voice. "There are other mines where we have more troops than we need. I know we are bound by law to maintain the Colonial Guard detachment, but every one of these soldiers is costing the Directorate. That money could be better used to improve yield."

Danysaan considered his reply carefully. "Troop numbers have been significantly reduced year on year, sir. It was felt that security might be compromised if we cut them even further."

Talazeer looked at the troops, then turned back to the governor. "You have, what, forty soldiers?"

"Forty-four, sir."

"Vellerik, that's more than enough, isn't it?"

"Possibly, sir. Governor, how many operational combat shells here?"

"Six."

Vellerik shrugged. "They're an older design—only the assault cannon and the grenade module—but even three or four would be enough to deal with a revolt, even in significant numbers."

The governor held up his hands. "There is no possibility of revolt. But we also need the guards to monitor different crews. On some days we have workers in ten different sections, several kilometers apart. It is not practical to use the shells underground. The guards are often very thinly spread."

The count inhaled through his nose and pointed at Danysaan. "Look into it—I will not tolerate waste. Speaking of which, let's see these workers; I want them back working within the hour."

As the count and his party strode up past the dormant conveyor toward the mine, Sonus could feel the fear spreading through the workers. Fear was something they'd all had to learn to live with, but this was something new. Something unpredictable. Sonus clenched his fists, but he couldn't stop his fingers shaking. Around him, others twitched and shuffled, unsure whether it was best to look forward or down. One particularly broad pair of shoulders in the line ahead of him remained upright and still.

Tanus sniffed loudly. Sonus had been so preoccupied by Karas and Qari's problems that he'd scarcely given the man a thought. He hoped everyone else had refused to help him too. Surely he wouldn't try anything here? Now? Sonus berated himself for joining this line without checking Tanus's position, but he was relieved to see Karas and Qari were on the other side of the path. Karas was as close as he could be without touching her. Qari was holding her arms over her stomach.

The count looked very young and was dressed in immaculate clothing. Sonus had discovered that morning that his was a very senior rank. This Talazeer came from an important family and was more powerful than anyone on the surface or on the *Galtaryax*. Sonus had only heard about the great ship that watched over his planet; he had never seen it.

As Talazeer approached, his attention—and that of all the workers and most of the guards—shifted to the creature behind the count. Sonus would never forget his first sight of a Vitaari (the giant soldier had kicked his way through the door of the house where he was hiding), but this was similarly remarkable. Though almost as tall as the Vitaari, the creature was incredibly lean and had skin like something that might be found in a swamp. The globular yellow eyes were constantly moving, seeming to take in everything.

Talazeer exchanged a few comments with the guards, then approached the workers in the front line, looming over them with the rest of the Vitaari behind him. Sonus now realized he recognized the officer; he could not remember his name, only that he held the rank of troop captain and commanded the Colonial Guard unit on the *Galtaryax*. He looked very old and very bored, watching the visitor with his hands behind his back, mouth turned down.

Sonus strained to hear what was being said; there was a slight wind blowing across the platform. The count concluded his discussion with one of the workers, then walked on, with only the strange creature, the governor, and the captain staying with him. Talazeer reached the end of the line, then headed up past the other side of the assembled workers. Sonus felt dread dry his throat as the visitor approached Karas and Qari.

But the count didn't stop. He continued on, then turned between two lines. The workers close by all moved forward or back to give him space. The Vitaari was looking down at each man and woman as he passed.

Vellerik had asked Talazeer not to get unnecessarily close to the natives, but the young noble ignored him, insisting that he wanted to look the workers in the eye; show himself, make sure they understood who was in charge. Vellerik had instructed all the governors to have the workers searched before their arrival, but there was always the chance one of them would try something.

He looked over Marl's shoulder as Talazeer stopped and peered down at a young boy standing with his parents. "And what's your name?"

Vellerik noted the father was trembling more than the mother.

"Madas, sir."

"Do you work hard, Madas?"

The lad seemed used to the delay and harsh voice of the translator. Vellerik supposed he had heard it all his life.

"Yes, sir. I always do what I'm told."

"Good boy. Do you know who I am?"

"No, sir."

"My name is Talazeer," said the count loudly. "But that's not important. What's important is that you keep working and you do what you're told. Understand?"

"Yes, sir."

Talazeer bent over and ruffled his hair, his silvery hand covering the lad's entire head. Vellerik was relieved when the count straightened up and moved on, but he took only a single step before stopping again. "Tell me, Madas. What happens to people who don't work hard and do as they're told?"

Madas thought for a moment. "They get hurt."

"Sir."

"They get hurt, sir. They get the rod. Or they get torn."

"You know about tearing, Madas?"

"Yes, sir."

Unlike the jolt-rods, Vellerik had heard of tearing before he arrived. Like most officers in the modern Colonial Guard, he viewed the practice as barbaric and ignoble, though it had been widely used in the past as a method of terrorizing enemies. He had been dismayed to learn that the guards had carried out several tearings under Danysaan's predecessor. Surely the count wouldn't countenance such an extreme sanction?

"I'm sure that won't happen to anyone here." Talazeer's tone did not match his words.

Vellerik looked at the few locals watching their new overlord. Try as they might, some of them couldn't hide their fury. Vellerik dropped his hand onto his sidearm, flicked the strap off the holster. Why didn't Talazeer understand how needless this all was. The mine functioned well—why get involved?

The count moved off. The boy's eyes widened as he transferred his attention to Marl, who moved between the lines like some spectral shadow.

Sonus saw now that the visitor was indeed young, younger than most of the guards, younger even than Kadessis. There was something unnervingly flawless about his features; he seemed almost unreal. He was about to walk past Tanus.

Please. Please don't. Don't do anything.

The big man's head was level with the count's chest. Sonus watched his right hand; the fingers were moving. They had all been searched before joining the line. Could he have made a weapon of his own?

But the fingers stopped moving and Tanus remained still as the count passed him. Then came the strange creature, and Sonus looked down at the ground, fearful of meeting his gaze. He only looked up when the captain and the governor had passed. Sonus let out a breath, then heard his name.

The count and the other three had stopped close to the wall. The governor was talking in Vitaari, pointing along the line straight at Sonus. Talazeer listened, then followed him over.

The governor spoke first. "I was just telling His Excellency about your technical knowledge."

Sonus clasped his hands together in front of him and said nothing.

"You understand our machines," said the count. "Is that correct?"

"I… do what I can, sir."

"He's Palanian, Excellency," said the governor. "The most advanced of the lot, though they had barely begun industrialization. Sonus here was some kind of engineer."

"An intelligent man, then," said Talazeer. "Amongst your own at least. I wonder what you must think of us."

Sonus had no idea how to answer that. As it turned out, he never had to.

. . .

Vellerik was behind Marl, who of course had followed the count. He saw the bald man turn and raise his hand. And he saw the tiny blade sticking out of his fist.

Vellerik's hand was already on his gun and pulling it out of the holster when the Drellen moved. His sword—a narrow blade with a square tip—scythed downward, severing the man's arm below the elbow. As the arm—and the knife—dropped to the ground, the man somehow stayed on his feet, watching the strange red blood geyser from the stump. Marl moved between him and the count, still with only a single gloved hand and the sword poking out of the cloak.

Vellerik had his finger on the trigger. He looked around in every direction, checking there were no more threats. By the time he looked back, Talazeer had seen enough to understand what had transpired.

His assailant was now sitting on his backside, mouth hanging open, eyes wide. Lying on the ground beside him was his severed arm.

Vellerik's men and the guards raised their rifles and converged on the scene, knocking the workers out of the way.

"Hold there," snapped Vellerik. "Everyone stay exactly where you are."

The governor was staring down at the butchered limb, his mouth also open. The count's method of recovering his composure was to smooth down the front of his uniform, then run a hand through his hair.

The mutilated man tried to get up, but he was losing color as fast as he was losing blood. He couldn't make his legs work.

"What's your name?" asked Talazeer.

Surprisingly, he could speak. "Tanus."

Marl put the blade close to the native's face. There wasn't a drop of blood or tissue upon the dark metal.

"Sir," said Vellerik. "Let's take him away. Move you out of this crowd."

"When I'm ready, if you don't mind, captain," said the count. "Marl, bring him."

Talazeer walked past Vellerik and back to the low wall. The Drellen reached down, gripped Tanus's good hand and dragged him away.

Sonus locked eyes with Tanus for a moment, and only then did he realize how strong the man was. There was no fear there.

One of the guards yelled orders. "Down! All of you down. Flat. Hands where we can see them."

Sonus dropped down on his front and stretched his arms out. As a soldier's boot narrowly missed his thumb, he looked toward the wall.

"Why?" asked Talazeer.

Tanus was on his knees, held up by Marl. Vellerik reckoned he would be dead in minutes if he wasn't helped. He doubted this would last that long.

"Speak," shouted Talazeer.

Marl put the blade against the man's throat.

"Are there more like you here?" demanded the count.

Tanus forced a lopsided smile. "These? They're weak. They're dead already."

"I suppose I should admire your bravery," said Talazeer.

Tanus looked up at him and spoke a short phrase. In Vitaari.

Vellerik imagined he must have heard it from the guards. A vicious insult that questioned the honor and integrity of a Vitaari and his family. For the guards it might have been used in jest; to a man of the count's class it was an affront to his entire being.

Talazeer touched his mouth, then spoke quietly to Marl, so quietly that Vellerik didn't catch a word.

Another flashing sweep of the blade sliced off one of Tanus's ears. Assailed by agony, he collapsed onto his side, whimpering like an animal. Most of the workers turned their heads away. Madas's mother had covered his eyes with her hands.

Talazeer casually placed a foot on a nearby rock and watched Marl line up the other ear.

Vellerik walked between them—reminded himself that these people's hearts were on the left—and put a bullet into Tanus. He lasted only seconds.

Marl gave him a sideways glance, then wiped the end of his blade on the dead man's overalls.

"I think the point's been made." Vellerik holstered his gun.

"Well, you've certainly made yours, captain." Talazeer turned around. "Governor, I suggest we put these people back to work immediately. Then you can show me the rest of the installation."

The governor took a long breath, then began issuing orders to the guards.

Sonus looked at Tanus, at his mutilated body and his open, still defiant eyes. He supposed some of the others might admire him. But he didn't. Tanus had died for nothing and made things worse for the rest of them. Sonus clenched his fists in the dirt. In truth, there had never been much hope that he would be able to help Karas and Qari. Now there was even less.

6

Cerrin had often dreamed of flying over the Great Forest. Her father had told her that the visions came from the birds that soared high in the sky: another part of the natural communion that linked all living things. But she could remember little of the dreams now; they could not compete with what she had seen with her own eyes.

Four times the Vitaari had taken her up in the flying craft and—despite the aches that struck her head and stomach—she'd spent almost every moment of every trip with her face pressed against a window, staring down at the endless beauty below.

This was the longest trip so far, and she had no idea where they were. The broad swathes of tasska trees with their pale green leaves were familiar, as was the occasional stand of spindly orange okka. But a few moments earlier she had spied a flock of dark birds flying in an unusual formation; she did not know the type. And then there was the meandering river they had just flown over. Cerrin had recognized neither its shape nor the yellow mud flats surrounding it. She understood that no one person could ever know all the forest or its creatures, but she was worried about what they might find at this new site. If the terrain, plants, and animals were unfamiliar, the Vitaari would have no use for her.

Cerrin was up on her knees, facing the wrong way in a seat twice her size. The shuttle would occasionally shudder so she retained her balance by gripping the seat straps. For only the third time since they had left Mine Fourteen, she glanced over her shoulder at the Vitaari.

They occupied the seats on the other side of the shuttle. There were four technicians: two were talking, two were poring over their data-pads. Cerrin recognized only one of them from Fourteen and reckoned the other three had come from either another mine or the *Galtaryax*. Governor Yeterris had once told her about the ship that flew so high that there was no sky, only blackness and stars. She could not imagine such a place.

Strapped to the deck in front of the technicians was a selection of equipment Cerrin had seen before: it would be used to inspect the site and take samples. The Vitaari had carried out the same procedure on the previous trips, but she knew that no mines had been built at those places. She wasn't sure why; they only ever asked her about trees and soil and animals and insects. The four guards were sitting with their guns across their laps. Cerrin was pleased that Stripe was not among them.

The governor was sitting alone. Before they had left, he'd spoken to her: reminding her that nothing less than complete obedience would be tolerated. They would be at the site for only one day; but if things went well, there would be return visits and she might be needed again. Cerrin had endured forty-two days of work in the mine for this; she could hardly wait for the moment when she walked out into her forest once more.

Just as she was about to turn back to the window, the communicator upon Yeterris's collar beeped and he pressed it. When the caller spoke, the governor snapped at the technicians to be quiet. Stiffening and sitting up, he listened carefully and nodded several times before the conversation ended. Yeterris then addressed the others, who in turn listened carefully to him. Cerrin observed the two guards farthest from the governor exchange a look, but nothing was said. Yeterris looked up at the roof and began to tap his hand against the empty seat beside him. Cerrin had picked up a handful of Vitaari words but had no idea what was going on.

As she turned around, the shuttle veered to the right, then began to descend. By craning her neck and pressing even closer to the window, she could just make out a distant gap in the canopy ahead. As before, the Vitaari had somehow blasted a hole in the forest so they could land their ships and do their work. Not for the first time, Cerrin felt a pang of shame that she was helping them. But as the ground came closer, such thoughts were forgotten.

Not long now. Almost there.

They could not spoil it: the noise of the technicians as they jabbered away and set up their equipment; the acrid stench of whatever they had used to create the clearing; the scorched, twisted remains of the plant life they had destroyed. It did not matter. Cerrin stood at the edge of the space and looked out into the forest.

Shafts of sunlight cut down through the trees, illuminating clouds of hovering insects. She had already spied a blue tapper hammering away and a pair of tiny skaala sitting together on a branch. Beyond the charred trunk of a nearby tree was a sprawling bush. One side was blackened, but in the middle was a handful of pretty purple flowers. Cerrin strode forward and cradled one in her hand.

She closed her eyes and said a prayer to the ancients and to the lost. They were all out there somewhere now: shades, wandering and content. She wanted nothing more than to be among them.

Go now!

Run!

Cerrin had to bunch her fists, set her feet; physically stop herself from moving.

"Girl, come away."

She spun around and found Yeterris right behind her.

The governor fingered his golden bracelet. He was flanked by two guards: uniform and hair dark, skin and guns the same silvery gray.

"I shall not repeat myself."

Cerrin walked over to him.

"We must work quickly this morning. Count Talazeer will be joining us later with a party from the *Galtaryax*. Once his inspection is complete, he wishes to embark on a hunt. You will assist him."

"A hunt?"

"Apparently a pair of these toothed creatures were seen near here. What do you call them?"

"Brown boar?" Cerrin knew that Stripe and some of the other guards had been into the forest before, returning with skulls and tusks. Hunting for sport was a practice forbidden by the Echobe, who killed animals only when other sources of food were unavailable. Cerrin herself had once been reprimanded by her father for chasing boar with a stolen spear. The custom didn't exist solely because of respect for fellow creatures; hunting large animals was dangerous.

"No," said Yerris. "These large things, with the yellow fur."

"They call them damareus, sir," said one of the guards.

"Yes—those," said Yeterris impatiently.

Cerrin had seen damareus only twice in her life and those had been solitary creatures, not pairs. The Echobe had never dared even consider hunting them and would move entire villages if one came near.

Damareus were not the largest creatures in the Great Forest, but they were considered by all tribes to be the most deadly. Six-legged and as tall as a man, they could reach twenty feet in length and leap three times that distance with ease. Cerrin had watched one pursue its prey across open ground, and her eyes had barely been able to keep up. The second damareus she had seen was dead. She recalled her father pulling back the mouth to reveal a pair of curved incisors as long as her arm. The teeth were so strongly mounted that her uncle had eventually given up trying to lever them out.

"Well?" demanded Yeterris. "Do you know these animals?"

"Yes, governor, but we do not hunt them. One alone would be dangerous enough. A pair—"

"Hunting is not an interest of mine, but I gather that an element of danger is part of the enjoyment. I'm sure the count will have enough weaponry to counter any threat."

"They work together, and they are too fast to shoot." Cerrin pointed at the nearest guard's gun. "Even with those."

"So they can outrun a shell?" said the other soldier with a sneer.

Cerrin just shook her head. If the count wanted to try his hand, she certainly wouldn't dissuade him. In fact, she rather liked the idea of being around to see a damareus tear the Vitaari to pieces.

Three hours later, Cerrin was finished. She knew that the sooner her work was complete, the more chance she would have of a little time to herself. As usual, the technicians' first task had been to release dozens of their little machines. These flew off into the forest or walked along the ground or burrowed into the soil. They later returned one by one and attached themselves to a larger machine mounted on tracks. Whenever one arrived, the technicians would eagerly read their data-pads and discuss the findings. They would show Cerrin pictures of plants and animals and sometimes take her to the edge of the clearing to discuss particular examples.

Occasionally it was clear to her why they needed her advice. They would ask her about certain species of tree: the hardness of the wood and what size they could grow to and what the root systems were like. And they were always very interested in how certain plants affected the soil; she knew that some of the substances within the ground could disrupt their machinery. And then there were the animals: their behavior, lifespan, breeding patterns, diet. Most of the time she could help, but about a quarter of the species here were new to her. Once satisfied she was still useful to them, Cerrin decided to be honest about what she did and didn't know.

The technicians were often impatient with her, and she saw they preferred to use their machines. One, however, was slightly less unfriendly than the others, and she gleaned from him that they were about six hundred miles northeast of Fourteen. This confirmed what

Cerrin already suspected: she was in an area far beyond the territory of her tribe. She didn't even know if any Echobe had ever occupied or passed through these lands.

Once certain she was no longer needed, she approached the governor, who was sitting on a chair in the middle of a pile of cargo containers. The guards were there too, eating from little boxes. Like most of the Vitaari food, it smelt disgusting.

Yeterris looked up from his data-pad. "Well done, girl. I'm told you've been most helpful. Would you like some food?"

"Not that," she said. "There are some desaai trees over there. The berries are delicious. I could fetch you some too."

"Probably poisonous," muttered one of the guards.

Yeterris glared at him. "No, thank you, Cerrin. But you must keep up your strength for this afternoon. Surely you can eat some of the biscuits?"

Cerrin had tried them before. They were horribly sweet, but she had to admit they seemed to provide a lot of energy. Compared to what they were given at the mine, it was an opportunity she could not refuse. She walked between two of the hulking guards and reached into the nearest container. The biscuits were wrapped in the transparent paper that the invaders used to cover everything. Cerrin took one packet and placed another in the pocket of her overalls. Leaning back against a container, she tore open the wrapper with her teeth. Yeterris gave an approving smile.

From the jungle came a high-pitched screech. The governor and the guards all froze and looked across the clearing. The technicians stopped their work. Again came the screech. Two of the soldiers dropped their food and grabbed their guns.

Yeterris stood up. "This… damareus?"

Cerrin surprised herself with a giggle. "Triterk. Female by the sounds of it. It's a bird. About six inches long. Will give you a nasty peck if you get too close to its nest though."

She laughed again as the men put down their weapons and returned to their food.

Yeterris cleared his throat. "How can you love this place?"

Cerrin ate her biscuits; there didn't seem much point trying to answer him.

The terrain was not easy going. The marshy ground was soft, and with every step the combat shells sank in deep. Though the motors had no difficulty pulling the legs free, this was yet another added drain on the energy cells. They could have continued flying, but the squad had used forty percent of their fuel reaching the natives' last known position. As usual, sensor information was severely disrupted by the mineral deposits strewn beneath the plain that surrounded the mine. According to Governor Sekithis, his troops experienced the same problems all the time; they would get a firm sensor fix, then arrive to find the troublesome primitives had disappeared.

As he popped his helmet screen and surveyed the ground ahead, Vellerik now realized how difficult this apparently simple operation might become. In amongst the undergrowth and occasional emaciated tree were clusters of rounded boulders as far as the eye could see. There were hundreds of them, any one of which might be hiding their prey.

The Colonial Guard were fifty kilometers north of Mine Ten, hunting a group who had finally succeeded in smashing one of the water pipes that supplied the installation. Vellerik, Lieutenant Triantaa, and half his men had been on the ground for two hours and had seen no trace of the natives known as "Batal."

"Sir, did you know it means 'without?'"

Triantaa also had his helmet screen up and was talking without his com-cell.

"What?"

"Batal, sir. In the Palanian language it means 'without.' Even the other inhabitants consider them primitive."

"Mmm."

"Probably off in a cave somewhere eating each other for breakfast," grumbled another of the men.

Vellerik couldn't be bothered to admonish him. He lifted his leg a fraction, and the shell did the rest, taking another squelching step forward. He turned to Perttiel, who was on tech duty and monitoring all of the sensor information coming from the shells and the Mine Ten drones up in the sky.

"Anything?"

"Sorry, captain. It's these formations. There's toronal and quelkite in all of them—life signs just aren't coming through."

"How much flying time left, excluding return?" asked Vellerik.

"Between fifteen and seventeen minutes, sir," answered Triantaa.

"Assign yourself and the others a search grid. Get as far as you can in three minutes. Check as many formations as possible from above, then re-assemble here."

"Yes, sir."

As Triantaa doled out the orders, Vellerik yawned and said, "Water." The pipe appeared from the right side of the helmet's interior. He closed his lips over it and drank.

Having expected an easy day, he had taken a double dose of Almana's Breath the previous night. He needed doubles every time now: his body was getting used to it again. He had fallen asleep straight afterward and woken late, feeling disoriented. Then he'd received the order from Count Talazeer: Vellerik was to deal with the problem at Mine Ten immediately, and immediately meant today.

But the operation was not going well, and the squad would look rather foolish if they failed against the least developed of the planet's tribes. Time was getting on, and the shells were designed for short-term use: devastating swift strikes, not lengthy search operations. Vellerik didn't want to find himself back in these stinking marshes the following day.

"Ready, sir," reported Triantaa.

"Go. Report any sightings immediately."

The troops fanned out.

"And don't spray me with that shit like you did last time."

The men all took another few steps, then started their engines. As they eased into the air, mud was sent flying, though none struck

Vellerik. The troop continued up to twenty meters, then moved away along five different routes.

A lizard nosed its way out of a bush, peered at the enormous hybrid of man and machine in front of it, then withdrew. Imagining the Batal doing exactly the same, Vellerik spat.

"Perttiel, any better from up there?"

"Yes, sir. Multiple readings. Either large animals or humanoids. I've got a grouping to the west. I think—"

"Captain, it's Saarden. Multiple contacts. Ten… no… twenty… more. They're coming out of the rocks, running away from me."

"Hold your position."

Vellerik checked the main display and powered up. His helmet screen came down, and the boot jets began to rumble. Within seconds he was up and flying toward Saarden's position.

"Troop, converge on me."

Vellerik watched Saarden ascend as spears flew up at him. He waited until the soldier had halted, then came along beside him. Forty meters below was a formation of three large circular boulders mottled with brown and black. The last of the natives pouring from between two of them followed the others north. Even those who had dared unleash their weapons were now fleeing.

"Pretty fast, eh, sir?" said Saarden. "Must be some tunnel or cave under there."

Half a kilometer ahead was a larger rock formation.

Vellerik checked his display again. "Triantaa, Dekkiran—get ahead of them and land. Zarrinda, cover the east; Perttiel, the west. Saarden, with me. Weapons ready but do not fire without my order."

Vellerik clicked another button, and his green tactical display appeared on the screen. Listed down one side were the four weapons available to him. Taking the lead, he eased the suit forward and downward at twenty kilometers per hour.

Stealing an occasional glance back at their enemies, the natives sped across the ground with sure-footed ease. They looked just like those in the footage Vellerik had seen: dark-skinned with long, matted hair. Barefoot and clad in animal hides, all appeared to be young males.

The Vitaari landed almost simultaneously, surrounding the Batal, who swiftly retreated into a densely packed group. Spears raised, they shouted at each other and their enemies.

"Keep your distance for now," instructed Vellerik.

"Doesn't even sound like language," said Saarden, who was five meters to his superior's right.

"A few on this side advancing toward us," said Triantaa.

Vellerik heard a loud impact through coms. "What was that?"

"Spear into my helmet, sir. Just bounced off."

"Brave," said someone, Vellerik couldn't tell who.

"Flamethrowers, Captain? Leave a few alive to tell the others what they saw?"

Vellerik knew exactly who that would be: Trooper Dekkiran had been desperate to kill something since arriving on the *Galtaryax*.

"Sir, they're advancing on me too," said Zarrinda.

"Hold your ground and hold fire," said Vellerik. "They can't hurt you."

Even in the event of a massed group of primitives grabbing a shell and managing to get the trooper on the ground, there was an unpleasant surprise waiting for them: an electrical shockwave that would stun or kill anything organic touching the shell's surface.

"Sir?" said Triantaa.

Vellerik had made his decision. "Triantaa, Dekkiran—take off, show them a way out."

"Yes, sir," said Triantaa after a pause.

"Zarrinda, Perttiel, Saarden—disruptor, beam only."

"Sir, what about—"

Triantaa snapped a response before Vellerik had a chance. "Dekkiran! You have your orders. Follow me."

The two troopers eased up into the air, sun flashing off the white shells. Slowly, warily, the primitives began to move toward the gap. A few were still shaking their spears at the Vitaari, but most had turned away from Vellerik and Saarden.

"Now, sir?" asked Zarrinda.

For a moment, Vellerik considered letting them all go. He imagined Seevarta at his right shoulder: watching, judging. But life wasn't that simple. If he didn't act now, these stupid creatures would continue what they had been doing. And Count Talazeer's orders had been unambiguous. He had no choice.

The Batal were all running now. They would have to fire into their backs. "Two targets each. No more."

Zarrinda fired first. The beam of yellow light sliced through the air and struck one of them between the shoulders. As he fell, a few others close by stopped. But when they saw what the disruptor had done to him, they bolted away at even greater speed. The other soldiers fired and more fell, the automated shots each finding their targets.

Vellerik already had his right arm up—the disruptor was mounted on the underside. He looked at his tactical display: the sight was flicking between targets. He selected two with his middle finger and felt the slightest of jolts as the disruptor fired. The others had already taken their second shots.

Triantaa reported in. "Remaining natives retreating to the north, sir. Not even looking back."

Zarrinda, Perttiel, and Saarden walked forward to examine the inert bodies lying upon the muddy ground.

"Look at this one. Is that the brain?" asked Saarden.

"No way—too big," replied Zarrinda with a snicker. "Perttiel, you can't shoot straight—missed the red zone on both of yours."

Saarden popped his helmet screen. "Look at their faces—the features. More like animals than men."

"Skull like that would fetch a decent price back home," observed Zarrinda. "Captain, can we—"

"Triantaa, round them up."

"Yes, sir."

As the troop lieutenant gave his instructions, Vellerik turned away. He hoped it would be enough: enough for the Batal, and enough for Talazeer.

7

The pile of flesh lay stinking and steaming in the heat. The sun had reached its zenith and penetrated even the dense canopy overhead. Insects whined and buzzed around them, but even they seemed slow in the thick, enervating air. Cerrin didn't know what the meat was, but it didn't seem to be working. And she didn't know what the count was saying, but it seemed that he was becoming rather bored.

The little machines had picked up traces of a damareus several miles from the clearing. As soon as the count arrived, he ordered one of the technicians and two of the guards to accompany him. Cerrin deduced that he didn't feel her help was needed; only after a prolonged discussion with Governor Yeterris had she been told to join the party.

Stripped of most of their equipment, the soldiers had used a remarkable tool to cut through foliage. Held in one hand, the device projected a spinning whirl of light that obliterated anything it touched. The Vitaari clearly thought they were moving quietly, but the only one who showed any feel for the ground was the count's bodyguard. Cerrin had previously seen him and his master only from a distance, but she now realized that Talazeer had chosen his defender well.

Marl seemed more animal than man and moved across the uneven terrain and tangled undergrowth with ease, clawed feet occasionally visible beneath his cloak. Though the soldiers did their work efficiently, there was always a root or a tuft of grass to trip on, and the count had done so several times, cursing upon each occasion. To begin with he had carried his gun: a long, thin weapon quite different to what the soldiers used. But as the going became harder, Marl had taken it from him.

The count had it back now though, and he seemed to enjoy holding it. He and the bodyguard were standing behind a huge fallen tree a hundred feet from the bait. Close by was the technician, who had been criticized several times for not properly monitoring his equipment. Strapped around his neck was a searching device that beeped at regular intervals. The two tired soldiers, meanwhile, had been told off for talking and were now sitting on the ground in silence, trying not to fall asleep. They seemed relieved to be able to take their rifles off. Cerrin could tell that great strength was required to wield the bulky, impressive weapons. She wondered if she would even be capable of firing one.

Eyes narrowed, arms resting on the vine-covered tree, the count surveyed the ground ahead. He was wearing military boots and trousers with a black sleeveless top. Cerrin noted now that he was more slender than the soldiers and his physique was as flawless as his face. Having studied animals all her life, she could not help admiring the size and power of the Vitaari bodies. Whichever god or goddess had made them had done a good job with that part of them at least.

Cerrin was standing alone, watching a spider spin an intricate web between three twigs. Determined to enjoy every moment, she tried to ignore the presence of the others and open up all her senses; these memories might have to sustain her for months.

The reverie was broken by a bitter curse. Talazeer slapped the side of his gun and turned around. He made some demand of the technician, who looked up from his equipment and shook his head. Talazeer kicked a pile of leaves. Marl glanced over his shoulder, then looked back at the bait.

The count walked up to Cerrin, one hand smoothing his long

black hair. His cheeks twitched as he looked her over. He reached up to the translator attached to his collar and activated it.

"I'm told you know this place—these creatures."

"I know the forest, but I've never been here. And I've only ever seen one live damareus."

"They can sniff out flesh and blood from great distances. Why do they not come?"

"Could be a hundred reasons."

"Call me 'sir.' What reasons?"

"Perhaps they prefer live prey, sir."

"Actually, I'd like you to use 'Excellency.' If they prefer live prey, perhaps I should send you out there."

Cerrin could think of worse ways to go. At least she would die in the forest.

"Perhaps you should go yourself, Excellency."

Talazeer smiled. "Some of you people seem almost to want death. It's strange, given how few years you live."

"There are worse things than death, Excellency."

"Such as?"

Cerrin suddenly realized the others were watching. She had heard what the count had done to troublemakers at the other mines. She decided to keep quiet.

He stepped forward, shadowing her. Cerrin felt a wave of nausea as she saw that odd, shiny gray skin up close.

"What's your name, girl?"

"Cerrin, Excellency."

"Do you know what I think, Cerrin? I think the creatures can smell you."

He ran his finger across her forehead, then showed her the droplets of sweat. The Vitaari did not seem to sweat.

"You stink." Talazeer wiped his finger down the middle of her overalls.

One of the others laughed as he walked back to the fallen tree.

They left not long after, trudging back along the trail the soldiers had made. Had it not been for the man posted at the rear behind her, Cerrin would have run. The combination of the pull of the forest and the encounter with Talazeer had convinced her that the time had come once more. She could not stand to spend another day with these… things. It didn't seem right to call them people. Though she knew she should be enjoying this last hour or so, she could not lift her head, let alone her mood.

Only when they passed close to the bend of a small river did her spirits rise a little. Though the water was green and thick with weed, the gurgling flow of the stream reminded her of beautiful places and happier times. Washing clothes and blankets and plates and bowls had been a constant occupation: how many countless hours had she spent with her mother and the other women of her tribe?

Beside the river was a sprawling fern that would make an excellent shelter. Cerrin indulged herself with thoughts of laying there, sleeping a peaceful sleep—among the green things, below the stars.

But the path angled away from the river, and soon the sight and smell of the water was lost. A few minutes later, the technician abruptly stopped in front of her. The boxy device was beeping again. He held it up to his face and examined the display. The soldier in front of him stopped too.

Count Talazeer—at the front with Marl—snapped something at them. The men continued on until the technician spoke. Then they all halted. Sweeping a branch aside, the count marched back to the technician and questioned him. None of them had their translators on so Cerrin had no idea what was being said, but the Vitaari had all turned in the same direction. The count continued to interrogate the technician, who answered without taking his gaze from the device.

Marl left the path and stared out at the forest, head moving slowly as he scanned the terrain. The vegetation here was less dense: tall, narrow trees well spread across a carpet of thick grass. For the first time on the trip, the bodyguard reached beneath his cloak and pulled out a gun. The weapon seemed different to the others; it was white and composed of curved, twisted parts. The only recognizable part was the cylindrical barrel.

The count joined the bodyguard and took his own gun from his shoulder. He said something to Marl, and the invader reluctantly lowered his weapon, then re-attached it to his belt. Grinning like an excited child, Talazeer barked orders at the soldiers. With Marl stationed to the count's left, they fanned out to the right but did not ready their weapons. The technician walked over to the count and pointed at the forest. Cerrin crossed the path and stood behind him. All of them except Marl continued to speak, voices now low and urgent.

Cerrin could not believe a damareus was actually approaching, but the truth was she didn't know how they behaved. If they had not encountered people before, the powerful creature had no reason to fear them. Perhaps it would attack.

One of the soldiers pointed at a stand of trees over to the right. The count dropped to one knee, and the technician retreated. Marl stayed absolutely still.

"It's there?" whispered Cerrin, but the technician ignored her. He looked as though he wished he were back in the clearing with his compatriots.

As Count Talazeer brought his rifle up, Cerrin caught her first sight of the damareus. Hunched low, the beast was moving slowly but purposefully through the grass toward them. The pale yellow fur was not difficult to see, but it seemed obvious to Cerrin it had no need or desire to hide itself.

Despite the count's orders, the soldiers readied their weapons and took aim. Marl turned his body toward the creature and reached inside his cloak.

Now no more than a hundred feet away, the damareus would soon have a clear run at them. The head was immense: ears upright, snout broad, and two huge white incisors stretching down well below the jaw. The eyes seemed to burn orange and were fixed upon the interlopers.

Cerrin recalled the feeling she had experienced with her father all those years ago. The creature was magnificent and—despite all she had witnessed since her capture—one of the most terrifying things she had ever seen. The tremors began in her fingers and spread swiftly up her arms. The Vitaari still did not realize what they were dealing with.

"They're quick," she said to the technician. "Quicker than you can believe."

The technician looked as frightened as she had seen a Vitaari. He activated his translator so he could understand.

"Tell them," breathed Cerrin. "They're very, very quick."

He spoke. Only Marl looked at her.

One of the soldiers moved to improve his angle on the beast, which was now higher on its four back legs. The head never seemed to move.

The technician's device was still beeping, but now another noise sounded. In his haste to bring the display closer, the Vitaari lost his grip and the machine slid out of his hands, the strap jolting his neck. He blurted something at the others, all of whom turned around.

Cerrin heard the thrum of large feet striking the ground, but the damareus was still advancing slowly. Then something crashed through branches to her left.

The second creature was a blur of movement. It powered between two trees and leapt at them, curved claws outstretched.

Its target had been Marl, but the bodyguard had already thrown himself to one side. As the damareus hit the ground and skidded across the grass, the unarmed technician tried vainly to scramble away.

Cerrin retreated, eyes fixed on the creature, which was between her and the count. *Ikala, god of battle, see me, hear me, help me.*

Roaring, the damareus spun. Its thick tail struck the technician's back, knocking him ten feet across the ground.

The guns of the soldiers rattled. Faces grim, arms shaking, they fired straight into the creature's side. Thick gouts of dark blood filled the air as metal pierced flesh. With one last attack, the damareus swept a paw at them. The claws raked across a soldier's gun and tore into his neck. He fell, screaming. Somehow the creature was still moving.

A line of blue light flashed in front of Cerrin, striking the damareus in the head. It slumped onto its back legs immediately, smoke rising from the scorched fur. With a final breath its head struck the ground, one tooth embedding itself several inches in the earth.

Marl fired a second shot to be sure, then looked over at his master.

Talazeer was down on his knees, staring open-mouthed at the dead creature.

Marl spoke quietly in Vitaari, then pointed at the first damareus, which was still moving toward them. He raised the strange weapon once more, but Talazeer again yelled an order. Just as the count turned and aimed his rifle, the damareus flew at them. Fifty feet became thirty. Thirty became ten. Talazeer fired and missed.

He was saved by a tree just in front of him. The damareus caught it a glancing blow and had to lunge again to reach him. But its claws scraped nothing but air.

Marl had already hauled his master to his feet and shoved him back toward the path. But as he let go, the strap of Talazeer's weapon snagged on his and pulled the bodyguard's gun from his grip.

The damareus's huge head smashed into the tree, and the branches whipped at Marl and Talazeer, sending them sprawling across the path. As the second soldier aimed his weapon, the creature spun its rear end, the tail catching the Vitaari in the head, knocking him away.

Cerrin knew she should be running, but the spectacular horror unfolding before her had rooted her to the spot. As Marl and Talazeer dragged themselves up, the damareus pounced onto the fallen soldier, claws tearing into flesh.

Cerrin reckoned she might be next, and the thought of it brought clarity. One of the few things she knew for certain about the creatures was that they didn't like water.

The river.

As Marl pushed his master across the path toward her, Cerrin considered telling them. She did not consider it for long: the pair would make a useful distraction as she fled.

Cerrin sprinted back along the trail, blood pumping in her ears. She cringed as the damareus roared and wood splintered behind her. She heard someone shouting: it might have been Talazeer. Glimpsing the river up ahead, she left the trail, leaping another fallen log and slipping smoothly through dozens of hanging vines.

Something behind her. Something moving quickly.

Not daring to look back, she ducked under a low branch and dived headlong off the bank, arrowing into the water. The weed pulled away as she sank deeper and kicked out. Only when she could no longer hold her breath did she allow herself to float upward. Just as she surfaced, something else struck the water.

She was twenty feet from the bank and had to push the clinging weed away to suck in air. Whatever had followed was splashing through the water toward her. When she saw the flailing gray arms and long black hair, she was relieved to find it was Talazeer. Cheeks twitching, eyes wide with panic, the count swam toward her, babbling in his own language.

Cerrin was no longer looking at him.

The damareus was so still that she had not noticed it at first. It was standing on the bank, chest heaving. Vines and other greenery hung from its body, and a wound upon its shoulder bled freely. The thick black lips trembled as it watched the moving shape in the water.

"Stay still!" snapped Cerrin.

The count's eyes somehow widened even further. Now close to her, he stopped swimming and turned. Muttering to himself in his own tongue, he began to move back past Cerrin.

"Still!" she repeated.

His translator clearly wasn't on, but this time the count understood.

The damareus paced one way, then the next. It looked down at the water, then sniffed it.

Talazeer smoothed his hair back over his ears and stared across the river.

"Don't look at it," said Cerrin. "Don't provoke it. Look away."

She had to show him what she meant. The count nodded and did as he was told, but Cerrin ignored her own advice as the damareus lowered its body onto the bank. One paw went in, then the other.

She glimpsed movement. Something black, springing from tree to tree about thirty yards back. It stopped. Marl straightened up, standing in the Y of a tree with a split trunk. His arm came up out of the folds of his cloak, the white gun in his hand.

The damareus retreated a step. Whiskers trembling, it turned its head.

"No!" yelled Cerrin. "Here!"

The damareus looked down at the water once more, then settled onto its haunches, ready to leap.

Cerrin had just begun to turn when the beam of blue light struck the damareus behind the neck. The entire body shook, dislodging clumps of mud and grass from the bank. Then the second shot hit. Suddenly still, the creature slid into the water, flesh smoking.

Marl lowered his weapon and leaped down to the ground.

After a victorious cry, the count swam back across the river. Cerrin was giving serious thought to making a try for the other side when several more figures appeared. The guards from the clearing joined Marl at the bank; one of them already aiming his gun at her.

Even though it was the bodyguard who had saved them, Cerrin thanked Ikala as she swam back, staying well away from the dead damareus. She was sure it was the god of battle that helped her hold her nerve and think clearly.

Once on the bank, Talazeer seemed quite full of himself, apparently berating the guards for not arriving in time. When he looked at the huge, dead creature, a manic grin spread across his face.

Once she could feel solid ground underneath, Cerrin pulled herself up through the mud toward the bank. The guards ignored her, of course, but she was surprised when a large gray hand gripped her wrist and helped her up out of the water.

Talazeer kept hold of her and held her gaze for a long moment. When he realized the others were watching, he let go.

. . .

Vellerik looked on as Triantaa and the others checked the combat shells. The cleaning drones had been working on them for hours, but the clinging mud seemed to get everywhere. He'd also insisted the troops inspect all the armament and other systems by hand; it wasn't strictly necessary but constituted another useful method of keeping them busy.

The half of the squad that had remained aboard the *Galtaryax* clearly expected some rather more exciting tales. Dekkiran and the others made little attempt to hide their disappointment at the low body count. Vellerik had even heard the trooper bemoaning his lack of trophies but left it to Triantaa to shut him up. He couldn't have cared less about the opinions of men half his age who knew nothing of real fighting, real war.

Triantaa walked over to him, holding a handful of small metal cubes. "Imager data clips showing the operation, sir. Remember Count Talazeer wanted them?"

Just as Vellerik nodded, his com-cell buzzed.

"Yes?"

"It's Danysaan. Meet me in bay three. The count's shuttle has just returned. Apparently there was some kind of incident."

"Incident?"

"We lost two men."

"On my way."

"Captain?" Danysaan offered him the data clips.

"Not now." Vellerik lowered his voice. "In fact, only if he asks for them." He pointed at the troops. "And make sure they don't go mouthing off in the canteen. If Dekkiran or any of the others has a problem with my decision-making, they can take it up with me."

"There won't be any problems, sir."

Vellerik marched out of bay two, along the adjoining corridor and into three. The shuttle ramp was already down, and Danysaan was waiting at the bottom of it. One technician came off first with their equipment, then two more leading a wheeled trolley upon which was a body covered by a sheet. With them was another tech whose arm had been bandaged and strapped. His cheek was heavily bruised.

"Who are they?" asked Vellerik as the trolleys passed.

"Levess and Staalter, from Mine Three. Governor Yeterris thought it best that they be brought straight here."

"What happened?"

"I—"

Danysaan was halted by the sight of Count Talazeer yelling at a trio of crewmen who were inspecting the shuttle's hull. He beckoned for them to join him inside, and a minute later another larger trolley appeared. It needed the three men and two more of the shuttle's crew to manhandle it down the ramp. Lying on top was the carcass of a huge creature with several dark wounds upon its body.

Striding along behind it were Count Talazeer and Marl. When the trolley came to a stop, one of the techs pointed at the carcass's stomach: some malodorous bodily fluid was leaking onto the floor. The count waved a dismissive hand at him and greeted Danysaan and Vellerik.

He pointed at the two dead guards and shook his head. "Terrible shame. Unfortunately, both men let themselves down. If it hadn't been for Marl and that local guide, I might not be standing here now." He turned toward the creature. "Incredible, isn't it? Called a damareus. I have never witnessed such a combination of speed and power. Danysaan, I would like to have it frozen. When I return home, I will have it displayed."

Vellerik peered at the wounds upon the creature's neck, then the old-fashioned hunting gun hanging from the count's shoulder.

"You are right, captain," said Talazeer. "Unfortunately, it was not I who administered the fatal shot. Good old Marl—always around when you need him. Perhaps it takes one beast to kill another."

The Drellen looked impassively at the dead creature. Vellerik noted the dirt upon his cloak and the mud on his clawed feet.

"Well, Danysaan, hadn't you better get moving? We're going to need a very large container to accommodate this." Talazeer looked down at his hands. "And I must go and get myself cleaned up at once. Oh, Vellerik—how did you fare at Mine Ten? I trust our spear-wielding friends won't be troubling us again?"

"Hopefully not, sir."

"Please remember to pass on the data clips. It's a shame I didn't think to have an imager to capture this beast in motion. Do you know how we got away? The native guided me to the river. It seems that these damareus don't like water. I must admit she handled herself very well. Name's Cerrin. Very tall and athletic. Rather impressive."

The count was all set to leave when Vellerik spoke.

"What about them?" He nodded at the dead guards. "What happened?"

Talazeer grimaced. "As I said, they did not perform well."

"They both had their rifles?"

"They did. And they both got shots away, but the creature was too strong and fast."

"It must have gotten close to be able to kill them. Why wasn't it taken down at range?"

Talazeer paused for a moment, then looked at Danysaan. "Don't the guards come under your jurisdiction, administrator?"

"Yes, Excellency."

"As I thought. It is most kind of you to take an interest, Captain, but it's really nothing you need concern yourself with."

"Sir, I am also concerned about your safety," lied Vellerik, who could not believe two men had lost their lives for Talazeer's trophy. "If I may say so, this seems like an unnecessary risk."

"Life is risk, isn't that what they say?" The count was already on his way out. "And captain, please don't forget those data clips."

8

The snow whipped passed them, blasted this way and that by the unpredictable winds that pummeled the walkway. Occasionally the metal squeaked and groaned, as if protesting at the assault.

Sonus kept his hands inside his overalls and watched his friend. Karas gripped the rail tight as he stared out at the snow. He had waited for Sonus there as the others descended; it was the first time they had met for several days. Three weeks had passed since their discussion in the caverns. Qari was struggling to get through each day, and Karas looked terrible, as if he'd neither eaten nor slept. Sonus spent every hour expecting to hear the worst. He could not imagine what they were going through.

Karas—who had not yet spoken—turned around. "We can't keep it. You will help?"

"If that is what you both want."

"It's for the best."

"Qari agrees?"

Karas gritted his teeth. "We… should have done it sooner. She says she can feel it moving now. I will persuade her. I must. There is no other way."

Sonus had not yet approached Kadessis. The atmosphere in Mine Three since Tanus's death had been as tense as he'd known it: workers fearful, the Vitaari on edge. But things were beginning to settle down, and with the increased workload, machines were break-ing down more often. He saw Kadessis almost every day.

And then there were the freighters, now landing even more regu-larly to collect the increased yield of terodite and aronium. Sonus had managed to strike up two conversations with one of the Lovirr pilots, a wary but polite fellow named Toroda. Before the invasion, he had travelled widely as a merchant and spoke passable Palanian.

"There might be."

"What?"

"There might be another way. If we could somehow protect Qari until the child is born, we might be able to get it out of here."

"Protect her? How?"

"I'm not sure yet. I don't want to say I can do it because I don't know. But there might be a chance."

"You have a way out, Sonus?"

"For you two, no. But for a little one who they never knew was here…"

Karas considered this for some time. "I cannot give her false hope."

"Do not. The chances are slim. But allow me a few more days. I will know by then. If not, I will help you do as you asked."

"I told her—it needn't be the end. We can try again. Later. After."

Sonus wasn't exactly sure how the chemical concoction might work, but he feared the damage to Orani's insides might be permanent.

"And if it comes to that—will she do it?"

Karas looked away for a moment. "I will make her. Even if she hates me for it. I cannot lose her, Sonus. I will not."

"Just give me those few days."

"Very well. I thank you, my friend."

"Shall we go down?"

Karas nodded but stopped after a few steps. "Someone said something today—during morning break. For three thousand years we Palanians prayed and gave offerings to the Maker. I myself would go with my mother to the old square and place offerings at the base of the pyramid mosaic. She would whisper prayers for every member of the family, alive or dead." Karas wiped his face. "But in the last century many of us gave up those beliefs. We looked to science and government and progress to improve our lives. We abandoned the Maker." Karas looked out again at the snow and the darkness. "I know you do not believe in such things, but it seems to me that he has now abandoned us."

It took Sonus two days to find an opportunity to talk to Kadessis alone. The Vitaari needed his help with the conveyor rail, one section of which was becoming unstable due to overuse. Their technicians had worked out a plan to shore up the mountings, but it was Sonus and his crew who completed the labor, and in very good time. Kadessis actually thanked him, remarking that his efforts would please the governor. Sonus made sure that he was still around when the administrator later left the tower heading for his own quarters. The compound was dark as he hurried out of the maintenance yard and caught up with the Vitaari.

"Sir, might I speak with you a moment?"

"Sonus, you're still here."

"Yes, sir. My apologies, but I wonder if I might ask your help with something."

The Vitaari looked around. They were alone and the closest building—the accommodation block—was forty feet away.

"What is it?"

"This will remain between us, sir?"

"You know I cannot make such a promise."

"Sorry. It's… a friend of mine. She has been talking strangely. She has not been herself. I fear that she is… having terrible thoughts."

Kadessis looked away for a moment and said, "I don't see what I can do."

"I am convinced, sir, that even a small change of scene would help. She is currently assigned to the secondary shaft, and all she talks of is the dark and the shadows and the noise. She is exhausted by it. All I wondered, sir, is if you might be able to re-assign her? Perhaps to a less taxing duty out here in the compound."

Kadessis scratched his neck and looked up at the sky.

Sonus kept his expression neutral, but he could feel his jaw trembling. So much depended on the Vitaari's response.

"I would need a reason."

While Sonus tried to force his addled mind to work faster, Kadessis continued. "A worker in such a condition might affect the morale and production of those around her. It might be beneficial for all if she was temporarily re-assigned."

Sonus had to stop himself grinning. "Yes, sir."

"The name?"

Sonus told him.

"I can make no guarantees. You do understand that?"

"Of course, sir."

"Good night," said Kadessis.

"Good night, sir."

By the time it actually happened, Sonus had almost given up hope. Four days later, at dawn, Qari was taken out of her line by a guard and escorted to the kitchens. She was to work there with the day shift, preparing food for the Vitaari. Sonus didn't hear the news until that night, when Karas came to his cavern.

"I can hardly believe it," he said, as he sat down on one of the stools Sonus had fashioned from metal off-cuts.

"How did you… I probably shouldn't ask."

"It's best you don't."

"Qari smiled today," continued Karas. "She smiled. The women in the kitchens were surprised that she'd been re-assigned, but they were friendly enough. She's in bed now, working on her overalls— she's adjusting them so that it's not so obvious. They wear aprons there—that will help. And there's hardly a guard near the place."

Though glad to see his friend happy, Sonus could not let himself get carried away. This was only a temporary solution.

"In truth I could not be sure that it would work out. I could easily have exposed Qari. You too."

"And yourself." Karas leaned forward. "I will never forget this, Sonus."

"That's not why I mentioned it. It was a risk. And now I have to take another one."

Again he had to wait; this time for the next freighter to arrive. He knew he had been fortunate so far: the increasing amount of repair and maintenance work had kept him out of the mines for over a week and the approach to Kadessis could hardly have turned out better. Now he faced greater challenge, and the outcome was far harder to predict. But whichever way he looked at it, he had to try.

By delaying repairs to a landing light, Sonus made sure he was around for the loading phase. Other than a couple of guards and a technician who were idly watching cargo crates ease along the conveyor and into the ship's hold, there were no other Vitaari close by. Sonus had been relieved to note the designation on the vessel's side—the same freighter had been used for the last few visits. He just hoped the Lovirr Toroda was on board.

Sonus made no attempt to hide himself as he walked along the side of the landing strip; he had an excuse ready if necessary. The ship had clearly not been designed with aesthetics in mind: the huge, angular hold took up three quarters of its volume and the engine block at the rear was similarly ugly. Sticking out at the front was a small cockpit; it reminded Sonus of a sand turtle's head.

He walked around one of the landing struts, then climbed up a short ladder and into the hold. Two Lovirr were at work there in wheeled loaders, stacking the crates one by one. Sonus waited until he could see their faces—neither was Toroda. He started up another ladder connected to a walkway that ran around the top of the hold and provided access to the cockpit. Sonus climbed quickly; Kadessis or one of the other administrators might call him at any time.

Once upon the walkway, he spotted two Lovirr leaving the cockpit and heading toward the front of the hold. One was Toroda, and when he saw Sonus, he left his colleague and walked over to him. Like all Lovirr, he was small: no more than five feet, with the squat, compact frame common to his race. Their custom was for all males to grow heavy beards, and his was dotted with gray.

"Good day, Sonus." Toroda spoke Palanian well but with a harsh accent that sometimes made him hard to understand.

"Good day. How are you?"

"Busy. You too, I expect. Can I help you with something?"

"I hope so."

The noise from the loaders below was loud; Sonus did not want to have to shout.

"Is there somewhere quieter?"

"Yes, but you must be quick. I am expected outside."

Toroda led him back into the cockpit but kept well away from the windows. "What is it?"

"You spoke before to me about the other mines that you visit. Have you heard of any people still free—outside, I mean?"

Sonus did not find it easy to read the expressions of the Lovirr, but Toroda appeared anxious.

"Rumors, occasionally."

"And where are they?"

"Why, Sonus?"

"Curiosity. We hear nothing else of the outside world."

"Is that all? You seem to me like a man with something specific on his mind."

Sonus tried not to gulp. "All right. I need your help."

"Then I must ask you to stop. I am sorry, but I will not endanger myself or my family. You know as well as I do what… they are capable of."

Toroda went to walk past him. Without thinking, Sonus placed a hand on his shoulder. Toroda shrank backwards, suddenly fearful.

Sonus held up both hands. "I'm sorry. But a life is at stake."

"And what of the lives of my children?" The Lovirr gestured at the cockpit. "I worked hard for this. To give my family a chance. You have no right—"

"I see that now. I apologize."

"You should go. We should not be seen talking. By anyone."

Sonus turned around, but Toroda had not finished.

"Please do not talk to me again. Stay away."

Once back outside, Sonus went to finish the job on the landing light, but his mind was buzzing as he knelt and took off his pack. It was bad enough that Toroda had refused to help, but he'd seemed so frightened; might he even go further and report the conversation to cover himself?

Gripping the edges of the light tightly, Sonus pried it free and laid it on the ground beside him. He glanced over his shoulder and spied the two guards standing near the front of the freighter. They were covering their ears, seemingly listening to their communicators. One of them said something to the other, and it seemed to Sonus that they were both looking at him.

They set off at marching pace—but not in his direction, toward the tower.

Sonus unscrewed the top of the light. He was about to examine it when a stone struck the ground and bounced off his foot. He looked around. A Lovirr was crouching behind one of the freighter's rear landing struts. He beckoned to Sonus.

Having checked he wasn't being watched, Sonus walked as casually as he could over to the strut. By standing close to the stranger he could remain well hidden. From above came a series of thuds and thumps as the loading continued.

The Lovirr was perhaps a bit younger than Toroda, also a little larger. He offered his hand, which Sonus shook.

"Name's Nomora."

"Sonus."

"I know. I hear you're a curious man."

Sonus wasn't sure how to respond or whether he even should.

What if Toroda had told him of his request? No tribe on Corvos had worked more closely with the Vitaari than the Lovirr. What if he was an informer?"

"Yes," added Nomora, whose accent was clearer than his compatriot's. "He told me. Toroda is not a curious man. Nor one to take risks. But he knows I am, and he is not entirely unsympathetic to what I do. We can trust him, and you can trust me."

Sonus knew he had little choice other than to do so. "Exactly what risks do you take?"

"I talk. I share information." Nomora gestured up at the ship. "I am in a good position to do so."

"There are more of you?"

"A few. We cannot tarry here long, Sonus. Tell me what you need to know."

"Are there free people out there? Anywhere?"

"Some, yes."

"Rebels?"

"That's not a word we use. For now we talk, and we watch, and we wait."

"What if I wanted to get something to them? Could you make that happen?"

"That depends."

"On what?"

"On you."

"I don't understand."

"I'm told you are very intelligent—that you understand more about the Vitaari machines even than we Lovirr. That knowledge is of great value. Tell me precisely what you require."

Sonus didn't know how long he had. Qari could be discovered at any time, and he could not know when he might be able to meet the Lovirr again. He told Nomora what he needed.

"That will be difficult. Very difficult. We will need a lot in return."

Sonus nodded. "Such as?"

"We will need *you*."

9

Cerrin sat against the cavern wall, well away from the glare of the artificial lights. The biscuits had run out long ago, and she was back on Vitaari rations. Today's midday delight came in a small transparent bag—a thick soup-like liquid that had to be squeezed out. It tasted entirely unnatural, but Cerrin was so hungry that she finished it quickly.

She was alone. The other women took their break in the tunnel where the air was a little fresher. It had been made clear that she was not welcome to join them. They somehow knew she had been on the trip with Yeterris and Talazeer, and the very mention of the count's name was enough to terrify them. As if her attempted escapes hadn't made things bad enough, she was now even more isolated. At least Dukas had stopped pestering her.

As she tried to wash the non-taste away with water, young Yarni trotted into the cavern. She held out her hand, and Cerrin passed her the empty bag. Yarni took it and put it in the sack she was carrying. She glanced toward the tunnel to check no one was watching, then abruptly sat down.

"Why does everyone always talk about you?"

"Good question."

Yarni's feet were only an inch or two from Cerrin's, who moved hers away.

"Did you try and escape again?"

"No."

"What happened then?"

Cerrin only answered because she hoped the truth might get through to the women and the other workers.

"The governor asked me to go along on a trip because I know about the forest. That's all."

"But you didn't try to escape?"

"No."

Yarni seemed disappointed.

"Not this time," added Cerrin with a grin.

"Is it true that you almost got across the river—the time before?"

"Almost." Cerrin was surprised by how much it hurt to say that.

"We lived by a river," said Yarni. She was a pretty girl with long, curly hair and intelligent eyes.

"Before? You can remember it?"

Yarni nodded.

"Do you speak any Echobe?"

"A few words."

"Where did you live?"

"Very far away. My father told me that no one from our tribe had ever seen the Empty Lands."

Cerrin knew that both of the girl's parents were gone; that was why the women were so protective toward her. "Do you remember the forest?"

Yarni thought about this for a moment, then shrugged.

"That's why I went with them," said Cerrin. "Just to spend some time there."

"My aunt says it's quiet. Here it's always noisy."

"She's right."

"My mother and father are there. They walk through the forest with the ancients and the other shades."

Cerrin's throat suddenly felt tight. "Yes."

"My aunt says I shouldn't say this but… sometimes I wish I was with them."

Without thinking, Cerrin leaned forward and gripped her hand. "No. You are young, Yarni. Young and strong. You will not join them. Not now. Not for a long time."

When the child pulled away, Cerrin realized she had scared her.

She reached out and this time held both her hands. "But I will show you the forest. We will go there together one day."

"Promise?"

"Promise."

Later that afternoon, she was called out of the line by Stripe, who explained that Yeterris wanted to speak to her. He escorted her to the tower and spoke most of the way. By the time they arrived, he'd asked her in five different ways what exactly had happened in the forest with Talazeer and the damareus. Cerrin didn't say a word.

She had never been up to the top of the tower before. With the hulking Stripe—now silent—behind her, she felt her stomach churn as the elevator zoomed upward, far faster than the ones they used in the mine.

When the doors opened, she was surprised by how few Vitaari were there. Four administrators sat in front of large displays, some of which showed different parts of the mine. Though Cerrin had occasionally seen such images on the data-pads, this was just another thing she could not comprehend—to watch something without being there?

When the Echobe had first witnessed what the Vitaari possessed, people had spoken about magic. But it was not magic the invaders depended on; it was their machines. They had machines to watch, machines to move, machines to talk to each other, and machines to kill. Cerrin sometimes looked at their silvery skin and lifeless faces and wondered if they were machines underneath, too. But though she had never seen black blood run herself, others had. She found the thought of it vaguely comforting: anything that bleeds can be killed.

The administrators had all turned around to look at her.

"This way." Grabbing a handful of her overalls, Stripe shoved her to the right and toward a smaller room. The door was open, and inside stood Governor Yeterris. He was standing over a large table, peering down at his own screen.

Noting the new arrivals, he touched the translator. "Ah. Cerrin. Come in."

Stripe pushed her forward but remained outside the doorway.

Yeterris ran a finger across the screen. It was set up on the table at an angle so Cerrin couldn't see what it showed.

What she could see was the grassy plain beyond the compound's northern wall. Like Yarni, she knew little of the Empty Lands; the thought of the endless, featureless terrain chilled her. Palanians and Kinassans and the other tribes felt the same way about the Great Forest.

"Yes," said the governor. "It is a fine view."

He wandered over to another table and poured himself a drink from an intricately carved bottle. The liquid was red. He sipped at it, then went to sit in a high-backed chair.

Cerrin glanced at a map upon the wall to her right. One part showed the surface of the installation, the other the mine itself: complete with all the tunnels and caverns. Cerrin had a picture of both in her head and reckoned they were as good as any map.

"You're probably thinking we need you for another scouting trip." Yeterris adjusted the folds of his tunic. "We may at some point but not yet. The findings from the site are still being analyzed; I'm not sure if we will proceed or not. But yesterday I spoke to Count Talazeer. He needs your help with a project of his. Come here."

Cerrin walked around the table. The governor moved his chair forward so he was closer to her and nodded at the screen. The display was divided into eight: each section showing a creature from the forest. Cerrin recognized all of them.

"Nothing as large or dangerous as those monstrous yellow things. And as I understand it, they can all be found relatively close to here."

The count aimed a finger at the screen. "Touch one. Any one."

Cerrin chose a picture of the sesskar—a large rodent noted mainly for its two tails. The change caused by her touch made her take a step back.

Yeterris snorted.

The whole screen had changed to show a larger image of the sesskar. Vitaari writing had appeared beside it, and various arrows pointed to different parts of the creature.

"A small team will be assigned to help you collect the animals."

Cerrin was confused.

"I thought you'd be happy," added the governor as she turned toward him. "More time in your beloved forest. You can start tomorrow."

"I don't understand."

"Count Talazeer wants the animals for his menagerie—a collection of live beasts. People like to see anything exotic—the count wishes to impress his guests back home with something they haven't seen before. I'm sure he will give you all the time you need. It seems he was rather impressed by the way you evaded that creature. I will have to send some guards with you, of course, but I'm sure you won't make any trouble while working for the count."

She shook her head.

"Good."

"No, sir. I can't do it."

"What? Why?"

She thought it best to be honest. "The others. They used to hate me because I tried to escape. Now they hate me because I help you. I can't do this as well."

"I am not offering you a choice, Cerrin."

"Governor, I have to live with these people."

"Girl, they are nothing compared to you. They do not have your… spirit."

"Please. I really would prefer not to do it."

"Come closer."

Cerrin took only one step. Yeterris sipped his drink and spoke quietly. "The guard outside. I do not particularly like him. But for a man in my position he does have his uses. If I so wish, I need not waste a single breath on attempting to persuade you. We both know that. Do we understand each other?"

"Yes, governor."

"I daresay you think me cruel."

She knew better than to reply to that.

"But the truth is, Cerrin—I'm the best friend you have."

"Well?"

Administrator Danysaan looked even more uncomfortable and anxious than usual. He cast a glance back at what had once been his office and shook his head. "Yield increases are still not enough. He asks the impossible.'

Clearly not in the mood for further conversation, Danysaan hurried away and could soon be heard calling for his deputy Rasikaar.

Glad he had been strong enough not to indulge himself in narcotic relief the previous night, Vellerik entered the office. As the door slid shut behind him, he once again found himself face to face with Marl. The Drellen was more interested in his sword; he was leaning against a wall and sharpening the edge with some kind of stone.

"Interesting encounter in the forest?" asked Vellerik.

"Not all that interesting," replied Marl. "I heard you've been killing natives. Or… not killing them. I know that Vitaari get soft in their old age, but I hadn't expected it of a former legionary."

Vellerik nodded at the stone. "That might be better used on your wit."

Talazeer strode out of an anteroom. "I must say you two are rather entertaining, but there are more pressing matters to attend to. Come, Vellerik."

He led him back through the door into what had now been transformed into his quarters. Garments were strewn across a large bed and a hunting gun lay on the floor, partly disassembled. Half of the largest wall screen showed an unlikely-looking creature with three curved tusks. The other half showed frozen footage from Vellerik's encounter with the Batal.

Talazeer waved a hand at the screen. "My uncle killed one of those on Sasalanga Prime. It weighs over three thousand kilos, would you believe? Unfortunately, the damareus is somewhat lighter. However—" The count held up a finger. "It is longer. By several centimeters. We will need an expert taxidermist, of course, but it's already frozen—should thaw out in decent condition."

Talazeer rubbed his chin. "I… I was reluctant to call you in, Erasmer."

Vellerik wasn't sure the use of his first name boded well.

Talazeer pointed at the other half of the screen. "We could watch it all, of course, but I don't really see the need. I think you know what I will say."

Vellerik could have played along, but he realized he was beginning to hate this young man. "Sir?"

"You wish me to spell it out?"

"Sorry, sir, I'm not sure what you mean."

"There were, what, fifty of these… Batal?"

"About forty, I think."

"You killed only eight. I would have left only eight alive—just enough to tell the others. And disruptors? Not much of a spectacle."

"I didn't realize I was there to create a spectacle, sir."

"You were there to stop these attacks. Every time the guards have to go out or your squad has to fly down, it costs. The Fleet needs the material, but it is the Resource Directorate that funds this operation. As well as improving production, I must keep expenditure down. Who's to say these bloody primitives might not return and cost me even more?"

"As far as I know, there have been no further sightings, sir."

"Not yet, Vellerik. Not yet." Talazeer let out a long breath. "This is the last thing I wanted. Please let me clear, I am not questioning your judgment. But I have certain targets in mind, and I must rule in a certain way. The incident with the assassin, now this? We must be strong, Erasmer. Hard."

The count paced around, wringing his hands. "I would hope to avoid any further such conversations. I feel awkward even now." He smiled. "I do so respect you, captain. Please tell me I will not have to feel awkward again."

Vellerik wondered: was this strange, arrogant noble as bad as he seemed or was it him? Hadn't he seen worse, done worse, many times before? Perhaps he was just too old.

It didn't really matter: the message was clear. If he defied Talazeer again, he might be removed from command. The shame would be intolerable—for him, for his family, even for Seevarta. He had been stupid to play these games. Stupid and unrealistic. He knew how The Domain worked. He just had to keep his head down, do as he was told, complete his last year; get out.

"You will not, sir. I assure you. It's just that I have seen how a strict approach can occasionally be counter-productive. Sometimes a strong response simply fans the flames. But you are right. The decisions are yours. I will do as you ask."

Three hours later, Vellerik received a message from Kerreslaa that made him suspect the count had known what was coming. But when he met the liaison officer in a quiet briefing room, Kerreslaa's panicked appearance and shaky voice convinced him that he had not been conspiring with his superior. In fact, Kerreslaa quickly disclosed that he didn't really want to involve Talazeer at all.

"He will be angry, captain. My initial report stated that there was no activity to concern us in the south."

"I thought there wasn't."

Kerreslaa gestured to the only active screen in the room, which showed a map of the southern sector. Vellerik was not familiar with the terrain, but he knew the Kinassans—the tough, nomadic people who occupied the south of Corvos's single continent—had been the most troublesome resistors during the invasion eighteen years ago; eventually an Imperial Legion battalion had been brought in to subdue them.

The remaining Kinassans had withdrawn, leaving the Vitaari to construct three mines. Without a local workforce, they had been forced to bring in laborers from other areas who simply wilted in the heat. When the extreme climate began to also have an impact on their machinery, the Resource Directorate decided to cut their losses and abandon the desert. Rumors occasionally surfaced of movement in the southern sector—from the mines closest to it—but no one had actually seen a Kinassan in five years.

Kerreslaa pointed to Mine Seven, which was the southernmost of the occupied installations. "Governor Fedriss has received some alarming reports since we visited with the count several weeks ago."

Kerreslaa moved his finger to a range of mountains several hundred kilometers east of Seven. "Never been much activity here. But long-range visual sensors have picked up smoke from manmade fires. First was here, second here, third here."

Next to each sighting was a reference detailing date and time. Kerreslaa had traced a path along a narrow pass, what looked like one of the few ways through the mountains.

"The southern end of the range borders the desert area. Could be Kinassans moving north. If they go much farther, they can threaten Seven and Nineteen."

"Any more from the sensors?"

"No. The long-range relays were scaled back about two years ago. Directorate orders—to reduce expenditure, of course.'

"Of course." Vellerik leaned over the display, studying the times of the sightings, using his finger to measure distances. "They're moving quite quickly."

"I believe they use some kind of animals well adapted to the desert. There's no one left here or on the surface who actually fought them. We have detailed files though."

Vellerik checked the last sighting of smoke, which was from the previous day. "They could reach Nineteen within a week."

"Yes."

Vellerik pointed at the northern end of the pass. "We need to get here, before they have a chance to spread out or move on Nineteen."

Kerreslaa ran two fingers across his brow.

"Tell the count," said Vellerik. "And tell him I'm dealing with it."

"But the costs—every time we use the shells."

"We're not going to use them. It's time my squad experienced some real soldiering."

"The Kinassans often attacked in force. Hundreds, at times."

"Thousands, as I recall. But I do not anticipate a problem." Vellerik glanced down at the display. "Especially as we will be there first."

He turned to Kerreslaa. "Tell him immediately or he will question the delay. And have the shuttle put on standby—I'll take the troop down tomorrow morning."

Kerreslaa seemed slightly taken aback by his enthusiasm. "Yes, captain."

"Send me all the files. Everything." Vellerik keyed his com-cell on his way out. "Triantaa, assemble the men. Cargo bay. Ten minutes."

10

Sonus was back in the mine. After his period of respite up on the surface, a full day's work in the tunnels came as a shock: the deafening noise, the weight of the drill, the juddering movements that seemed to shake every bone in his body. Worst of all was the dust. More than a dozen times he had to stop, put down the drill, take off his mask, and cough out the black muck. It left his throat raw and his stomach bitter; he longed for a job up top, but the communicator never came to his rescue. Unable to eat anything at lunch, he was almost on his knees when the shift finally ended.

He was in a team of four, but the others hadn't said much. His fellow workers could be roughly divided in two: those who viewed him as a collaborator no better than the Lovirr and those who saw him as a sensible pragmatist who did his best for himself and others where he could. It seemed these three were in the former group.

Sonus left his drill where it lay for the night shift and activated the drone that would collect the terodite he and the team had carved out in the last hour or so. The machine's magnetized tentacles hauled in the fist-sized lumps of terodite, ignoring the other deposits that came out during the drilling.

Sonus released his hot, blistered hands from the gloves, then followed the trio as they trudged up the sloping shaft; another crew would be down soon to continue their work. The men didn't even have the energy to talk to each other, and there was barely more conversation when their path converged with a larger tunnel and they joined the queue waiting for the elevator. A pair of Vitaari guards watched attentively—their behavior had changed notably since Talazeer's arrival.

When the elevator came, Sonus was one of the last inside. Ignoring a couple of sharp looks from some unpleasant characters he'd encountered before, he stared resolutely through the gap in the doors as they ascended. Two of the workers nearby discussed dinner, one describing how he would improve the tasteless rations from his stock of herbs and spices. Two others agreed to meet later to play an improvised board game that had been running for several months, each taunting the other about their performance. Another worker—a woman—spied a familiar face and asked a man about his wife. Sonus listened carefully, as he always did. Somehow, the people of his planet found ways to enjoy even these lives. He thought it rather wonderful.

Another coughing fit came upon him as the elevator shuddered to a halt. Standing aside to let the others out, he retrieved a handkerchief from his overalls and dabbed the dark spittle from his mouth. Others suffered, of course, though few as badly. He had no more of the medication left, but he could hardly ask Kadessis for another favor now.

It was a price he was happy to pay. Qari was now settled in the kitchens, and the Lovirr Nomora had promised to help. The precise nature of what Sonus had to provide in return remained vague—Nomora had said that he and his compatriots would ask for nothing until they had shown good faith by holding up their end of the deal. This surprised him, and after a lot of thought he'd realized it was because of the value they placed on what he could offer.

Sonus had often wondered if there was some kind of organized resistance movement out there, but the last place he'd expected to find it was amongst the Lovirr. He was curious to know how many there were. Surely it couldn't just be the Lovirr involved? And where? He suspected they might be after the same thing Tanus had wanted—weapons.

Dragging his eyes off the gun in the hands of the guard stationed outside the elevator, Sonus ambled after the others, wiping grime from his face with his sleeve.

"You all right?" Karas was suddenly beside him, arm over his shoulder.

Sonus was glad to see him. "First day back in a while. You?"

"I will be when I get home."

Karas noted the stained handkerchief in his friend's hand. "It's bad again?"

Sonus forced a smile. "I'm all right."

"Quiet," hissed one of the workers. Occasionally a guard would hold up the line if there was too much noise so most didn't speak until they were outside. Karas and Sonus exchanged a look but kept quiet.

They were not far from the fading daylight when the group ahead began to slow down. Before long they had moved to the right side of the main shaft and stopped. The two Vitaari behind them barked orders. Most hurried onward, but a few remained by the wall.

Sonus saw that there was a pair of women there, standing at the mouth of another tunnel. One of them noticed him and Karas and tugged the sleeve of the other.

"You. Karas."

He and Sonus stopped.

"It's Qari." The older of the two women pointed along the tunnel, which had not been used for a while and was dimly lit by a few weak lamps.

"What?" said Karas.

"Qari—she's there." The woman was still pointing. "She was taken to the infirmary this morning, then we heard she'd been seen heading toward the mine. She's standing by one of the old vertical shafts. Right at the edge."

Sonus felt a chill wash over him.

"You lot—move along." While one of the guards corralled the other workers toward the entrance, the other halted behind them.

Karas didn't even seem to have noticed.

"His wife is in there," explained Sonus. "Will you just give him a moment to fetch her?"

"What's she doing down there?" demanded the Vitaari. "Hasn't been used for weeks."

"I know. He'll be as quick as he can." Sonus switched to Vitaari. "Please."

Karas suddenly sprinted past the women and into the gloomy tunnel.

"What about you two?" asked the guard.

The two women hurried away, holding hands.

The guard glared at Sonus. "You—go and hurry them up."

Just to reinforce the point, he tapped the jolt-rod held in a holster on his belt.

Cold sweat trickling down his back, Sonus broke into a run. His boots kicked through piles of dust as he passed through the yellow light of a lamp, then into darkness again. His mind seemed numb, incapable even of trying to work out how this had happened. He just had to get to them, do what he could.

He stopped just before the last light. Karas was standing at the far edge of the lamp's reach, back illuminated. One hand was outstretched toward Qari, who was ten feet beyond him at the side of the vertical shaft. Sonus shivered as he saw the wide black maw just inches from her feet.

"Qari, what happened?" asked Karas.

She was standing completely still, arms by her sides.

"Qari!"

She turned her head toward her husband. "They took it. They cut me open and took it out."

Sonus squeezed his eyes shut as the words leeched into him. Someone must have told them. Was this his fault?

Karas struggled to control his voice. "Will you… come away from there, my darling?" He moved toward her, then stopped.

"It was a boy," whispered Qari. "I'm sure of it. I must go to him."

"You will, my darling—one day. But not now. Not like this."

"I love you, Karas."

With a single step she was gone, swallowed by the dark chasm.

There was no cry or sound. Just the shock of it.

Karas seemed to break in two. His head dropped and he hunched over. From within came an animal cry.

Sonus was already moving when Karas ran forward and threw himself after his wife, bellowing her name as he fell.

Sonus dropped to his knees, unable to absorb what he'd seen. He thought of following them, but something held him there.

He had no idea how much time had passed when he heard heavy footsteps behind him. His mind seemed to have emptied itself of all thought and feeling, but when the guard gripped his shoulder, he tore himself free and launched himself at the Vitaari, smashing a fist into his chest.

Startled, the guard took a step back. Sonus hit him again and had his fist back ready for another blow when pain exploded into the side of his head. The last thing he felt was his face hitting the dust.

He awoke. He took in the cold, metal floor on which he lay and the thumping ache in his head before succumbing to sleep once more.

He runs through the streets of the capital. Looking back for a moment, he sees one of the ships looming over the Great Church, its vast hull gleaming in the sun.

On he goes, hearing more of the distant explosions that haven't ceased since dawn. He passes corpses of soldiers in the road: some still holding firearms, some spears or clubs or swords. Crouching in an alleyway is an old woman, hands gripping her head. She recites a prayer loudly, voice defiant. In the Old Square, beside the sundial, a whimpering dog circles its dead master.

At last he reaches his home. He finds his mother and father there. Mother is gathering supplies; Father is sharpening a spear. They argue. She wants to run for the mountains, he wants to stay and fight.

Shouts from the street. Father runs past him, joins the men who have appeared outside.

Mother holds onto him, keeps him with her. They watch from the doorway.

There are only two of the invaders, but their weapons cut down most of the defenders in an instant. Father is still alive. The invaders kick bodies aside as they advance. When Father tries to get to his feet, one of them picks him up by the neck. The other grabs the spear from his hand, peers down at it, then drives it through Father's chest. The bloodied tip punches out of his back.

The invader drops the body. They move on.

He and Mother hide in the house, hands over their ears, tears darkening the floor. Hours pass before she can speak again.

Promise me you will not fight. You must not fight.

Sonus awoke again to find the pain had lessened. The power of the dreams faded, and his mind began to work once more. But then he remembered, and the horror of those moments in the darkened tunnel struck him like a physical blow. He hauled himself into a corner and sat there, arms wrapped around his knees.

This was real. After what had happened, after he'd attacked that guard, they would put him somewhere like this. He supposed he was lucky the Vitaari hadn't killed him. He did not feel it.

The door opened. A woman he did not recognize brought in a mug of water and placed it on the floor. As she left without looking at him, a larger figure entered. Kadessis shut the door behind him. He folded his arms across his chest and stared down at Sonus. The Vitaari's sleek black hair—usually tied back above the collar—now hung over his shoulders, making him appear rather wild.

"How are you feeling?"

Sonus found it strange that the administrator thought they could just talk. As they had before. As if things were the same. Nothing was the same, and Sonus wished he had constructed a weapon as Tanus had asked him to. He wished he had it in his hand right now so that he could blow the Vitaari's head off. He looked at the floor and tried not to vomit.

"We are fortunate that the governor appreciates your abilities, Sonus. Having lost two workers yesterday, he is not keen to lose a third. The use of the jolt-rod is to be considered punishment enough. You will return to your usual duties as soon as you are able."

Punishment enough. Kadessis obviously didn't understand that the real punishment would never fade. The memory. The guilt.

"You are still affected by what happened," continued the Vitaari. "That's understandable, I suppose." He walked slowly to the other side of the little room. "Or perhaps you blame yourself? You should not. I do not appreciate being lied to—or used—but I can see you were trying to do your best for your friends. But the blame lies with them for allowing this situation to occur at all. It was never going to end well."

Sonus saw only the tunnel, then Qari and Karas. He pictured them lying together at the bottom of that dark hole, bodies bloodied and broken. How he wished he could believe in the Maker. How he wished all three of them were in a better place.

"You should drink your water." Kadessis dropped a packet of tablets beside the mug. "I got these from the infirmary—they will help with the pain. You will be released later today."

Kadessis opened the door, then stopped. "Perhaps you think it was me who alerted the governor. If I had realized she was pregnant, I would have. But it was not me, Sonus. I know who did, but I am not permitted to tell you, nor should you try to find out. I'm afraid you will have to put all this behind you and carry on—focusing on your work will help. I am sorry about your friends."

He left, closing the door gently behind him.

. . .

They let him go as darkness fell. A single guard escorted him from the room within the tower to the walkway. The Vitaari departed swiftly, leaving him standing there alone. Sonus looked back at the lights twinkling at the top of the tower and the landing strip. The mouth of the mine was illuminated, too; he could make out the hunched figures of the night shift as they traipsed inside.

He thought again of the two bodies lying together, and tears formed in his eyes. He let them come and soon he was sobbing.

By the time he stopped, both his sleeves were wet. He put his hand on the rail of the walkway. He could follow them. He could throw himself off and join them in the Kingdom with the Maker.

But he didn't believe in it. Never had. When he was dead, he was gone and he could affect nothing.

Yet, however bad things were, there was a glimmer of hope for Corvos: what he had learned from Nomora had shown that. A faint voice told him that perhaps this had happened for a reason. He had lost everyone who had ever mattered to him now, and along with the pain came clarity.

He had deluded himself. He had convinced himself that survival was all that mattered, that there was a chance some of them might endure beyond Vitaari rule. He had thought himself rational, but in truth he had merely been weak.

They were all gone now. Family, friends, every last one. His promise to his mother didn't matter now. There was nothing left but the fight now. And he was ready to fight.

Sonus wiped his face again. There would be no more tears. He would carry on tomorrow as if nothing had happened, but he was already making plans. He had work to do.

11

The third guard was the problem.

Cerrin and the three Vitaari had been out in the forest for several days—observing, planning, setting traps—and they had now captured six of the eight creatures the count wanted. She had remained cooperative throughout and, despite her reputation, two of the guards had become far more relaxed. They no longer kept their hands near their jolt-rods and seemed happy to help with the work.

But the third guard—who rarely spoke, even to his compatriots—always kept his eyes on her. Cerrin reckoned he'd been specifically instructed to do so. Though they had ventured as far as three miles into the forest to locate and trap the creatures, he had maintained his vigil with a relentlessness that Cerrin begrudgingly admired. Her nemesis was named Kezzelet.

He was even sitting next to her now—in the rear of the vehicle behind the other two. Cerrin had thought several times of jumping off and making a run for it, but there was little chance of getting away. When lightly equipped and armed, the Vitaari could outrun her with ease. Worse still, they had two of the trackers like the technician had used on the hunt. Without them, they would not have found all the animals—the machines could somehow "see" movement and heat. Even if Cerrin got far enough away to hide, the guards would have located her. She had also not forgotten the governor's threats: attempted escape would bring more punishment and end what had actually been a comparatively pleasant few days.

Cerrin took no satisfaction from capturing the creatures—and was far from sure that any of them would survive—but she had to admit she was almost enjoying herself. In the unlikely event that a chance arose, she would take it. Until then, she intended to milk this opportunity for all it was worth.

Kezzelet activated his translator and turned to her. "You better get one of those rats this morning. It's taking too long."

"Rats?" said one of the guards at the front. He paused as the vehicle bumped over some tree roots, then continued. "Did you see the size of that thing yesterday?"

Kezzelet shook his head.

"The lightflies could be difficult, too," said Cerrin. "We've not seen any yet and they're very fragile."

"Waste of time," mumbled Kezzelet.

"Why don't you tell the count that?" asked Cerrin. "Perhaps he'll give you another duty."

The remaining guard was sitting in front of her. He pointed ahead. "Girl, we're close to those big trees. Where are we starting?"

"Anywhere. We've got plenty of traps."

The Vitaari had spent much of the morning putting them together. Transparent containers of various sizes had been sent down via a shuttle, and a technician assigned to rig them as traps. Cerrin had no idea how it worked, but some small device clamped to the door sensed when an animal entered and shut it. All she had to do was place bait inside. They had tried numerous different foods the previous day but, despite seeing several sesskar, hadn't managed to entice one of them inside. Today, they had double the amount of traps and a greater variety of bait.

The vehicle slowed and stopped well short of the trees. They were not particularly tall but had wide trunks that splayed out and split above the ground. The cool, dark recesses beneath could harbor all types of creatures and were particularly favored by sesskar.

Cerrin jumped down, then walked to the rear of the four-wheeled vehicle and the rack containing the traps. The Vitaari had laughed at the way she gripped her seat during her first trip in what they called the "runner." The craft seemed to her almost as fast as their shuttles, and she had been amazed to discover that the guards didn't even control it. Apparently, they just gave it the destination and the machine did the rest. Though it could cope with flat terrain and smaller obstacles, Cerrin had noted that it avoided steep slopes and very slippery ground. Over a long distance, it would be no more useful to the Vitaari than their combat shells, which struggled with dense forest.

Cerrin waited for one of the guards to untie the straps used to secure the containers, then helped take them off the vehicle. As usual, Kezzelet stood to one side and watched her. She had been surprised that the other two hadn't said anything about him never helping with the work and guessed he was either older, more senior, or both. Apart from the obviously old and young, she found it hard to judge their age.

The other guards grabbed two containers each and—not for the first time—Cerrin found a jolt-rod within easy reach. She doubted the weapons were particularly complicated, but it was too risky to make a move. She also couldn't be sure what effect the rods might have on a Vitaari. Though it would be almost impossible for her to reach the head, she imagined a blow anywhere might put them out of action temporarily.

Feeling Kezzelet's eyes on her, Cerrin looked over her shoulder. There he stood, motionless, one hand on the top of his gun. His cheeks were less angular than some of the others; but his brow was heavier, and those dark eyes didn't miss a thing. Unlike Stripe, he didn't say much, but Cerrin felt sure he was another who would enjoy the excitement of foiling an escape.

"Girl." One of the other guards handed her the bag containing today's bait. Cerrin thought it possible that her scent—or more likely that of the invaders—had put off the sesskar, so all of the food had been carefully wrapped. She would use gloves to place the warbler eggs in the traps.

"Let's hurry it up," growled Kezzelet.

She led the Vitaari toward the trees.

The rock formations were bizarre: colossal chunks of orange stone that seemed to have been stuck together and then dropped onto the desert floor to form towers. A line of them ran as far as the eye could see both east and west, many marked with glittering red where erosion had torn at the surface.

"They looked like mountains from the map," remarked Vellerik, as he and Triantaa strode across the plain. Thankfully, they were now through the rock field, and instead of watching his footing, he could admire the view.

Triantaa was fiddling with the sensor unit attached to his forearm. "That one to the east is the highest. Almost three kilometers."

"How far to the pass?"

"Five."

Vellerik looked back at the troop. Clad in light brown fatigues, the ten soldiers were laden down with heavy packs containing shelters, sleeping gear, and provisions. It had taken them a full day to prepare, and Vellerik realized he'd been remiss in not properly training for such a mission. He could have used the shuttle or the shells, but the pass was narrow and flying close to the towers would be risky. On the ground, however, they would have a perfect opportunity to intercept the Kinassans before they could pose a threat. Cutting costs and widening the experience of the troop were added benefits. Vellerik was finding the mission refreshingly authentic. The barren, hostile landscape and lack of air support robbed them of most advantages and, to him, recalled a dozen such missions on dangerous, unpredictable worlds—facing dangerous, unpredictable foes.

But when he reminded himself they were facing an enemy who hadn't advanced beyond bladed weapons, he suddenly felt rather foolish.

"Any reading on them?"

The troop had disembarked from the shuttle two hours previous, and the last update had shown a significant number of lifeforms twenty kilometers from the end of the pass.

"Not yet, sir," said Triantaa. "But range is much less at ground level."

Vellerik—who had a display of his own but left it off when he was with Triantaa—pointed ahead at a gap between two of the taller rock towers. "Is that it?"

"Yes, sir."

"Reminds me of Tangaara back home," said Vellerik after some time. "Same heat. Same emptiness. Ever been there?"

"No, sir. Flown over it a couple of times."

Vellerik examined the ground ahead. Though the wind was currently light, over time it had crafted elaborate swirls into the sandy plain. It seemed almost a shame to walk across them.

He checked the troop again; they had clearly dropped back. "Pick it up, you men."

"Sorry, sir," said Triantaa quietly. "Hard to keep up stamina aboard ship."

"Not your fault. Soldiers get less fit every year. And most of them aren't even past fifty. What are you again?"

"Forty-eight, sir," said Triantaa, adjusting the visor attached to his lightweight helmet.

Vellerik was actually feeling rather spry, having augmented his exercise regime and stayed off the Almana's Breath for five days.

"The High Ridge was terrain like this, wasn't it, sir?"

Vellerik smothered a grin. Triantaa used any opportunity he could to bring up one of the famous battles at which his superior had fought. The Imperial Legion's defense of an isolated fortress against a massive enemy force had turned the tide of a stuttering campaign. It was one of the few victories Vellerik was proud of; the battle hadn't been conducted to secure an operating base for the Fleet or a mineral field for the Resource Directorate. It had been fought to wipe out a race who had attacked the Vitaari: the inhabitants of the Erax system.

Taking exception to Vitaari ships flying through what they

perceived as their territory, the advanced Eraxi had launched several strikes, including one raid that vaporized almost a thousand civilians. It had taken two years for the Vitaari to defeat the Eraxi ships and another three years on the ground. The Battle of the High Ridge had taken place close to the start of that campaign, when the surrounded Fourth Legion held out against a fearsome Eraxi counter-offensive.

"A little," said Vellerik, though in truth he had only a handful of clear memories. He had been a lowly trooper back then, with not a single decoration to his name.

"The real problem was that the High Ridge wasn't actually all that high. If it had been, we might have had an easier time. Once they'd given up trying to bomb us out, they sent in their best assault division."

"Five thousand, wasn't there, sir?"

"So they say. Must have been three thousand of them dead on those slopes when it was done."

"And just the six hundred of you, sir?"

"About that."

Triantaa seemed keen to exploit this rare opportunity. "I saw a preserved Erax at the imperial museum. Very hard to bring down, weren't they?"

"Very—thick carapace protecting the head and the vital organs. Then they had all that armor too. Sometimes took six or seven direct hits. But you know why we won? Really?"

"Commander Xersiix, sir. His speech on the third night."

"Couldn't tell you what he said. I slept through it."

Triantaa's eyes widened.

"No, soon after we secured the ridge, a supply officer arrived and worked out we were running low on food. There was a crippled eight-wheeler a few hours away, but Xersiix didn't want to risk losing any men before the Eraxi hit us. The supply officer asked time and again, but Xersiix refused. He was confident we would be re-supplied, but the freighter sent our way was shot down. The supply officer went out on his own in a runner—came back with enough ration packs to get us through. Without him we would have run out of food two days before the battle—we wouldn't have been able to even lift our guns."

"I didn't know that, sir."

"Not many people do. And you know what, I don't even remember the man's name. Everyone's heard of Xersiix, of course."

Triantaa looked thoughtfully up at the sky.

"You're a good troop lieutenant," Vellerik told him. "But you never disagree with me. Never. Remember—a good second-in-command questions his superior. You think I'm wrong or I forget something—you tell me. I may well ignore you, but you tell me. Understand?"

"Captain."

They marched on. Though he eventually began to feel weary, Vellerik didn't stop for a break, even when Trooper Dekkiran stumbled into a hollow and twisted his ankle. They would still reach the pass by the middle of the day, though the temperature was soaring. And when another trooper complained about keeping his helmet on, Vellerik reminded him that he had the advantage of self-cooling clothing and skin specially treated to resist extremes of heat and cold. These treatments—and an accompanying mix of booster medicines—were administered annually to all the armed forces of The Domain. There was also the option of newer augmentations that could improve concentration, reaction time, and so on. Vellerik always refused them; he felt safer with his own narcotics.

Only when they neared the pass was it really possible to appreciate the huge dimensions of the rock towers. In some places, erosion had left larger chunks close to the top, giving the impression that the structures might fall at any moment. The surface was pock-marked and seamed by white and gray.

Vellerik finally called a halt in the shadow of the tower to the left, fractionally the higher of the two. The pass was no more than fifty meters across at its widest and stretched away out of sight, bounded on both sides by more towers and lower, flatter formations.

"Take a few minutes," said Vellerik. "Get some liquid down, food if you want it. Then get the shelters up." He walked a few paces into the pass and started adjusting the settings on his visor. Even with the range at maximum he couldn't see any movement to the south.

"Got anything?" he asked Triantaa.

"Only smoke, sir. About ten Ks away, right side of the pass. Wouldn't pick up any lifeforms unless they were line of sight."

"Ten—if they keep moving, they could be here before night. Check every half hour. I'll get us set up." Vellerik walked back to the men, who were now lying on the sand in shade, slumped against their packs. "Trooper, get your gun barrel out of the sand."

"Sorry, sir."

Dekkiran, whose neck was dotted with green tattoos in the style of his native region, lifted his gun and placed it on top of his pack. The troop—Vellerik included—were armed with the Mark 8 Assaulter: a lightweight, reliable weapon that had been in production for years. With a long effective range and a one hundred shell clip, it was ideal for the mission. Each man also carried three spare clips and five anti-infantry missiles for the pod attached to the top of the gun. Two also carried mines, which Vellerik intended to plant before they left—to discourage any further incursions along this route.

"Any sign of them, sir?" asked Pertiell, who was holding a huge water flask in both hands.

"Just smoke. But close. It'll be today or tomorrow."

"Unless they travel at night, sir."

"Unlikely, I would think. Primitive peoples tend to fear darkness."

"I wonder why they're coming north now, sir?" asked Perttiel.

"To attack," suggested another soldier.

"Or they might be hungry," said a third. "Looking for food."

"Doesn't matter," said Vellerik. "All that matters is we stop them."

Cerrin sat alone with the animals, knowing she had only the rest of the day before she was thrown back into the grinding routine of Block A and that accursed cavern.

"Stupid thing," she whispered, watching the sesskar as it scurried from one side of the transparent container to the other. Upon their return to the traps in the afternoon, they'd found the greedy creature unable to resist the warbler eggs. Cerrin had been dismayed to see it and wished she had been less conscientious with her choice of bait. Worse still, they had captured a dozen or so lightflies at the first attempt: the winged insects adored tree syrup.

The three Vitaari—especially Kezzelet—had been glad to finally get the job done and left her with the creatures in a storeroom close to the landing strip. The door was, of course, locked so Cerrin had occupied herself by checking on the animals. Though all were showing signs of anxiety, she had provided a good supply of food for each and added vegetation to the containers.

Of the eight types of creatures, it was the climbing karki she felt most sorry for. She walked over to the container in which the animal was housed. It was lying in a corner on a pile of branches, long legs and arms hanging loose. Karkis were usually noisy and were said to have their own language, but this one—a young male by the looks of it—was silent. It looked dolefully up at her with its big brown eyes.

"I know. I'm sorry."

Noting how smelly and stuffy the storeroom had become, Cerrin walked over to a control panel and keyed the button to open the window wider. The transparent pane was situated close to the top of the wall—about fifteen feet up—and, as it eased open, Cerrin realized how broad it actually was. She looked around. The store room was full of empty containers; it wouldn't be difficult to make a stack and climb out. Better still, darkness was coming.

But even if she could get out, what about the wall? She had gotten over it twice, but the Vitaari now ensured that no vehicles were left close enough to be climbed upon. There were also rumors that they had installed some other security measure on top of the wall, but no one knew for sure. And even if she got over and as far as the river? There was no reason to think it would end any better than last time.

Then again, she had been close—closer than ever before. And

with this work for the count done, it was possible the Vitaari might not need her. For all she knew, she might never see the forest again.

Almost before the thought was fully formed, Cerrin had her hands on a large container and was dragging it under the window. Once she had pushed it into position, she looked around for another.

The sesskar began its scurrying again, and the karki let out a whimper. Cerrin realized she could hear two Vitaari approaching outside. As they got closer, she heard the familiar voice of the governor.

Her mind was made up now. When they came in, she would try for the door. She couldn't think any farther than that. She just had to try.

But she would also have to put them off somehow, pretend she was in no state to escape. She sat on the floor close to the animals. By the time the door opened, she had her head in her hands.

"Cerrin."

She looked up and knew instantly her chance had gone. The governor had Kezzelet with him, and the soldier's gun was aimed right at her.

"Are you all right?"

"Yes, governor." She slowly got to her feet.

"I will have some food brought to you soon." Yeterris's expression turned sour with one look at the sesskar. "You are to remain with the animals for the moment."

As Kezzelet moved up alongside his superior, Cerrin tried to process what this meant.

"A change of plan," continued Yeterris. "Without your knowledge, the creatures may not survive the trip back to the home world. You will go up with the next freighter to the *Galtaryax* in two days' time. You will pass on all that you know so that the animals have the best chance of survival. The count has ordered this."

12

Sonus felt as if he were in a nightmare within a nightmare.

His friendship with Karas and Qari had sustained him long after everyone else he'd ever known was gone. When he'd arrived at Three, Karas's had been the only familiar face. They had not seen each other since school—and were not even from the same cohort—but each remembered the other well from visits to the painted caves and the lake region. From the very beginning they had agreed to watch out for each other. And when Karas had struck up his relationship with Qari, they had become a three, with no hint of jealously or awkwardness, only the warmth of affection and loyalty.

Now they were gone too, and Sonus spent hours running over the events of recent weeks: examining each decision, every possible outcome. When the guilt struck him, it was Karas's voice he heard, reassuring him this was not his fault. He again considered joining them in the oblivion of death. If—like Qari, like his parents—Sonus believed he would find his way to a better place, he might have done it. But awful though it was, this was the only life he had; the only life Palanians had, the only life the inhabitants of Corvos had. Unless something could be done to change it.

But that was proving even harder than he'd imagined. There

had been only a few jobs on the surface recently, reducing his opportunities to be around the Vitaari and pick up news. He didn't even know when the next freighter was due, though he was desperate to make contact with Nomora. Sonus needed something to focus on, something concrete. But until he could speak to the Lovirr again, he was on his own.

With a last glance back down the tunnel, he stifled a cough, then set off at a run. A guard had come down to order their midday break and as soon as he'd left, so had Sonus. He was still with the same work crew and had needed something very persuasive to buy their silence. Each man had been given a pack of painkillers from the supply provided by Kadessis some time ago. Designed for large Vitaari bodies, the tablets were very effective and highly prized by any worker who could get their hands on them, either for an emergency or for barter. The guard usually returned promptly at the end of the break, so Sonus had twenty-five minutes at the most. The journey would take him eight.

Only at the far end of the tunnel would he be safe to move up an access ladder to the level above. There were more guards there and a larger work crew, but—like his—they were currently drilling close to the elevator. Sonus had to hope he could find what he needed and get back before the guard. He had enough tablets to buy one more trip but no more than that. He would need to be quick, and he would need to be lucky. He reckoned he was due some luck.

Stopping at the base of the ladder, he looked both ways—no sign of any guards or anyone else. He climbed up into darkness (only the tunnels were lit, and those only weakly). Amongst the pieces of equipment strapped to his chest beneath his overalls was a flashlight, but using it here would produce a shaft of light that might give him away. Grimacing at the musty air, Sonus kept up a steady pace and soon emerged into the tunnel above.

To his relief, the work crew was several hundred yards away: dark figures moving around between powerful lights. Even the guards had no reason to come in this direction. Sonus turned and ran along the middle of the tunnel, staying well away from the yellow glow of any active lamps. It took another minute to reach his destination.

The pit was an accident. Several years previous, one of the heavy drills had been boring downward when it struck an impenetrable seam of rock. Even when some special equipment had been flown in from another mine, the Vitaari had been unable to break through. They had eventually decided to simply bore elsewhere, leaving a vertical shaft that had become a useful receptacle for waste. Over the years, the pit had filled up with all types of trash, including extraneous, damaged, and outdated machinery.

Standing at the edge, Sonus looked down at the murky morass of refuse some ten feet below. Then he glanced up at the dim light of the opening far, far above. He could not help thinking of Karas and Qari, though that shaft was in another part of the mine.

Pushing such thoughts aside, Sonus pulled out a rope from inside his overalls and attached one end to the nearest lamp, the workings of which had been removed. He then swiftly knotted the other end around his waist and took out his flashlight. Only when he had slid down the sloping edge of the pit did he turn on the light, and only on low power.

Over the years, he had seen numerous items that might suit his current needs, but one in particular would be perfect. The Vitaari machinery depended on several different types of power cell, and Sonus had come across most of them. Some were tiny enough to hold between two fingers; others—like those in the heavy drills— were as big as a man. One of his jobs had been to replace the cells in the cargo conveyor, and he'd learned the hard way that there was a certain method to removing them. Though he'd done his best to follow the Vitaari instructions, he had missed a vital step and succeeded in blowing a hole in the housing.

The cell that had caused the damage was no larger than a coin, and a later conversation with one of the engineers revealed that these particular cells were being phased out. Despite their remarkable durability, they were unstable when close to the end of their life. Several months later, the Vitaari engineers were instructed to dump all of the remaining cells (Sonus recalled some mutterings about cheap foreign technology). Left in the housings for safety's sake, hundreds of the cells had been thrown away. Most had been dumped the previous year—and would probably be deeply buried by now—but Sonus remembered seeing three or four more of the housing boards quite recently. They were in there somewhere.

With one hand on the rope, he stopped at the edge and moved the flashlight across the refuse. He tried to recall everything he could about the housings—they were narrow and rectangular, about a foot long, colored silver and white. Each contained twenty cells.

A minute passed. Two. Three. Sonus moved the light across the waste in methodical fashion, but every glimpse of something promising turned to disappointment. The pit was perhaps forty feet across, and he could see little of the far side because of a huge metal panel that had landed in the middle. Sonus checked his communicator, which also included a clock. He had twelve minutes before the guard returned.

He moved to the far left of the tunnel to change his view. Wedged against the wall on this side were the remains of a discarded loading machine. It was only three feet below the lip, and Sonus reckoned that by climbing across it he could get an angle over the panel and see more of the pit's far side.

He lowered himself over the lip, both hands on the rope, and soon had both heels on the loader. After a delicate turning maneuver, he was facing the right way. The machine was a little unstable but retained its position even when supporting his full weight. Having made sure the rope was running free behind him, Sonus put his arms out for balance and walked forward. Once at the end, he raised the flashlight high, aiming it over the panel. His view was still limited, but he continued his search.

Once he had illuminated all he could see, he checked the

communicator again. Ten minutes. He had to leave. But he couldn't resist turning the light on the front of the pit now that he had a different view. Within only three sweeps of the flashlight he saw it. The housing was upside down and lying behind a barrel—he would never have spotted it from above. It was ten feet away and a similar distance from the side. He would have to climb across the pit. There was no time now. But he could come back.

Sonus retraced his steps across the machine, keeping the rope taut to steady him. Only when he reached the other end did he realize how much harder it would be to get back, especially with such unsteady footing. He stretched out his arms, gripped the rope as high as he could, then pressed his left boot against the rock and pulled himself up. He had almost levered both elbows over the lip when his foot slipped.

He came down hard on the edge and cracked his chin but somehow retained his grip. Both feet were dangling, but he eventually got his left boot over the edge and hauled himself up. He rolled onto his back and was struck immediately by a coughing fit. Used to concealing his symptoms, he suppressed the noise but could feel the black bile rising up his throat.

Once on his feet, he hurried over to the lamp and untied the rope. He looped it, stuffed it inside his overalls and ran back to the ladder. Still coughing when he reached the bottom, he had to take a swig of water from his flask. As he ran, he checked the communicator. He had seven minutes.

Vellerik had been watching the Kinassans for over two hours. His half of the squad was behind the larger tower to the left, Triantaa was on the right side of the pass with the rest. The men had packed up the shelters and were now waiting in the shade.

"How close now, captain?" asked one of them.

"Three hundred meters. Looks like they're stopping."

Wary of sunlight sparking off his visor, Vellerik was using only his eyes and was lying at the corner of the tower. Earlier, he had risked a quick look with the visor at a greater range and seen what he supposed might have once been called a warband. There were around a hundred of them: all male, all of fighting age, wearing pale flowing robes that covered their heads and bodies. Most seemed to be armed with spears, but a few had bows and arrows. Toward the back of the group were some of the creatures Kerreslaa had mentioned. They were tall, lolloping, long-haired creatures, each one laden down with bags.

But—even though the Kinassans were now stationary—what had struck Vellerik most was the purposeful look about them; that and the red triangle daubed across the front of every warrior's chest. Triantaa had been trying to research the symbol using the files Kerreslaa had passed on but was having some sort of problem with his display.

Zarrinda—one of the youngest, keenest members of the troop— was sitting close to Vellerik. "I'm glad they didn't come through last night, captain."

The hours of darkness had passed without incident, and there had been no sign of movement until the morning. Triantaa had suggested the Kinassans might wish to avoid moving in the hottest hours of the afternoon.

"What if they turn around?" added Zarrinda. "Will we go after them?"

"That's up to the captain," grunted Dekkiran, who seemed anxious to regain some ground after his poor performance the previous day.

Triantaa's voice came over coms. "Got it, sir. The red triangle signifies they are preparing for battle. Oh… it appears they use their own blood. They really are savages."

Vellerik recalled what he'd read about previous Kinassan attacks. They had struck in waves and fought with almost suicidal bravery against whatever they faced. The Legion had eventually employed artillery, decimating thousands of the locals, who had foolishly continued to fight on open ground where the Vitaari could maximize the effects of their firepower.

Vellerik checked they still hadn't moved, then withdrew into cover and considered his options. He could mine the pass now as a precaution, but that would alert the Kinassans to their presence. He thought it unlikely they could have heard or seen the troop arrive, and he had two men stationed further back looking for any scouts who might appear on the formations.

If the Kinassans did know he and his men were guarding the end of the pass, surely they would either fight or withdraw? Vellerik glanced at his observers. Neither had reported anything.

He heard a shriek, then watched with bemusement as his half of the troop scrambled to their feet and scattered. Vellerik grabbed his gun and looked around. Lying on the ground where the men had been was an object that looked very much like a head. Having established that it was no danger to him, he got to his feet and backed away from the tower, gun aimed upward.

"Anyone see anything?" he asked. None of the soldiers replied.

"Sir?" Triantaa sounded worried.

"Await orders." Vellerik saw Triantaa and his men hadn't moved from the second tower.

"They couldn't climb up there, could they?" said Dekkiran, as he and the others followed their commander.

When he was twenty paces back, Vellerik stopped and looked again at the head.

"I think it's one of ours," said Perttiel.

The gray skin was shriveled but intact. The size and features suggested the trooper was right.

"They must have kept it all these years," said Zarrinda. "Since they last fought us."

"It's a warning," said Vellerik.

"Sir?"

"They just dropped an old head on top of us," he told Triantaa. "At a guess I'd say they'd like us to le—"

"There!" blurted Perttiel. "Captain, look."

The Kinassan was perched in a well protected position upon the tower, about fifty meters up.

"Got him, sir," murmured Dekkiran, gun aimed high, stock against his shoulder.

"Hold fire," snapped Vellerik.

When he realized he was not under immediate threat, the Kinassan straightened up and shouted something. He then pointed at the desert.

"They definitely want us to leave," observed Perttiel.

"How did he get up there?" asked another of the troopers.

"Quiet," ordered Vellerik. "Both squads, retreat to thirty meters."

Still facing forward, the soldiers on both sides of the pass withdrew.

Dark face visible under his hood, the Kinassan pointed at the Vitaari, then at the desert once more.

"We got the message, friend," said Vellerik.

"Sir, they've gone," said Triantaa over coms.

Vellerik looked across at him as he and the rest of the troop stopped. "What?"

"The others, sir. They've gone. Can't see any of them in the pass." Vellerik moved to his right and saw immediately Triantaa was right; the hundred warriors had disappeared. All he could see was a few of the pack animals.

"Sir, I'm now getting more readings close by. I think there might be more of them on the towers."

Vellerik ignored the lone warrior and ran his eyes across both towers, but he could see no sign of any others.

"Where'd he go?" said Pertiell. Now the Kinassan messenger had disappeared too.

"Maybe they're retreating," suggested Zarrinda.

"There's one," shouted a soldier with Triantaa's group.

Just as he pointed up at the tower, Vellerik heard something hit the ground. He turned and saw a two-meter wooden spear embedded in the dusty earth.

"And there," yelled Dekkiran.

Suddenly shapes appeared on both towers, and more spears

were hurtling down toward the Vitaari. Vellerik knew the helmets and body armor would protect them, but a lucky shot around the face or neck could do some damage. He could not understand how so many of the Kinassans could have climbed the tower so quickly.

A spear clattered off Pertiell's helmet. The trooper staggered backwards.

"Open fire!"

Vellerik clicked the activator on his gun but left his finger over the trigger, instead watching as the rest of the troop poured shells up at the formation. As the Assaulters spat fire, dust and chunks of rock flew up and the first of the Kinassans fell—a whirl of robes and dark skin that thumped into the ground close to the head.

Some of them had the sense to duck back into cover, but others continued to fling their spears. One stood up wielding a bow but hadn't even drawn the string when a line of shells ripped across his position, tearing into his torso and splashing blood across his robes. The warrior slumped back against the rock and dropped his bow.

Vellerik glanced over at Triantaa's squad. The lieutenant and every man were aiming at the tower, picking the natives off from an ever-decreasing supply of targets. One trooper was hit dead center by a spear, which bounced off his plate armor, and he continued firing.

Because he was the only one not looking up, Vellerik was the first to see the Kinassans break cover at the base of the tower close to where he had been lying. There were about ten of them, all armed with spears, all charging across the ground toward the Vitaari.

Vellerik took two steps to the right to give himself a clear field of fire. Selecting the anti-infantry missile, he fired from the hip, aiming at the ground ahead of the quickest warrior. The last he saw of him was his open mouth and wild eyes. The blast sent earth in every direction, and Vellerik felt the ground shake beneath him.

He turned to the right and saw another group of warriors

running at Triantaa's men. Several got spears away before the troopers turned their guns on them and cut them down. At such close range, the Assaulters were brutally effective, blowing the Kinassans backwards and halting their charge in seconds.

As the dust cleared, Vellerik realized his men had stopped firing.

There wasn't much left of the Kinassans, just a blackened crater in the ground and some bloodied body parts and tunics. He glanced up at the tower and spied a single warrior scrabbling across an exposed rock face. Before Vellerik could raise his gun again, Dekkiran fired. The trooper gave a triumphant roar as the shells blasted the Kinassan away. When he was done, he turned to his superior, grinning inanely.

"Nice work with the missile, captain."

"Could someone help me here?" The unfortunate Perttiel dropped his gun. A long wooden arrow was sticking out of his shoulder.

"Think it must have gone between two plates."

"You'll be fine." Vellerik again scanned both towers and the ground, but there were no more Kinassans moving. He pointed at four of his men who were standing close together. "Cover. Keep your eyes forward. Zarrinda, break out the kit and check the manual for procedure."

"Sir, look." Despite his injury, Perttiel was pointing across at the other troop, where the men had gathered around a figure lying on the ground.

Vellerik shouldered his gun and ran across to them.

"Let me through." When the men separated, he saw the rank insignia on the arm of the fallen man. Triantaa. He was on his front, head twisted as he looked up at his commanding officer. His eyes were already turning yellow, a sign of internal trauma Vellerik had seen countless times.

"Sorry, sir."

Vellerik knelt beside him. They had already removed the spear. The wound was on the side of Triantaa's neck. It had torn out a large chunk of flesh, and black blood was seeping onto the ground. One of the men already had his kit open and now placed the sealer drone next to the wound. Once it had inspected the injury, it would staunch the bleeding and prevent infection until Triantaa could be operated on. The lieutenant's eyes flickered, then closed.

As one of the troopers used another piece of equipment to check his vital signs, Vellerik stood up and keyed his com-cell. "Vellerik to *Galtaryax*, requesting immediate medical evacuation."

The reply came within five seconds. "Captain Vellerik, this is Kerreslaa. We have a shuttle at Mine Five. They can be with you in fifteen minutes. Passing on your position now."

"Tell them to hurry. Vellerik out." He turned back to the others. "Well?"

"Looks fairly stable, sir. Sealer will be ready soon."

"Keep him warm."

Vellerik called over to his squad. "Perttiel, shuttle's on its way. Zarrinda, help him over here. The rest of you follow me."

Vellerik strode forward with his gun up, the men falling in behind him as he entered the pass. He turned left and right every few paces, examining every fissure and boulder, aware there might still be more of them alive. In the distance, he could see the pack animals; they appeared to have broken their tethers and fled.

Suddenly a single warrior sprinted out of a gully and away along the pass.

"Leave him for me."

Vellerik raised the gun and fired.

The shells ripped into the earth behind the Kinassan, and he stopped.

As Vellerik walked toward him, the warrior slowly turned. He appeared to have no weapons, and his hood had fallen down. He was young, his hair a matted mess and only a few wisps upon his chin. Like all Kinassans, he was brown-skinned with black hair and pale green eyes. Brow furrowed, he glared up at his enemy.

Vellerik reached for his translator, then remembered there was no program for Kinassan. He pointed south. "Go back. Do not come here again. Go."

Suddenly the Kinassan lunged at him.

Vellerik stuck out a hand and clamped it around his neck. He could easily have lifted the youth or crushed the life out of him. But he just held him there.

"Go. Do not come back."

He threw the Kinassan the way he wanted him to go. The youth landed heavily, then dragged himself up and kept walking.

Vellerik cursed to himself, then ambled back to the squad. "Take a few of the intact bodies and string them up where anyone approaching from the south will see them. Dekkiran, bring me the proximity mines."

13

Cerrin was starting to wish she were back working in the cavern. Half of the lightflies and one of the two illari birds had perished before they'd even left, and now the creatures were locked away in the hold of the shuttle. And if they were finding the journey as unpleasant as she was, she wasn't sure how many would still be alive when they arrived. What would the count do then?

She currently had more pressing matters to attend to: trying not to vomit as the shuttle lurched and shuddered and shook. Kezzelet had been assigned to escort her to the *Galtaryax*. He was strapped into a seat at one end of a row; she was at the other. The guard had soon given up trying to secure her there—the straps were too wide and too loose—but as soon as the ship began to move about, she'd found a way of wedging herself in place.

"How much longer?" she asked between waves of nausea.

"Don't know," said the Vitaari. "Relax, girl. It's normal."

Cerrin couldn't think of anything less normal. She didn't understand why anyone would want to fly up into the sky and keep going. Looking out the nearest window, all she could see was a red glare.

After some time, the sickness abated, replaced by a numbing chill. She remembered asking her father what lay beyond the clouds. He'd answered no one really knew, but some thought there was nothing but endless darkness, a place where only the gods could go.

She did not belong here. Cerrin clasped her hands together and bowed her head. *Ancients, please protect me. Please protect me.*

She closed her eyes, trying to imagine she was somewhere beautiful, somewhere safe.

"Settling down," said Kezzelet. "Not far now."

Cerrin felt a wave of cool air come from somewhere and a rumbling beneath her feet. Outside the window, red had become black.

He could not turn back now. Though it had taken him far too long to clamber across the treacherous pile of scrap, Sonus was within two feet of the housing. Smothering a cry as he scraped himself on something sharp yet again, he put the flashlight in his mouth and heaved a thick cable out of the way. Once over an angular, greasy chunk of machinery, he could finally get his hands on the housing. He grabbed it with both hands, turned, and threw it up into the tunnel.

Not daring to check the time, he started back, forcing himself on as he climbed and stretched and slid. He was ten feet from the wall of the pit when something smashed into the refuse behind him. He looked up and saw a light far above.

"Oh no."

A second impact sent a chunk of metal flying past him. He had already freed the troublesome rope from around his waist, but the bit he needed was still hanging from the lip, with knots tied to help him climb.

The third impact was the heaviest, sending tremors through the entire pit. Whatever Sonus was standing on shifted, and his foot slid down into a hole. As he struggled to free himself, a barrel landed just a couple of feet away, spilling over his arm. For a moment he feared acid, but he caught enough on his hands to see it was nothing more than blue-tinged coolant.

Trying to stay calm, he pushed his toe down and managed to pull his leg free. He gripped a pole sticking up ahead of him and used it to haul himself onward. Then came a useful length of paneling, which he crawled along, gaining vital feet. More junk crashed into the pit behind him as he finally reached the rope. Knowing he was safer this close to the edge, he threw the flashlight up first, then climbed steadily, feet and hands gripping the knots. Once he could get his arms over the lip, he pulled himself up.

Though he knew time was desperately short, Sonus had to lay on his back for some time, sucking in air. He struggled to his knees, then to his feet. Once the rope was untied from the lamp, he threw it into the pit. Nothing else fell from above.

Sonus put the housing inside his overalls, where he had sewn in some webbing to make sure his secret cargo wouldn't be visible; it would have to stay there until he got home that night. With a brief look along the tunnel—he saw only lights, no one on the move—he ran back to the ladder and clambered down.

Only when he reached the bottom did he check the time: five minutes left for an eight-minute journey. Holding the base of the housing through his overalls, he set off at a loping run; he simply didn't have the energy to sprint.

Before long he was struck by another coughing fit. Halting in the near-dark between two lamps, he forced the breaths out to get it over with. No spittle came this time, but the pain in his throat was so acute he had to hold onto the wall for a moment. When it had passed, he drank some water and set off again. By the time he felt able to move quickly, the five minutes had elapsed.

Sonus looked ahead. He had several hundred yards to go, but the Vitaari guard might appear at any time. He could not arrive there looking like he was about collapse. Trying to maintain a swift walking pace while regulating his breathing, he pressed on. His arms and legs were leaden, and sweat was pooling under his arms.

Passing the passageway that led to the elevator, he looked inside. There no was no sign of the guard, and the door was closed.

As he entered the cavern where his crew were currently drilling, Sonus began to relax. He saw his three compatriots all at work, chipping chunks of stone from a high expanse of wall. Then he glimpsed something to his right, and the guard materialized out of the shadows. The Vitaari towered over him, hand already on his jolt-rod.

"Where have you been?"

"Sorry, I had to… I'm not feeling very…"

Before Sonus could say any more, he felt a convulsion in his stomach and knew instantly he was about to be sick. He bent over and coughed up a thick, dark fluid, splattering the earth between his feet.

The Vitaari made a noise that sounded like disgust, then stepped backwards.

Sonus dropped to his knees and reached for his water bottle. He drank, then looked up at the Vitaari. "Sorry, sir."

"Perhaps you should go to the infirmary."

"No, no. I'm fine." Sonus forced himself back to his feet.

"Then get to work." Without another word, the Vitaari stalked out of the cavern.

The medical bay contained four beds, each surrounded by banks of equipment. Perttiel seemed to be sleeping. Triantaa was in the bed next to him, but Vellerik couldn't see him; the surgeon was blocking his view.

He backed away from the window and sat down. Noting the dusty earth on his boots and fatigues, he leant back and crossed his arms. He supposed he should have been relieved: both men were stable and the surgeon had assured him they would recover, though he seemed concerned about the location of Triantaa's wound.

Vellerik thumped a hand down onto his leg. He could not believe his troop had sustained casualties fighting these bloody primitives. His mistake had been not moving the men further back from the towers. Twenty meters? Should have been fifty. And now Triantaa might suffer because of his stupidity. If things went badly, he might not be able to return to duty.

He wondered: was it the narcotics? His age? The posting?

Probably a combination of all three. So much for his attempt to reinforce the value of "real soldiering" to his men. And so much for his attempt to reassure the count he could do the job. No Vitaari had been seriously injured by a native in years. This was nothing less than an embarrassment.

Had he not been so anxious to hear an update from the surgeon, Vellerik would have retreated to his quarters. He pressed a hand against his brow.

"Captain!"

Count Talazeer was marching along the corridor, the ever-present Marl two paces behind. Vellerik knew the debrief was inevitable; he'd just hoped to be able to delay it.

Talazeer walked up to the window and looked into the medical bay. "How are they? Two injured, wasn't it?"

"Yes, sir. Two."

Talazeer studied the patients intently for a moment, then caught sight of his reflection and began rearranging his hair. Vellerik locked eyes with Marl and saw what might have been a smile.

"Well," said the count. "What happened?"

Vellerik gave his report, even though he'd had imagers running throughout the engagement as instructed. Talazeer seemed interested in the Kinassans, particularly details like the bloody triangles and the head, even asking if Vellerik had recovered it (he had not—it had been buried along with the rest of the bodies). Talazeer remarked that he was looking forward to watching the battle in his room later.

When it came to discussing the casualties, Vellerik felt it best to admit his mistake. To his surprise, Talazeer seemed unconcerned.

"Nonsense, captain. We hope for their recovery, of course, but surely we must expect our men to be able to avoid such a basic weapon. Let us consider it a lesson learned. Now, what of enemy casualties?"

"One hundred eleven, sir. We displayed some of the bodies upon the rocks as a warning to others. I planted three lines of mines across the pass. The Kinassans won't be passing that way again."

"Excellent. And all achieved without the combat shells. This was a victory for the honorable traditions of our infantry forces. I congratulate you, captain. I was glad to hear of you taking such a proactive approach to this problem."

Vellerik nodded stiffly.

"It makes me wish I could have been down there with you. Perhaps next time."

"Sir, I don't think—"

"We will have to talk about decorations," added the count. "Aside from yourself, did anyone else distinguish themselves?"

Vellerik wouldn't have dreamed of recommending any of his troop for such a short, one-sided engagement, and he certainly wouldn't accept one for himself. While he was trying to think of a diplomatic answer, Talazeer's com-cell buzzed with a three-tone signal. A broad grin spread across the nobleman's face.

"I must go, Vellerik—the animals for my menagerie have arrived. We can talk again later."

Talazeer turned and hurried away and did not seem concerned that his bodyguard had not followed.

"This head," said Marl. "Where did it come from?"

Vellerik had little interest in conversing with the Drellen but found himself replying. "They must have had it a long time. There were some fairly major engagements a few years ago. They had to bring in a battalion of Imperial Legion to suppress them."

"Maybe these natives aren't so weak, after all."

The bright lights in the corridor illuminated the Drellen's scaly skin. Vellerik observed that it was made up of thousands of over-lapping hexagons of various shades of green.

"They are weak in body, not in mind." Vellerik looked into the medical bay. The surgeon had now moved and he could see the unconscious Triantaa.

"You seem upset, captain."

Despite the words, Vellerik sensed that Marl was not seeking to provoke him.

"I do not like to see my people hurt."

"Then it is fortunate that you are Vitaari."

. . .

Sonus was struggling. Though he knew the guard would check his work before the crew was dismissed, at one point he just dropped his drill and sat down. Out of water, he begged the others for some, but they said they needed it for themselves. With their transactions complete (and his supply of tablets finished) they had reverted to ignoring him. Hardly caring if he was discovered away from his drill, Sonus walked some way to find a water barrel and replenish his supply.

By the end of his shift he was as exhausted as he'd ever been. In a way he was glad; the weariness took the edge off his fear as he endured the end-of-shift check and then the tense walk out of the mine to the walkway. Once past the last guard, he made his way downward in the middle of the crowd.

Back at his dwelling, he slumped down on his bed and lay there. Only when satisfied all his neighbors were preoccupied did he open his overalls and pull out the housing. He already had a suitable hiding place with a reasonable chance of surviving an inspection— a container of spare parts he maintained to effect repairs. When he had first began collecting the components, the guards had reported the matter to the governor, who had permitted him to continue as long as he obtained permission from an administrator or an engineer. Also secreted at the bottom of the container were the other parts and tools he would use to start constructing the weapon.

He had no idea if it would work. The design was simple, but it was connecting the components that might cause him the most problems.

That could wait; he was too tired to begin work tonight. Hiding the housing beneath a blanket, he poured himself more water. If he'd had any of the tablets left, he would have taken one—his stomach was churning with bitter bile and his throat felt raw.

He was about to move the housing into the container when he heard a familiar friendly voice in the passageway. Evening meals were distributed by four women who did so in exchange for the occasional extra portion.

Sonus knew Orani well; she had been bringing him his food for years. A stout woman of about sixty, she placed the plastic box on the barrels that formed the front of Sonus's dwelling.

"Evening."

"Evening." For once he was actually looking forward to eating; apart from sustenance, the food would ease the pain in his throat.

"It's the light brown stuff, I'm afraid," said Orani. The general consensus was that the light brown stuff was even more bland than the dark brown stuff.

As Sonus smiled and picked up the box, he could feel Orani examining his face. On previous nights since his return, she had simply asked him how he was. But now she reached out and touched his arm.

"You couldn't have done anything, you know."

Sonus looked at her kindly face and felt tears form in his eyes.

"They are in a better place now," she added.

"I hope so," he said, largely for her benefit.

"I better hand the rest of these out." Orani squeezed his arm and continued on to the next cavern.

Before Sonus had a chance to sit down, another visitor arrived. Litas wasn't really a friend, but he seemed impressed by Sonus's attempt to help Qari and had offered to find the informer. Concerned about anything that might affect his own plans, Sonus had tried to put him off, but Litas was insistent. Though not known to have ever organized anything that could be considered resistance, he had been a friend of Tanus and previously attacked those suspected of collaboration.

He was around Sonus's age but looked older due to a hunched back that worsened every year. His hair was long, lank, and gray.

"Still nothing. Sorry."

Sonus wiped his eyes. "Litas, there's nothing we can do. We'll probably never know."

"How can you give in just like that? One of those bitches gave

Qari up. Might as well have killed her and Karas herself. I'll get the name one way or another."

"It won't change anything."

"We look out for own. We lose that, we have nothing."

"You'll just cause more trouble for yourself. Me too."

"I'm not stupid, Sonus. I can wait, take my time. But when I get that name…"

"Whoever did it, it's not really their fault. It's the Vitaari."

Litas gave a grim smile. "A shame it took this for you to see the light, Sonus. You back on our side for good now then?"

"I was never anywhere else."

If he had been more intelligent, Litas might have made a good ally. But he was too impetuous, too narrow-minded. "I don't suppose you… have something in mind?"

"No," said Sonus. "I do not."

14

Cerrin watched Count Talazeer prowl up and down. He had his hands clasped behind his back and would stop occasionally to peer down at the animals. She, Marl, and Kezzelet were standing at the other end of the storeroom, close to the door. Physically, Cerrin was feeling better, but what she had seen beyond the great ship's viewports had shocked her as much as the flight. That endless black seemed to her a dark sea that might wash them all away at any moment.

Kezzelet shifted around impatiently. Cerrin and the guard had already been waiting for some time before the count arrived, and he had not spoken a word while inspecting his new collection. Clad in a black tunic striped with gold, he bent over the box containing the climbing karki. The animal pressed itself against the back of the container, long limbs scrabbling in the leaves.

Talazeer straightened up and ran a finger down his neck, then gestured to Cerrin without looking at her. Kezzelet gave her a shove in the shoulder that almost knocked her off her feet. When she reached the count, he turned to her.

"They are frightened."

"Yes, sir."

"I am having an expert sent to collect them, but I must have everything you know. We've set up a recorder in my quarters—you will spend this evening passing on the information, then return to Mine Fourteen tomorrow."

"Sir, it will not take long. Can't I go back—"

Talazeer was already on the move. He marched to the doorway and was joined by Marl as he continued out into the corridor. Kezzelet waved Cerrin forward, and she almost had to run to keep up. When they passed another long, high viewport, her stomach tightened and she made herself ignore the darkness. Two Vitaari coming the other way bowed to the count, who did not acknowledge them. They were dressed like the administrators at the mine; she had already seen at least a dozen of them aboard the *Galtaryax*.

The count rounded a corner and stopped beside an elevator. Mounted on the wall beside it was a large, colorful picture. It showed an elderly Vitaari sitting on a richly decorated throne. In one hand was a large staff with a glowing ball at the top. The old man was wrapped in a purple robe and was staring resolutely forward.

Talazeer said something to Kezzelet, who hesitated, then walked back the way they had come, gun hanging from his shoulder. Cerrin wasn't sure what this meant, but she was glad to be rid of him, at least for the moment. When the elevator doors opened, it was Marl who put his hand on her shoulder and guided her inside. His touch chilled her. Though the Vitaari didn't seem to smell or sweat, their large bodies gave out a lot of heat. The spindly, scaled fingers of the bodyguard, however, were utterly cold.

As the doors closed and the elevator eased upward, Cerrin observed the blurred reflections of the two tall beings behind her: Marl, head round and smooth, body upright and still; Talazeer, mane of hair framing his angular face, body twitching and restless.

When the doors opened, they set off again, Marl walking beside Cerrin as they passed more administrators and a pair of soldiers wearing blue uniforms and carrying equipment unlike any Cerrin had seen. When they reached a junction, she looked along another corridor and spied a man dressed in the same gear. It was the old commander who'd been with Talazeer on his first visit. She couldn't remember his name.

Once beyond the next broad doorway, the corridor divided into two, curling around the sides of a large room. Pausing momentarily for a beep to sound, Talazeer led the way into a space that looked to Cerrin like a bigger version of Governor Yeterris's office. There was a large table in the middle with a seating area to the rear. On either side of the main space were smaller rooms.

As the door shut behind them, Talazeer pointed at the table and a screen mounted on a flexible arm. The display showed a huge, gleaming building with arches and domes and towers. Cerrin had never seen such structures, though she had heard them described by Palanians.

"Sit," said Talazeer.

She did so but was barely able to touch the ground. The count adjusted the chair somehow so it descended.

"Do you people not say thank you?" He turned the screen toward her.

"Thank you, Excellency."

The count's fingers danced across the screen, and suddenly Cerrin found herself staring at a picture of a lightfly. Talazeer pointed at a symbol in the corner of the screen.

"Touch this when you want to talk, then again when you want to stop. When you've finished, you just press here for the other creatures."

Now she realized there were little boxes at the top showing the other seven animals.

"Everything you know about them. Especially food—I want them to last the journey."

Cerrin nodded.

Talazeer deactivated his translator and issued a few orders to Marl. He then walked to the back of the room, poured himself a drink, and checked his appearance in a mirror. Marl returned from one of the smaller rooms, holding a black jacket with a red line across the front. Muttering something to himself, Talazeer walked over and put the jacket on.

Marl rounded the table and stood over Cerrin. "Do not leave that seat." His thin black lips hardly moved, yet she glimpsed the dark red tongue and triangular teeth. "We won't be here, but we will be watching."

The two sides of his cloak separated momentarily, and Cerrin spied a bladed weapon hanging from his belt. The count summoned him and they left.

She slumped back and let out a long breath. Perhaps things would be all right after all. Her eyes were drawn to the rear of the room; behind the couches was another viewport. She turned the chair away from it and faced the screen.

Cerrin awoke to the sound of scraping claws. Sitting up, she looked across the darkened storeroom toward the containers. The movement drew more noise from the animals: she heard the sesskar squeaking and the illari bird pecking at something. It was hard to know how long she'd been sleeping; she was surprised she'd been able to.

Having completed her task in around an hour, she had then waited for Talazeer and Marl to return. Ignoring her, the count had walked straight into what looked like his bedroom. Marl had then escorted her back down to the storeroom. She found they had put out a bed for her, well away from the animals. There was also some water, but no food. Cerrin reckoned it was exhaustion that had sent her to sleep: the strain of coming to this strange place and being alone amongst the Vitaari.

The animals began to settle down again. She pulled the covers over herself and laid down. Just as her eyes closed, the sesskar began its scraping again. Then the karki began to grunt and move around.

When the door opened, light flooded the room. Shock or fear quieted the animals as a tall dark shape entered and walked toward Cerrin. She pushed the covers off and stood up. By the time the interloper arrived, his distinctive silhouette had given him away.

"Come with me," said Marl.

"Where?"

"Do as you're told and no harm will come to you."

He reached for her, but she sat down.

"Girl."

Instead of answering, Cerrin reached for her nearest boot and put it on.

Marl withdrew and waited for her.

When she was ready, she followed him out into the corridor. The bodyguard shut the door, then looked around warily before leading her away, cold hand on her arm. Every time they reached a junction or a doorway, he would check that they hadn't been seen, and instead of using the elevator, he took stairways and a route through what seemed a quieter part of the ship. Cerrin did not know what was going on, only that she wished she were back in the storeroom with the animals.

At one corner, she didn't move with him. Marl stopped and looked down at her, eyes alert and bright in the round, green head.

"What if I scream?" said Cerrin.

"You wouldn't dare," replied the bodyguard.

He was right about that.

Talazeer was sitting on one of the couches, a glass in his hand. Marl escorted her that far, then left them alone.

"Please," said the count, gesturing at a chair close to his end of the couch.

Cerrin sat down. On the table between them was a drink of the same pale orange liquid Talazeer was holding. There were also six bowls filled with different foods, none of which she recognized.

"Destrian honey wine and delicacies from my home world. You will never drink nor eat anything better."

Cerrin stared blankly at the floor.

"I know you must be hungry, girl. Please."

"No, thank you."

"Will you look at me?"

She did so.

Talazeer was once again clad in another of the tight sleeveless shirts like he had worn in the forest. His feet were bare below a pair of flowing trousers—black like the shirt.

"I understand that you people refer to your star as the 'Wild Sun.' Nobody seems to know why."

"Many centuries ago, the sun was calm. Then we began to see fire flashes."

"Solar flares, I expect."

"Some said the fire gods were angry. Others thought the end times were coming. There was a time when a person was lucky to see a fire flash once in their life. Now they happen most years. Perhaps the end is near."

"Perhaps. And your name, Cerrin—does it have any meaning?"

"Just a name."

The count nodded slowly, then picked something off his lean, muscular arm. "I've been…" Talazeer looked at the door, then at Cerrin. "I've been unable to forget it. You. Since the forest."

He suddenly stood up and walked to the window. "It's a kind of sickness, I suppose. Perhaps there is something wrong with me. But I'm hardly the first. And I have always found that once I want something, I… I simply have to have it."

He returned and offered her the second glass. "Please drink, Cerrin. It will help you relax."

She was certain now; the Vitaari expected her to lie with him. Cerrin had never been with a man in that way; it was forbidden by the Echobe before betrothal. She had kissed boys occasionally, but nothing more. Her father had told her there'd been offers of betrothal but none of the young men had been worthy of his bright, strong, beautiful daughter.

The very thought of being close to the Vitaari sent her hand into the glass, which spun away and smashed to the floor.

Marl appeared from the room to the right in an instant, but the count waved him away.

Talazeer cleared his throat and ran a hand through his hair, as if trying to calm himself down. "There is plenty more honey wine,

Cerrin. It is important that you be relaxed. Of course, our species are different but I have done some research, and we are… compatible. However, you will have to clean yourself up first."

Talazeer leaned over her again. "Everything you need can be found in my quarters. I have put out one of my robes. It is rather long but of a fine material and red in color. It will suit you, I think. Off you go now."

Vellerik couldn't sleep. It was not thoughts of Triantaa and Perttiel that disturbed him, nor the dead Kinassans at the pass. His imagination had created a scene he simply could not dispel—the lone warrior returning to a Kinassan village. Dozens of women and children weeping together when they heard that their men had been killed, that they were now defenseless and alone. All thanks to Vellerik and the Colonial Guard.

He could not face a night of this. He sat up and downed half a glass of water. It contained a mild sleeping aid, but Vellerik was already starting to think he might need something more powerful.

No. I am stronger than that.

He lay back and closed his eyes.

Cerrin was relieved to get out of the shower and find herself still alone in the restroom. Glimpsing her naked form in a mirror, she turned away and quickly dried herself. Outside, all was quiet.

She put on her underwear, then took the robe. The material was horribly smooth and clingy, and she somehow felt even more exposed when wearing it. She tied the belt around her waist, then looked for a weapon.

As soon as she'd played along, the count had sent Marl out. Cerrin wasn't sure if the bodyguard was close by or not, but at least now she might have a chance of keeping Talazeer off her. Either that or she would die trying.

On a shelf close by was a large selection of vials and tubs, mostly containing liquids and lotions. There was also a long rack of narrow cylinders, all of which contained some kind of needle. She took one of the larger ones and unscrewed the top, then tipped out the needle. She slipped it into one of the robe's broad pockets.

"Come, Cerrin," said the count from right outside the door. "I'm getting impatient."

She turned back toward the mirror and recognized nothing of what she saw. Her dark skin seemed almost yellow under these strange lights, and her eyes did not seem to be hers.

I am alone. This man–this thing–does whatever he wants to. No one here will help me.

She choked back tears.

No. I am not alone. Ikala, god of battle, see me, hear me, help me.

"I'm waiting." The count sounded farther away.

She reached into the pocket and moved the needle so it would be easier to grab. The eye perhaps, or the throat. Throat would do more damage—might even keep him quiet, give her some time.

Cerrin undid two of the buttons on the robe to show more of herself, then walked out across the quarters and into the main room. The count was back on the couch. As she approached, he looked her up and down.

"I never expected to find such beauty out here, Cerrin. Come to me."

She walked along the side of the table, then perched on his left knee, facing toward him. As the robe slipped open, the count put his drink down and moved a hand onto her leg. He stroked the inside of her thigh, eyes fixed on hers.

"Do you kiss with tongues? As a rule, my people do not, but I rather like it."

"We do," replied Cerrin honestly.

"You are shaking." The count put his other hand on her back. "You must try to relax. I will be gentle. At first, anyway."

Talazeer raised his knee, tipping Cerrin toward him. He ran his hand farther along her leg, then up between her breasts. Circling her neck with his fingers, he turned her head toward him.

"There is something wonderful about this, don't you agree, Cerrin? To be the first of our kind. To… discover each other."

She let him move her head toward his but kept her right hand out to the side and free. As their mouths met, she reached into the pocket and gripped the needle. The count's tongue ran along her lips. Struggling not to pull away, she opened her mouth, knowing she had to distract him. As his tongue entered her, she pulled out the needle and jabbed it at him, aiming for the prominent vein on the side of his neck.

At the last moment, Talazeer sensed something was wrong and jerked away. Cerrin missed the vein but plunged the needle deep into the silvery skin.

The count bellowed with agony and lashed out, catching her on the chest and sending her flying onto the table. As glasses and bottles smashed, she rolled off onto the floor.

Talazeer stood up and gripped the needle, which swayed as it hung there. Whimpering, face wracked with pain, he pulled it out.

Trying to ignore the thumping ache in her chest, Cerrin dove between two chairs and ran for the door. The count gave chase and made a grab for her over the corner of the table. He tore away part of the robe's sleeve, but Cerrin wrenched herself free.

She was five yards from the door when it opened and Marl sprang in. She could not stop herself screaming as she turned and fled back around the other side of the table, only to find the enraged Talazeer coming straight for her. He wrapped her up in those two long arms, but Cerrin clawed at his face, catching him close to the eye. She pulled away from him again, but he stuck out a leg and tripped her.

Cerrin landed on her side. Light glinted off something nearby, and she spied a sliver from the glass she'd knocked out of the count's hand. Gripping the wider end, she sprang to her feet.

Spitting curses as blood leaked from his neck, Talazeer lurched toward her. Marl shouted something at his master as Cerrin slashed at him with the glass, catching him on the finger.

She had just turned toward the onrushing bodyguard when he picked up a chair and threw it at her. The solid lump of metal and plastic caught her on the legs, and she fell heavily onto her back. She had time only to register the spreading pain when Marl whipped his hand into her wrist. She dropped the shard of glass instantly.

Then his hands were under her arms, lifting her up off the floor. Then they were gripping her elbows, holding her from behind. The robe was torn and open, but there was nothing Cerrin could do.

Talazeer gazed down at his fingers.

At last, Cerrin had drawn black blood. But when the count bent down and picked up the glass she had cut him with, she began to think it might be the last thing she ever saw.

"Hold her still," he said.

Marl replied but Cerrin didn't understand; the bodyguard had deactivated his translator.

"All for nothing, I'm afraid, girl," hissed Talazeer as he advanced, light twinkling off the glass. "For I will still have you, and I shall give you something to ensure you always remember me."

When he heard coms buzzing, Vellerik came around so slowly that he first thought he must have taken more Almana's Breath. But then he remembered he had stayed in bed, left the container alone.

"Accept."

No visual on the wallscreen; just the panicky voice of Deputy Administrator Rasikaar. "Captain Vellerik. Something is happening in the Administrator's—in the count's quarters. Danysaan doesn't want to do anything but… someone heard a scream."

"A scream?"

Cerrin could taste blood. When she felt her head against the floor, she realized she must have passed out. Something dripped onto her mouth and she saw the drops of red, bright and glistening beneath her. She touched her face, igniting a line of fire across her cheek. Then she saw the bloodied shard of glass lying close by, and she remembered Talazeer cutting her.

He and Marl were standing by the door, the count shaking his fist as he gave his orders. Marl replied but Talazeer snapped back instantly and reached for the control panel. Once the door was open, Talazeer shoved his bodyguard outside, then punched two buttons.

When she realized he had locked the door, Cerrin tried to get up. But her arms gave way and more blood fell from her face.

"Don't worry," said Talazeer, "you can barely see it against the robe."

He scooped her up easily in his arms and held her tight as he walked into the bedroom. Injured and without a weapon, Cerrin knew she didn't have a chance.

Talazeer dropped her onto the middle of the bed, then stretched her arms up above her with one hand. With the other, he pulled the belt off the robe, then began tying her wrists together.

She watched him. Those dark eyes were without depth or feeling, his face even more lifeless than before. Black blood dripped onto the covers beside her head. Somehow she got some words out.

"You're bleeding."

It didn't even seem to register. He had finished tying her and now ran both bloodied hands through his hair.

Cerrin screamed again, a scream that shook her entire body. This was not fear but rage. As tears streamed down her face, she spat at him and cursed with every oath she knew.

Talazeer covered her mouth with one hand and reached for his belt with the other.

Then he suddenly let go and turned around.

Cerrin looked past him and saw the old soldier standing there, dressed but barefoot like the count. When she saw the expression on his face, she knew she would live.

15

Vellerik found himself outside the medical bay again.

The girl had tried to run past him, but he could hardly let her loose on the ship with blood pouring from her face so he'd grabbed her and picked her up. When she realized he meant her no harm, she stopped struggling. Neither Talazeer nor Marl had followed him as he carried her away, ordering Rasikaar to wake the surgeon. The physician was currently examining her while the two curious soldiers looked on. The girl— whose name Vellerik still did not know—was letting the surgeon treat her but was breathing heavily and staring blankly up at the roof.

He reckoned half an hour had now passed since he'd activated his security override to access Talazeer's quarters. Though Danysaan and Rasikaar had followed him there and seen the girl, the Administrator had just made an announcement that all personnel were to remain in their cabins. Vellerik assumed the count was already moving to keep the incident quiet, limit the damage. He glanced at the clock inside the bay—it was the middle of the night. Despite its gruesome outcome, Talazeer had evidently put some thought into his plan.

Vellerik moved up to the window and watched the surgeon work. Once the bleeding was staunched, he used a scanner mounted on an arm to check the wound. Having briefly disappeared into an anteroom, he returned with a beaker full of liquid. He tried three times to get the girl to drink it, but she refused.

The surgeon then came outside to join Vellerik in the corridor. He was of a similar age, probably not far off from retirement himself. "I wonder if you might try in a moment, captain. It's a sedative. I have no experience in dealing with the species, so I had to use files from the planetary installations for reference."

"She needs it?"

"Certainly. You didn't say exactly what happened?"

"Did you get a name at least?"

"She did speak a little, but I couldn't make much sense of it. Don't have a translator, do you?"

Vellerik gestured at himself—he was barefoot and wearing only trousers and shirt.

The surgeon glanced through the window. The two injured soldiers were talking to each other. The girl had turned onto her side, away from them. Even from ten meters away, Vellerik could see she was shaking.

"The cut is quite deep," continued the surgeon. "If we can get her to take the sedative, then I can administer anesthetic before the operation."

Count Talazeer marched around the corner and along the corridor. He had now dressed himself in formal attire, but what Vellerik noted first was his hair: he had taken the time to arrange it in his preferred swept-back style.

"Sorry about all this," he said to the surgeon without a hint of shame. "How is she?"

"Very anxious, sir. I was telling Captain Vellerik, I need to administer both a sedative and an anesthetic. The cut is deep but clean and straight; I believe I will be able to…"

"There will be no operation," said the count.

"Sir?"

"Excellency."

The surgeon accepted the correction with good grace.

"Excellency, once the anesthetic takes effect, I can conduct the operation in a matter of minutes."

"That's not necessary. As long as you've stopped the bleeding. I've arranged for a shuttle to take her back to the surface immediately. We have the information we need from her." He shook his head. "I blame myself really, but I thought Marl had his odd predilections under control. These Drellens… if it weren't for his abilities as a bodyguard, I would have got rid of him years ago."

Vellerik stared into the medical bay; he feared his reaction if he actually looked at Talazeer.

"But, Excellency, why leave the girl scarred? If I start now—"

"No, no. Marl should not have forced himself on her, of course, but the little bitch attacked him. I cannot be bothered to go through all the rigmarole of an official sanction—we shall leave her with the scar to remind her and her people of the importance of obedience. I think that's best. I suggest you finish your treatment so she's ready for that shuttle."

The surgeon seemed to think about persisting for a moment. "As you wish, Excellency. If I may, your neck… were you injured?"

"No, no. It's nothing."

"Very well."

As the surgeon walked away, Vellerik took the opportunity to do the same.

"Captain, a word?"

Vellerik took two more steps before halting. His whole body felt rigid and his head ached. But he turned around.

"Perhaps here?" Talazeer pointed further along the corridor, which led to an isolated junction where they would not be heard.

Once there, the count interlocked his fingers and raised his chin, the very picture of composure. "Captain, I would just like to ensure that you understand exactly what happened. It would be unfortunate if differing versions of this incident were to emerge."

Vellerik put his hands in his pockets and said nothing.

Talazeer looked along the corridor and grimaced. "Back home, reputations are so easily tarnished. Even unfounded rumors can be dangerous. Perhaps if you were to tell me now your account of what occurred, I could be sure there is no danger of anyone getting the wrong idea."

It was so tempting.

Vellerik could delay until the morning, compile a written report for Colonel Ferrinor, his immediate superior.

But what then? He was in no doubt about whose side Danysaan and Rasikaar and all the others would take. He could call in a few favors, but his connections were nothing compared to Talazeer's. And once he'd stood up to him, the count would undoubtedly go on the attack. It simply wasn't worth it.

He was surprised by how easily the lies came. "I was awoken by Deputy Administrator Rasikaar—there were reports of screams coming from Count Talazeer's quarters. I arrived there to find Marl attacking the native girl. I intervened."

"I too attempted to stop him," said Talazeer, somehow sounding more convincing with this than any previous statement.

"I then took the girl to the medical bay where she was treated by the surgeon."

Talazeer nodded enthusiastically. "Best to keep it simple, I agree. You thought it odd Marl had taken her to my quarters, but it later emerged that he wanted to have his way with her in his own room. He thought he could keep her quiet, but she fought back."

"So you will be reporting the incident then, sir?"

Talazeer pretended to give this some thought. "No. And neither will Administrator Danysaan. Though it was unfortunate, I can control Marl and I will ensure it won't happen again. But the account needs to be clear for our colleagues aboard the ship and anyone who asks. People do like to talk." Talazeer stood aside. "You would probably like to get back to sleep, captain."

Vellerik reckoned he had earned one moment of candor. "You're going to let her live?"

With the matter settled, it seemed Talazeer was also prepared to drop his guard. "Yes."

"With what she knows? What if she speaks of it?"

"I don't think she will. I don't think she will dare. But what if she does? It will only be to her own kind. And what do they matter?"

Certain he would not be able to get back to sleep, Sonus decided he might as well use the time before his shift started. He retrieved a few key parts from the container and sat in a corner, well away from any prying eyes.

He was still not sure he could create the weapon. He had a design, and most of the parts, but without access to the maintenance yard he didn't have the tools to modify them. He would just to have to hope there would be more work up on the surface at some point, and if the occasion arose, he would need to be ready.

The weapon was to consist of three key parts. The first was the barrel, the second the magazine, the third the firing mechanism. The barrel was a length of metal tubing from which the weapon would discharge canisters of shrapnel (his current idea was to use scraps of metal housed in plastic cylinders). The weapon would fire only once before reloading, so he would have to configure a method for inserting the ammunition. He retrieved a sheet of notes and began to imagine how he might put them into practice. Progress came quickly, and he was soon marking up the cylinder and listing exactly what he needed.

After an hour or so, however, his thoughts drifted to the other parts of the weapon, particularly the troublesome firing mechanism, and belief began to wane. He considered other devices—a bomb perhaps? He knew there had been some attempts at other mines years ago, but the saboteurs had either been discovered or blown themselves up. There were undoubtedly stocks of explosives stored in the armory or main warehouse, but it had been a while since the engineers had cleared new shafts and tunnels. It seemed unlikely he would be able to get his hands on the necessary material, let alone develop a workable method of detonating it.

Then he began to think about targets. Nomora and his allies

clearly hadn't taken any action yet, but they wanted weapons. Who would they try to kill? Someone significant surely. A guard? A commander? Even the Planetary Administrator or Count Talazeer himself?"

Sonus admonished himself for wasting time. He had long since learned that little could be achieved by tying yourself in knots thinking about endless possibilities. He spent a few more minutes on the barrel, then heard the familiar sounds of the cavern coming to life: shuffling feet, muted conversations, boiling water. Soon the alarm would sound and the women would appear with the morning meal. He hid all the incriminating materials in the container, then tidied his bed and began to dress.

As ever, there was so much he could not control. He resolved to think solely about the weapon. Only by focusing on that could he make a concrete contribution. He wanted it ready and working within a month.

Cerrin felt nothing. Her mind seemed blank, empty. Her body seemed somehow both heavy yet weightless. The wound upon her cheek did not hurt at all.

"Girl." The surgeon pointed at the bed.

Cerrin rubbed her eyes, then realized there were other people in this room. At first she thought it was the Vitaari in the medical bay, but these were women. Echobe women. One of them sat up in her bed. She looked at Cerrin but did not speak.

"There, girl. Lie down."

She turned toward him and recognized his face, and then she remembered she was back on Corvos, back in the infirmary of Mine Fourteen.

The Vitaari put a hand on her shoulder. She shrank away from him and sat down on the bed. Another woman came along and stood in front of her.

"Mari will help you undress," said the surgeon. "I understand you were given some medication?"

The woman repeated what he had said, but her Palanian accent wasn't a great improvement on the Vitaari translator.

Though her arm felt like it was made out of wood, Cerrin moved her hand into her pocket and pulled out the packet of tablets. She showed it to the Vitaari, who took it and said something she didn't understand. He then left, and she felt the Palanian hold her hand.

Cerrin shook it off.

"Are you all right? What happened to you?"

Her pale face was a blur, but Cerrin now remembered Mari from her time in the infirmary after her last escape attempt. Mari was kind. She sat next to Cerrin and put an arm around her shoulder.

"What did they do to you?"

Mari took her hand again, and this time Cerrin gripped it tight.

When she awoke later, it was getting dark outside. Reaching up to rub her eyes again, she felt the sting of the wound. Wincing, she gently put a finger against her cheek and traced the two lines of dried blood, the edges of the wound. It was reassuring to know the whole side of her face hadn't been opened up, which was how it now felt. She let go, then looked around.

There were three beds on each side of the infirmary. On her last visit she had been in one by the window, but now she was close to the corridor. There were small weak lights beside the beds of the other two patients—one next to her, one on the other side. Cerrin thought she recognized the woman opposite from Block A. She was staring out of the window up at the sky. The other woman was covered by sheets, facing away from Cerrin. She seemed to be sleeping. In a little room on the other side of the corridor, the surgeon and Mari were sorting through trays of multi-colored vials.

Cerrin was so thirsty she drank the entire mug of water on the table by the bed. Apart from the pulsing pain in her cheek, her head still felt fuzzy and her back ached from where she had been thrown onto the table. The thought of those moments with Talazeer sent a shiver through her, and she put her cold hands under the sheets. It did not seem real. She had thought the worst was over when she'd settled down for the night with the creatures, before Marl had come for her. Before…

Suddenly she was sobbing, her whole body shaking. Shamed by it, she stifled the noise and eventually forced herself to stop by reciting one of her mother's favorite prayers—an invocation to the Lake Goddess that asked for calm and serenity. By the fifth repetition she was beginning to feel better.

Lights came on in the corridor. The surgeon exited the little room to greet Governor Yeterris. Cerrin turned away and pulled the sheets over her, pretending to sleep. She stayed like it even when the door hissed open, even when the surgeon spoke to her. Only when a shadow fell across her face did she open her eyes.

Yeterris—the surgeon standing behind him—was peering down at her. To be precise, he was looking at her cheek.

The governor activated his translator. "Ah, you are awake."

Cerrin sat up, mainly to move away from him.

At a look from the governor, the surgeon quickly left. Yeterris glanced briefly at the other two women, then spoke quietly. "Who did this to you?"

Cerrin did not want to talk about it, certainly not to a Vitaari.

Yeterris fingered one of his gold bracelets. "Was it the bodyguard? He is known to be fond of blades."

Cerrin looked down at the clean white sheets.

"I'm not surprised you don't want to talk. You must have been very frightened. It is unfortunate I had to send you up there."

The governor smacked a fist into a palm. "That bloody Drellen. Talazeer needs to keep him in order."

Then Cerrin did want to speak. She remembered Marl arguing with the count; perhaps he had even tried to stop him. She wanted to tell Yeterris the truth, but the words wouldn't come. In fact, she couldn't even make a sound.

"What?" Yeterris leaned over her. "Can you not speak, girl?"

She tried again. She opened her mouth, but all that came out was breath.

It was him. Talazeer. He did it. It was him.

She could think the words, but she couldn't say them.

Yeterris shook his head, then called out. The surgeon returned, and the two of them began a long conversation in Vitaari. At the end of it, the surgeon checked the screen of the machine beside the bed. He then reached downward and pulled out a cable attached to a metal band.

"It is to help you," said the surgeon.

"Don't worry, girl," added Yeterris.

Cerrin glanced warily at the band, but the surgeon had previously done more frightening things to fix her ankle; she trusted him not to harm her.

He attached the band to the back of her neck, checked the screen again, keyed a few buttons, and spoke to Yeterris in Vitaari. Then he removed the band. "I will send Mari in. That might help."

The governor waited until he had gone before speaking again. He whispered. "You are still beautiful, Cerrin. I hope you feel better soon."

She did not watch him leave. She stared down at the sheets, struck by the realization this had happened to her before: once when she had heard about her father, and again when her mother died. The affliction had taken several days to pass.

Mari came in and tried her best. She spoke softly, spoke of the old days, asked about the forest. To Cerrin's relief, Mari quickly realized she couldn't help and left her in peace. Cerrin leant back and covered her face with her hands. She prayed to all the ancients and gods that she would fall asleep and wake up somewhere else.

16

Sonus stood with a group of about a dozen others outside Orani's dwelling. Maker's Day was approaching, and some of the more enthusiastic workers—Orani included—always managed to cobble together some sort of celebration. There would be singing, small presents, and games for the children. In years past, the Vitaari had allowed them to finish an hour or two early, but the governor had made it clear there was no chance of that happening this time. Behind Orani, her husband was sitting in a chair, carving wooden figures for gifts. Another man was painting them. Three women were discussing the treats they could make from the limited ingredients available. Real food had become increasingly hard to come by, even though the workers were occasionally allowed to barter with the Lovirr, who could offer dried fruit and nuts, even some preserved cakes. But over the years, the mine inhabitants had run out of anything to trade with.

Sonus moved past Orani to a man named Arkus, who he did not know well but now needed to. "Hard to find anything for barter, eh?"

"Very. The Lovirr don't know how lucky they are. They live in luxury compared to us."

"Do they talk about what it's like on the coast?" asked Sonus.

Arkus—a wiry fellow who wore a homemade sleeveless jacket over his overalls—was one of the few laborers other than Sonus permitted to work outside the mine. He had been a sewer engineer before the invasion and was used to working in confined spaces; the Vitaari could not find any drone or individual more effective at clearing the drainage channels they'd had to install. Though there was rain only in the summer months, melting snow was a constant problem. One of the main access points to the channels was close to the landing strip, and Arkus spoke to the Lovirr more than anyone else.

"Now and again." Arkus dug the toe of his boot into the dust. "Some are better than others, but as a people they are selfish. They don't care about us Palanians, or the Echobe, or anyone else. They live almost as free men in their four cities—they can tend their fields, fish if they want to. And every family is allowed to have a child, as long as they can feed it."

Arkus's face changed when he realized this might be a subject he should avoid with Sonus.

"The cities are heavily guarded though, aren't they?"

"There are perimeters but nothing like here. The Vitaari know they hardly need guard them. The Lovirr have what they need to live, why would they cause trouble?"

"It is not in their nature," said Sonus, mainly to see if Arkus agreed.

"They do what is convenient for them. The Vitaari view them almost as children—as long as they provide some free labor and do what they're told, they know they'll be safe. They must know what we go through here though—and at all the other mines."

Sonus thought of the Kinassans. If rumors were to be believed, they were the only people who had successfully fought off the Vitaari. Few Palanians had ever seen one of the tribesmen and viewed the southern people as exotic, mysterious, and dangerous. He wondered if they even knew they were now heroes to the enslaved peoples of the north.

Arkus shrugged. "Ah, who's to say we'd be any different if we were given the chance? There is an irony to it, eh? We Palanians used to think we were so superior. Doesn't look that way now, does it?"

"I remember those dried apples we used to buy," said Sonus. "The children loved those. Do you think one of the Lovirr might still be able to get some?"

"Maybe. Guards used to check everything, but there's so little traded now they've probably forgotten about it. Probably best to just show them or tell them though, in case they got the wrong idea."

"Do you know when the next freighter's due?"

"Won't be long," said Arkus. "Once you can see cargo containers stacked up almost to the warehouse door, the freighter usually turns up. Next few days probably. Keeping you down below most of the time, aren't they?"

"Yes."

"Punishment, is it? For… you know."

"I don't think so," said Sonus honestly. "Just not much work in the maintenance yard."

Arkus watched someone walk past. Sonus turned and realized it was Litas. Arkus nodded in his direction: "I've seen him pestering you—still trying to find out who told them about Qari?"

"Yes."

"Probably prefer to forget about it, would you?"

"I would."

"He means well. Just puts his energy into the wrong things. He always used to go on at me about the channels. Where do they lead? What can you see from down there? Where do they come out? I told him, they all come out the same way—two thousand feet above a sheer drop onto solid rock."

"He doesn't ask anymore?"

"No. I suppose he's given up. Like all of us."

Vellerik took the call from Kerreslaa while sitting on his bed. The update had been as tedious and routine as ever, but the liaison officer seemed very proud of himself. There had been no serious incidents at any of the mines; Talazeer's new regime was proving very effective.

"—and lastly the Kinassans. Sensors have picked up nothing since your operation, captain. I don't imagine they'll be venturing north when they see what you left behind."

"Is that it?"

"Yes. I do hope you feel better, we—"

Vellerik cut him off.

He was pretending to be ill. Pathetic, he knew, but he couldn't face going out there and lying—helping the count conceal the truth. And he didn't want to run into Talazeer himself. The last he'd heard, the count had let one of the larger creatures loose in a cargo bay and was watching it run around.

Vellerik thought of Seevarta. He wondered what she was doing today. Visiting one of her friends perhaps or taking a walk? He had received his last message from her the previous week. She had been worried about her back but was now feeling better. She missed him. She was counting the days until his return. Apparently, there were only ninety-eight left.

Earlier that day he'd tried to record his own message. He thought it would be good for him to get it out, tell the truth. Though the subspace transmissions took days to reach the home world, the lines were secure. But he couldn't even start speaking because he didn't know where he would end up. The thought of taking even one more order from Talazeer appalled him.

If he could just get through those ninety-eight days, it would be over. He could forget the count, forget Corvos, forget all the killing, all the death. He had done it before. Even the worst memories faded, especially if you wanted them to. He could get through it. But he would need some help.

Cerrin was released after two days.

She didn't particularly want to leave, but the surgeon made it clear she had no choice. He gave her the medication and told her to take half a tablet every day for a week. Mari asked if she wanted to use the showers and Cerrin willingly accepted, using as much soap as she could and staying under the water so long Mari eventually had to tell her to come out.

She stood there in a new pair of overalls, watching as the Palanian woman took her sheets from the bed. There were bloodstains where the wound had rubbed against them. That morning, the surgeon had applied some kind of glue-like liquid to it; he said this would help it heal and prevent what he called "infection." Cerrin was also surprised to hear a second apology from a Vitaari surgeon: he said he'd like to "remove" the wound but was forbidden from doing so.

A guard arrived as Mari said goodbye in the corridor. She held Cerrin's hand again and told her everything would be all right. Cerrin knew she should thank her, but the words didn't come. They would soon enough, though.

The guard pointed to the exit and walked along beside her. Cerrin had to shield her eyes as she stepped outside; it was a bright, cold day. Ahead were the two accommodation blocks, silent with the day shift working and the night shift asleep. Two cleaning drones were sliding up and down the tower, cleaning off brown leaves blown in from the forest. Over at the landing strip, a squad of guards was running circuits. Among them was Kezzelet, who did not notice her.

The guard shoved her forward.

Cerrin spun around, snarling. "Don't touch me. Don't ever touch me."

The guard laughed. "They told me you were one to watch." His expression changed abruptly. "I wouldn't try that again though or I'll have to introduce you to my friend." He tapped the top of his jolt-rod.

Cerrin only actually noticed her voice had returned when she spoke for a second time. "Where am I supposed to be going?"

"Straight to the mine—top level, cavern four."

She walked quickly across the compound, past the tower and the accommodation blocks. As she passed under the cage, she recalled being looked at day after day. It would be the same now.

The entrance to the Mine Fourteen was a colossal, square tunnel that sloped downward into the earth. A drill had obviously been through recently because a crew of laborers were at work with shovels, levelling out the deep ruts left by the vehicle. The four Vitaari guards on duty had a gun laid out on a table and seemed to be dismantling it. One of them was Stripe, and he looked up as Cerrin and the guard started down the slope.

"Wait there."

Both she and the guard obeyed.

Stripe came close and expected the wound. "Look at that. Who have you annoyed this time, Longlegs? Knowing you, you probably thought you could escape from a starship—that right? Or maybe one of your pets did it?"

She hadn't ever expected help to come from this quarter, but it was as good an explanation as any. She would not be telling anyone the truth. She felt ashamed; not that it had happened but that she'd gone along with it. Because she had gone with Marl. Because she had cleaned herself and wore that horrible red thing even when she knew what was coming. She should have fought back earlier.

"Yes, it was one of the animals."

Stripe reached forward with one great gray hand and tipped her chin up. "Didn't do much of a job fixing you up, did they? Probably decided you weren't worth it."

By Ikala, I will kill you. One day I will kill you.

"Probably." She pointed into the mine. "Can I go?"

"Oh, don't let me stop you."

He let her and the guard take several paces away before continuing. "You know you made history, Longlegs. It's ironic. Who would have thought an ignorant fool like you would be the first of your kind into space?"

The others laughed, but his words meant nothing to her. For once, all she wanted was to be amongst her own people, and she was surprised to find renewed strength in her body as she hurried on, the guard several paces behind.

The fourth cavern was one of the largest in the mine. Two Vitaari engineers were on movable gantries close to the roof, operating larger versions of the cutting blades used to clear vegetation in the forest. They were slicing off the enormous pale roots of the enkemika tree that regrew at a prodigious rate and could find their way down through the tiniest hole in search of water. Cerrin had done this work before: the Vitaari were concerned about the roots destabilizing the roof and obviously thought it easier to do this every few months than pull down the huge trees. Like much of the sprawling mine, the cavern was situated below ground far beyond the walls.

There were about twenty women from the day shift, divided into two groups. The Vitaari engineer in charge directed Cerrin toward the second, on the far side of the cavern. Passing the first group—who were shoveling the roots into crates—she saw a few familiar faces, one of which was Yarni. When the girl waved at her, Cerrin couldn't stop herself from smiling. She realized it must have been the first time she had done so because the movement of the skin tugged at the wound. All of the women watched her.

The second group were collecting clumps of root cut by the Vitaari and piling them up. Again she saw many women she knew, and again they stared at her. Cerrin set about her work and found a strange comfort in the banal routine of it. She spoke to no one until the midday break.

Even then, the two groups were kept separate, and Yarni had to ask for permission to go and see Cerrin. Like the others, they had been given the usual tasteless food-packs, but Cerrin had also grabbed some softer sections of the root—it was a tad bitter but edible and known to provide energy.

"Nobody knew where you were," said Yarni, trying not to look at the cut.

The pulsing ache had returned, so Cerrin took another half-tablet with her water.

"I had to collect some animals for… for the Vitaari. Then I went with them to their ship, to tell them how to look after them. While we were moving the karki, it attacked me." She gestured at the cut. "Did this."

"You went to their ship?" The girl's eyes widened as she chewed on a length of root. "You went above the clouds?" She said the second part loudly, drawing looks from the other women.

"I did."

"What was it like?"

"I don't want to go back there."

"What does it look like—is it black?"

"All black—like a sea. The ship is as big as a mountain, but it floats there like the ones that fly here."

"Did you see the gods?" asked Yarni.

Cerrin shook her head. She had never felt farther from the gods in her life than up there. Though what she'd seen of the Vitaari should have convinced her it was futile to take them on, that was the opposite of how she felt.

"Some new faces," she said quietly, nodding at the women.

Yarni shuffled closer. "Five on our shift. Two men and three women. They came in a few days ago—they were moved from Mine Six. Do you know where it is?"

"Out in the Empty Lands, I think. Do you know why they were moved here?"

"For work, they said. But we haven't lost anyone to be replaced, so some don't believe it."

Cerrin glanced at the three newcomers. One in particular had caught her eye: a powerfully built Palanian woman with short spiky hair. She too was sitting apart from the others and staring thoughtfully down at the ground.

"Sadi," whispered Yarni. "She's not very friendly."

Though it hurt to eat, Cerrin knew the root was good for her and she kept some for later. Yarni continued to question her about her trip beyond the clouds, but Cerrin was more interested in her and why she was now working with the women.

"I asked to," said Yarni proudly. "They will still give me the little jobs, but for the rest of the time I will work with the women. Can I work beside you sometimes, Cerrin?"

"Of course you can. I was watching you earlier—you didn't stop. Remember to go at an even pace—you've got to last all day, and the next one comes around quick."

"But I'm young." The look of innocent enthusiasm upon the girl's face almost drew tears from Cerrin, but she covered her reaction by pretending the cut was bothering her. When she thought of how all Yarni's hopes would be battered out of her by years of enslavement, she could have easily struck out at the Vitaari there and then. While the girl told her how she planned to work hard so she would be strong when the Vitaari left, Cerrin looked over at the two engineers and two guards, who were at the other end of the cavern. The guards had no guns, only jolt-rods. It was a shame the engineers had left the light-knives up on the gantries. She imagined they would take off a leg with ease.

But it was not them she wanted to attack. Not just them, anyway. And there would be no more thoughts of escape. Not just her, anyway. She'd had a long time to think while working that morning, and it suddenly seemed an age since she'd lay in that bed, unable to speak.

Ikala, god of battle. See me, hear me, help me with what lies ahead.

It was as if Ikala had heard her already.

Midway through the afternoon, the new arrival, Sadi, moved subtly across the cavern, unnoticed by the Vitaari but not by Cerrin. The Palanian helped her shift a particularly heavy section of root and eventually broke the silence.

"Cerrin, right?"

"Right."

"Sadi."

They continued to talk quietly as they collected scraps well away from the others.

"You came in from Six?" asked Cerrin.

"Yes."

"Why'd they move you?

"Labor reasons. That's what they said."

"That the truth?"

"Who knows?"

Cerrin decided she couldn't read much from Sadi's pale face. She knew that in the past the Vitaari had put spies and informers into mines where there might be trouble. Was it possible Talazeer had decided to return to such measures?

Sadi said, "I heard you tried to escape from here—even got close once?"

Cerrin didn't mind talking about that; everyone knew anyway. "Not close enough."

"Me too. Long time ago."

"They let you live?"

"I think they were impressed I managed to survive." Sadi turned around and pointed to an area on the back of her head where no hair grew.

"Three jolt-rod shots in the same place. I was back on my feet within a day."

"You never tried again?"

"Not much point out on the plain—nowhere to go. I heard you know the forest? That the Vitaari even use you for a guide?"

Cerrin stayed quiet. What had seemed lucky now seemed suspiciously so. Were the gods helping her, or was she being lured into revealing too much?

"You don't trust me," said Sadi. "I don't blame you. You shouldn't." She threw a hefty root onto the nearest pile. "Not yet."

17

Sonus worked in the mines for six consecutive days before he was summoned to the surface by Kadessis. Strangely, his cough barely troubled him and, physically, he felt better than he had in months.

Work on the weapon was progressing. The barrel was complete, and the method for loading the ammunition functioned well. The magazine (a converted plastic container) sat atop the rear of the barrel; a simple bolt opened a slot in the tube, and gravity did the rest. Sonus reckoned he would be able to reload and fire within two or three seconds with a bit of practice. But now came the last and most complicated element: the firing mechanism. It would be difficult to construct and dangerous to test, but he couldn't even start without a few key components. And those could only be found in the maintenance yard: to be precise, the maintenance building.

As he walked in from the compound, he realized instantly why he was needed. Mine Three had four Vitaari engineers, all of whom he had worked with at some point. They remained utterly dismissive of his abilities but were happy to use him for monotonous "unskilled" tasks. Today, two of them were standing by a drill, examining the tracks. Two more were inside the maintenance building, which was situated at the rear of the yard. Close to the open doors, they were standing on either side of one of the combat shells. Sonus knew that these only occasionally needed repair and were regarded as more reliable than much of the Vitaari technology. The white exterior of the four-limbed shells was composed of curved, armored sections, giving the impression of a tall, broad humanoid. There was no head, only a reinforced window for the pilot.

"Sonus. Over here."

He trotted over to Kadessis, who was standing next to the fence. Lying in a row alongside it were more than twenty of the large lamps used in the tunnels. All were filthy and many had broken bulbs.

"You can see the problem."

"Yes, sir." Sonus tried not to appear happy. This was a lot of work; he might be able to stretch it out for two or three days.

"Those without damaged bulbs have other problems," said Kadessis. He then gestured at two other items. "You'll need the diagnostic unit, and there are your tools." Sonus had assembled this box over the years but was not permitted to take it from the yard. Within it were several implements he needed.

"Yes, sir. Thank you."

"Any questions, come to the tower and ask for me. Do not bother the engineers."

"No, sir."

Kadessis did up his bulky jacket; there was a chill breeze blowing in off the mountain. Sonus knew he would be freezing by the end of the day, but the thought did not concern him.

"I must be going," said Kadessis, though he did not leave. "How are you?"

"Better, sir. Thank you."

"You know, what happens amongst our people is not so very different to what happens here. You remember what I told you about the twelve clans—those who command The Domain?"

"Yes."

"They have done so for centuries. Not because of any particular reason, not because they are particularly gifted, but simply because that is the way it has always been. Some have been murderers, thieves, even pederasts. My uncle wrote a book about one of them, dared to tell the truth. My cousins didn't see him for twelve years because he was imprisoned for his "crimes." They may wreck the economy, neglect their people, make awful, ridiculous mistakes. And yet they remain at the top, looking down upon the rest of us. And we are not permitted to say a word about it."

Sonus had heard remarks like this from Kadessis before. He sometimes wondered if this was why he'd been posted to Corvos.

The Vitaari paused for a moment, then spoke again. "Your… effort to assist your friends. You were attempting to do what you thought was right, what would be right in an ideal world. But there is no ideal world, Sonus, is there? There is only the one we have. You must accept that."

Sonus tried to answer like his old self. "I have, sir. I did what I did out of friendship. I thought I could save a life."

From Kadessis, a trace of a smile. "One day we Vitaari will leave."

"How long do you have to stay here, sir?"

The administrator suddenly seemed a lot less keen to talk. "Work as quickly as you can. We need to get those lights back in the mine."

"Of course, sir."

As Kadessis departed, Sonus opened the toolbox and got to work. He fixed the first two lamps quickly—elementary problems correctly identified by the diagnostic unit—but then came to the third, which required a new bulb. Kadessis had forgotten to bring them out. Sonus wasn't about to give up this opportunity to get inside the maintenance building; he had to get those parts.

Lugging the big lamp with both hands, he walked across the yard and up to the doorway. One engineer was now sitting down, consulting a data-pad. The other was standing on a large box next to the arm of the combat shell. He had a panel open and was examining the machine's complicated innards. Sonus was fascinated by the shells but had never had a chance to examine them up close.

The engineer with the data-pad said something in Vitaari. With them both looking at him, Sonus nodded down at the lamp. The engineer on the box went back to his work, but the other pointed over his shoulder toward the stores where the bulbs and other spares were kept.

Sonus thanked him, put the lamp down next to the door, and hurried toward the back of the building. He passed a damaged section of conveyor and a loading vehicle, then entered an area of storage shelves. He knew exactly where the bulbs were but took a route past a long rack containing smaller parts. Having checked that the engineers weren't watching, he swiftly located the two components he needed. One was a self-powered spring, the other a connector rod he reckoned he could reconfigure into a trigger. He tucked them into his overalls, then went to get the bulbs. Knowing he would need a few, he grabbed a box of six.

On his way back, he passed the table where the engineer was sitting. Lying on it was a large metallic case, clearly part of the maintenance package. As he neared the door, Sonus scanned the variety of parts laid out beneath the shell. There seemed to be no weapons there; presumably they were kept in the armory along with the functioning shells and the ammunition.

Sonus narrowed his eyes against the wind as he crossed the yard. He had never been inside the armory but now found himself looking at it. The building was attached to the guards' barracks, the rear close to the edge of the platform and another vertiginous drop. He put the box of bulbs down, then headed back for the lamp.

The engineers now had both their heads buried in the access hatch, which gave him a moment to inspect the features of the shell: the enormous metal hands and feet, the thick panels of the armored body, the propulsion system, the numerous attachments for guns and ordnance.

On his way back, Sonus thought of the single, small weapon he was trying to construct. He could not avoid the conclusion he was wasting both effort and time.

Vellerik met the troop outside the cargo bay. He couldn't be bothered to inspect them but was glad to see Perttiel back on his feet. There was also good news about Triantaa: though the main artery in his neck had been nicked by the spearhead, the damage had been successfully repaired. The lieutenant was unable to talk for the moment due to his medication but was expected to make a full recovery and be out of the medical bay within weeks.

With his second-in-command out of action, Vellerik should have been spending more time with the troop, but he had temporarily promoted Zarrinda and let him lead the daily drills. He hadn't actually seen the men for two days and felt curious eyes upon him as they gathered by the doorway.

"Any idea what this is about, sir?" asked Zarrinda.

"None." Vellerik had only been up for half an hour. Two nights with a double dose of Almana's Breath had taken their toll, and he suspected it showed. The first night had brought him relief: images of his woman, his friends, his home. Good things.

Last night had been different. Talazeer and the girl. Vellerik could not forget the look on her face: the same blend of hatred and fear he had seen on the young Kinassan warrior and countless times before.

He led the men to the meeting room, where they arrived to find most of the staff already present. Without greeting Danysaan, Rasikaar, Kerreslaa, or anyone else, Vellerik placed the men in two lines behind the crew and the administrators. As the last few arrived, Rasikaar hurried forward to make an adjustment to the wallscreen. He sharpened up the color and the focus of the image: the Imperial standard—a gold circle on a black background to symbolize the home world. It was surrounded by twelve stars, one each for the noble clans.

All of the chairs and tables had been removed from the room; the only piece of furniture was the platform on which the count would stand. He kept them waiting, during which time the only sign of exasperation came from Vellerik himself. It seemed Talazeer had succeeded in engendering almost as much fear in his fellow Vitaari as the natives. Predictably immaculate, he left Marl outside and strode straight up to and onto the platform.

"Welcome to you all. It is now sixty days since I arrived on the *Galtaryax* to take charge of the Corvos operation. My sole aim was to increase yields of all minerals from all facilities. Let's look at the numbers."

Rasikaar came forward and handed him the screen controller. The first image was a graph showing yields broken down by mineral. The second showed them by installation.

Having hammered home his point about production, Talazeer then displayed two messages of congratulations, one from the chief of the Resource Directorate, the second from his father. He read the second letter out, and Vellerik was sure he actually heard the count's voice waver with emotion at one point.

He imagined himself walking into the office of Lord Talazeer and telling him what his son had tried to do to a native female.

The count then turned to security and was soon boasting about the reduction in "incidents." He described both operations the troop had undertaken, and Vellerik had to suffer a round of applause. He wished he'd stayed in his room.

Just when the briefing seemed to be over, Talazeer revealed he had received another message. This communique came from Viceroy Mennander, whose regional command included the Corvos system. Talazeer explained that—due to the remoteness of the planet—Mennander had never visited before but, because of the "unprecedented success of the last few weeks," he wished to attend as The Domain's representative—to commend the leadership and staff. Vellerik doubted that was the whole truth; more likely Mennander felt he had to do so because of Talazeer's family connections.

The count clasped his hands. "This is, of course, a great, great honor. The precise dates are yet to be finalized, but Viceroy Mennander will be attending in around four weeks. There will be a tour of the *Galtaryax* and the surface installations. The climax of the trip will be a dinner held on one of the islands south of Mine Twelve, where we will present the viceroy with a statue of himself carved from a mixture of terodite and blue diamonds. I thank each and every one of you for your contribution and trust you will do your part ensuring our success continues. We shall show the viceroy and his party the very best in Vitaari efficiency and endeavor!"

Danysaan and Rasikaar led the applause.

Talazeer changed the display back to the imperial standard. "And now we will say the vow."

All of the fifty or so Vitaari men gathered there knew it by heart and delivered it in perfect unison.

Honor, loyalty, pride...

It was a long time since the words had meant anything to Vellerik. He mouthed them but did not make a sound.

As they left the meeting room, Vellerik was intercepted by Marl.

"The count would like to see you."

"Now?"

"Immediately. In his quarters."

As they set off, soldiers and administrators alike were careful not to get in their way. Vellerik drew level with Marl as they turned along an empty corridor. "Haven't seen much of you around the ship lately."

"I've heard the same said of you," countered the bodyguard. "And you are supposed to be a leader."

Vellerik couldn't think of much to say to that. They reached the elevator and travelled up two levels in silence.

He spoke again as they neared the count's quarters. "It doesn't affect you—these lies? About you?"

Marl scratched his teeth together before replying. "What else would the Vitaari expect of a 'skinner?'"

They stopped. "But it is untrue."

"Captain, do you really think I care what a bunch of Vitaari think of me?"

Vellerik could deduce nothing from those bright yellow eyes. "Actually, I do."

Marl opened the door and walked inside. "Excellency." He gestured at Vellerik, then went and stood against the wall.

"Ah, captain, do come in." Talazeer did not look up. He was standing, staring at the screen mounted on the table.

Vellerik walked over to him.

"I do love the vow," said Talazeer, running a hand through his hair. "Makes me feel… warm. You know—inside."

Vellerik considered a series of colorful replies but said nothing.

Talazeer nodded at the screen. "As I mentioned, details are yet to be finalized, but I would like you to organize security. It sounds as if the viceroy will be coming in his own cruiser; I suggest we take that down to the surface. We wouldn't want him to have to "rough it" in one of the shuttles, or indeed the *Galtaryax*. I was thinking of a simple flypast for most of the mines but visits to Nine, Eighteen, and Three—mainly for the views. I imagine he'll depart straight after the dinner. You and some of the troop could provide an escort at various points—be flying around as we take off and land."

"The cost, sir?"

Talazeer made a face. "This is the viceroy, Vellerik. He has seen the ice mines of the Far Belt, the waterfalls of the Kaitan Lakes. We must at least try to make an impression."

Talazeer pointed at the screen. "I have sent you my suggestions. Please get back to me by tomorrow evening at the latest."

Vellerik nodded.

"It might do you good to have something to get your teeth into," added the count. "If I may say so, you do not look very well. And it has come to my attention that you have been spending a lot of time in your quarters."

"A minor illness, sir. I'm feeling much better now."

"I also could not help noticing your expression during the briefing, captain. It did not convey what is generally considered an appropriate level of enthusiasm."

"Apologies, sir. I am not yet fully recovered."

"Not been to see the surgeon though, have you? I checked."

Vellerik put his hands behind his back.

Talazeer continued: "It's just that your men are young, impressionable. A man of your standing—"

"Sir?"

"Vellerik, it pains me to say this, truly. I hesitate to use the word unprofessional, but—"

Any thoughts of lasting ninety-eight days instantly vanished. Vellerik knew then he had to settle the matter once and for all.

"Count Talazeer, I would like to formally tender my resignation."

Talazeer couldn't get a reply out before Vellerik continued. "I know you will not be able to find a replacement before the viceroy's visit so I will gladly make the security arrangements. But I would like to leave as soon as possible afterward."

He could see Talazeer thinking. And he knew Marl was now looking at him.

"Captain, I'm shocked. I had not expected this."

"Sir, I'm afraid I can't see an alternative. Will you accept?"

"I suppose I must. In fact, it might be best for both of us."

"My thoughts precisely, sir."

"General Eddekal will want to know why, of course."

"Illness and… and my age. I am no longer able to function effectively in the role."

Vellerik felt as if the words were being spoken by someone else. He just had to get away.

"Very well. But I have one condition."

"Sir?"

Talazeer glanced around the room, collecting his thoughts.

For once, Vellerik decided to make it easy for him. "I will never speak of it. I doubt I will ever speak of Corvos or a dozen other worlds like it. I plan to never return to the capital."

Talazeer could not hide his relief. "Then, with regret, I accept."

When the two engineers working on the combat shell took a break, Sonus realized he had an opportunity too good to miss. The other pair had already finished with the drill and were long gone. There were guards on patrol in the compound, but the cold kept their walks past the maintenance yard to a minimum. Though dusk was still some hours away, the bank of gray cloud overhead cast a helpful gloom over Mine Three.

Armed with a genuine reason for his trip (more bulbs), Sonus returned to the building. On his way past the table, he noted the case contained some specialized tools and a series of data clips. There were three copies of each. One group was labelled "general."

Once at the rear of the building, Sonus went straight to the long, untidy work desk behind the shelves.

Please still be there.

On his last visit several weeks previous, he had noted an abandoned data-pad with a broken screen. It still worked, and he'd considered asking if he could take it but had never summoned the courage. After a minute of searching he found it buried under some plastic sheeting. Sonus secreted it within his overalls, then quickly grabbed another box of lamps. He paused at the end of the shelves and stared at the well lit front of the building.

If he went through with this, there was no going back. If he were discovered, there would be no jolt-rod this time.

He stepped forward, then stopped again.

The Vitaari would do something terrible to him. He would die in great pain.

He doubted it would be as bad as what Qari and Karas had felt.

Once he reached the table, he put the box down and stole the data clip from the case as if it were the most natural thing in the world.

18

It was one of the more unusual jobs assigned to the women of Mine Fourteen, but most of them clearly preferred it to their usual labors. For the past five days they had been sent into scores of old unused tunnels, collecting up the small quantities of aronium left behind. Used to spending weeks and months in the same location, it came as a welcome relief, especially as the older tunnels were closer to the surface and unsullied by the dust of recent drilling. Every day they were split into groups of four and sent off with two flashlights and a handcart to fill. The task involved hours of walking and searching, but with no guards around, nobody was complaining.

Cerrin had tried to make sure she worked with Yarni, but Stripe had managed to frustrate her efforts on previous occasions (she presumed he just did it to annoy her). He hadn't been on duty today though, and Cerrin's crew was Yarni plus two older women. As they hauled the cart through the tunnels, Cerrin did most of the heavy work and encouraged Yarni to sit on the cart and relax.

Though it was labor for the Vitaari, she actually enjoyed it. She liked the feeling of building up her body and being too tired to think at the end of the day. The cut was healing, but now that the swelling had reduced, she could see the full extent of it. It ran three inches, from just below her right eye to her jaw. But even this had one benefit: the other women—including the older pair—seemed friendlier. It was perhaps easier for them to understand her position now: she was just another victim of the Vitaari, like them.

Cerrin's own view of the scar changed almost daily. It enraged her to know Talazeer had marked her for the rest of her life, but she knew it would also drive her on. More than one of the women had pointed out it might help her in another way: she would not catch the eye of the Vitaari now—perhaps they might leave her alone. Cerrin reckoned there was some truth to that though it clearly didn't apply to Stripe. It seemed she provided him with a source of entertainment he did not want to give up.

There was another reason she was feeling better: for two of the past five days she had worked alongside Sadi. Nothing had been said openly yet, but the new arrival had disclosed a great deal about her time at Mine Six. Like Cerrin, she was one of the last captured (though that had been four years previous, not two), and she had faced hostility from those less minded to provoke their captors.

Neither of them had spoken explicitly of escape or resistance, but it was clear from Sadi's attitude that both subjects were on her mind. Cerrin had been planning to expand their conversation that day, but Sadi had gone with another group. As they'd already discussed the fact that they were spending too much time together, Cerrin knew it was probably a sensible move.

Though she'd told herself several times to be careful, she craved a true ally. She had not expected that ally to arrive in the shape of a Palanian woman who seemed tougher and stronger than a lot of Echobe men.

"Look, there's some," said Yarni, jumping off the cart and running to collect some white-veined chunks of aronium ore. The others went to help her.

They worked on until they all agreed it was lunch time. The meals had been doled out in the morning, and they sat beside the cart at a four-way junction. When they finished eating, Yarni pestered the older women into singing, and the pair struck up a harmonious version of a traditional Echobe song. Yarni wanted to learn it, and soon Cerrin was the only one not singing along. Though the sound brought back pleasant memories, she could not make herself take part. After a while, she felt so uncomfortable she left them to it.

She hadn't gone far along one of the adjoining tunnels when someone called her name. She turned around to see a woman walking quickly across the junction. As the interloper passed a lamp, she saw it was Esteann, a woman who lived in the row beneath her in Block A.

"What are you doing down here?"

"I wanted to speak to you." She pointed along the tunnel and continued past Cerrin, who followed, frowning. Esteann only stopped when they were well away from the others. She too was Echobe, from a village not far from Cerrin's own. She was also around her age, with hair and skin the same hue as Cerrin. The two had been on good terms before Cerrin's first escape attempt.

"About what?"

"I've seen you talking to that Sadi."

Cerrin said nothing.

"You should know what people are saying."

"Which is?"

"That she and those others were transferred here because there was something going on at their mine. They were planning something. The Vitaari couldn't work out exactly who was behind it, but they split them up and sent them elsewhere. You should not let yourself be seen with her, Cerrin—with your history and hers. If the Vitaari even think you're—"

"Who told you this?"

"Several people."

"How do they know?"

"It adds up, Cerrin. We don't get many new arrivals these days. Especially not groups."

"If the Vitaari suspected anything, they would have just killed them."

"A whole shift of workers? Not easy to replace."

Cerrin paused. A lot of what Esteann said made sense, yet it only affirmed what she suspected: Sadi really was someone who could help her. But if Sadi were already under suspicion, she might be more trouble than she was worth.

"Cerrin, what has she told you?"

Even if Esteann were right, Cerrin needed to counter her suspicions. "She said they were moved because there was less work at the mine."

"And you believe her?"

"Why should I believe you?"

Esteann cast a despairing look at the roof of the tunnel. "Cerrin, do you not understand? If they think you two are planning something, who's to say they won't divide our shift? Things are bad enough without being sent to gods know where. If not for us, think of yourself." She pointed at the scar. "Look what they've done to you already. You know I wouldn't betray you, but there are some who would."

Cerrin thought for a moment about grabbing her, pinning her down and demanding the names. Dukas would be among them, she was sure. But that was the wrong move. Esteann and the others like her had to be convinced nothing was going on.

Now Cerrin pointed to the scar. "Just so you know, I did not get this because I tried to escape. Why do I speak to Sadi? Perhaps it's because no one else but Yarni speaks to me."

Esteann's expression was one of regret. "We were close once. I came down here because I don't want to see you hurt again."

With that, Esteann turned and left.

Cerrin was long past the point of trying to see the other side of things. To her, Esteann and her kind were weak. When the moment came, she and the others would have to make their choice.

The caverns were silent but for the distant sound of snoring. Sonus was lying on his side, body obscuring the data-pad in case anyone happened to pass. The display occasionally flashed and one corner of the screen was obscured by the crack, but he could read most of the manual and what he saw fascinated him.

Though much of the technical language was beyond his understanding, the data clip was full of immaculately rendered schematics. All he had to do was touch a certain part and it would magnify and rotate, showing him every single section of the combat shell and how it worked.

One of the first things he'd noticed was how flexible the shells were in terms of how they attached to the body. There were supports and belts all over, and he realized after a while it could be adjusted for humanoids of different sizes and shapes.

This conclusion tallied with his other observations of the literature within the clip: the shells were not made by the Vitaari. It seemed they were manufactured by some foreign enterprise whose name and symbol appeared everywhere. Intrigued by this discovery, Sonus continued his survey, scrolling through pages showing the controls, the engines, and the armaments until his eyes ached and he had to look away.

When he returned to the first page—which listed the contents of the clip—he realized he had missed the most important section of all. Touching the Vitaari word for "access," he was soon looking at dense text and several diagrams. After several partially successful attempts at translation, he established the basics of how the shells were activated before use. It seemed users had to be in possession of an authenticator chip. He surmised these were contained within the triangular ID cards the Vitaari all carried, some on cords around their necks. Without these, the shells wouldn't even power up.

He made a mental note to add this to his list of questions for Nomora. According to Arkus, a freighter was due the following morning, and Sonus was almost tempted to pray the Lovirr would be on it. He'd been assigned to the maintenance yard ever since the lamp repairs and had ensured his present assignment—cleaning drill tracks—would take at least another day.

He turned off the data-pad, then got up and walked over to the container. Lifting out the spare parts quietly was not easy, and it took him a while to secrete the data-pad and then replace them on top. It was a measure he felt he had to take; though the Vitaari had not conducted an inspection of the caverns in months, they might do so at any time.

Sonus returned to bed. He watched the white mist of his breath and pulled the blankets up to his neck. When he closed his eyes, all he saw was the triangular ID cards. Somehow, he had to get one.

Cerrin was also cold. She stood in complete darkness behind Block A, waiting for Sadi. Yarni had come up to her compartment just before lights out and whispered the message without the Palanian sisters noticing. Cerrin reckoned an hour had passed, but it was hard to be precise.

Hearing footsteps, she glanced around the corner of the container and watched a man leave the block and cross the five yards of ground to the latrine building. Occasionally—if the Vitaari guards on patrol heard someone step outside—they would shine their lights, but Cerrin had seen no sign of them tonight.

She recalled her first attempted escape. It had taken her almost an hour to get across the compound unseen before climbing the vehicle and getting over the wall. Unbeknownst to her, a pair of guards had been flying back to the mine in combat shells, and the machines had somehow detected her. The gate had opened, and more guards had tackled her fifty feet from the river.

Cerrin had seen Sadi in the elevator earlier but had purposefully avoided her, particularly as Esteann was there. Anyone awake and observant enough to have noticed her leave would know by now she had been gone a suspiciously long time, but she felt the risk was worthwhile.

The man returned to the block. Another figure came out not long after and walked straight into the shadows.

"Cerrin?"

"I'm here."

They moved farther into the darkness.

"I had a visit from Esteann today. You know her?"

"I think so."

"Looks like she and a few others have noticed us. She warned me off, told me you and your lot were moved here because the Vitaari thought you were up to something. That true?"

"What if it is?"

"Just answer me. Please."

"It's true."

"And were you up something?"

"Me personally?"

"No games, Sadi. Just tell me."

"Why should I, Cerrin? What if you're an informer?"

The change in the Palanian's tone startled Cerrin. It had been years since she'd met another female who might be able to take her on physically. Sadi was a foot shorter than her but undoubtedly as strong.

"Well? Are you?"

"You should not say that to me," replied Cerrin. "Don't ever say that to me."

"You haven't thought the same thing of me? Why all this dancing around the subject then?"

Cerrin sighed. "Sooner or later, we're just going to have to trust each other. I'd prefer sooner."

"Me too. Yes, we were moved because there was something going on. The Vitaari realized they were missing some materials: mining equipment, explosives. They knew the theft had taken place on our shift, but they didn't know who'd done it. This was months ago. Ten of us were sent to Eighteen, but after a few weeks they realized they didn't have a lot of work so they moved us here."

"Will Governor Yeterris know that?"

"No idea. But new arrivals are always watched anyway. We should be careful. Yarni can keep passing messages if we need her to."

"I don't think we should involve her."

"We may not have a choice. Anyway, involve her in what? What are we doing, Cerrin?"

"You still haven't told me if you were involved."

Sadi stepped closer. "Was I involved? It was my idea. I wanted to blow every single Vitaari in that place into a thousand pieces."

It was actually shocking—to hear someone else say something like that.

"Now what about you?" continued Sadi. "You've tried to get out of here before. Looking to try again?"

"Yes. But not just me. As many as will come with me."

It felt good to say it.

"Us."

"Us, then. And that's not all. I want to burn this place to the ground."

Cerrin saw a flash of teeth in the darkness as Sadi smiled.

"Do you have a plan?"

"I have an idea. I'm pretty sure they've done something to the wall—something to stop us going over."

"They have. I've seen those wires before. It's some sort of electrical charge."

Cerrin wasn't sure what that was, but it didn't particularly matter. "If we can't get over the wall, we have to go under."

"A tunnel? From here?"

"Maybe."

"The closest point of the wall has to be a hundred feet."

"More like a hundred twenty," said Cerrin. "But we won't have to dig half of that."

"What do you mean?" asked Sadi.

"I've had an interesting few days, touring around the top level. If I'm right, we'll only have to dig two small tunnels instead of one big one. The Vitaari have already done most of the work for us."

19

Sonus was running out of time.

Twice he had tried to access the landing strip only to be foiled by the appearance of Kadessis. The administrator would want to know why he was outside the maintenance yard, and Sonus had to keep any meeting with Nomora secret.

Cursing quietly, he bent over the length of drill track but kept his eyes on the strip. He had glimpsed the Lovirr shortly after the freighter landed, but that had been almost an hour ago. The loaders were filling the hold quickly, and the ship would be gone before long. Weeks would pass before another chance arose, and the previous wait had seemed eternal.

Sonus coated the exterior of the track with the cleaning spray he had been provided with, then picked up a big chisel. The tracks grew so hot when the carts were moving that some types of rock actually fused to the metal. Removing it was a task beyond the drones, another failing for which Sonus was extremely grateful. He made himself work for five more minutes before checking again. To his immense relief, Kadessis had returned inside the tower.

He dropped the chisel and picked up the small cloth bag sitting beside his tools. There was no one else working in the yard, and the only guard he passed ignored him as he hurried through the biting wind to the landing strip. Once there, he continued purposefully along the edge, past an engineer and two Lovirr. They also ignored him.

Lined up close to the ship were row after row of large, cubic containers, each containing chunks of ore. There were three Lovirr manning the loaders. Nomora was one of them.

When he saw Sonus, he subtly held up a hand. Sonus nodded an acknowledgement and used the closest container to hide him from any watching Vitaari. Nomora maneuvered the vehicle with great skill, bringing it up close to a container, then extending the arms that locked underneath. Once the container had been lifted, he reversed and headed back up the long ramp into the freighter's hold.

Sonus glanced at the cockpit but could see no one inside. If he stayed where he was and none of the Vitaari moved, he would be able to talk to Nomora unobserved. He watched the loaders continue their work. After a while, Nomora's vehicle emerged with a different driver. The Lovirr exited the ship via the smaller hatch and hurried around the edge of the landing strip. He made an admirable effort to appear relaxed, but Sonus noted a wary glance across the compound.

"Good to see you again."

"If anyone asks, I came to trade with you." Sonus held up the bag. "I have some wooden figurines here, and I'd like some dried apples."

"Very well, though it's better if no one sees us at all." Nomora ushered Sonus closer to the containers. "I heard what happened. I am sorry."

The Lovirr's small dark eyes bored into him. If he knew about Karas and Qari, he probably knew about Sonus attacking the guard—and about his imprisonment.

"I have been cooperating. I am not under suspicion. But I have not been idle."

Nomora scratched at his beard. "Go on."

Sonus did not like revealing his intentions. But as he did not want to involve anyone else at Mine Three, he would need help from outside. Only Nomora could provide it.

"I believe I can break myself out of here."

"That is not quite what we are looking for."

"Even if I stole one of the combat shells? Even if I destroyed most of this installation?"

Nomora's brow furrowed as he looked up at him. "You really believe you can do that?"

"I do. I will need an authenticator chip, correct? Are they contained in the triangular cards they carry? All of them?"

"Only the soldiers."

"I want to try within weeks. But if I get out alive, where would I go? Where else do we have... friends?"

Nomora took a while to reply. "I'd prefer not to mention specifics—names, places, and such—but I can make inquiries. You must understand, though, things are still at an early stage. So far, it has been about making contact, establishing a network. Some operations have been planned, but—"

"Who else is out there? Who else is doing something?"

Nomora opened his mouth but stopped himself.

"What about the Kinassans? They defied the Vitaari, didn't they?"

The Lovirr shook his head. "No one has heard from them in years. They withdrew far to the south. I believe an attempt was made some time back, but there was no confirmation of contact."

"Where else? Where else are people taking action?"

Nomora held up his hands. Sonus noted how small they were, like a child's. "Let me talk to my contacts. But I ask you to do nothing until we have spoken again. I am assigned to this ship for the next few months. I will be back before too long. Make plans if you wish, but please wait."

"Very well."

"Sonus, you have a rare gift. I understand you may want revenge, but you must not risk your life too readily. We need you; we need what you can do."

Sonus leant over him. "I do want revenge, you're right. But I want something more. And I can't do it alone."

"I understand."

Nomora peered around the corner of the container. "I should go."

Sonus handed him the bag of figurines. "If anyone asks, we must tell the same story. There are four in there. How much apple will that get me?"

"About eight pounds."

Sonus offered his hand. Nomora shook it. "Be careful."

"You too."

Cerrin made good use of her last day of freedom. The guards had revealed that the women would be back with a big crew the following day, though no one seemed sure what the work would be. She was not with Yarni nor Sadi, but while her fellow laborers were eating, she found time to sneak off. There was an area she needed another look at.

Without a reference, it was difficult to work out how the layout of the tunnels corresponded to the surface. But she had found just such a point on the second day of the job. The top layer of tunnels was fitted with air ducts. Cerrin had never paid much attention to them before, but by pacing out distances, she had established that one came out below a grill situated on the far side of the latrine. It was too narrow to fit through, but the tunnel underneath ran roughly parallel to the accommodation block. Cerrin could only guess at the distance to the surface, but she and Sadi agreed it could not be much more than fifteen or twenty feet.

Cerrin now stood directly below the base of the air duct. Brushing away a wispy cobweb, she continued on along the darkened tunnel. Ten paces. Twenty. The closest lamp was now a long way behind her. She reached into her overalls and took out a candle Yarni had been saving and a fire-lighter supplied by Sadi. She lit it and continued on.

The yellow light pooled across the rusting remnants of some piece of machinery. Cerrin climbed over it. Beyond were more cobwebs and some pale roots that had broken through the roof. Thirty paces. Thirty-five. At forty, she felt sure she was beyond the wall of Mine Fourteen. The tunnel ended five yards ahead. If her estimates were correct, a continuation of it would come out on the slope above the river. She gave no thought to getting across it, or anything else that might distract her from her current concern.

She walked up to the solid wall of earth and held the candle close. Scattered amongst the hard-packed soil were jagged lumps of rock. It would not be easy to dig through, but again, that was not something that required consideration yet. She and Sadi had agreed on their approach: one step at a time.

As usual, the meeting was arranged through young Yarni. Entering the latrine, Cerrin found Sadi washing her face in a trough of water. The Palanian shook her head and pointed at one of the cubicles. They spoke only when the occupant had left.

"Well?"

"It's out of the way. Dark. Perfect. If we can get to it."

"I had a quick look between Blocks A and B yesterday. I agree it's not right on top of the tunnel, but there's nowhere else out of sight to start digging."

"No good," said Cerrin, who had given the issue a great deal of thought. "The noise. It's not only me who made a window by knocking out a ventilator. Yarni's been checking. There are seven or eight holes in the back of the container. Someone will hear us."

"Where then?" asked Sadi. "On the far side of B are those other containers, but they're packed tight as can be."

"Not quite. I had a look. There are gaps. And it'll be out of sight. And quiet. We can check now."

Cerrin led the way. The greatest risk came as they passed through the light from the lamp above the latrine door. There was only a little patch of darkness between it and the one on Block A. Any Vitaari looking in that direction would see that they were not returning to the container, but the pair heard no shout or sound of movement. There was little noise at all: just the rumble of some drill far beneath and the rattle of the conveyor as it moved the never-ending supply of rock from the mine to the warehouse.

Block B was quiet; all the laborers were working below. Cerrin hurried past the open door to the stack of containers beside it. They were four across and three high. Beyond the last of them was unused space, then the compound wall.

With only moon and starlight to guide them, they headed right and stopped at each point where the containers met. Cerrin was correct: there were gaps, but the first two were only of inches. They could not move between them, and certainly would not have space to dig. But the gap between the last two containers was larger, perhaps ten inches.

"Careful," whispered Sadi. "Might be stuff on the ground."

Cerrin turned sideways and entered the gap. She shuffled along with hands against the cold metal, taking each step slowly. Eventually she reached an intersection between four of the containers. The shortest distance between the corners was about thirty inches. Not much space. But enough.

"We can dig here," she said. "No one will see. No one will hear. These containers haven't moved in years. They'd have to shift both blocks to get to them. What about tools?"

"We can get a shovel or two out of the mine," said Sadi. "But we're, what, forty feet from where we need to be? On a diagonal, total distance might be sixty. Even if we could get someone from the night shift to help, we can't do it in daylight—what if a patrol flies overhead? And between us we can do at most half an hour a night. It would take months."

Cerrin had arrived at the same conclusion days ago.

"We need more people," added Sadi.

"I know. A lot more people."

The cloak was made from a thick, hardy blanket. Qari had given it to him for his thirty-fourth birthday. But even as he pulled it tight around him and tied the clasp below his neck, Sonus did not think of her. He tried to think of her and Karas only when he felt prepared for it, and now was not one of those occasions.

At first, he thought no one was on duty, but then he spied the light coming from the small cave closest to the walkway. His approach startled Orani and her husband, who were sitting close together, wrapped in layers of their own blankets.

"Who—" The old man's sight was not good.

"It's Sonus," said Orani. "What are you doing up at this hour?"

"Just realized I left some equipment switched on in the yard. I'll be in trouble if it stays on all night."

"Ah."

"Sit with us a while, lad," said the husband, who was named Keras.

"I really should get up there."

"Just for moment. We've some hot tea. It'll warm you up a bit before you brave the walk in this snow."

Sonus admitted to himself a few moments with the old couple might be pleasant. He could not remember the last time he had just talked to someone. Keras found a stool for him, and he sat down between them, facing the snow streaking through the darkness. From above came the weak glow of the lights attached to the walkway.

This duty had been divided amongst the inhabitants of Mine Three for as long as he could remember. It was not a result of Vitaari orders, but something the community had decided on. There were several reasons why it was useful to have someone watching the mouth of the cavern. The first was they could give adequate warning if the guards came down the walkway. Their considerable weight caused the scaffolding to shake in unmistakable fashion, and early word could give a crucial minute or two to anyone who needed it. The second reason was to provide help to anyone who got into difficulty. Over the years, several people had been lost over the side, and one unfortunate had been found clinging to the bottom of the shaky structure.

The last reason was perhaps the most important. In the first few months, there had been several suicides. People simply got up and walked out of their caverns, leaving someone or no one, and threw themselves off. There had been even more deaths from this spot than within the mine. Sonus had a theory about it; people felt most alone in the dead of night.

"To be honest, I didn't realize you still did this. Have there been any… incidents?"

"No, not recently," said Orani.

"Apart from the hawk," said Yeras.

Orani tutted.

Yeras continued: "One night last week, the wind died for a few hours. A snowhawk landed on the rail, just a few yards from here. Beautiful creature. Magnificent."

"I wish I'd seen that."

"If Orani hadn't been here too, I might have thought I imagined it."

She poured Sonus's tea—from a flask into a mug.

He kept his gloves on while he drank.

"Would you like me to cut your hair again?" asked Orani.

Sonus did his best to rearrange the shaggy mess that now hung down over his brow and ears. "Yes, thank you, Orani—when there's time."

"Such a nice color, just a little unruly."

Sonus's mother had always told him his hair was his best feature. She had also told him he was handsome, but he had long ago realized he was middling at best. He had at least inherited his father's athletic frame, which had given him an advantage over most of his peers at the University.

"I hear you've been back in the yard a lot," said Keras.

Sonus nodded as he sipped the tea: it was weak but pleasant. "Cleaning drill tracks."

"Any luck with those figurines?" asked Keras. "The freighter was in today, wasn't it?"

"It was. I did a deal—all four for eight pounds of dried apples.

Won't be here in time for Maker's Day, but we can still hand them out to the young ones."

"Well done," said Keras.

"Was there any news from the Lovirr?" asked Orani.

"Not much. You know how they are. It was all I could do to persuade them to trade."

"Arkus speaks to them now and again," said Orani. "He says they have forgotten us."

"So has everyone," added Keras. "We are alone up here."

"The Maker has not forgotten us," said Orani, turning to her husband. "You said that hawk was a sign. A sign from him."

Keras seemed embarrassed. "I don't know why I said that."

"We are the only living things up here," said Sonus.

"Apart from them," said Orani.

"They do not count," countered Keras. He looked out at the snow for a time, then spoke to Sonus. "You are an intelligent man. You were at the University. You must agree with me that everything we Palanians had achieved in the last decades improved us—medicine, exploration, science, politics. We made our society richer, more advanced, more fair."

"We did."

"The invaders are far, far more advanced. Rich beyond imagining. And yet they are so cruel. I do not understand why."

After he'd finished his tea, Sonus left them. He had known stronger winds, but the snow was incredibly heavy: dense flurries of inch-wide flakes that whipped across the walkway. He kept at least one gloved hand clamped to the scaffold all the way, and it took him twice as long as usual to reach the top.

He knew from the night shift that the Vitaari hadn't bothered to post a guard at the top for more than a year; they had obviously concluded there was no need.

Hunched over, holding his hood tight with one hand, Sonus walked across the slushy ground to the corner of the closest building:

the generator station. He looked up at the tower and spied a figure move away from a window. Two guards could be seen trudging toward the mine, powerful flashlights lighting their way.

Sonus peered around the corner toward the armory and gained the solitary piece of information he needed. The guard was clad in a bulky jacket, with a visored helmet upon his head and wrappings to protect his face. His rifle was over his shoulder, and he was walking circuits between the armory and the barracks to keep warm. He was alone.

The visions were getting better. Without even opening his eyes, Vellerik reached over to the box and grabbed another capsule.

He walks out onto a terrace bathed in sun. The wind is light but strong enough to refresh. Barefoot, he strides down the slope to the water. She is already on the little island. Sand yields under his feet until he pushes off. The water is perfect, and he enjoys every moment of the swim because it brings her closer. As he walks up the beach, she stands, pale robes clinging to her form. She smiles, eyes enchanting and kind.

Happiness.

20

The workers stood in silence. Three Vitaari guards watched while a fourth paced up and down, eyes fierce.

"Who was it? I know it was one of you."

They had been on their way to a freshly cut shaft. They'd passed numerous male drilling crews and several tracked loaders. They'd been through clouds of thick choking dust, through tunnels none of them had ever seen before. The guards had revealed they would be ferrying wheeled crates of aronium: the crews were cutting so much that the loaders couldn't keep up.

A vehicle had broken down ahead of them so they'd been told to wait. Two of the Vitaari had gone ahead; the other pair had stayed with the workers. Eventually the loader was repaired, and the vehicle came past them. The two guards returned. One of them had left a pack against the tunnel wall. It had disappeared.

"Who took it?"

Like the others, Cerrin was keeping her head down. She knew the guard's face, and he knew hers.

"I'm waiting."

He turned off his translator and spoke to the other guards. They didn't seem particularly concerned.

Everyone present knew he wouldn't wait long. If they were late to their work, it was he who would be in trouble.

He stopped by one of the younger women, clicked his translator back on, and nudged her chin up with his hand. "See anything?"

"No, sir."

He toyed with his jolt-rod. "Sure?"

"Yes, sir. I was just waiting like the others."

He eyed a couple more, continued along the line in Cerrin's direction.

"You—you were running around, as usual. You must have seen something."

A murmur of concern from the women. Cerrin peered forward and realized he was looking down at Yarni. Dwarfed by the guard's enormous bulk, the girl had fixed her eyes on the ground, hands clasped in front of her.

"Speak!"

"I don't know anything about it, sir."

Cerrin could not stop herself. She was already moving through the others when a strong hand gripped her wrist. She turned and saw Sadi, face resolute. The Palanian eased her grip and gave a barely perceptible shake of her head.

"Liar," said the guard. "You'll all lie to me. Unless you can be persuaded to tell the truth."

He reached for his belt, pulled out his jolt-rod.

One of the other Vitaari walked toward him.

The guard grabbed Yarni by the shoulder and turned her around to face the others.

"Someone better start talking." He moved his thumb over the controls of the rod. "There—weakest setting. She's still going to smoke a bit though."

Yarni's eyes scanned back and forth. Realizing she was looking for her, Cerrin stood as tall as she could. When she saw her, Yarni somehow smiled.

The guard glanced at his colleagues, then back at the women. "Still waiting."

He held the jolt-rod an inch from Yarni's head. She kept her eyes on Cerrin, who was already moving forward again.

Sadi tightened her grip once more and whispered into her ear. "Don't do it."

"Last chance," said the guard. "Someone better say something quick."

Cerrin had just shaken herself free when the other Vitaari—who looked quite a bit older—spoke and pointed at the ground on the other side of the tunnel. The guard holding Yarni snapped something back at him. His compatriot kicked at the dusty ground, then gestured at one particular spot.

The guard walked over to him, then reached down and plucked his pack from the dirt. It appeared to have been squashed by the passing loader. As he checked the contents, the other three laughed.

The older guard turned on his translator and walked up to Yarni. He stroked a finger across her hair, then ushered her back to the group. One of the women held her close.

"Let's move out," said the guard. "Quickly."

The younger man was still inspecting his crushed belongings.

As the others moved off, Sadi whispered to Cerrin once more. "Same place, same time tonight. We need three names each. Got it?"

Cerrin nodded.

As Sadi moved away, Yarni broke free of the woman holding her and grabbed her hand. Cerrin held it tight.

The hours of the morning passed with agonizing slowness; a single line from Kadessis had thrown Sonus into a panic. Just as he'd reached the maintenance yard that morning, the administrator had walked past. "I need to speak to you later."

Sonus always found it hard to read the tone of the Vitaari, and he had replayed the incident countless times. Had the phrase seemed casual? Serious? Grave?

He tried to focus on his work—cleaning the last section of track—but he could not dispel the fear. He had taken more items from the building: a few small components for the weapon, which he now reckoned he would need after all. It was perfectly possible someone had noticed what was missing.

Just before midday, Kadessis exited the tower and spoke to the guards outside. Sonus reached inside his jacket and touched the hilt of the sharp blade he now kept on him at all times. If it came to it, he would slice his own throat rather than allow the Vitaari to torture him. He continued his work, chiseling away until the shadow loomed.

"Sonus."

"Sir."

Kadessis walked along the length of track, occasionally bending over to examine it. "How much longer?"

"I should be finished by tomorrow."

Kadessis adjusted the sleeves of his robes. "I had a conversation with one of the engineers yesterday."

Sonus stood up straight and tried to ignore the tremors running through his body.

"He has been watching you."

Kadessis scratched at his cheek; the bone beneath was twitching. "He is of the opinion—and I agree—that you are taking far too long over this job."

Sonus hoped the relief didn't show. "Sir?"

"If he has noticed, it is possible others have noticed too. It goes without saying your reputation is not what it was. You would be unwise to attract attention. Otherwise you may find that you are not excused regular duties so often. There are limits to what I can do."

"I understand, sir. I shall make sure I am finished by the end of the day."

"Good." The Vitaari rubbed his eyes, then looked up at the sky. "Cold today, isn't it?"

"Very, sir. No cloud."

Kadessis gestured to the tower. "It is unusually clear. This morning I used our viewing equipment to look up at the mountain. Quite beautiful. There was a discussion amongst the staff—we could not remember, did any of your people ever reach the top?"

"No, sir. The most successful attempt was made some decades ago by a Palanian man named Tellus Sangar. He used some specialized breathing equipment and clothing designed at the University. He reached what's known as the Black Ledge, a plateau on the southern flank of Origo."

"What height is that?"

"Around twenty-two thousand feet, sir."

Kadessis didn't look impressed. "Long way to go."

Sonus had been a young student when Sangar had finally accomplished his lifelong mission of reaching the Black Ledge on the fourth attempt. He recalled watching the parade pass the University.

Kadessis said, "Some of the others were of the opinion that a weak-willed people like yours would never have achieved something requiring such courage. I disagreed."

"Perhaps one of us will do it one day, sir."

"Perhaps." Kadessis glanced back at the tower. "I should not delay you. You must get on."

The Vitaari took several steps before stopping and turning around. "You shouldn't be stuck back in the tunnels for too long. There will be quite a lot more cleaning work for you in the next few weeks. It seems we will be receiving a prestigious visitor."

Sonus tried not to look too interested. "The count, sir?"

"No. Someone even more important. Imagine that."

Cerrin had listened carefully to Sadi's names. Two were from the group that had arrived with her: both men who worked on the day shift. The other she knew by name but little more. Sadi had spent hours working and speaking with them and felt sure they would all be prepared to help.

Then Cerrin took her turn.

In truth, she was not sure of any of them. Other than Sadi, she had never had a conversation with anyone within Mine Fourteen about organized resistance or escape. But there had been the odd comment, the occasional expression of approval, and incidents where others had shown an attitude toward the Vitaari not entirely unlike her own.

"I don't know any of them," said Sadi when Cerrin had given her three names. "Who are our best bets, do you think?"

They were standing outside, behind the latrine; it was too risky to remain inside for long with people coming and going.

"Bet?" She didn't know the word.

"Gamble."

"Gamble is right. We get this wrong, it's over."

"I know," said Sadi. "But we need more bodies, and we have a chance at this now. Who knows what could happen? The Vitaari might alter the shifts, or put a guard on the block, or fill in that tunnel. We have to get started, at least. I can talk to Trantis and Erras tomorrow. Ralar too, if I can."

"You're sure about her? She just doesn't seem right."

"You said yourself you don't know her. You worry about yours who's first?"

"Torrin is on my crew. I can probably get to her tomorrow."

"Only her? What about Kannalin? He's in the compartment below you, right? And he's in there on his own. You could talk to him now."

"At night? No."

"When else will you get the chance? You have to start—"

From the other side of the compound came the boom of a heavy impact. They moved up to the corner and looked toward the warehouse. A shouted conversation in Vitaari ensued, then all went quiet again. They withdrew into the darkness once more.

"Listen," said Cerrin. "It's complicated. Kannalin, he... likes me. When I first arrived, he was always trying to talk to me. Once he even tried to climb into my compartment."

"What happened?"

"I kicked him in the face."

Despite the circumstances, Sadi began to laugh. And suddenly Cerrin found that she did too. They laughed so much they had to move farther away from the accommodation block. It took a long time for them to calm down.

"By the Maker, look at us," said Sadi. "Well, will you talk to him now? Listen, Kannalin is big, strong. He could be very useful."

"I haven't spoken to him in months. He probably hates me."

"Then you must change his mind."

"What do you mean?"

"I think you know."

Cerrin could not believe what Sadi was suggesting. Even the words brought back memories of Talazeer's assault.

"I would never do that."

"I'm not saying that you should… give yourself to him. But you are a very attractive woman, Cerrin, and he is one of your kind. We must use whatever means we have to."

There was no denying it made sense, and Cerrin realized she had to be realistic. The truth was, she was terrified of ruining their plans before they'd even made a start.

"I haven't done this kind of thing before. What if one of them refuses? What if they tell others? Or the Vitaari?"

Sadi gripped her by the shoulder. "We didn't, Cerrin. We each took a risk, and it paid off. We cannot do this on our own. We trusted each other, and we trusted our instincts. We just have to keep doing that."

Cerrin put her hand on the ladder and looked into the compartment. The only light inside Block A came from the compound, allowing her to see only the silhouette of Kannalin's bulky form. She reached out and tapped his foot. At the second attempt to wake him, he kicked out.

"Who's there?" he said, sitting up. His voice was a low rumble, his Echobe accent harsher even than Cerrin's.

She leant into the compartment and spoke in their own language. "Quiet. It's me, Cerrin."

"What?"

She sat and moved up closer to him. She could just out make out the shape of his head and broad shoulders.

"What?" he said again, rubbing his eyes.

"Keep your voice down. I want to talk to you about something."

"Now?"

"It has to be now."

"By the gods," he sighed. "What is it?"

She didn't know where to begin, how to say it.

"Well?" he demanded.

"I haven't worked with you for a while. But when I did, you used to make signs at the Vitaari behind their backs. Do you still do that?"

He gave a little laugh. "When I can be bothered. Stupid, I know, but it seems to make me feel better."

"Why do you do it?"

"What else can I do? I suppose I'm not as brave as you. Then again, I'm not the governor's favorite, so I can't afford to take risks like you can."

Cerrin said nothing.

"Maybe you're not his favorite anymore," added Kannalin. "Who did that to your face?"

She couldn't be bothered to repeat the lie; it didn't particularly matter what Kannalin believed.

"Will you just tell me what you want, Cerrin? I need my sleep."

"If there were a way out, a way to escape, would you help?"

He did not reply immediately. She listened to his breathing.

"That depends."

"On?"

"On whether I trust you. Up to a few weeks ago, you were the last person I would ever think a traitor, even though you'd been out scouting for the governor. But helping the count with these animals? Going up to their ship? And then coming down with that scar upon you?" Maybe they did that to warn you, make sure you did as you were told. Who better to root out troublemakers than you?"

Cerrin couldn't see how she was going to make any progress. "Do you want me to leave?"

"No. I want you to tell the truth. What happened up there?"

She had decided not to tell anyone. Ever. But a lot had happened since then. Suddenly the prospect didn't seem quite so bad.

"If I do, will you help?"

"I'll need to know exactly what you're doing, but… yes."

"The count—Talazeer—he tried to force himself on me. I fought back. He cut me. I got away before—"

"All right. All right. I'm sorry."

"I haven't told anyone else."

"Neither will I. I shouldn't have asked."

"It's done now." She actually felt relieved. Perhaps it was best she had told someone.

Kannalin's breathing became louder. She heard him thump a fist into a palm.

"Shall I tell you what we're planning then?"

"We?"

"Me and Sadi."

"Are there others?"

"We'll see."

Kannalin shifted closer, but she felt no fear of him. "Yes, tell me. But I can give you my answer now. I'm in."

21

"You all right, sir?"

"Fine," replied Vellerik, though he felt anything but.

Officer Kerreslaa turned his attention to Deputy Administrator Rasikaar, who was sitting on the other side of the table.

Vellerik was relieved to have made the meeting at all. Despite setting three separate alarms, he had slept through them all. The double and triple sessions had to end. In fact, it had to end completely. He pledged to himself he would destroy the box that night, kill the soarer: that way he couldn't be tempted again.

Now that he was leaving earlier than planned, he'd expected it to get easier. But it was getting worse. He had begun to wonder if life away from it all with Seevarta would be so perfect after all. Would he really be able to forget everything? Start again?

There was an undeniable irony. Only now—when he was about to leave the service of The Domain—was he preoccupied by all he had seen and done.

Administrator Danysaan was last to arrive. As he sat down, Vellerik went to fetch himself some water from the machine in the corner. He drank it there; he didn't want them to see his hands shaking—a side-effect that was notably worsening.

"I'll keep this brief," said Danysaan, elbows on the transparent table. "This is the first of our meetings to oversee planning for the visit of Viceroy Mennander. As you all know, the date has now been fixed and we have only twenty-two days until he arrives. I have assumed overall command for the day itself, while Captain Vellerik is responsible for security. Officer Kerreslaa will liaise with the mines to be visited, and Deputy Administrator Rasikaar is in charge of certain specifics. Firstly, I shall run through the schedule."

Vellerik just about kept up. When Danysaan finished, the two junior men fired questions at him. Now they seemed to be talking about this ridiculous statue.

"Obviously the terodite is not a problem," said Rasikaar, "and apparently the engineers can manufacture a decent likeness. But blue diamonds? We've already ordered them, but they'll arrive only a day or two before the tour. And the cost!"

"But it's the viceroy," said Vellerik, mocking Talazeer's previous words. "The *viceroy*."

Danysaan glared at him. "Captain, you may enjoy the privilege of disobeying the count, but the rest of us do not. Now is as good a time as any to discuss the dispositions of your men. I suggest you and one of your senior officers accompany the party for the entire day."

"No. I need to be with the troop. The count has his Drellen, and the viceroy has his own detail."

"Have you mentioned this to him?"

"No, but I will. He was very insistent that an escort of my men accompany the shuttle in combat shells. The party are flying over every mine and visiting six locations so that will be a rather hazardous and complicated operation. I will use three of my best men, but I will need to be with them."

"Very well. And the arrangements at the location for the meal? Presumably you will coordinate this with Officer Kerreslaa?"

Vellerik offered a nod and leaned back in his seat. Danysaan had a few more questions for him, which he answered as cogently as he could. It was evident the other three were highly anxious about the viceroy's visit. Vellerik told himself he should at least ensure he did his part well; it would be his last duty as a soldier of The Domain.

When they eventually ran out of things to discuss, the Administrator concluded the meeting. Officer Kerreslaa still seemed very happy about the Kinassan operation and informed Vellerik there had also been no further trouble with the Batal. Vellerik was relieved to hear it; he wasn't sure he had it in him to lead another massacre. Kerreslaa also asked about Triantaa. Vellerik told him that he would be back on duty within a week or so, possibly even in time for the visit.

Danysaan made it clear to the other two that they should leave, then took a seat beside Vellerik. He waited for the door to slide shut before speaking.

"If I may say so, Erasmer, you do not look well."

"Nor do I feel it. Some… illness. The surgeon hasn't been able to work out what it is. I will seek further help after I leave."

"I saw the confirmation of your resignation. General Eddekal will be sorry to lose you. As will I. No reason was mentioned. I assume it is this condition?"

Vellerik nodded and finished the rest of his water.

Danysaan ran a finger down his neck. "It is obvious that relations between yourself and the count have been strained. And that you are not particularly enthusiastic about your role in the viceroy's visit. But I must ask that you do your part. We all need it to go well."

Vellerik almost snapped at him. But Danysaan was not the worst of his type—not by a long way—and Vellerik couldn't blame him for being concerned.

"My men and I will do our duty. You needn't worry about that. As long as Talazeer and the viceroy keep a safe distance from the locals, there should be no danger."

"Mine Fourteen is first on the itinerary, of course—where the Drellen killed that suicidal native. Perhaps the count wishes to make a point."

"Perhaps. I can't claim to understand the working of that young man's mind."

Danysaan cast a look toward the door before continuing. "That night… with the girl. Those of us who were there know what we saw. If that information were to ever reach certain parties…"

"Administrator, I suggest you proceed no further along that line of thought. We both know that making an enemy of him is unlikely to end well. My advice—hope for the continued deterioration in the health of his father. If the count fulfills his ambition, you will be rid of him for good."

So far, recruitment was going well. Sadi had spoken to the two men who had arrived with her, and they were eager to help. She had decided not to approach Ralar—having changed her mind about how the woman might respond—but Cerrin had made solid progress. As well as Kannalin, she had approached an older Palanian women named Sirras.

Sirras had lost both her husband and son in an accident in the mine the previous year. Grief-stricken, she had vowed revenge. It was common knowledge that Dukas had dissuaded her from a plot to poison the Vitaari food. As soon as Cerrin said the words, Sirras gripped her hand and agreed to do whatever she could.

Another approach had not gone so well. Torrin was a young Echobe woman who had been captured the year before Cerrin. They had only ever spoken briefly, but Cerrin had seen her stand up to the Vitaari guards on several occasions. Torrin had been transferred to the night shift for a while but was now back in Block A. Cerrin had taken her aside while queuing for the elevator. The conversation seemed promising until she mentioned she was working with Sadi. Torrin simply walked away and refused to say any more to Cerrin or even look her in the eye.

This was just the type of thing Cerrin had feared. Torrin now knew they were up to something, but she was not with them. Cerrin was also concerned that it was Sadi's involvement that had put Torrin off. What did she know?

"Has she gone in yet?" asked Kannalin.

"Just now." Cerrin was waiting with him outside Block A. She couldn't afford to leave it any longer, and he had agreed to help. They had to wait a while for the line to clear, as people entered their compartments and climbed the ladders.

"How are we going to handle her?" whispered Kannalin, head bowed. He was one of the few Echobe men taller than Cerrin. She supposed he was good-looking in his own way: a strong, broad face marked with several scars.

"Not sure. But we're not leaving her alone until either she joins us or she swears to say nothing."

It didn't take long to find Torrin's compartment, which was on the lower level. Unfortunately, she was not alone. Both women were about to take off their dirty overalls when they noticed they were being watched.

Cerrin smiled at the second woman. "I'd like a word with Torrin. Can you give us a minute?"

The woman—also Echobe but middle-aged—glanced at Torrin, who nodded her agreement. When the woman left, Cerrin sat on the edge of the compartment. Torrin came forward and sat with her legs crossed in front of her. Kannalin loomed over them.

"I have nothing to say to you."

Like Torrin, Cerrin kept her voice down. "You did earlier. Then suddenly you walked off. Why?"

Torrin reached up and rubbed the large metal ring in her left ear. "If it were just you, I would help. But not with Palanians. Never."

"That's it? That's why? Listen, we have to forget the old ways. We're in this together—"

"It has nothing to do with the old ways. On the night shift, some of ours won't even work with the Palanians. The Vitaari keep them separate just to avoid trouble. We've had six informers here. Five were Palanian."

"But there's been nothing like that for years."

"How do you know? We only found out about those six because either someone worked it out or the Vitaari moved them on. Now suddenly this new lot arrive and you're in with them straight away? Not me."

"What if you wouldn't have to work with them?"

"If they're involved, I'm not." Torrin pointed at the corridor. "Now go. And take your big friend. I'm not afraid of you, Cerrin."

"I need your word—that what I told you goes no further. To anyone. Ever."

"Wishing you hadn't told me your plan?" A smile tugged at the edge of Torrin's mouth. "Not very good at this, are you?"

She saw it coming and tried to pull away, but Cerrin was too quick for her.

She gripped Torrin's collar and pulled her face in close. "I'm sorry you said no. I wish you'd change your mind. But if you don't, know that I'm watching. If I even suspect you've opened your mouth, our next conversation will be a lot less pleasant. Do you understand me?"

Torrin tried to pull away, but Cerrin was too strong.

"Understand?"

When Torrin nodded, Cerrin let her go and stood up. She was about to leave when the woman spoke again:

"It's not me you should worry about."

Ignoring the curious looks, Cerrin turned and walked away, Kannalin beside her.

"Not good," he said.

"No. And we still need another body."

"Leave that to me."

Sonus examined the components. He had begun work on the firing mechanism, starting with the spring, which would fire a piston into the faulty power cell. If his theories proved practicable, the cell would detonate and the resultant blast would launch the shrapnel-filled casing out of the barrel. He had already taken the spring apart in order to understand its workings. Now he had to reconfigure it as part of the weapon. But he was tired from a day's work back in the mine; his mind was foggy and slow.

He would not use the data-pad tonight. He'd already spent

countless hours reading the documentation and now felt he understood the basics of the combat shells. Recently, he'd been studying the controls, a wondrous but worryingly complex system involving sensors mounted on fingers and various screens. Though the guards never seemed to have much trouble controlling them, Sonus imagined they had been through hundreds of hours of training. He was determined to know every last sentence of the manual by heart but appreciated that no amount of preparation could compensate for actual experience. In truth, he reckoned he would do well to get one of the machines off the ground.

But what gave him hope was what he could do with that machine. He'd only had time for a cursory glance at the section detailing weapons and equipment, but if the armory had even half of it, there was almost no limit to the damage he could inflict. The targeting systems seemed simple by comparison with the controls, and the shells could be equipped with up to four weapon modules including assault cannons, disruptor beams, anti-personnel clusters, anti-structure missiles, flare-bursts, and incendiary bombs. As interesting were the defensive measures: deflector fields, anti-missile systems, armor plates, jamming nodes.

Once more, Sonus looked down at the components laid out on the floor. He was squatting behind a barrel, working under a weak light he didn't have time to fix. There was still so much to do, but if he were to ever get close to the combat shells, he would need a weapon; and it would have to be lethal.

They had decided on a few rules. Firstly, everyone was to work in an order decided daily by Cerrin and Sadi (and passed on to all involved by Yarni). Secondly, no one should communicate during the hours of night unless there were an emergency. Thirdly, no one was to work longer than twenty minutes.

Cerrin was to dig last on the first night, and she did not sleep at all. Sadi began, followed by the two Palanian men, then Kannalin, then Sirras. Kannalin's new prospect was his cousin, but they had decided as a group not to approach anyone else until they were up and running.

Cerrin was scared. Not for herself, but for the others and the possibility they might be discovered. She could not be absolutely certain of anyone other than Yarni, and Torrin's warning had stayed with her. She could not see that the Vitaari would gain a great deal by going to the trouble of planting someone like Sadi, yet Torrin had seemed so sure she was not to be trusted. Cerrin remembered a time when her attitude toward the Palanians had been similar—as it was amongst many Echobe. She told herself she had to go with her instincts, and they told her Sadi was no liar.

When the time finally arrived, it was only eagerness to do her part that overcame her exhaustion. Assuming Sirras had finished her turn, she slipped out of the doorway and into the darkness. They had even discussed the dangers of leaving a visible trail on the ground so she took an indirect route toward the containers.

Startled by a cough from Block B, she composed herself before moving on. The noise had probably come from someone too ill to work who had not yet been admitted to the infirmary. Cerrin reminded herself to be doubly careful on the way back; it was possible the Vitaari might send someone over.

She reached the gap and moved between the containers. There was a lot of drilling going on below, enough to cause a tremor in the walls of metal. The hole was covered by plastic sheeting: another of Sadi's ideas. Cerrin pulled it away and stared down into the darkness.

It was surprisingly deep: she was impressed by what the others had achieved. Lying next to the hole was a shovel and a large bucket, which had been liberated from the latrine. Tied around a strut at the base of one of the containers was a rope that ran down into the hole. Attached to it were several loops to help the digger climb in and out. The level of the ground was already higher where the excavated earth had been dumped and then flattened. Sadi had been the first to point out that redistributing the waste would soon become a major issue; yet another problem they would have to solve.

Cerrin took a last look around. Even the high lights of the tower and the wall were obscured by the containers. Directly above, streaks of silvery cloud drifted past. She listened for a moment, but there was only the buzz of the drills to be heard.

She placed the shovel in the bucket, hung the bucket over her arm, and climbed down. Finding the loops with her feet in the darkness wasn't easy, but she reached the bottom safely, estimating it was at least ten feet from the surface.

The shaft was four feet wide as agreed; they needed that much space to work. Cerrin put the bucket down in a corner and took out the shovel. Even the memory of tiredness was long gone. With a grim smile, she bent over and started digging.

22

Litas was waiting for Sonus at the top of the walkway. Most of the workers were already on their way down and the rest were filing past quickly. The wind was light and no snow was falling, but the plateau was bitterly cold.

"Can I speak with you?" asked Litas, eyes narrow under his hood.

Sonus nodded and stood to one side with him. He would have preferred to avoid the conversation—he had a day of work behind him and an evening of work ahead—but it was more circumspect to speak to the man here than in the busy cavern.

Litas waited until the last worker was out of earshot. "I've arranged a meeting. Someone you should talk to."

"What do you mean?"

"Wait two minutes, then follow me down."

Without another word, Litas hurried away.

Sonus watched him, then looked back across the compound. The temperature ensured the only Vitaari outside were those who needed to be there. There seemed to be some problem with the conveyor, which had been stopped. The four engineers had gathered at one particular section, all wearing bulky jackets over their overalls and now deep in discussion. A pair of guards had just emerged from behind the tower. They noticed the lone figure immediately. Sonus made for the walkway; he didn't need that kind of attention.

Far below the plateau, the barren plains were lit orange by the setting sun. Few people had ever ventured to this region before the invasion, and Sonus often stared down at the distant ground, looking and hoping for a speck of movement. He saw nothing but a flight of dark birds, arrowing west.

There were twelve sets of steps down to the cavern, one hundred twenty individual steps in all. Below the seventh set, two hooded figures were waiting. Litas saw him coming and swiftly switched his attention to his companion. As Sonus took his hand off the icy rail, the second figure turned. When she saw him, she tried to flee.

Litas pushed her back, then reached inside his jacket and pulled out a rusty metal spike about five inches long. "Take down your hood."

She did so. Sonus knew only her face and name. Eldi was a woman of about fifty. She had thin gray hair, and her features were pinched and pale. She wrapped her arms around herself, eyes darting from one man to the other.

"It was her," said Litas. "It was her that told them about Qari."

"No," said Eldi. "I would never—"

"Don't even try," he snapped.

Though it should have been obvious, Sonus had not anticipated this. He dragged his eyes off the spike. "How do you know?"

"It took a while. Those bitches in the kitchens stick together. But I've been asking around. Asking everyone. Her name came up once at the start, but I couldn't be sure. Then old Jansarri at the infirmary overheard the surgeon talking last week. About Qari—getting rid of the baby. He knew who told the Vitaari." He jabbed the spike toward Eldi.

She shook her head violently. "I would never do something like that. Never."

Litas nodded down at the grating beneath them. "Slippery today. One wrong step and off you go."

The sun had almost set. Beyond the rock face was darkness.

Eldi shrank back against the rock. "I didn't do it, Sonus. I swear by the Maker."

Sonus didn't consider himself a great judge of people. Nor did he consider the opinion of Litas particularly reliable, but when he looked at her, he was sure. He glanced again at the black depths below them and thought of the shaft where Karas and Qari had fallen.

"Give me that."

With a sly grin, Litas handed him the spike.

"I'll scream," said Eldi.

"Not for long." Sonus turned toward her. "Tell the truth."

"There are six of us work in those kitchens. Any one of them—"

"Tell the truth," repeated Sonus. "Do it and I'll let you go. You have my word."

He expected a protest from Litas, but none came.

Eldi peered at him, hands bunching into anxious fists.

Sonus spoke gently and lowered the spike. "You have my word."

She was still shaking her head. "It wasn't me. You can't believe him."

Sonus took a step toward her. "But you must tell me."

Her teeth were chattering, her mouth twisting.

Sonus gripped the spike, felt the uneven metal beneath his fingers. "The truth."

It came suddenly. "Some of the others knew. They were covering for her. They're my friends. I thought the Vitaari would kill them all. I didn't know her. I thought it would be better for her anyway. I didn't know she would…"

"Do it now," hissed Litas. "There's no one around. *Now.*"

Eldi slid to the ground and covered her face with her hands. "I'm sorry. Sonus, I'm sorry."

"You traitor whore," spat Litas. "What else have you told them over the years?"

She dropped her hands, looked up at them. "Nothing. Nothing, I swear."

Sonus said, "It's not 'her.' Or 'she.' Her name was Qari. He was Karas. You should never forget those names."

"I will not," cried Eldi. "I pray for them. Them and the little one. I will pray for forgiveness from the Maker."

Sonus closed his eyes for a moment, then stood aside. "Go."

She got to her feet.

"Let her past."

Litas shook his head in disbelief but moved aside.

Back pressed against the rock, Eldi slid past them. She stumbled on the first step, then hurried downward.

Litas rubbed a knuckle against his brow and grimaced. "I didn't think even you were this pathetic."

Sonus threw the spike into the darkness.

Litas said, "You haven't changed much at all, Sonus. Still a weak-willed traitor, just like her. Maybe that's why you let her go."

"Is she the enemy, Litas? Am I?"

He walked past him and did not look back.

Five nights of good work had given them a new set of problems. The tunnel itself was not one of them. Having dug fourteen feet straight down, they were now moving horizontally and had progressed twenty-three feet. They would have to cover a similar distance again before cutting diagonally downward to intersect the top level of the mine. The earth was not easy to dig through, but its firm consistency meant the tunnels kept their shape well. They had taken the precaution of adding a few supports to the horizontal section (thin plastic panels liberated from the Block A beds), but this was largely to put the diggers at ease. They knew they would not be able to find materials to reinforce the tunnel properly. There had been only one small collapse, during Sadi's shift, and she had never been in danger.

The first problem had arisen once they started the horizontal section. Whoever was digging had to lie flat and use a trowel and fork. The earth was placed in the bucket as before, but if the same person had to remove it, work would be painfully slow. So now they had to operate in pairs: one to dig, one to remove the soil. The bucket was attached to a string so the second person could pull it back, haul it onto their shoulder, then climb up the shaft and distribute it.

They found themselves scattering the earth on a layer already three feet high. The layer ran to the end of all four gaps between the containers. Any Vitaari guard flying above wouldn't notice, but anyone on the ground who took a closer look couldn't miss it. Cerrin and Sadi estimated it would reach at least six feet by the time they finished.

The third problem was also connected to the horizontal section. Though willing, Sirras couldn't stand the confined spaces and was also not strong enough to haul the bucket up the shaft. She had reluctantly given way to Kannalin's cousin, Jersa, who had soon proven himself just as efficient and committed as the others. The two worked together, as did Cerrin and Sadi, with the final pair being the Palanians, Trantis and Erras.

The three crews alternated times, never left or entered the block as a pair, and did everything they could to obscure the footprints leading to the containers.

Cerrin had always thought of the fourth problem as inevitable. However careful and organized they were, people were bound to notice. The inhabitants of Block A lived literally on top of each other. New arrivals always aroused curiosity, and familiar faces who started acting differently attracted suspicion. The simple fact that the same six people were going out for some time every night was unusual.

Cerrin and Sadi did not agree on what to do about it.

"We stop for a few nights. Three, maybe only two."

Cerrin shook her head. "Meanwhile the tunnel just sits there? Covered by a bit of sheeting?"

They were currently working close to each other. At the midday break, they had met close by a small pit used by the workers as a latrine.

"If anything, we should be going faster," she added. "Let's get it done before we're found out."

"Cerrin, don't get carried away. We've done well, I agree, but we haven't even talked about what we do when it's finished. We can't just crawl through and hope the Vitaari don't notice. Especially if you're still insisting on trying to get as many out as possible. We'll need a way of keeping them occupied."

"Like what?"

"You talked about burning this place to the ground. A fire or two would attract the Vitaari's attention."

"Where?"

"Generator station? The tower? The armory—take the shells out before they can get after us."

"How would we do it?"

"We'd made some plans before. The fuel they store at the landing strip is very flammable. If we can get some of that in the right places and set it off—"

"With the guards around? How?"

"We'll find a way. But let's focus on tonight. Everyone's exhausted anyway. One night off won't make a difference."

Cerrin took a deep breath and thought about it.

She heard quick light footsteps. Yarni ran past the small dark cavern.

"Cerrin?"

"Here. What is it?"

The girl darted in and spoke between hurried breaths. "We got word from one of the men's crews. Kannalin was pulled out of the line this morning. The guards have him."

Vellerik looked down at the remains of the box. He was surprised no one had heard him smashing it up, but then everyone else was probably working. He had used the butt of his sidearm, shattering the plastic in several places and destroying the regulator. He had also pulled off all the remaining capsules and crushed them under his boot.

He sat down on the floor beside the box. The soarer was atop a leaf, wings quivering. It wouldn't last long without the regulator. He shivered as the reality hit him. He could not find solace any more. He was alone with his thoughts.

The dreams had been exactly as he wanted. But after he had woken from them and gone back to sleep, only more nightmares followed. Some were as much memory as invention.

He saw the Batal, cut down as they fled. He saw the bloodied Kinassan bodies laid out on sand and rock. And so much more. Things he had forgotten. Things he wasn't even sure he had seen. Enemies of The Domain blasted and mutilated and blown into pieces. Natives of all creeds and colors hunted and imprisoned and used. Resistors tortured and executed.

He had protected The Domain and helped it expand, done his sworn duty. But what did he have to show for it? Some pretty pieces of metal and enough money to live on until the end of his life. He would have swapped both for peace of mind.

The narcotics had helped in the beginning, but ultimately they had made things worse.

He would face this on his own, conquer it, and make sure he returned to Seevarta ready for their new life together.

He stood up and dressed quickly. He wanted to get down to the cargo bay, start briefing the men about the viceroy's visit. By the time he dragged the broken box into a corner and covered it, the soarer was dead.

There was no news that afternoon or evening.

Cerrin asked anyone who she thought might know something, but the answers were all the same. Kannalin had been taken away along with three other men from his crew (none of whom were connected to Cerrin or Sadi).

She was surprised to wake up the following day because she had not expected to sleep. As the siren finished, she pushed her blankets aside. The sisters were already up and whispering Palanian prayers—to their Maker. Cerrin always did hers too, partly out of habit, partly to honor her mother, who had never let Cerrin or her father begin the day without a few words for the gods and ancients.

Cerrin crawled into the corner and touched one of the plants while she first uttered the prayer of communion. Then she spoke to Ikala. She felt she was already in a battle and he had already answered by helping her, Sadi, and the others help themselves. She asked him to continue to watch over them and that Kannalin be returned to them safe and well.

But when the day shift lined up outside Block A, he was still nowhere to be seen.

There was no news during the morning break. Cerrin was with five others, shoveling chunks of aronium ore from a huge pile into wheeled crates. The nearest guard was stationed at an intersection fifty feet away. She had to force herself not to look in his direction every few seconds. She could not escape the feeling she would be joining Kannalin soon.

There was no news at midday. She could not eat and had to fight the urge to run when the guard approached. He was simply checking on them, but she still couldn't eat when he'd left.

She heard nothing for the rest of the day. She lined up with Sadi, Sirras, and all the others as they filed out of the mine but didn't dare speak to them with so many watching eyes.

The answer came an hour after lights out. She heard some people come in and voices below. It was Yarni who climbed up to the compartment. She crawled under the blankets with Cerrin and whispered to her.

"He's back. All four of them are back. They're fine. The Vitaari wanted to rearrange some of the rooms in the tower. They kept them working all that time, but they got double rations from one of the governor's men."

Cerrin thanked the gods.

"Can I stay here tonight?" asked Yarni.

Cerrin held her close.

23

There was a skill to it: putting aside all other thoughts and concentrating entirely on what was in front of you. Whether trying to spark a flame, hone an arrow point, stalk an animal—the best results came when you removed each and every distraction.

Having developed the ability over many years, Cerrin had recently made a very specific adaptation. When she was lying in the compartment, waiting her turn, she let the fear come: fear that someone would start asking too many questions, fear that the tunnel might collapse, fear that the Vitaari would discover them. It was not pleasant—and she often found herself sweating and shivering—but by the time she reached the tunnel, her mind was clear and she attacked the work with an energy that surprised even Sadi.

Reach forward; dig in; pull back.

When enough fresh earth had been carved out, she would push her body flat against the side of the tunnel and Sadi would pass up the bucket. Cerrin would fill it and then—while Sadi took it for disposal—tidy up the newly dug section, keeping the shape and the four-foot width.

The tunnel was now angling downward at forty-five degrees. Both women were working with even greater urgency than usual because this night—the fourteenth of digging—was when they expected to finally hit the top layer of the mine.

The Palanian men had taken the previous shift. Though she had not spoken to them, Cerrin knew they would be disappointed not to have been the ones to make the breakthrough. To her, it was only right that she and Sadi should do so, but there was no sign they were even close. Previously confident, Sadi now seemed unsure whether they had ended up in the right place. Cerrin had entrusted this to her, hoping the endless calculations and measurements using a length of rope would do the job. That same rope now connected them: if they did reach the mine, there was considerable danger that the digger would fall.

Cerrin worked on, only giving way to Sadi when she knew she had done significantly more than her allotted fifteen minutes. The Palanian wriggled up beside her and took the trowel.

"Really thought we'd be there by now."

"It's as thick as ever," said Cerrin as she slid backwards.

The dense, sticky consistency of the earth was both a blessing and a curse; it gave the tunnel form but was very difficult to dig through.

Cerrin drew in some deep breaths.

They were a long way from the surface, and the air was stale. It now took so long for the person with the bucket to haul their load back to the shaft, climb up and dump it, that their work was almost continuous. This task, however, was still not as arduous as the digging. Here, all effort was concen-trated in the shoulders, arms, and hands. All of them were suffering continual pain in their muscles and joints. The veins on Cerrin's forearms now bulged like roots under the ground.

There was another challenge. Crawling back and forth in the confined space, they would emerge from the tunnel covered in earth. So now they all kept their spare overalls solely for their nighttime efforts. Standard practice was to change before and after completing the shift.

Cerrin lay on her back to make the most of the short break. She listened to Sadi's panting breaths and the thumps and scrapes of the trowel. She ran her hands across the caked mud on her arms and started picking it off to save time later.

Sadi suddenly stopped and moved the lamp, one of two Yarni had pilfered from the Vitaari stores. "Bloody great stone."

"Can you get it out?"

"Think so. Yes, earth's quite soft here."

Cerrin watched Sadi push her fingers into it, then grip the stone. It was at least a foot wide—one of the biggest they'd come across.

"There, I think that's—"

It was as if a great hand pulled Sadi out of the tunnel. Cerrin stuck out her feet to anchor herself, but the rope around her waist went tight and hauled her several feet downward. She shut her eyes as clumps of earth peppered her face.

When she came to a halt, her neck was on the edge of something. She could smell the fresher air of open space. The rope had cut into her side and stomach, leaving her winded and coughing. She covered her mouth to reduce the noise.

"Cerrin. Hey, I'm down here."

Wincing at the pain, Cerrin turned over and realized she was hanging out of a small tunnel that now joined a very big one.

Sadi picked up the lamp, which—like the stone—had landed near her. "You all right?"

"Yes. You?"

"Bit sore."

Cerrin propped herself up on her elbows and tried to get her bearings. To the left was a dim trace of light.

"Is that—" Sadi untied the rope, then hurried away to the right. Stopping after about twenty paces, she held the lamp close to something. Cerrin spied the metallic surface of the machine she had climbed over. Not far beyond it was the end of the tunnel and their way out.

She no longer felt the pain; it was submerged beneath a flood of relief and jubilation.

Gods and ancients, I thank you.

Sadi returned and stood on the pile of earth that had fallen with her. "We did it."

Cerrin felt around with her hands and eventually located the trowel, which she dropped at Sadi's feet. "Tidy up as best you can—in case anyone comes along."

Sadi grinned. "Yes, chief. Why don't you come down and help?"

Cerrin pointed at the rope. "I need to save my strength—for pulling you back up."

Sonus had waited a week for the strong winds; he needed something to cover the noise. Given the season, he'd known it was only a matter of time, but every night that passed took him closer to the next meeting with Nomora. The warehouse was filling up again, and the freighter would be back before long. He wanted to be able to tell the Lovirr he was ready.

He knew the man on duty and stopped outside the little cave.

"Not going up, are you, Sonus? At this time of night?"

He had yet to invent a better excuse: "Just realized I left some equipment switched on. They'll be angry."

Barris was an amiable man with a graying beard. Sonus had fixed a lamp for him several weeks previous.

"Might you lose your privileges?"

"I suppose so." In fact, the only privilege he still received was working on the surface—and he was due to be back drilling the following day.

"How are you feeling?" Like Sonus, Barris had been made ill by the work.

"Not bad, thank you." In fact, Sonus hadn't felt better in years, a development he could not account for. "Sorry, I really should—"

"Go, go," said Barris. "Just be careful. The Maker is angry tonight."

Sonus checked the pack on his back was secure, then set off up the walkway. Not for the first time, he wondered how believers like Barris accommodated the presence of the Vitaari into their system of faith. The teachings of the Maker had mentioned nothing about a race of invaders that would lay waste to his creation and enslave his people. He advocated generosity, tolerance, forgiveness, and other positive traits, few of which were of any practical benefit to those housed at Mine Fourteen.

Sonus—who had sat through religious lessons in school—could think of only one tale that provided him with a little inspiration: the story of the bridge-maker.

A solitary farmer needed to use the pasture on the other side of a river. Nobody else from his village would spare him the time to help build a bridge, and they mocked him when he told them he would do it alone. The farmer's initial attempts failed. His first structure of stone and wood was washed away in a flood. But he rebuilt it even bigger and stronger the following year. Eventually, dozens passed over it every day, and it lasted for centuries. When the farmer died, the bridge was named after him. A simple tale of tenacity and persistence but one often mentioned fondly by Sonus's professors at the University.

He continued upward, wind howling through the darkness around him. Though the previous day had been a little warmer, patches of ice had appeared on the metal, making the journey even more hazardous. But, for Sonus, the conditions were ideal; he could do what he needed to without fear of interruption.

At the sixth flight of steps, he stopped and squatted by the rock wall, well away from the nearest lamp. He clicked on his flashlight and took the weapon from the pack. Next, he opened a small case containing the plastic canisters: five had been produced, all filled with nails and other metal scraps. He took one and dropped it down the barrel, reminding himself to keep the weapon aiming upward—there was nothing to stop the canister falling out. Sonus was even more careful when he took the power cell from the case. He had selected five of the oldest cells, hoping they would be more unstable and therefore more prone to detonation. He pulled back the bolt, opened the slot behind the barrel, and placed the cell inside. He then retracted the bolt and took a deep breath.

Only now would he discover if his theories were any more than that, if all his efforts had been worthwhile.

He held the weapon in both hands and stood up. It was unwieldy and heavy, due largely to the thickness of the barrel and the other components.

Sonus walked to the front of the walkway and placed a finger on the trigger. Once depressed, this rod would fire the piston into the power cell, hopefully igniting a contained explosion and blasting the ammunition out of the barrel. Eyes narrowed against the stinging wind, Sonus set his feet and held the weapon well away from him. He pushed the trigger down and winced as the piston fired.

Nothing happened.

He was, however, relieved the piston had retracted itself and he could try again. He pulled the trigger three more times. Still nothing. He shook the weapon, then tried once more, to no avail.

As the walkway rattled and groaned, he opened the slot and tipped out the firing cell. The sides of it had been crushed, but the impact had not been sufficient to ignite the charge. Sonus had known this might well happen, but he needed some idea of how often—or how rarely—a detonation might occur. He threw the power cell into the darkness, then returned to the pack and loaded a new one.

Once back at the edge of the walkway, he struggled to stay upright as the wind somehow grew even stronger.

He gripped the handle and depressed the trigger. Again, nothing. He tried twice more, then discarded this cell too.

By the third attempt, all enthusiasm and conviction had left him. So much so that when this cell did detonate—and the weapon kicked backwards—he dropped it. Surprised by how quiet the blast had been, he knelt beside the weapon and examined it with the flashlight.

Apart from a slightly bent trigger, it seemed to be undamaged. He checked inside the barrel and saw the metal was blackened and scratched but intact. He also noted traces of plastic seared to the surface, but the canister seemed to have been ejected smoothly.

But he had fired into the air; he needed to know what damage the weapon could do. Sonus retrieved a heavy chunk of machinery from his pack: a drill part made of various metals. He placed it against the rock wall.

The fourth attempt showed him nothing: another misfire.

He loaded the last cell, then aimed it at the target. Gripping the barrel and the handle firmly, he fired. The blast gave him a jolt, but he kept his feet steady and the barrel straight. He put the weapon down and grabbed the flashlight.

What he saw made him smile. The shrapnel had shredded the piece of machinery, blowing apart all but the most solid chunks of metal. He had no doubt it would make a real mess of anything organic.

Two out of five; not a great success rate. But it worked.

Cerrin hadn't been able to sleep after the eventful night's work, and the day was becoming a struggle. Though none would admit it to each other, the constant strain of days in the mine and nights in the tunnel was taking its toll. When midday came, she slumped against a cargo container, downed her food and closed her eyes.

"Cerrin."

The tone of her fellow worker seemed to hold a warning. Fearing it was a guard standing over her, she looked up to see Trantis, one of Sadi's Palanian allies. Though he had worked on the tunnel as much as her, she had only spoken to him a couple of times.

"Got a minute?"

Without a word, she followed him around a corner, well away from the three members of her crew.

"Sadi's way off in one of the new shafts. She asked me to speak to you."

Cerrin couldn't help feeling slightly afraid of Trantis. He was a large man—not as tall as Kannalin but very broad—and his bulging eyes never seemed to blink. Cerrin didn't want to get too close.

"You know Erras has been on that crew up in the yard? He managed to get a couple of words with one of the Lovirr while the freighter was loading yesterday—an associate of ours."

Cerrin knew from Sadi that her group had previously established some limited contact with the Lovirr and that a few of them were far more sympathetic to the plight of the other tribes than was commonly known.

"He passed on information about a friend in Mine Three. There's a man who believes he can steal one of the Vitaari vehicles and escape."

Cerrin absorbed this. She admired the courage of whoever this man was, though she could not begin to grasp how anyone could do such a thing.

"Apparently he understands the Vitaari equipment. The Lovirr think he may actually be able to do it. But if he does, he will need somewhere to go."

"The forest?"

Trantis nodded. "Mine Fourteen is around two hundred miles from here. There are some caves a similar distance away, but he would have little chance of evading the Vitaari there. The Lovirr say he wants to move quickly. They are suggesting we work together—time both escapes to cause maximum confusion. And if he gets here at the right time, he may be able to help us."

"What did Erras say?"

"That he would discuss it with us. When the freighter next returns, we can pass on our decision, perhaps even suggest a day and time."

The siren signaling the end of the break sounded.

Trantis glanced along the tunnel; Cerrin knew he was working some distance away.

"You should go."

"Sadi will be in touch."

As he jogged away, Cerrin walked back to the others. She wasn't entirely sure how to feel about what she'd heard. It was both reassuring and exciting to know others were on their side, but there were now a lot of individuals who knew about what they were planning. The risks grew with every passing day. She wasn't sure they could afford to wait for anything or anyone. When they finally broke through, she wanted to be gone the next day.

Even though there was no sign of a guard, the other three in her crew were already up and working: collecting small chunks of aronium ore spilled when a malfunctioning loader ploughed into the tunnel wall. They had already filled two containers.

One of the women watched Cerrin pick up her shovel. "I remember when you never had a friend in this place, girl. Now, whenever I see you, you're talking to someone."

Cerrin shrugged. "Maybe I've just accepted that I'm stuck here. Maybe I just want to make the most of it."

She could not decipher the meaning behind the woman's smile. "Maybe."

24

Sonus awoke to the sound of shouting.

"Guards coming down! Inspection! Inspection!"

He pushed his blankets aside and rolled off his bed. Outside his dwelling, others were already up and passing the message on. Sonus pulled on his boots and overalls, then stood there, unsure what to do.

He looked at the container. Inside—close to the bottom—were the various components of the weapon. He had dismantled it after the second test, which he'd carried out the previous night. By carefully inspecting the power cells that had not detonated, he reckoned he'd made some progress in identifying those that would: there had been only two misfires out of five this time. Also secreted in the container was the data-pad. He'd considered other hiding places outside his dwelling but that risked bringing suspicion on others; something he was not prepared to do.

After all he had planned, all he had achieved, the thought of discovery was almost beyond comprehension. As the Vitaari shouted their orders, he went to stand in the passageway. Not much was being said, but the fear within the caverns was as palpable as the cold. Opposite him was a family of three, mother and father each with a hand upon the shoulders of their teenage son.

The Vitaari were taking each dwelling in turn, pushing the

workers aside and rifling through their things. Sonus watched men, women, and children staying close together and out of the guards' way. Guns strapped to their backs, the Vitaari flipped over beds and furniture and emptied containers onto the floor. One of them came across a stash of food packs. As the man in possession was not one of those assigned to distribute them, he was sent to the cavern entrance.

By the time they reached Sonus, he knew he was dependent on fortune. Though they were making a big show, the Vitaari were not conducting the search in a methodical way. Some were actually examining what they'd found; others were simply making a mess. He could hear an officer giving more orders, but he was out of sight.

"Move," said the first guard to reach him. Holding up his hands, Sonus hurried out of his way. The Vitaari was the one known as Faraway, the one teased by the others. A well aimed kick sent Sonus's bed spinning into the wall. Faraway used his boot to sort through the selection of water barrels and wooden scaffolding he found underneath. It wasn't long before the cylindrical container caught his eye. He wrenched off the top and inspected the contents.

"What's this?"

"Sir, I do work up in the maintenance yard, also some repairs down here. I am permitted to keep all of that."

Faraway turned off his translator and called across to the guard who had just arrived at the dwelling opposite. The second Vitaari glanced at Sonus and nodded. Tapping one hand against the other, Faraway peered down at Sonus, then made his decision. The container hit the ground with a heavy slap, spilling its contents across the floor. Sonus had no light on so Faraway activated the flashlight affixed to his wrist and ran the yellow beam over the plastic and metal parts. He again used his boot to move the objects around.

Sonus tried to slow his breathing and forced himself back into the dwelling, to see what the Vitaari was looking at.

The guard bent over and picked something up. He shone the light on it. "What's this?"

He was holding a relay coupling, the three prongs of which could look rather dangerous to an untrained eye. When he heard what it was, Faraway turned it over and examined it, then dropped it. Sonus watched the yellow beam pass over the box in which he kept the power cells, then the trigger mechanism, then the barrel. The light skirted the edge of the data-pad, which was face up, the display screen quite clear. Faraway moved the light past it to the wall, then began to move it back—straight toward the data-pad.

Sonus stepped forward and pretended to trip, inadvertently landing on the Vitaari's foot.

"Sorry, I—"

The next thing he knew he was hanging in the air. Faraway had grabbed a handful of his overalls and lifted him off the floor with one hand. Sonus shut his eyes as the flashlight was shone straight in his eyes.

"What are you doing?"

"Sorry. I fell."

The guard dropped him. Sonus's left foot came down on a component and twisted under him. He cried out as landed on something hard and angular. He wasn't surprised to hear the low rumble that constituted Vitaari laughter.

"So weak." Faraway stepped over him. "Tidy up."

Sonus waited until he was sure he was safe, then got to his feet. His ankle ached a little, but worse was the pain in his side. He found that the sharp edge had torn through his overalls. He reached inside them and found blood. The wound was tender but not deep.

"You all right?" asked his neighbor.

He nodded. It had been a small price to pay.

Other than the man with the stash of food and a woman who possessed some casks of liquid the Vitaari couldn't identify, no one else attracted suspicion. The officer gave a last check of the caverns, then ordered the guards out. After they'd left, the talk was of what might happen to the unfortunate pair. In times past, Sonus might have acted on their behalf, but he could not afford to draw any more attention to himself.

Though the pain in his side was getting worse, he turned on a lamp and got to work. He had most of the components—including all the essential ones—back in the container when Arkus appeared.

"Can I help?"

"I'm fine, thank you."

"They pretty much left me alone," said Arkus, "because they see me every day, I suppose."

"That didn't help me."

"They can be very unpredictable. I thought this might be coming though."

"Why's that?"

"You've heard about this important visitor? I reckon that explains the inspection—must be the first one in months."

"I heard about it. Not long to go, I believe."

"Twelve days. Some man ranked higher than the Administrator and even the count—known as a viceroy. Apparently, he's responsible for many different groups of planets. What they call systems." Arkus shook his head. "I must admit it's all beyond me."

"And he's coming here—to Fourteen?"

"Yes. I suppose they're being careful because they can't risk anything going wrong—anything happening to him."

"Twelve days, you say?"

"That's what I heard."

Cerrin's foot was already on the ladder when a hand touched her shoulder. She turned to find Dukas's pale, spherical face staring at her.

"Can I talk to you?"

Around them, the silent, exhausted workers were still coming in through the door of Block A.

Cerrin pointed at Kannalin's empty compartment; he and a few other men had been kept back by the Vitaari to help the night shift with something. She pushed his blankets up to the other end and moved inside. Dukas did the same; clearly, he was also keen to ensure their conversation was not overheard.

"What is it?"

"Perhaps you would like to tell me what's going on?"

She kept her expression neutral. "What *is* going on?"

"A number of people have come to me with concerns. About you and a few others leaving the block at night, about a lot of whispering and secret meetings. They all seemed fairly sure you are involved. You and Sadi."

Cerrin shrugged. "I am friends with her, yes."

Dukas rubbed a finger across his chin. "If our people are noticing, it's only a matter of time before the Vitaari notice. And what then?"

"Wish I could help. But I honestly don't know what you're talking about." Cerrin gestured at her face. "You think I want another scar like this? You think I'm going to risk more trouble for myself?"

"I knew you wouldn't tell me anything."

"Nothing to tell."

"It's one thing to take risks yourself, Cerrin. Quite another to put others at risk. I hope you've considered that." He pointed toward the door, where the last of the workers were coming in. "Something's going on. Some important visitor. The Vitaari are unsettled. Now would not be a good time to upset them."

She shrugged again. "Thanks for the advice. Are we finished?"

The inspection came just before lights out. Cerrin was watering her plants when she heard noise from below. She crawled to the edge of the compartment and looked down. Six Vitaari were ordering everyone out. The laborers were not slow to obey.

Cerrin moved aside to let the sisters past. Her first thought was relief that the inspection hadn't come later; they were due to carry out the second night of work on the new tunnel. Then she thought about what the Vitaari might find. All the tools and other equipment were kept within the tunnel. Some of the conspirators—herself included—had the dirty overalls, but these could be explained away if necessary. As long as no one had made a mistake, there was nothing else to incriminate them.

"You—come down."

She quickly put her boots on and did so. As she reached the door, one of the guards shouted.

"That's the third time. Come here now!"

She turned back and realized it was Stripe. The Vitaari bent over a compartment and reached inside. Suddenly a man came flying out and landed heavily on the floor. He rolled over, groaning. Cerrin had seen such things many times before; despite all of the years dealing with the natives, the Vitaari did not understand how fragile their bodies were. As if they even cared.

"Get up," snapped Stripe, looming over him.

Cerrin looked at the dazed figure on the floor. It was a Palanian; she didn't know his name.

Stripe reached down and grabbed the man's arm. As he tried to lift him, the man kicked out, catching the Vitaari on the leg. Stripe immediately pulled out his jolt-rod, placed it against the man's forehead, and fired. Cerrin saw the flash of blue light and the man fall back to the floor. Wisps of smoke drifted up from his skull. His body spasmed once, then went still.

Teeth grinding, fists clenched, she only just stopped herself from moving.

Another guard close by turned around. "Out."

She took a breath and obeyed, and soon found herself among the rest of the shift gathered outside the door.

"Who is it?"

"Poor Serisus."

"His leg—he was slow because of his leg."

"I think he said something."

"What happened?"

Cerrin kept quiet and pushed her way to the back of the group.

Not long afterward, one of the guards dragged Serisus out and dumped his prone body on the ground. He pointed at two men and ordered them to carry him to the infirmary.

The rest of them stood in silence while the Vitaari searched the compartments. Many hadn't had time to dress properly; one of them was Yarni. Cerrin knelt down and wrapped her arms around her to keep her warm.

"They won't find anything, will they?" whispered the girl.

"There's nothing to find."

Stripe was the last out, just behind a guard clutching two handfuls of plants. Cerrin knew a few others kept them too; they had not been specifically forbidden from doing so.

"You can't have these in there," said Stripe. "For all we know, you could be making narcotics—or poisons. No plants. And there are dirty clothes everywhere. That's why you have two sets—so you can wash them. You have water and cleaner in the latrine. Anything dirty, you wash it. I know you'd prefer to live like animals, but you should have learned by now. Get back inside and get tidied up. We'll give you another half hour of lights."

Stripe stalked away but then stopped. "And remember—when a guard gives you an order, you do it the first time. Otherwise, you might end up with a little headache like your slow friend. Sleep well."

As he strode away with the others, Cerrin heard a familiar voice in her ear.

"Want to go ahead tonight?" asked Sadi.

"Yes."

"Agreed."

On her way back to the block, Cerrin received speculative looks from Kannalin, his cousin, and Erras. She nodded to all of them.

Sonus reckoned his luck had run out. It was evident from the state of the warehouse and the preparations being made on the landing strip that the freighter was due in. But he had not been given any work by Kadessis and the com-cell had remained silent since he'd returned to the mine two days earlier.

Angrily jabbing the point of the juddering drill into a wall of rock, he considered his limited options. Of course, he could just walk straight up to the surface. The guards wouldn't question it; he had done so many times before. But once up there? Did he dare cross the compound and try to meet with Nomora? If he was seen by Kadessis or questioned by the guards, the excuse of making the trade would not be sufficient to keep him out of trouble. He would also expose the Lovirr. Another alternative was to approach the guards and ask to make the trade. But this again would bring scrutiny. Yet in either case, the risk might be worthwhile; he had made a significant change to his plans—Nomora and the other "friends" needed to know.

When the siren for morning break sounded, he dropped his drill and pulled off his gloves. While the other workers sat down and drank, he walked toward the main shaft, indecision tearing at him. He was close to the elevator when he stopped. What if they were discovered? If the Vitaari interrogated Nomora, he might give up the whole network. Was he even entitled to take such a risk?

Light bloomed up ahead—the elevator doors opening. A small figure walked out, spied Sonus and walked toward him.

"There you are." Wearing his sleeveless jacket as usual, Arkus held up the small sack in his hand.

"They let you come down?"

"They did—one of the more pleasant guards was on duty. I had to give him a handful of the apples, but here's the rest. Nomora said he gave the figurines to his family for one of their festivals."

Sonus took the sack from him. "Thank you."

"I better get back up there."

"Wait. Is…"

"What is it?"

"Is the freighter leaving soon?"

"Within the hour, I should say."

"If I… had a message for Nomora. Would you be able to pass it on? Perhaps he might need the sack returned?"

"I suppose he might. He didn't say he did."

"You could do it without the Vitaari… interfering?"

"Probably."

"I could write it down."

Arkus scratched his arm and glanced back at the elevator. "This message…"

Sonus told himself he had to do it. He had to contact Nomora now, and he had no choice but to use this man. "It's… well…"

"If I didn't know if it was in the sack, I wouldn't read it, right?"

Sonus gripped his arm. "It's important. Very imp—"

"I'm not going to read it, so I don't need to know."

Sonus let go of him. "Thank you."

"Just be quick. Do you have something to write with?"

"Yes. But nothing to write on."

Arkus reached inside his overalls and pulled out a corner of paper. Sonus took it from him, then retrieved his pen and started writing. He supposed a code would have been preferable, but nothing had been agreed. Arkus looked away.

The message contained only three sentences.

Will attack here in twelve days and try to kill the viceroy. If I survive, will head north to Mine Three. Tell them.

25

"Up and about already? I'm impressed."

"Thank you, sir."

Troop Lieutenant Triantaa was sitting on a chair with a data-pad on his lap, neck still heavily bandaged. Lined up to his right on metal pallets were five combat shells. Most of the troop and a few engineers were gathered around them, checking and re-checking the innumerable parts and systems. Even though there were still seven days until the viceroy's visit, Vellerik wanted to make sure they were ready. He hadn't chosen who would accompany him yet so most of the men were doing their best to put themselves in contention. It would be a long day in the shells, and the previous training sessions had focused solely on stamina tests. Having participated in some himself, Vellerik now realized just how badly he had let himself go. His legs still ached.

"So how are we doing?"

"As you requested, sir. Four plus one spare—the five with optimal performance records."

"Remember what I said about reliability—that's the key. Those engines and systems will be running for three, maybe four hours."

"Yes, sir."

"And the fuel?"

"Apart from the reserve pods, we will have another ten barrels transported onto the viceroy's ship along with the spare shell. If necessary, you will be able to refuel at one of the mines."

"Did you work out the overall distance?"

"If the schedule remains as is, you will cover almost nine hundred kilometers."

Vellerik took a moment to absorb this. They had never used the shells over such a distance.

"I'm sure they'll perform well, sir. The engineers are on top of it."

"What's the cruising speed of the viceroy's ship?"

Triantaa moved a finger across the data-pad screen. "It's a Mark 6 Conveyor—somewhere around two hundred fifty."

"Those shells are going to get very hot."

"The engineers will recreate those conditions in the tests, sir. Have you thought about armament yet?"

"If I had my way, it would just be disruptors, but apparently the count would prefer something that can be seen. We'll go with the assault cannon—just be sure to keep the ammo packs light. "

"And the missile module, sir?"

"Then we won't have weight for the deflector fields."

"Are you likely to need those, sir?"

Vellerik conceded with a grin. "The biggest danger is either an in-flight malfunction or one of us getting sucked into that conveyor's air intakes."

"Sir, I think the best configuration might be two on either side, parallel with the rear of the ship. A minimum proximity of one hundred meters is recommended."

"Make it one-fifty."

"Yes, sir."

"How are you feeling?"

"A little sore, sir. Not too bad. The surgeon says I can start proper exercise in a week or so."

"Good." Vellerik watched the men congregate around one combat shell to detach a leg. Once they had laid it down, the engineers opened an access panel.

"Have you met the viceroy before, sir?" asked Triantaa.

"No, but I remember hearing him speak once at some function. He was just a regional governor back then."

"Of the Tennaren Plains, sir?"

"I think so, yes. You seem to know more about him than me."

"I've not had time to do anything much but read, sir."

"Wasn't he sent there to get the place in order after some… incident?"

"Yes, sir. That was eight years ago. The weapons testing facility. There was a communication breakdown—seventy infantry out testing masking tech got caught by a stray gas capsule. One of them was a distant relation of the Emperor."

"Ah yes."

"Viceroy Mennander ran the facility for four years—some major advances were made and not a single life lost."

"Family?"

"He is a member of the Duss-Viskar clan, sir."

Of the twelve clans that controlled the Domain, the Duss-Viskar were known for their interest in exploration and trade.

"Well, they seldom miss an opportunity for advancement. I wonder what he has his eye on next."

"Perhaps a more central quadrant."

"Perhaps."

"Sir—" Triantaa hesitated.

"What is it?"

The lieutenant glanced warily at the nearest troops and lowered his voice. "Sir, I overheard a few conversations while I was in the infirmary. The surgeon seemed to think you might be leaving."

Though he had not wanted to tell the men until the last possible moment, Vellerik knew Triantaa could be trusted.

"That's right." He liked the young lieutenant, and he felt he owed him an explanation. "I suppose… I've had enough."

Triantaa seemed surprised, and Vellerik saw disappointment in his eyes. He did not want to be pitied.

"Captain, it has been an absolute privilege to serve under your command."

"Thank you. I trust you will not mention this again until I tell the men."

"Of course, sir."

"Can you walk for a bit?"

"Yes, sir."

"Let's have a look at these shells then."

The garden was housed in a disused cargo bay toward the rear of the *Galtaryax*. Vellerik had only been there once before; he usually preferred his quarters if he craved peace and quiet. But on this day, something made him walk past his own door.

Just inside the entrance, two engineers were dispatching maintenance drones in various directions. Before they noticed him, Vellerik heard one moaning that the viceroy probably wouldn't even come near the place.

He wasn't generally one for artificial re-creations of the natural world, but this was actually done rather well. Danysaan had insisted on it, having read some research about how it boosted staff morale and productivity. Vellerik was surprised the count hadn't had it stripped out—surely another unnecessary expense.

Upon the walls were convincing vistas of a lakeside scene. Underfoot were earthen paths that followed circuitous routes through banks of grass and beds of plants and flowers. There was even an audio track of appropriate sounds. Vellerik was most interested in the water: the circular pool of clear, fresh-smelling water.

Pushing aside a particularly expansive frond of grass, he discovered Marl standing over the pool, utterly motionless, as ever almost entirely covered by his cloak. The head didn't move as the yellow eye turned.

Vellerik couldn't resist. "Feel like jumping in?"

Marl did not reply.

"I suppose that doesn't really merit a response." Vellerik had little desire for a conversation with him, but—having walked all that way—he didn't want to leave either.

He sat down on a bench apparently made of archaic-looking stone. Touching the surface, he realized it was in fact some kind of moulded plastic.

Marl continued to face the water while he spoke. "It helps you, captain, I suppose—to think of all those you conquer as primitive—savages, animals."

"Perhaps. Can't say it ever particularly occurred to me."

"Do you know how far back Drellen history goes?"

"I must confess I don't."

"In some of the most ancient caves there is evidence of language dating from two hundred thousand years ago. We were writing while the Vitaari were still walking on all fours."

"I suppose one might argue that we rather overtook you."

"I suppose."

"And if the Drellen had moved off their own world first—would they have left other peoples alone? Acted peacefully?"

"Who knows?" said Marl.

"I am not entirely ignorant of history. One of the reasons your people lost was in-fighting."

"The Vitaari had a long time to learn how to conquer. You turned us against each other."

"That's politics," said Vellerik.

"And you are just a soldier—who does as he is bid."

"Exactly. Like you."

As he turned, Marl ran a scaly hand across his head. Vellerik noted how long his fingers were, how dark the nails.

"What will you do, captain? When you leave."

"I will go somewhere a little like this—except it will be real."

"Alone?"

"No. Don't expect any more detail than that."

The display of triangular teeth on the rare occasions the Drellen smiled was always alarming.

"How old are you, Marl?"

"Thirty-one of your years."

"Is that young or old?"

"Males generally live to around fifty."

"Then—like me—you are over the hill and coming down the other side. What will you do? Remain with the count?"

"Yes."

"I hope he pays you well."

"Well enough."

"I have a strong suspicion that you hate him."

"You are wrong. I have good reason to hate every Vitaari, but the count has shown me kindness. And loyalty."

"I haven't seen much evidence he is capable of demonstrating either of those traits. Surely you must see that he keeps you only for what you can do for him?"

"I do not have to explain myself to you, captain."

"True." Vellerik watched a cleaning drone suck dust from the ceiling. "Where is the count? I've hardly seen him these last few days."

"Preparing for the viceroy's visit."

"Ah yes. Menus, drinks, his outfit. That type of thing."

"I think it is you who hates him, captain."

"Soon he will be nothing more than a memory."

"I am sure there are other memories you will find less easy to forget. From what I have observed of you, you are rather more prone to guilt and regret than most Vitaari."

After a long moment of silence, the Drellen walked away along the edge of the pool. Vellerik had to credit him with landing that one, but he could not allow him the last word.

"Oh, Marl—about the viceroy's visit."

"Yes?"

"Try to keep that blade of yours sheathed. We wouldn't want any mutilation or disemboweling that might put our esteemed guest off his dinner."

"You do your job, captain. I shall do mine."

Feeling the need for physical activity, Vellerik took an elevator down to the practice range.

Thankfully, it was empty. Sensing his ID card, the system screen flickered into life. Vellerik selected his preferred program, then used the same card to access the weapons rack. As the transparent cover retracted, he picked up the Mark 8 Assaulter. Apart from the fact it contained no live ammunition, this version was identical to his own weapon, currently housed with scores of others in the loading bay.

Vellerik waited for the door to open, then walked into the large cubic chamber. It was a rudimentary version of the ranges found in Colonial Guard facilities and Fleet ships but would suffice for his purposes.

"Start."

The two target drones detached from the wall, then each projected a black, humanoid figure. The figures began to move: circling around him, darting left and right, shifting up and down, swooping closer or pulling away.

The system spoke. "Sequence F, program 2. Sixty targets sixty seconds. Three, two, one... begin."

The weapon even sounded and jolted like the real thing. Every hit registered as an orange flash. If it was in a vital area, the black figure would explode then reappear. Vellerik made no attempt to keep track of his score. He just moved and aimed and fired.

He had been running drills on this type of range for more than four decades; he reckoned he must have totted up thousands of hours. Thirty years ago, he would regularly score ninety percent or above: that was for one-shot kills; anything else was considered a mistake. Ten years previous, he was still at over eighty percent—more than what most of the young men in the troop could manage.

He only just got his last shot away before the sixty seconds elapsed. Standing there, fingers aching, slightly dizzy, he waited for the bad news.

"Score: one-shot kill percentage—sixty-five."

Vellerik cursed. It had to be because of the drug, even though he hadn't ingested a thing since destroying the box.

"Restart sequence."

He lifted the weapon again, then realized he wasn't ready.

"Pause."

Vellerik went and leaned on the wall and took some deep breaths. On the other side of the room, the targets hovered side by side, ready to start.

"Continue."

Now re-acquainted with the movement and rhythm of the sequence, he did a little better. But the final score still appalled him; he couldn't believe he had fallen so far so fast. He took a longer break and went to drink some water before returning.

Once back at the range, he completed three more sequences. Not one score exceeded seventy percent.

When he heard the last one—sixty-eight—he felt like swinging the gun into the wall and smashing it to pieces. But his anger faded as he returned the weapon to the rack. He glanced at the scores again, then deactivated the display. He stood there in silence for what seemed like a long time.

By the time the door of the range shut behind him, he realized it didn't matter anymore. He did not intend to ever fire a weapon again.

26

After four nights of digging they had covered fifty feet. It was not easy going: there was more stone in this area and the soil was loose—the tunnel therefore more liable to collapse. They also had no material left to bolster the structure with.

But their spirits could not have been higher, and the prospect of actually reaching the surface spurred every one of them on. Erras and the hulking Trantis outperformed everyone to such a degree that when Cerrin and Sadi took their turn after them, they knew theirs would be the last session of work.

Cerrin was first down, and she steadied the rope while Sadi lowered herself from the original tunnel. The line was anchored inside and could be withdrawn out of sight when they didn't need it. Though she'd said nothing, Cerrin knew this was largely pointless: any significant search would have revealed their presence. Though they'd tried to cover their tracks on the near side of the old machine, on the far side was a volume of waste earth that would betray the operation in an instant. Yet it seemed they were safe. The Vitaari never came this way and Cerrin prayed that would continue for just a few more days.

Once Sadi was down, they hurried to the new second tunnel.

The pair clambered over the rusty machine and trudged through the waste soil. Cerrin took the trowel and bucket from inside, handing the bucket to Sadi. She then turned on the flashlight—which was now mounted on a head strap—and dived straight in. The best way to ascend was a rhythmic crawl, during which the diggers would inevitably encounter crawling insects, awkwardly placed stones and increasingly stale, bitter air.

After a few minutes, she reached a key marker. Two days previous, Kannalin had clanged his trowel against the foundations of the mine wall. He—and the others—had feared it might set off some kind of alarm, but nothing happened. Other than an enforced horizontal detour, the structure caused them no further problems: in fact, negotiating it provided another boost to morale.

Having checked that Sadi was behind her, Cerrin ploughed on until she reached the end. After a quick swig of water from the bottle in the pocket of her overalls, she jabbed the trowel in and tore out a clump of earth.

To her disappointment, it was Sadi who made the final break-through. Cerrin had just returned with an empty bucket when the Palanian turned and threw something back at her. Cerrin's flash-light illuminated a handful of fine white roots and green stems: grass.

Employing the usual technique, Sadi was pressed up against the left side of the tunnel. Cerrin crouched below her, watching as more and more grass appeared. Sadi hauled herself further up, then dropped the trowel so she could tear the vegetation away. After a time, she stopped and whispered.

"By the Maker. Stars."

Cerrin crawled up beside her.

There they were. Two tiny bright dots visible through the small hole.

"Flashlights," warned Cerrin.

They both turned them off and lay there together in silence. After a while Cerrin realized Sadi was crying. She said nothing but used the time to keep working until they could see more sky and there was enough space for her to poke her head out.

The clean, fresh scent of the air was almost overpowering. She could hear some kind of animal moving about close by. She turned and looked up. The dark wall of Mine Three looked impossibly high, lights blinking on top. She looked back down the slope. Cloud was currently obscuring the moon so she couldn't make out the river. But she could hear it, or at least she thought she could.

I could go now. I could go right now.

The thought came out of nowhere. The river lilies would be past their best, but with this much of a start she could swim across. By the time the Vitaari got moving, she would be in the forest and safe.

"I know what you're thinking," said Sadi.

Cerrin cast the notion aside, almost ashamed by it. She lowered herself back down into the tunnel. "Let's get finished."

Sonus needed one more piece of information. He'd spent some time up on the surface working on the maintenance drones and had picked up certain facts from Arkus, Kadessis, and the guards. He knew the viceroy was visiting in three days' time and he would attend Mine Fourteen in early morning. This was fortunate; it meant he could infiltrate the armory in darkness, then make his escape.

He would have to do so before the guards entered to ready the combat shells; they invariably put on a show of force for a prestigious visitor. He could then disable the other vehicles and hopefully be in the air before the guards could stop him. But where would the viceroy be then? Could he get to him before the element of surprise was lost and more Vitaari were sent to hunt him down?

Despite his best efforts, Sonus still did not know the visitor's precise movements. What he did know was there was an itinerary and he needed to see it. With midday approaching and only one more cleaning drone left to service, time was once again running out. For all he knew, there would be no more opportunities.

He closed the access panel of the penultimate drone, wiped coolant off his hands and looked at the tower. While waiting for

Kadessis there, he'd observed that the guards kept a single data-pad on a rack just inside the doorway. He imagined it provided orders or updates. (His damaged data-pad seemed incapable of receiving such information.)

Though in previous times, the tower guard—or guards—would occasionally wander off, under Talazeer's regime they did not stray far. Seeing the single man was still in position, Sonus grimaced. He couldn't think of any other way to access a data-pad: there were no engineers in the yard today and the building was locked up.

The Vitaari was tapping a finger against the side of his rifle, staring up at the clear blue sky.

Though he had already been through numerous ideas, Sonus considered his limited alternatives again. Kadessis—who would probably check in on him soon—usually kept his data-pad in a sleeve attached to his belt. Sonus supposed he could ask to use it, but he was yet to come up with a convincing explanation.

The drone he had been working on beeped. He looked down and saw a message appear on the screen. Now repaired, the robot was asking for work.

A moment later, Sonus walked out of the yard.

The Vitaari watched him approach, face glistening in the wintry sunlight, dark eyes implacable. Sonus had recognized him from his finger-tapping habit. He didn't know his name but recalled he was not one of the most aggressive guards, not by a long way.

Sonus ran a hand through his newly trimmed hair, having visited Orani the previous evening. He then clasped both hands together and bowed low. "Excuse me, sir."

The guard clicked his translator on. "What is it?"

"I've been repairing the cleaning drones, and now I have to program them. I was instructed to ensure they are able to do a final sweep of the compound just before the visitors arrive." Sonus felt it sensible not to specifically mention the viceroy. "I believe they're coming sometime in the morning—do you know exactly when?"

"08:00, I think."

An hour after dawn.

"Ah."

"Mine Five first, then here."

"I see. Thank you. It's a beautiful day, isn't it, sir? Very clear. Sometimes I wonder if your gods can see you here—so far from home."

The guard frowned, then pointed at the yard. "You should get back to it."

Sonus bowed once more, then hurried away. His hope was that the guard would remember the strange comment, not what had gone before.

As he entered the yard, numbers filled his mind. He had quite a few calculations to make.

Cerrin's day passed with grinding, suffocating slowness. Where previously she had been scared the escape plan would be discovered, now she was terrified. The path to freedom was open, and yet she and the others found themselves working like any other day. They had not yet agreed when they would go, but Cerrin was determined to leave no later than the following night.

By the evening—when she visited Sadi's compartment under the pretense of examining the knee the Palanian had twisted earlier—she reiterated her intention.

As they were surrounded by people preparing for bed, Sadi whispered her reply. "We're not ready."

"But you have the flares."

Yarni had pilfered four from a supply depot within the mine. They were usually used by the Vitaari for marking drilling areas but—according to Sadi—they were the easiest method of igniting fuel. Whoever set them off would be at great risk but, if correctly situated, the resulting blasts could cause considerable damage.

"That's not all we need," added Sadi. "What about these weapons you promised us?"

Unless the Vitaari were very slow to react, the escapees would probably have to defend the tunnel or the others while they crossed the river. Cerrin's idea was to turn a collection of wooden stakes she'd found behind Block B into spears. She had sharpened one of the trowels to do so but hadn't had time to fashion them. In truth, they would be next to useless when facing the Vitaari—with or without the shells—but Cerrin reckoned she and the others would all feel better with a weapon in their hands.

"I'll get to work on them tonight. Kannalin said he'll help me. But we go tomorrow."

"Cerrin, we haven't even established who's doing what."

"That's easy enough. We—"

Sadi looked up. The broad figure of Trantis was blocking out most of the light.

"What's going on?" he said loudly.

"Knee," answered Sadi.

The big Palanian knelt in front of her and pretended to examine it. "Another message from our friends," he said quietly. "This man at Mine Three will attack at dawn in three days' time. They want us to start an hour before."

"Why?" asked Cerrin.

"Because he may be able to help us and we may be able to help him."

Cerrin shook her head. "An hour of darkness isn't long enough. Why take the risk? We don't need his help."

"How do you know?" replied Sadi.

"One hour?" said Cerrin. She couldn't believe their "friends" would suggest such a thing.

Trantis did a better job than the women of keeping his voice down. "The Lovirr think striking together aids us both. If he's inside one of their fighting machines and he gets here in time, he could make the difference."

"And if we start earlier, we could all be in the forest by then."

Trantis fixed his eyes on Cerrin. "The Lovirr want us to help him. If he gets to us, he will have killed this important Vitaari. No offense,

Cerrin, but there are many like us. This man is special. We need to keep him alive."

"If he's so special, he can look after himself. We have another ninety-three to think about."

Sadi turned to her. "We should wait. We should do as they ask. Act together. As one."

As she looked at them, Cerrin reminded herself that the tunnel would not exist without the enterprising Palanians. She still didn't believe this man was worth altering their plans for, but she owed them loyalty. The thought of waiting even longer horrified her, but now was not the time to argue.

"It's decided then. Let's just make sure we're ready."

Sonus had drunk three large mugs of water but could not rid himself of the headache. It probably didn't help that he was reading the data-pad under a blanket or that he seemed to have encountered a potentially intractable problem.

Mine Five was one hundred sixty kilometers to the south of Mine Three, situated beyond a line of sand dunes known to Palanians as Skakka's Bight. Assuming he somehow survived the attack on the viceroy, he would then have to reach Mine Fourteen, which was another ninety-five kilometers to the northwest. This was possible if he travelled at the optimum speed and did not make drastic maneuvers. But he planned to travel south from Three at maximum speed and maneuvering was inevitable. He could add extra fuel modules but was not prepared to sacrifice any of the key armaments and equipment. He'd been unable to find out anything about the viceroy's ship and its capabilities, but it seemed obvious such a craft would have defensive systems. Sonus reckoned his best hope was to rely on surprise.

It took him another half an hour before he found a solution. A single fuel tank could be stored in the locker mounted on the back of the shell. It would have to be attached manually, but he reckoned it might just be enough to get him to Three.

Sonus left the data-pad under the blanket and gazed up at the darkened cavern. It seemed almost ridiculous to be looking so far ahead. Even what he had to accomplish here at Fourteen seemed more of an optimistic vision than a feasible plan. He had tried to put the very first stage of that plan firmly to the back of his mind, but soon the moment would arrive when he had to kill.

He looked across at the container and thought of holding the weapon in his hands, aiming at the armory guard. To his mother—a believer to her dying day—taking a life was an affront to the Maker. Sonus could never know how more than a decade spent in the grip of the Vitaari might have changed her mind, but she had been a woman of conviction. Perhaps she would have held firm, believed the Maker would eventually somehow free his chosen people. Or perhaps she would have said it didn't matter, they were all better off in the Kingdom anyway.

Sonus wiped his aching eyes and turned off the data-pad. Once it was well hidden, he drank more water, then returned to bed. As usual, he wrapped himself up well and kept his arms under the blankets to get warm. There was a familiar comfort to these moments, and he knew from talking to others that many thought this the best part of the day. The body could rest and the mind too—free from the noise and dirt of the mines, the cruel whims of the guards. He recalled what Qari used to say: every night a part of her truly thought she might wake up and find it had all been a dream, that she might find herself back in her family home, in the time before the Vitaari.

Sonus gazed up at one particular patch of the cavern. Even in darkness he could always make out the streak of pale green. Though he knew it was in fact caused by deposits of a rare mineral, he'd always found the splash of color encouraging. It seemed to suggest that the unexpected was always possible.

Before he finally succumbed to sleep, he forced himself back to a place he did not want to go: the abandoned shaft where Qari and Karas had thrown themselves to their deaths. He forced himself to remember how suddenly they were gone; every hope and dream of the future snuffed out in an instant. He thought of how it could have been, imagined the three of them together. He thought of the baby as a boy; that's what Qari had wanted.

Sonus cried. But he also felt that fire in his gut, that anger. He would need his rage. He would depend on it.

27

Vellerik watched the *Tarikan* ease closer to the *Galtaryax*. The shuttle was a converted exploration ship that allowed Governor Mennander to visit both space-bound and surface installations. A third the size of the *Galtaryax*, it was a lot newer and equipped with a state-of-the-art communications array mounted below the cockpit. The high fin above the ship's body displayed one of the biggest imperial insignias Vellerik had ever seen. He felt certain the viceroy and the count would get on well.

"*Tarikan?*" said Triantaa, whose recovery was continuing well. Like Vellerik, he was in full ceremonial garb. "General, wasn't he?"

"Indeed," said Vellerik. "Sotthan campaign, I believe—thirty-third century."

"To your places." The order came from Count Talazeer himself, who had grown increasingly insufferable as the visit neared. Vellerik and Triantaa joined him, Administrator Danysaan, and Deputy Rasikaar in front of the accessway.

The imperial anthem began: the full orchestral version, of which Vellerik was not fond. He preferred the original style, which was usually performed by only five players with classical instruments. It had always struck him as rather understated and noble. The new incarnation seemed bloated by grandeur, utterly devoid of subtlety.

The accessway locks thumped into place. Vellerik looked around;

Marl was still nowhere to be seen and it occurred to him perhaps Talazeer was wary of alarming the viceroy. The accessway doors eased apart. First to appear were two bodyguards, both in the black of the Imperial Guard. Judging by their decoration bars, the pair were veterans. Like Vellerik, they carried only holstered sidearms.

As the pair separated, Viceroy Mennander strode forward. He was a small man, with white streaks in his hair, which Vellerik guessed might be artificial. He wore the gray robes of a civilian administrator covered by a long scarlet cloak. Holding it together was a large metallic clasp, again showing the imperial standard, the golden circle surrounded by twelve stars.

Talazeer greeted him politely, and they shook hands. "Viceroy, may I welcome you aboard the *Galtaryax* and to the imperial territory of Corvos."

"Count Talazeer, it is a pleasure to see you again."

"How was the trip?"

"Uneventful, though yesterday we received some troubling news."

Vellerik couldn't see Talazeer's face, but the viceroy had clearly noted the count's alarm.

"Nothing to do with yourself or this operation, rest assured. We will discuss it later. "

Talazeer looked relieved as he turned around. "Viceroy, allow me to introduce my staff."

Once they were free of their duties, Lieutenant Triantaa declared he would test out his stamina with a trip to the cargo bay. Vellerik decided to accompany him, and they were not surprised to find it empty. All the troop—the three selected to accompany Vellerik the following day and the others—had been given time off. According to Triantaa, the majority were holed up in Perttiel's quarters watching the latest clip from home featuring a famous actress.

Vellerik had decided the lieutenant was fit enough to participate: he would travel inside the *Tarikan* and coordinate the escort.

"I'll feel better with you there," he said as they sat down on a cargo container close to the combat shells. "Then I can concentrate on flying."

It had been agreed that the shells would leave the ship to form the escort as they approached every mine and return when they were a safe distance away.

Vellerik shook his head. "All this effort. And for what? So the count can put on a show."

"Sir, I know you said the biggest threat came from flying into each other, but I have identified another." Triantaa's expression was grave. "Flocks of birds."

"Are you serious?"

"Yes, sir. Kerreslaa told me ships in the northern zone have had the odd problem, and apparently it's a migratory season. Once I've patched into the *Tarikan*'s array, I'll see anything that can cause us trouble."

"Very well."

The cargo bay was utterly silent. The combat shells had been left close to the main doors. They would be transferred to the *Tarikan* later on.

"Maybe they'll name a ship after you one day, sir."

Vellerik laughed out loud at that, even though he knew the young lieutenant was being genuine. "I certainly hope not."

"You wouldn't consider it an honor, sir?"

Vellerik took a long breath. Count Talazeer had agreed he could depart aboard the *Tarikan*. In two days he'd leave Corvos behind. In five days he'd reach Nexus Eighty. In eleven days he'd pass the Core Boundary. In twenty days he'd be reunited with Seevarta.

"Devan." Vellerik put his hand on Triantaa's shoulder. He had not used his given name before. "I simply do not care anymore. I am an old man, and I should have listened to myself sooner. I fear I have grown weak."

"That is the last word I would ever use to describe you, sir."

Vellerik smiled. "You're a good officer. You'll do well. When I was your age, I couldn't even imagine a time when I would leave. I just did what I needed to: listened, learned, moved up. Nothing else mattered. To make captain I knew I had to complete every order, go above and beyond. Then when I got there, I realized there was nowhere else to go—not without becoming a glorified administrator. Do you know I am one of the longest serving captains of all time? Not something to be very proud of."

"I don't agree, sir."

Vellerik could see no reason to censor himself now, even with his subordinate. "I'll tell you something else. I have no idea how many beings I have killed. Not just by the odd one or two, or even five or ten. It could be two hundred, it could be four hundred. I have no idea. I must admit sometimes the thought of it shames me."

Triantaa stared down at the floor. "Our enemies, sir. The Domain spreads civilization, advancement. This may sound stupid, but… well… it's not our fault we are superior. "

"You sound like me. Forty years ago." Vellerik ran a knuckle down his face. "I don't think anyone will ever stop us—any people, any race. It is simply in us to do this. Fight. Conquer." He turned to the younger man. "Just promise me this, Devan—you'll only kill when you have to."

He could not avoid the dinner. It was to be held in a small room specially adapted for the purpose. He arrived as late as possible and found Talazeer and Danysaan anxiously awaiting the viceroy. Once again Marl was nowhere to be seen. Vellerik continued to speculate: perhaps Talazeer feared talk of the attack on the native girl had somehow reached Mennander, perhaps he thought it best to keep the Drellen out of the way so the subject was never mentioned.

While Talazeer interrogated the ship's chef and the serving staff, Vellerik took a glass of wine and stood with Danysaan on the far side of a large rectangular table. He nodded at the hangings on the walls: ersatz versions of tapestries showing ancient emperors and classic imperial scenes.

"I didn't even know we had those."

"Neither did I. Rasikaar dug them out of storage."

"Enjoying yourself so far?"

Danysaan made sure he was facing away from the count when he rolled his eyes and answered, "I envy you, Erasmer."

"How much longer will you have to stay?"

"I've already applied for re-assignment. As Rasikaar is more than happy to do the count's bidding, I am surplus to requirements."

"I still find it hard to believe his methods really made much difference."

"Increased work hours had an impact," confided Danysaan. "But we've had more illness and missed days as a result—as I predicted."

Vellerik kept his voice down. "So the figures are false?"

"No. What the count has brought to this operation can be summed up in one word."

Fortunately, Talazeer was still deep in discussion with the staff.

Vellerik nodded. "Fear."

"Precisely. From myself down to the lowliest guard and the workers themselves—nobody dares gives less than their best. It all adds up over time." Danysaan smirked. "Didn't manage to have quite the same effect on you, did he?"

Vellerik took a hefty swig of wine. "What is this?"

"Red Eldar. Strong."

"Good. Spoken to the viceroy?"

"A little."

"And?"

"As I have noted on previous occasions, his reputation for direct speaking is well deserved. My advice—watch your step."

Shortly afterward, the chef disappeared and the viceroy arrived. One of the attendants hung up his cloak for him while another poured more drinks. At Talazeer's invitation, the four of them sat down. Neither the count nor Danysaan appeared keen to face the viceroy so Vellerik was forced to sit opposite him.

Mennander sipped his drink with mannered precision. "Excellent. Red Keccbar—a fine choice, Talazeer."

No one corrected him. Vellerik was more interested in the fact

Mennander used the count's name instead of his title. He doubted Talazeer would make an issue of that either.

"I hope you feel refreshed, sir," said the count, after an adjustment to his uniform.

"Indeed, I do. The ship seems to be run very smoothly. I'm sure I'll be similarly impressed by the tour of the installations tomorrow. Captain Vellerik, I understand your trip will be a little less comfortable than ours?"

"A little, sir."

"Must be quite enjoyable, zipping about in those shells?"

"Some might say I'm a bit old for it, sir." Only now did Vellerik consider the fact he had a few years even on the viceroy.

"Not at all. I know General Eddekal is sorry to be losing you."

Vellerik gave an appreciative nod.

The two attendants returned, carrying plates with the first course. Mennander spoke as the four men picked up their cutlery. "To be honest, I'm afraid you may well find yourself recalled before long."

"Sir?"

"As I was telling the count earlier, there have been some worrying developments in the ninth quadrant: an escalation in the conflict with the Red Regent. It's just as well that operations like this one are providing the Fleet with the resources they need. But if the situation worsens, every branch of the armed forces will be affected."

"An escalation, sir?"

Mennander glanced at Talazeer. "I did not disclose the full details earlier, but I know this will not leave the room. Eight ships—a double patrol—were ambushed close to the Great Nebula. Four were destroyed, two crippled."

"Cruisers, sir?" asked Vellerik.

Mennander chewed his food before answering. "All but one."

Vellerik lowered his fork. Cruisers were the second most powerful designation in the fleet, each with a crew of almost four hundred. The Vitaari hadn't sustained losses like this for a generation.

"Enemy losses?"

"Twelve, but the ships are comparatively small. Apparently, the attack showed considerable tactical progression in comparison to earlier strikes."

Danysaan weighed in. "There are no notable systems in that area. Do we know the motivation for the attack?"

Mennander had clearly heard the administrator but ate for some time before answering. "That is a point causing considerable speculation. Some—myself included—believe it is retaliation for our actions on Yera III."

Vellerik was unaware there was still an imperial presence on Yera III. The primitive planet had been colonized decades earlier. Other than the fact it hosted a usefully positioned supply depot, the whole system was a forgotten backwater. It was also situated a long way from the Great Nebula. In fact, it wasn't that far from Nexus Eighty, where he would soon meet his connecting flight.

Noting the confused looks, the viceroy continued. "Recently, we have become aware of… infiltrators on some of our less well protected territories. We don't know a great deal yet, but there is some evidence they are part of the Regent's efforts against us. These agents equip the locals with armaments and encourage them to conduct guerilla operations."

"Drag in our men and material so we've less to face their conventional forces," observed Vellerik.

"Precisely," said Mennander. He seemed more interested in his wine than continuing his explanation.

Vellerik forced himself to wait. "You mentioned 'our actions,' sir?"

"Yes, well, a group of these guerillas somehow got inside the depot on Yera III and did a lot of damage. No fatalities but an explosion took out most of the fuel, which meant Prince Telerrion found himself stranded—his ship was due to re-supply there. Anyway, he missed the birth of his first child—you know how long they've been trying. So on his way back, he took charge of the reprisals himself."

Vellerik put down the forkful of food and leaned back in his chair.

"Quite imaginative, really," said Mennander. "They used one of the black ghosts."

"I didn't know there were any left," said Talazeer.

Administrator Danysaan frowned. "What are they?"

Vellerik answered. "They were found in some kind of temple in the mountains of the Ossarr home world. They can manipulate the minds of others; at first only their own kind, but our scientists eventually got them to the stage where they could affect most other humanoids."

Mennander seemed to have quite an appetite for a small man. He ate a large chunk of bread before continuing. "In any case, our forces on Yera III purposefully let the captured rebels escape. The ghost then took control of them and sent them first to eliminate their leaders, then their allies, then their families. Over two hundred."

"And then themselves, I imagine," said Vellerik.

"When the ghost let them go? Yes, probably."

For a while no one spoke.

Vellerik knew he would not eat anything else. Telerrion had always had a nasty streak, but this was beyond viciousness.

"That was stupid. A commensurate response would have sent a strong enough message. Now every man on that planet will want our blood. The Red Regent will have allies flocking to her."

"Captain." Talazeer's warning came through gritted teeth.

Danysaan's wine glass stopped halfway to his mouth.

The viceroy sat up straight and stared across the table. "I do hope I didn't just hear you insult a member of one of the twelve clans."

Vellerik knew he had no choice but to act immediately. He could hardly believe the words had come out of his mouth. "Please forgive me, all of you, a poor choice of words. I meant merely that—"

"I think you have said enough," snapped the viceroy. He took a deep breath in through his nose and rubbed his hands together. "Captain, I am tempted to say that I will not have you aboard my ship. That your presence might offend me. But I think it is best you leave this place—and end your term of service."

The words struck Vellerik like a blow. Though he already disliked the viceroy almost as much as the count, he had gone too far. Whatever his private thoughts, he had dishonored himself and his uniform by criticizing the prince. He would just have to hope Mennander didn't report him; he could face charges, even after retirement.

"Will you excuse me?"

Talazeer gestured at the door without looking at him.

Despite his shame, Vellerik couldn't bring himself to apologize to Talazeer. He stood up and walked around the table to the viceroy. "I am truly sorry, sir. Rest assured I will fulfill my duties to the best of my ability until they are complete."

He was relieved to see the viceroy offer a nod.

The wait for the door to open seemed endless.

28

Sonus had done most of his work before darkness fell. On the floor next to the spare parts container was his pack. Within it were a flashlight, a flask of water, the data-pad, and the weapon—including spare power cells and ammunition. During the past few days he had taken every opportunity to practice re-loading: if the first cell didn't ignite, he would have to load another one instantly.

At the bottom of the pack was one other item. His mother had given him her copy of *Our Maker's Teachings* on his eighteenth birthday. Though this was a family tradition, she had known by then her son would never believe as she did. Sonus rarely opened it, but the book was his most treasured possession—because it had been hers and because it was a gift from her.

Once out of his sleeping clothes, he put on as many layers as he could under his overalls. He knew from the manual he would be exposed to cold while flying at speed and his clothes would offer none of the insulation of the advanced Vitaari uniforms. Though he would be protected by the armored hull of the shell, the machines did not waste much power on making the pilot comfortable.

He had been through every procedure many times. In theory, he knew how to activate the shell, how to fly it, how to arm and use the weapons, and how to land.

In theory.

Sonus knew reality would be far more complicated and unpredictable, but he drew comfort from the fact he had made every preparation possible.

He made his bed, then picked up the pack and put on his gloves. He would need them to negotiate the walkway but would have to take them off later to operate both the weapon and the vehicle. He looked around at his home of so many years but did not indulge himself with regret. He had resolved to put all emotion aside from this point onward. Unless he needed it.

He reached into a pocket and took out his com-cell. The time was 05:20, about an hour and a half before dawn. He had estimated the viceroy's ship might arrive at Mine Five around 07:30.

As he walked quietly through the caverns, he told himself not to think that far ahead, nor about what he might eventually find at Mine Fourteen should he reach it. For now, all that mattered was getting inside the armory undetected.

By the time he neared the walkway, he had spied several pairs of eyes watching him from the darkness. Outside, the wind was light but the snow thick; heavy flakes had settled at the mouth of the entrance. Sonus thought this a good thing, for now at least: it would help him move unseen across the compound. But if it persisted, it might add to his difficulties later on.

Orani was on duty alone.

"Not again," she said when she saw him. "You're getting forgetful, Sonus."

"It's not that. A special job."

"Ah." She tapped the seat next to her. "The old boy was yawning so I sent him to bed."

Sonus nodded.

"Sit me with a while," said Orani.

"Sorry, I can't." He walked on but paused after a couple of steps. "Orani, I... I... would just like to say thank you. You have always been very kind to me."

. . .

Several inches of snow lay on the ground. One side of the tower had turned white, including the windows close to the top. Two containers of ore were currently on the conveyor, rumbling slowly across the rear of the compound toward the warehouse. There would be at least one engineer on duty there. The powerful lights beside the mine illuminated the flurries falling across the face of the mountain. Two small figures—guards—could be seen just inside the entrance, looking out.

The closest building was the generator station, which was protected by a high wire fence. Keeping low and staying in the shadows, Sonus scuttled toward it. Hearing the low hum of machinery within and his boots cutting through the slush, he then skirted the rear of the station. Halting at the far corner, he removed the pack and squatted down.

He waited there for several minutes to see if the guard was patrolling, but the only movement came from the falling snow, which was already settling on his pack. He was about to move forward to locate the guard when the Vitaari appeared dead ahead, walking around the far corner of the armory, no more than forty feet away. Sonus retreated. All his clothing was dark, and he had painted anything with a metallic surface that could betray him. He kept his head down but watched the guard.

By the time the Vitaari reached the near corner, Sonus had to clench his fists to stop himself shivering. As the guard turned back toward the compound, Sonus was surprised to hear he was singing to himself.

Keep moving. Come around again.

Hoping he hadn't missed his opportunity, Sonus removed his gloves and opened the pack.

Cerrin knew there would be no time later. She said the prayer of honor to her mother and father.

Yarni—who was lying beside her—shifted under the blankets. Cerrin could not believe the girl could sleep. She thought of the others: Sadi, Trantis and Erras, Kannalin and his cousin Jespa. All there in Block A, lying awake, waiting. She already felt exhausted but told herself her body had rested; she was ready.

The first step would be the tap on her foot; Kannalin telling her Sadi had given the signal. Then he, Cerrin, and Jespa would go outside to the tunnel entrance. While Jespa guarded it, Cerrin and Kannalin would take the ten makeshift spears they had made and return to the block. And then…

Cerrin didn't even try to make any predictions. She shut her eyes and closed her mind to all distractions.

Ikala, god of battle. I face the hardest battle of my life. My enemies are strong, but my will is stronger. Harden my heart, strengthen my body, guide my hand. In return, I pledge myself to the warrior, the rage, the bloodlust, the conqueror.

Ikala, god of battle, see me, hear me, help me.

Sonus sat hunched over in the snow, freezing fingers clasping the weapon.

Head still bowed to obscure his face, he watched the guard walk toward him once more. The black silhouette seemed immense, as did the rifle hanging in front of his chest. He was wearing a hood, which would at least limit his hearing.

Sonus was confident he could get behind him. What he could not be confident of was the power cells. There was no chance he would have time for more than two shots. On his right hand, one finger was on the trigger. The other three were gripping a spare cell. He had practiced reloading so much that blisters had formed. He could do it without thinking or looking.

Bizarrely, the guard was still singing. He kicked up snow like a youngster as he turned the corner.

Sonus stood. He had to move quickly: though the Vitaari was walking slowly, his stride length would quickly take him toward the front of the armory—and the light. Sonus reminded himself not to let the barrel drop. Fingers tight on the weapon, he followed the guard. At a range of no more than six feet, he raised the barrel, aimed at the back of the head, and depressed the trigger.

Misfire. A noisy misfire. A low popping sound he hadn't heard before. Sonus grabbed the bolt and drew it back.

As the guard turned, he flicked the power cell out and replaced it. He shoved the bolt back in and raised the barrel once more.

The Vitaari didn't seem to understand he was in danger. He saw Sonus standing there, but all he did was speak in his own language.

The blast illuminated him. Shrapnel tore into his upper chest and face. One piece of metal blew a fist-sized hole in his jaw. The huge figure rocked back for a moment, then toppled into the snow. He hit with such force that his rifle flew into the side of the building, landing several feet away.

Sonus just stood there, paralyzed. The noise had probably been no worse than any of the detonations, but he felt sure someone would have heard.

Forcing his limbs to work, he ran past the guard to the front of the armory. He looked up at the tower and across the compound. There were no Vitaari visible. He made himself count to twenty to ensure no one was coming, then retraced his steps.

The guard had disappeared. At first Sonus thought he had simply lost his night vision, but there was no sign of him.

Gripped by panic, he backed against the wall. His foot caught something. As his eyes began to adjust to the dark once more, he realized it was the rifle. Why hadn't the guard taken it?

Sonus exchanged his weapon for the Vitaari's and was surprised how light it was. He had studied them over the years and knew they were activated by a square firing stud beneath a protective cover. He flipped the cover up and walked along the side of the armory. He also knew the rifles had a built-in flashlight. He activated it, then reduced the power to minimum. After several yards more, he realized he could see something upon the snow. Something very dark— black, in fact. Vitaari blood.

He found the guard face down, still crawling. His breath was coming in halting gasps. When Sonus stopped beside him, he began to moan. The guard rolled over, eyes glinting. He raised one of his arms, opened his palm, asking for mercy.

Sonus let the cover down over the firing stud, then held the weapon firmly in both hands. Without even thinking, Qari and Karas came to him when he needed them.

He drove the butt of the weapon down into the Vitaari's face.

Bones cracked. The guard moaned, quieter this time.

Sonus hammered the weapon down again and again and again. At the fourth blow, blood splattered his hands. He fell to his knees and dropped the rifle. The guard was silent.

Trying not to look anywhere near his face, Sonus undid the top of his jacket and reached inside. Still warm, the Vitaari skin felt unnaturally smooth. Possessed by a desire to get away from the corpse, he nonetheless found the cord around the neck, followed it down to the triangular ID card, and pulled it free.

Once this was out, he also removed the com-cell from the Vitaari's ear. The guards communicated with the tower fairly regularly. Even if he couldn't convince them he was the sentry and there was nothing to concern them, he would know if they were coming.

Sonus was about to leave the body when he realized he needed something else. He shone the rifle's flashlight on the guard's fatigues. His name was Nullerik.

Taking the weapon with him, Sonus walked around the far corner of the armory. The next building along was the barracks. There was no noise coming from it, no other sign of activity. He glanced up at the mine. More fresh containers were on the conveyor, but the guards at the entrance had disappeared.

The armory's main door was at the front, a wide entrance for the combat shells. The secondary door was on the right side, halfway along. A powerful lamp was situated above it. Sonus had already decided that taking it out was more likely to draw attention; he would just to have to hope none of the Vitaari looked at that precise location at that precise moment.

Please work. Please work.

He walked straight up to the door and held the ID against the sensor panel. A light turned from red to yellow, and the door slid open. He threw himself inside and slammed a hand into the controls. As it shut, the armory's interior lights came on.

The purple-tinged rays of the Wild Sun speared the cargo bay of the *Tarikan*. The five combat shells were hanging from the storage rack upon which they had been transported. The rack was attached to rails that ran the length and breadth of the bay. Cables had been strung from the walls to secure the shells during the trip down.

The worst of the turbulence now past, Vellerik was relieved all the precautions had worked: the shells had moved around a bit but had not sustained any damage. He glanced down at the outline of the central ramp. He and the other three men would exit the ship via this door as they approached Mine Five.

He'd been unable to read anything from Talazeer or Mennander, who had given the soldiers only a cursory greeting on their way to the passenger lounge behind the shuttle's cockpit. He had, however, received a message from Danysaan. Not daring to use the ship's coms system, the Administrator had slipped a note under his door during the night. He explained the count and the viceroy had discussed Vellerik for some time at the dinner after his departure. Talazeer contended that Vellerik's mood had been affected recently by this mysterious affliction. Mennander seemed to accept this and was only interested in assurances that Vellerik would perform professionally for the remainder of the visit.

Vellerik was determined to do precisely that. He had briefed the men twice and had run through the itinerary several times in his head. The shells had been checked three times before departure, and there were no outstanding issues. The spare fuel pods had been loaded aboard and were secured in a reinforced container situated in the corner of the bay.

To his right, the three members of his team—Perttiel, Zarrinda, and Saarden sat in silence. Vellerik harbored concerns only about young Zarrinda: he didn't have as much time in the shells as the others and was occasionally given to panic. But Vellerik knew he would follow orders to the letter and far preferred him to some of the overly aggressive troopers, such as Dekkiran.

To his left, Triantaa was fiddling with the field-scanner on his lap. The unit had a large screen and would enable him to monitor the ship, the shells, and the surrounding area. He'd already confirmed the scanner had successfully linked with the *Tarikan*'s powerful sensor array.

"How are you feeling?" Vellerik had to speak loudly above the shuttle's engines.

"Fine, thank you, sir," said Triantaa. "I meant to ask earlier—tonight will be your last on the *Galtaryax*. Will you eat dinner with myself and the rest of the troop?"

Vellerik felt the unfamiliar sensation of a smile forming on his face. "Of course."

Though Sonus knew all he could know about the combat shells, he had only ever glimpsed the armory's interior once before. At first, he simply stood there, waiting for an alarm or the sound of approaching guards. Only when he was satisfied he had not been discovered did he look around.

The rear of the building was taken up by racks of weapons, helmets, and armor. Most of the rest of the space was occupied up by a high, semi-circular structure he knew to be something called the support station. All six white combat shells stood dormant in front of the station, three on either side, facing the main door. Between them was a broad central panel that contained all the various pods and modules that could be attached to the shells. On the floor below it was the legend "FUEL": the station was connected via an underground pipe to the main tank beneath the landing strip.

Sonus hurried over to one of the shells beside the central panel. He put the rifle and the pack on the floor and the com-cell on top of the rifle. He then took the ID card and approached the shell. The cockpit door was up, revealing the inside of the machine. Every space not occupied by the soft sections that molded themselves to the pilot was packed with cables, boxes, screens, and numerous other components Sonus couldn't identify. His stomach turned over as he thought of locking himself into the thing.

The shell's bulbous arms hung down straight, hands resting on the floor. Sonus knelt down beside the left hand and spied the rectangular sensor inside the palm. He held the ID card against it. Two seconds later, the shell began to hum. As the main cockpit screen activated, he turned to the central panel.

There, another screen was now active. Sonus knew he could use this to control the shell remotely. He walked over to the display and checked the status of the craft. It presently had no pods or modules attached. The tanks were empty but fueling time was listed as only a minute and a half so he made the command. Something clicked at the back of the shell, and he heard liquid on the move.

By the time Cerrin and Kannalin returned to Block A, there was already too much noise.

She found Sadi, Yarni, Trantis, and Erras gathered by the door. Sadi had one of the lamps in her hand and a few other workers had lit what lights they had, mostly candles and lanterns. The buzz of confusion and fear was growing ever louder.

"Now?" asked Sadi.

"It's time," replied Cerrin. "You others watch the door." Leaving her share of the spears with the men, she gave Yarni a reassuring squeeze on the shoulder and then followed Sadi into the middle of the block. As the men and women moved aside, Cerrin tried not catch anyone's eye.

When they stopped, Sadi spoke as loudly as she dared. "Let's have quiet, please. Can everyone come down here—we need to talk to you all. As quickly as possible."

Cerrin was surprised how cooperative they were. Several more people came down ladders, and in moments they were surrounded by dazed, wide-eyed faces. Questions were already being asked. As they waited for the last of the workers to arrive, Esteann pushed her way to the front.

"What is this, Cerrin? You told me there was nothing going on."

"You'll hear along with everyone else."

"I knew it," said the Echobe woman, eyes narrow. "I knew I couldn't trust you."

Cerrin spied the spherical face of Dukas, watching her over the shoulder of another man. Sadi was waving everyone forward so they could address the group as one. Even those not involved in the plot were reminding their compatriots to be quiet; they knew they would all suffer if the Vitaari found them assembled like this.

Cerrin and Sadi had agreed to both speak. Though Sadi was new, she shared Palanian heritage with a good portion of the laborers. Cerrin would do her best to convince the Echobe, though she knew most probably still disliked her. She had no idea how the people would respond. The press of the crowd and those expectant faces already made her want to turn and run.

"Speak up then," said someone.

Sadi continued. "Whatever happens, let's keep the noise down." She took a breath. "Now, we'll keep this simple because there's no time. Ever since each of you was brought here, you have not had a choice. Now you do. For the past few weeks we have been working on a tunnel."

Cerrin heard sharp intakes of breath and curses.

To her credit, Sadi pressed on with great composure. "It is now complete. The entrance is hidden amongst the containers beyond Block B. It runs down into the mine, then back up under the wall and comes out just above the river. We can get through in under ten minutes. If we stay together and work together, we can get everyone out before dawn."

For a moment, no one said anything. Then came the questions.

"What do we do then?"

"How did you do it?"

"Won't the sensors pick us up?"

"Surely the Vitaari must know?"

Sadi held up her hand, but the noise didn't stop. "Listen, we can all go; we'll take you in small groups. You can be free."

The questions continued. Some of the laborers even turned away.

"You had no right. No right." Dukas hadn't spoken loudly, but the others quietened. He came forward and stood beside Esteann. "What you have done will bring great suffering to all. You have betrayed us."

"By giving you a way out?" asked Sadi.

"All you have given us is a death sentence. They'll catch us—either here or outside. And then?"

"Tearing," said another man. "They'll tear us for this."

"Shut your mouth," snapped Cerrin. She couldn't believe the spineless Dukas and his ally would use fear to control the others.

Sadi held her by the arm.

Kannalin came forward on her other side. She took the spear he offered but held it low.

As the noise grew again, help came from an unlikely quarter.

"Just listen!" said Esteann, holding up both hands. "Where exactly does this tunnel come out?"

"To the south," replied Sadi. "There are trees for cover. Cross the river and we're safe."

"And there are still some lilies," said the Echobe woman. "Those who can't swim can use them."

"You really think we'll get that far?" countered Dukas. He nodded at Cerrin. "She's tried four times already."

"They can't get to us once we're in the forest." Esteann pointed at Cerrin. "Me and her and others of us here stayed free out there for years."

Torrin—the Echobe woman who had refused to work with the Palanians—also weighed in. "If we keep moving, we can get away. We can do it. "

"We can," said Cerrin. "But we have to go now. There's not long until first light."

"Why now?" asked someone from the back. "Why not in the middle of the night—so we had longer."

They had discussed this: they would not reveal what was happening at Mine Five.

"We have our reasons," said Sadi. "You just have to trust us. We can get every one of you out of here."

"Even if you don't, I'd rather die trying."

Though she couldn't see her, Cerrin knew Serras's voice.

"And shame on any who wouldn't."

"They'll assume we were part of it," said the man who had agreed with Dukas. He was Echobe, but Cerrin had never spoken to him; she knew only that he had been at Thirteen as long as anyone. "The only way is to tell them—at least then only you fools will suffer."

Kannalin touched Cerrin lightly. She nodded. The big man sprang past her and grabbed his fellow Echobe. As they grappled, the man cried out. Cerrin kicked him hard in the knee, felling him in an instant. As he landed, she knocked others aside and placed the point of the spear against his cheek. Lights fell on his terrified face.

"I didn't want it like this," she said. "We're all going. And we're going now." She looked up. "I have to tell you all—for once in his life, Dukas is right. They'll take out the entire shift for this. So you stay, you'll die. Painfully."

Though some of the children and women were crying, Cerrin kept going.

"You can each take one small bag, nothing else. We will go one row at a time. So quietly collect your stuff and start lining up. You don't have to worry about the Vitaari; they'll have plenty to keep them busy."

She moved the spear away from the man's face. "I'd rather use this on them. You with us?"

He nodded. Cerrin and Kannalin helped him to his feet.

People were already hurrying back to their compartments. Cerrin noticed Dukas had not moved. Spear still in her hand, she walked up to him.

"You too."

The Palanian spoke quietly. "These people will die. And their blood will be on your hands."

Cerrin moved toward him so their faces were close. "You do anything to stop us and the only blood on my hands will be yours."

Vellerik was first out of the *Tarikan*. Once clear of the hull, he jumped off the ramp and held the shell in a hover. He turned himself around, then descended, looking up as the others came down the ramp. He checked the scanners were clear, then backed off another ten meters and ordered them to follow.

As the men complied, Triantaa spoke over the open channel.

"Captain, tactical info link established."

Below the cockpit window was the main display. Vellerik had the image set to terrain and now saw his position, that of the other shells, the *Tarikan*, and Mine Five—all indicated by green dots, lines, and arrows.

Once the others were out, he ordered Zarrinda and Saarden to the left while he and Perttiel moved to the right. As he cleared the wing, he adjusted the window's visibility settings once more. The shuttle's passenger lounge was situated at the base of the fin, just behind the cockpit. Among the faces watching the escort, he could make out Talazeer and Viceroy Mennander.

Another reading showed distance to the *Tarikan*'s hull. He and Perttiel eased outward until they reached the agreed one hundred fifty meters.

"Rightward shells in position."

Saarden was in charge of the other pair. "Leftward shells in position."

The pilot answered, "Proceeding on a bearing of 080, height two hundred meters, speed one fifty."

"Acknowledged."

"Departing in three, two…"

Triantaa had already fed the itinerary into the shell's system. "Select waypoint one."

"… one."

The *Tarikan* leapt away. Vellerik and Perttiel stayed together and caught up in their own time. Vellerik kept track of the other two and saw they had maintained positioned well.

He leaned forward and looked down at the ground. Through the darkness, he could just make out the curves of the sand dunes far below.

Sonus was relieved to find his weight calculations were correct. He had finished entering the module selection into the station and now double-checked them before initiating the loading process. The weight limit was two hundred kilos. The twin assault cannons and one thousand rounds took up ninety of that. The extra fuel tank weighed fifty kilos, the deflector field pod just twenty, leaving him with enough capacity for five of the seeker missiles.

He had no idea of the size or strength of the viceroy's ship; he just hoped he had enough firepower to bring it down. His finger was over the EXECUTE command when a voice came through the com-cell.

"Compound patrol, status check."

Sonus ran over to it and picked it up. He knew enough Vitaari words to respond but not what a sentry would typically say.

"Compound patrol, status check."

Sonus found he suddenly couldn't form the right sentence.

"Nullerik—all well?"

Sonus had only ever spoken Vitaar with Kadessis. With no clue of how the guard might sound, he decided to imitate the administrator. He moved the com-cell away from his mouth.

"All well. Repeat, all well."

No reply. Was that a good thing or a bad thing?

The guard's default position was standing in front of the armory. If the man on duty in the tower walked to the window and looked down, he would see he wasn't there. If he didn't see him once, that might not cause alarm: he could be patrolling. But twice? Or if he realized he hadn't reappeared?

Still no reply.

Sonus didn't have time to stand there and think about it. He hurried back to the station and pressed EXECUTE. Two cables attached to the rear of the shell retracted. The arms rose up, and the combat shell stepped forward.

29

Vellerik was almost beginning to enjoy himself; he had forgotten how exhilarating it was to fly the shells at high speed. The approach had passed without incident, and his team hovered over the gloomy compound as the *Tarikan* descended onto the landing strip. Once the shuttle had touched down, he gave the order. Swooping in low over the assembled staff and laborers, he and the other three landed on one corner of the strip.

After a quick check on the status screen, he powered down. The arms of the shell dropped, then the cockpit door popped up. Leaving the com-cell in his ear, he stepped out of the machine and waited for the others before striding to the edge of the strip. There was no need for refueling yet, but they would have to do so later in the morning.

"Good morning, captain."

Governor Urdiss and the rest of the Mine Five reception party had walked over to greet him.

"Governor."

Urdiss anxiously gathered his senior staff around him as a technician declared they were safe to approach the ship. The *Tarikan*'s ramp began to descend.

. . .

Cerrin stayed in the block with Sadi. Kannalin and Trantis escorted each group of five to the tunnel entrance, where Jespa remained on guard. Serras had been sent ahead to the watch the exit beyond the wall while Erras was in charge of getting the escapees from one tunnel to the other.

So far, twenty-five had already left. There seemed little point in dividing the groups into individuals or pairs to avoid attention. If any of the Vitaari bothered to look down at the Block A entrance for any amount of time, they would see what was going on. Cerrin and the others remained sure this was less likely to draw attention than covering or destroying the light.

While Sadi waited by the door to corral those ready to follow Kannalin and Trantis, Cerrin worked on those few who still hadn't come forward. She knew it was best not to give them any chance for doubts and second thoughts, to exploit the passivity many of her fellow prisoners had fallen into.

Yet the questions were endless.

"Won't they see us leave?"

"How big is this tunnel?"

"Surely they must know?"

"What do we do if they discover us?"

Cerrin answered none of them, choosing to repeat only two lines. "Keep moving. This is your chance to be free."

She was holding a lamp, checking the compartments and climbing the ladders where she had to. A few of the faces she glimpsed seemed almost happy—or at least relieved. Most looked terrified.

"We're coming," snapped Dukas as the light hit him. Behind him were five of his fellow Palanians, some of those he claimed to speak for. He led them past Cerrin, who continued on toward the rear of the container.

She then encountered two more Palanians kneeling in front of a compartment. At first, she thought they were praying. Then she realized they were pleading with their son. Cerrin recognized him: Maxis, the youngest child in Mine Three. The Vitaari sometimes used him to clean inaccessible parts of their machines.

The father turned toward the light and stood.

Cerrin had attached a strap to the top half of her spear. She hung it from her shoulder as she approached. "What's wrong?"

"The tunnel," whispered the man. "He can't do it. He can barely stand the mines."

"He must."

"He can't. He will scream."

"You *cannot* stay here."

"You think I don't know that?" hissed the Palanian. "Thanks to you and your friends, we have no choice."

"Gag him—do whatever you have to. But we are all leaving. Now."

"You really are a heartless b—"

Cerrin felt something brush past her. She turned the light and watched Yarni go and stand with the mother, in front of Maxis.

"You can do it," said the girl. "I've been through the tunnel. All the way."

In fact, she had only been through half of the first section: a test to see if the eight children in Block A could manage it. But even she had found it difficult, and Cerrin knew that only fear and relentlessness from her and the others would ensure they got the children and everyone to the river.

Realizing she could do no more good there, she continued her search.

Sonus placed the rifle and the pack in the storage space inside the shell. The main fuel tank was full, and the extra tank attached, along with the other modules. The deflector field pod didn't look particularly impressive: a circular device studded with bronze-colored nodes that had attached itself to the top of the shell. The assault cannons were double-barreled units mounted on the forearms, each with a loading tube running back to the magazines. Affixed to the rear of the shell on one side of the exterior storage pod was the seeker missile system. Sonus had watched as each of the five projectiles was loaded. The half-meter long cylinders were green apart from a single band of orange around the middle; they appeared rather innocuous.

With a final glance at the shafts of sunlight now filtering through the high windows of the main door, he stuck the com-cell into the top pocket of his overalls. He then stepped up into the voluminous interior of the combat shell. His first job was to locate the left-hand sensors, which controlled the vehicle's basic functions. As soon as he reached into the upper arm, a flexible ring fitted itself around his middle finger.

The language was set to Vitaari. There were two steps to complete before anything else. He moved the finger, which in turn moved the indicator on the main screen across a series of option boxes.

security>safety>ally restrictions DISABLE

Sonus had permitted the shell to fire on those carrying ID cards. It unfortunately meant that any other shell could also fire on him, but he didn't plan on leaving any of them usable.

security>command>exterior control override DISABLE

Sonus knew from the manual that shells could be remotely controlled via not only the support station but another hub. He had no idea if the Vitaari had such equipment in the tower, but he wasn't about to risk it.

pilot>position>comfort ENABLE

The flexible padded interior of the shell moved like something organic, fitting itself to Sonus's frame. Straps snaked across his chest and around his legs to hold him in place. He was lifted up at least a foot so he would have a good view through the cockpit window and the main screen mounted beneath it. The arms came up until they were horizontal.

control>terrain ENABLE

Sonus felt movement around his feet—the walking sensors taking their place. He could now move the shell simply by lifting his feet: the machine would replicate the movements.

His next command closed the cockpit door. Sonus took his last few breaths of unregulated air, which reminded him to make a further adjustment he had forgotten.

pilot>environment>detect MODIFY

After hours of studying the manual, he'd eventually realized this was the way to make the shell adjust to the breathing habits of a body type it might not recognize. The door clicked shut, and the interior lights came on.

Sonus paused for a moment. His first few breaths seemed normal but then his throat became tight, as if he wasn't getting enough air into his lungs. Then it seemed as if there were no air in the shell at all. He glanced at the screen.

modifying...

He began to feel faint.

control>cockpit>

The next breath was better, though the air tasted odd. He left the controls alone and waited until his head cleared.

"Nullerik? Where are you? We cannot see you. Nullerik, report."

Sonus knew there was no use continuing the pretense. He reached into the right arm. Two rings attached themselves to his hand: one to his thumb, one to his middle finger. Movement of the thumb dictated direction commands in all three dimensions. Movement of the finger indicated the pace of that movement.

He double-checked that he hadn't yet enabled the flight controls, not knowing what effect that might have while still on the ground.

flight motivator>status

-active-

As soon as Sonus enabled the controls, he could take off.

The broad window seemed go hazy, then abruptly cleared itself. Dread gripped him as he spied a beam of flashlight light outside the armory door. Soon there were several. Any one of the Vitaari could open the door with their IDs.

display>tactical

Green symbols and lines appeared on the window.

weapons>all ARM

equipment>defense>field ENABLE

The field could run for five hundred seconds at full power. Sonus wanted to be away from Fourteen without using more than half of that.

control>automated evasion sequence ENABLE

The last command instructed the shell to switch to auto-pilot in the event of an incoming missile or other heavy ordnance. Sonus knew some of the guards' rifles fired more than just bullets. With no time to consider navigation, he made one more command.

sensors>audio>exterior MAGNIFY

He could hear the Vitaari shouting.

He lifted his left foot, then the right. His legs barely reached into the top of the shell legs so there was little sense of walking, only moving forward as if suspended in mid-air. A sideways movement with the right foot initiated a turn in that direction, which the shell carried out independently.

When they entered, the Vitaari would be looking ahead, toward the support station. He would attack them from the side.

Cerrin knelt beside Yarni. She, Sadi, and the girl were standing together in darkness beside Block A. Kannalin had just taken another group of five to the tunnel. He'd reported that sixty were now with Erras, waiting inside the mine for the others. No one would make for the surface or head for the river until Cerrin and Sadi began their attack. Those who could not face the tunnel had taken themselves to the back of the queue. Trantis was inside the block with the last few.

"You can go to the tunnel now," Cerrin told Yarni. "To help that boy and anyone else you can."

"What about you?"

"I'll be along soon."

"Will you show me the forest?"

"Of course. Now go."

The girl was soon swallowed up by the darkness. Cerrin stood. "By the time we're ready, they should all be underground."

As well as their spears, both women were also carrying two signal flares. They had already discussed their route many times. Cerrin, who had crept around the compound during previous escape attempts, led the way.

There were small lamps placed at regular intervals upon the wall and more powerful lights illuminating the space around buildings, but whole swathes of the compound were left dark. The Vitaari generally deployed only three sentries outside the mine, and Cerrin and Sadi were yet to see any of them.

They ran along the side of the block, then cut across to the landing strip. Reaching the cover of a loading machine, they paused and looked up at the tower. They saw no Vitaari at the windows; it was almost as if they were the only ones in the compound.

"The guards?" whispered Sadi.

"I know. I don't like moving farther until we know where they are."

From what she'd observed, one would always patrol near the armory, also keeping watch on the generator station and the barracks. Another would stay fairly close to the tower, and the third wouldn't stray far from the main gate.

"Come on."

Hunched low, they used the endless rows of fuel barrels to hide them as they jogged along the side of the strip. These containers were no good to them: hard to move and impossible to lift.

Cerrin suddenly felt a hand slap her back. As she halted, Sadi came up beside her. "Look there, past the corner of the warehouse."

The two Vitaari were standing together, half-illuminated by a lamp. Their position was roughly halfway between the tower and the gate.

"That just leaves the armory guard. He won't move far. Let's get the barrels."

They hurried across the middle of the strip, straight to where they knew the smaller barrels were kept. Though a quarter the volume of the standard containers, the women were only just able to lift them—but they could easily be rolled along on their side.

"Remind me again," said Cerrin, who was never confident with anything complicated made of metal.

Sadi took her hand and put it on the lid of the closest barrel. "Find the cap—turn it twice clockwise, then it should detach."

Cerrin had told herself to think of clockwise as to the right.

"Make sure it's laying on its side first. Some of the fuel will leak out, which is what you want. Drag it away to create some distance for when you light it. Then the flare. Take the end with the hollow. Reach inside and pull off the protective strip. Then just push down on the stud. Make sure you're well away from the barrel when you do it. And remember how bright it will be. Throw it onto the fuel and get out of there."

"Got it."

"Remember where you're going to leave it?"

"By the side door, where the protection is weakest."

Cerrin glanced up at the sky. The first smudges of dawn light were beginning to appear. She had a lot farther to travel than Sadi.

"I should go."

"Cerrin, listen, if I have time, I'll move some more barrels in—we might be able to put the tower out of action permanently."

They had agreed Sadi would act first.

"With the two guards near the gate, I'll have to go the back way."

"Agreed."

Sadi gripped Cerrin's shoulder. "See you at the tunnel."

primary weapon>assisted aim>threat identification ENABLE

Sonus waited until the last possible moment. The tactical display superimposed green boxes over each of the Vitaari guards as they approached the armory. The door finally reached the top with a metallic thud.

A large red circle appeared at the bottom of the main screen. Sonus moved the indicator over it.

He heard shouts. One of the Vitaari had seen him—he turned his weapon toward the shell.

Sonus tapped his finger down.

The shell's arms juddered. Artificially dimmed flowers of light bloomed from the assault cannons.

The green boxes turned to green Xs as the cannons shredded the guards. The weapons readjusted constantly, moving to the next target, then the next. The Vitaari bodies were blown backwards. Limbs, weapons, and helmets flew through the air.

Sonus tapped on the circle again, and the firing stopped.

Somehow, one of the Vitaari was still standing. He lurched into the armory and fell face first onto the floor. His rifle spun away into a corner. His outstretched left arm was missing a hand. Black blood seeped out from under him.

Sonus moved his feet, and the shell stomped out of the armory. He closed his eyes and cringed when he realized he was walking across the bodies, but it made no difference to the vehicle.

Feeling suddenly vulnerable once outside, he checked the main screen. The shell's sensors were picking up what looked like dozens of Vitaari on the move, but he couldn't actually see any of them.

The side of the tower was dead ahead. The door opened, and administrators ran—in several different directions. The tower would have to wait: that was not his first target.

Turning the shell to the right, Sonus walked it toward the mine to get some distance. Just as he began to turn back toward the armory, he heard a tapping somewhere behind him. A beep sounded, and the display showed a flashing target to the rear. Realizing the tapping was probably rifle fire striking the shell, he continued the turn.

The guards found cover quickly, running straight into the armory. That helped him.

secondary weapon>target select

He aimed the indicator at the center of the armory. Another green square appeared, then the red dot. He tapped down.

At first, he thought the system had failed. Then he heard a popping sound from above him, and something orange streaked straight through the doorway and into the building.

The blast lit up everything in front of him, and he felt the shell rock back. By the time he'd opened his eyes and the window had adjusted itself, flames and thick black smoke were pouring out of what was left of the armory. A ragged hole had been torn in the roof.

-target destroyed-

By the Maker. The power of this killing machine is incredible.

Again came the popping sound of rifle fire hitting the shell.

control>flight ENABLE

Sonus moved his thumb upward. A cold hollow formed in his stomach as the vehicle rose off the ground. The noise and the display told him that the shell was still taking fire so he pushed his finger forward.

Too fast.

His head was thrown back but protected by the cushioned interior. Stomach twisting, head buzzing, he heard a different tone of warning. A voice spoke in Vitaari.

"Proximity warning, proximity warning."

Only now did he realize he was still flying up. The quickest method of stopping was to tap the rings together.

The shell halted itself smoothly.

All Sonus could see was snow. Then he looked to the right and spied gray slabs of stone: he was staring at Mount Origo.

He checked his altitude: one hundred five meters.

The tower.

The Vitaari would be alerting the other mines of the attack. He had to strike now.

The tactical display wasn't showing any targets. He looked at the main screen. It also showed nothing but darkness and sheeting snow. He couldn't remember how to instruct the sensors to focus on a distant target.

In desperation, he simply moved his thumb down, descending slowly at first, then quicker to a height of forty meters. By then the shell had automatically worked out what he wanted to see.

Lights were coming on all over the compound. He glimpsed figures running from every building. The armory fire seemed to have already spread toward the generator station.

He aimed the missile at the base of the tower and fired.

This time he followed the streak all the way in. The blast sent flame, dust, and material in every direction.

-target destroyed-

The shell swayed slightly. Sonus remembered he could alter the pitch and adjusted it so he was looking down at the compound.

The lights at the top of the tower seemed to be moving. They lurched one way, then the other, then the entire structure fell. The top landed close to the main gate, debris smashing into the wall. A section of scaffolding bounced across the compound and came to a rest on the generator station fence. The resulting cloud of dust actually dampened the fire at the armory, but there were now pockets of flame all over, some not far from the landing strip.

Suddenly, Sonus could hear how hard he was breathing. He knew only two or three minutes had passed since the armory doors had opened. The destruction he had wrought seemed beyond compre-hension.

The alarm pierced his ears.

-auto evade-

The shell seemed to drop out of the air. It hadn't fallen far when Sonus felt as if he had been kicked in the back. Snow streaked past the cockpit as the shell blasted itself forward. Then it veered away to the right. Sonus spied the streaky surface of the mountain coming closer.

Closer.

Too close.

"No!" He actually put his hands up, as if that would do anything.

The shell abruptly dropped straight down again, then he heard a booming explosion from above. What he guessed to be fragments of rock showered the top of the shell. One cracked the window, but it didn't break. The shell swayed from side to side again, then stopped.

-auto evade sequence complete. move to regain control-

Water sprayed onto the screen and a small rod moved across it, cleaning off dust.

Sonus found himself looking at a shadowy hollow within the rock face. He noticed now that the shell did not quite hover smoothly but bobbed up and down as if it were in water.

He spun it around and adjusted the pitch. Far below him, Mine Fourteen burned. He counted eight pockets of flame, the worst of which was where the tower had stood just seconds earlier.

He was so far above the compound that the shell was taking its height reading from the plain—one hundred three thousand meters.

With a moment to breathe, all he had studied began to return to him.

sensors>long-range FULL SPECTRUM

While the systems did their work, Sonus eased the shell away from the rock face and began to descend. He spied the most southerly light on the plateau: the one at the top of the walkway. He imagined Orani hearing the first explosion, the others running out of the caverns.

"Stay there, all of you. Just stay there."

The long-range scans were slowly adding detail to a map, including terrain and artificial structures. It had picked up four mines, including Five and Three.

control>destination>select

He tapped the indicator over the icon for Mine Five: a blue triangle surrounded it.

control>speed MAXIMUM
control>auto-pilot ENGAGE

As the shell swooped down past the edge of the plateau, Sonus checked the diagnostic screen. The only damage listed was to the rear armor paneling and was described as *-superficial/minor-*.

Suddenly he was through the snow and dropping toward the dark yellow surface of the plain. Away to the east, the rising sun was split by the horizon.

30

Gathered outside the tower were the installation's senior adminis-trators and Mennander's bodyguards. Marl was standing alone some distance away, hands clasped behind him, completely still. Vellerik watched the staff watching him; most had seen the Drellen only once before.

Talazeer and the viceroy had been in the tower for some time. Vellerik reckoned they were already behind schedule and Mennander was still scheduled to inspect the workers. He turned and saw the rows of figures lined up in front of their accommodation block. The natives also stood still, heads bowed. Vellerik was relieved to see there were no children.

One of the officers suddenly stepped away from the others and covered his ear, listening intently.

Vellerik's com-cell beeped and Triantaa spoke. "Captain, priority message from Officer Kerreslaa."

"Captain?" Kerreslaa sounded anxious.

"Vellerik here."

"Five minutes ago someone at Mine Fourteen activated a general alert, but we can't raise anyone there."

Vellerik didn't bother asking if any personal coms had been pick-ed up. Due to the facility's unusual position on Mount Origo, only signals sourced through the main array had any chance of getting out. "Has that ever happened before?"

"Not once."

"We'll move the count and the viceroy back to the shuttle. Keep me informed."

Vellerik hurried over to the bodyguards. "We've lost contact with Fourteen—it's not far from here. I suggest we get them back in the *Tarikan* and stay mobile. At least until we know more."

"Agreed," said one of the bodyguards. The other ran into the tower.

Though difficult, Cerrin had decided it was a lot quieter—and therefore a lot safer—to carry the barrel. Had she not done so, she may never have heard the footsteps behind her.

She'd just passed Block A and was heading straight across the compound toward the generator station when she halted and turned. A large figure flashed past the light outside the block, heading toward the tower. It took her mind several seconds to process what she had seen.

Dukas. Alone. Moving quickly.

Cerrin put the barrel down and followed the shape through the darkness. She glanced over her shoulder. The guard on duty at the armory was leaning against the wall, at least a hundred feet away. She slipped her spear from her shoulder, held it in one hand and gave chase.

Having sacrificed stealth for speed, she wasn't surprised when Dukas turned around, his eyes catching what little light there was.

"Who's there?" he asked, voice faint.

The reply came swiftly.

Holding the shaft of the spear with both hands, Cerrin ran at him and jabbed the blunt end into his face. The wood struck with a low crack. Dukas tottered backwards then fell. Cerrin didn't give him a chance to react. She knelt down beside him and placed the shaft against his throat.

As he spluttered something, she pushed it down. "I'd speak very quietly if I were you."

"Cerrin?"

She looked up. They were worryingly close to the reach of the lamp over the tower door, and the sky was getting lighter all the time. The only Vitaari she could see was the armory guard, who thankfully hadn't moved.

"Cerrin, is that you?"

Ever since she had risen from her bed, Cerrin had felt an unshakeable confidence in her every action, a certainty Ikala was with her. After the endless worry and fear, now there was only what needed to be done.

"What were you doing?" she demanded.

"I—I—"

"Where were you going? The tower?"

"No. I—"

He stopped. There was nothing he could say that would convince her; it seemed they both knew it.

All she could see of him was his eyes. They were no more than pale dots; they didn't seem to belong to a person.

"Cerrin, I swear—I will go now. I will come with you. You can use me, I—"

She spun the spear and drove the sharpened end into his throat. As he struggled, she stood on his chest and held the spear down on him. His body began to shake. Choking breaths escaped so she pushed even harder.

Noise.

An administrator stepped out of the tower. Cerrin dropped low and bowed her head to obscure her eyes. She kept her weight on the spear and listened. When she heard fast-moving footsteps, she looked up and glimpsed the Vitaari's robes as he strode away toward the barracks.

Dukas had gone still beneath her. She lifted the spear and moved off him. He was not breathing.

She had only ever killed animals before. But she knew some of those kills would trouble her more. Those creatures hadn't deserved it; she could easily have let them be. Dukas had given her no choice. Even so, it took her a few precious moments to compose herself.

She put the spear over shoulder and retraced her steps. It took a frustratingly long time to locate the barrel, which she eventually did by walking into it. Knowing Sadi might start the attack at any time, she took a wide route around the lights at the front of the generator station but moved as fast as she could. Other than a brief sighting of the armory guard and an engineer exiting the mine, she spotted no Vitaari.

Once at the station's side door, she tipped the barrel over and pulled out the cap. As the fuel glugged out, she dragged the barrel several meters away, then let go. She retrieved a flare from her overalls, stepped away from the barrel and removed the protective strip. As the light might easily give her away, she turned away from the compound and pressed down on the stud. Green light fizzed from the other end.

She was about to throw it when darkness became light. Something whistled over her head and a wave of heat hit her. Instinct and shock sent her to the ground. When she recovered herself, she saw a fountain of flame beside the tower. A moment later, an alarm sounded.

Cerrin held up the flare. It had gone out. She threw it aside, pulled out the second one and ignited it. Having seen the size of the blast Sadi had caused, she took five more steps backwards, then threw it. The flare landed in the tongue of liquid left on the ground.

The fuel was already alight when she turned and ran for the accommodation blocks. She had taken no more than ten paces when the barrel went up. Another wave of heat hit her back, but so did a concussive force that sent her sprawling. She threw out her hands but came down hard on her front, scraping her hands and knees.

Wincing at the pain, she forced herself up. The explosion had taken out much of the fence and blackened the side of the generator station, but the flames were already dying. She saw two Vitaari guards run out of the barracks and more approaching from the gate.

Another administrator exited the tower just as another blast went up. Momentarily blinded, Cerrin turned and lurched away. Then came a third explosion. When she looked back, the whole of the tower was enveloped by flame. From within came a figure.

Hair, face, and clothes aflame, the Vitaari slowed to a walk, then pitched forward. As he burned, Cerrin felt a surge of satisfaction. Seeing the invaders suffer was as pleasurable as she'd hoped.

Now she knew why Sadi had taken so long: she'd moved two more barrels into position by the tower. As Cerrin neared the block, she heard a shout over the noise of the alarm.

"Here! Stay out of the light."

Cerrin rubbed her eyes, which still hadn't recovered from the flash of light.

"Sadi?"

"With me."

The Palanian emerged out of the darkness and grabbed her arm. Together, they ran around the rear of the latrine and toward Block B. Cerrin could hear bellowed commands coming from the mine.

"Don't look back," said Sadi. "Are you hurt?"

"No."

Once past Block B, they turned into the gap between the containers.

But their path was blocked—by people.

"What the—" Sadi didn't finish her sentence.

Cerrin couldn't see their faces, and none of them spoke. The only light was distant and faint, close to the tunnel.

"What's going on?" said Sadi. "You should be through by now."

Cerrin pushed her way forward. "Move. Out of the way."

When she eventually reached the tunnel entrance, she found Jespa holding the light.

"What's going on?"

"Someone got stuck. Kannalin went down to help." Jespa aimed the light downward. A woman looked up, her dirty face streaked with tears. From below came the sounds of weeping and shouting.

"You have a knife, don't you?"

Jespa took out a short blade.

Cerrin snatched it from him, knelt down and gave it to the woman. "Pass this down. And an order to Kannalin. He is to use it on anyone who won't move."

The woman just stared at the blade.

"Do it," hissed Cerrin.

As the woman took it, she turned to Sadi. "You'll keep them moving?"

"Yes. What about you?"

Cerrin took the spear from her shoulder. "I'll stand guard. They'll be coming."

Mine Five was not difficult to spot. Sunlight sparked off the metal walls, and it was the only visible structure upon the apparently endless plain. At five kilometers, Sonus halved his speed. He had used more than two thirds of his fuel: even now he would not have enough to reach Mine Three.

The shell had picked up a brief burst of communications on a general channel, but now that had gone dead. The scanners were showing a large vessel within the compound beginning to ascend. Sonus could not be certain it was the viceroy's shuttle, but it seemed likely: the shell was also detecting coms emanating from the vessel, but the messages were encoded.

During the journey across the great dunes of Skakka's Bight, he had kept himself occupied by constantly checking the shell's numerous systems. He didn't want to give himself time to think.

He cut his speed to one quarter and disengaged the auto-pilot, then moved to the east to ensure he had the sun at his back. The window took a moment to adjust. Now he could see detail: the reinforced gate at the front of the mine, the glittering tower, the roof of the warehouse. And now the fin of a large Vitaari ship.

deflector field ACTIVATE

secondary weapon>target select

The system began listing the ship's designation and characteristics. One sentence was flashing,

-capability: counter-measures-

Sonus selected a command box he had already used three times, usually with helpful results.

-recommendation?-

The shell's system gave no answer.

Talazeer had resisted, which meant Vellerik had to enter the tower and reason with him. The count refused to believe anything could really be wrong and only relented when Mennander agreed the sensible course of action was to return to the *Tarikan* until they knew precisely what had occurred at Mine Five.

The result of this delay was that Vellerik was last into his shell. The other three were ready to take off, and the shuttle was already up and maneuvering.

"Sir, shall we follow the *Tarikan*?" asked Zarrinda.

Before Vellerik could reply, Triantaa cut in.

"Captain, we have a shell approaching from the east. Kerreslaa thought it was trying to get a message out from Five, but it's not answering hails from the tower."

"Notify the shuttle pilot, tell him to get out of here. Maximum speed. Men, get up and intercept that shell."

Vellerik's cockpit door had only just shut. As he activated the controls, he glimpsed the first of the others take off.

Sonus kept low, almost below the top of the wall. Above him, the ship shadowed half the mine as it turned. The sheer size of it was startling, and the gold circle of the imperial standard blazed under the sun's glare. Toward the rear were the three cylinders of an engine block not unlike that of the planet's shuttle, though twice the size.

secondary weapon>target select

Sonus knew he didn't have long. He locked the green square on the middle of the engine block as it swung away from him. He tapped down.

He heard the pop, saw the missile streak toward the ship. Something flashed on the side of the shuttle. The explosion was disappointingly small and some distance from the vessel.

Counter-measures.

Sonus cursed. What now?

He spied two white shapes zooming up from the mine, then a third.

Combat shells.

Sonus told himself to concentrate on the shuttle, which was now moving across his field of vision, building up speed. He ascended and guided the shell toward it.

-threat detected-

Now in a triangular formation, the Vitaari pilots came up quickly between his position and the shuttle.

-deflector field: active-

Sonus never saw what was fired at him: only the shimmering blue light that flashed in front of the shell for several seconds. He had no idea how the field worked, but the vehicle seemed to have sustained no damage.

Resisting the urge to watch the enemy shells, he saw a heat haze appear behind the shuttle's engine block. The green square was still locked onto it.

He tapped down, and the second missile blasted away.

-threat detected-

-threat detected-

Again came the blue light, but this time he heard popping sounds and impacts on the shell. One of the Vitaari was flying straight at him.

Sonus froze. Should he trust the field or engage the auto-evade?

Then came the explosions. The first was a bloom of fire just like those at the armory. A curved section from one of the three cylinders fell from the shuttle's engine block, followed by dozens of bits of debris. The nose of the vessel dipped slightly, but it continued to accelerate away.

The second explosion was a colossal blast that sent huge sections of the engine block spinning through the air. One tore into the fin, shredding panels off it. Another shot downward, hitting the wall of the compound before crashing into the dust.

Sonus glimpsed one of the Vitaari shells spiraling toward the ground.

Then the shockwave struck. Warm air suddenly filled the cockpit, and his body was pressed backwards. As invisible forces tugged at him, the shell was sent spinning away, end over end.

Vellerik cleared the wall of Mine Five just as the *Tarikan* came down.

The rear of the shuttle was a blackened mess, with smoke issuing from countless places and ragged sections of the hull hanging at unlikely angles. Most of the engine block was gone.

He could see emergency maneuvering jets firing on the underside, but with no propulsion from the main block they would not keep the vessel in the air. The pilot—who had been shouting ever since the missile strike—had now gone quiet.

"Triantaa?"

Vellerik received no answer.

At a height of about eighty meters, the ship suddenly listed to the right, then fell out of the sky. Picking up speed quickly, it plummeted downward, bow now aiming at the ground. Vellerik knew those in the cockpit stood no chance. The lounge was behind it, where the passengers would be.

Tarikan hit with a noise he heard even inside the shell. The delicate masts of the sensor array snapped off first. As the bow crumpled, the rest of the vessel came after it like the body of some great fallen beast. When the underside struck, the impact seemed to shatter the fin, the top third of which fell to the ground. Clouds of dust blew up, but there were no further explosions.

"I've got him."

Vellerik recognized the voice. Zarrinda sounded frantic.

"Zarrinda, where are the others?"

He checked his display—there were no signals coming from either Perttiel or Saarden's shells.

"Engaging now, captain."

"Zarrinda?"

Sonus tried to focus on the main screen, but everything was moving. The next spin was too much for his stomach. He vomited down his chin and the front of his overalls. He tried to suck in air, but it was so warm it almost made him throw up again.

Then the shell seemed to slow. It righted itself and eased to a holding position. The warm air dissipated. Sonus looked out through the window, but all he could see below was yellow earth. He wasn't even sure of his altitude. The diagnostic screen offered various messages, none of which he really understood.

The tactical display showed a shell closing in rapidly.

-threat detected-

The Vitaari was coming at him from his left. Sonus couldn't see him.

-deflector inoperable-

Multiple impacts struck the shell. The left arm suddenly sagged and sparks burst out of something below one of the minor screens.

-auto-evade inoperable-

Then Sonus remembered he had a missile left. The system was already tracking. He confirmed the target and fired. Once the missile was away, he took command of the controls and sent the shell toward the surface.

The enemy assault cannons did no more damage. He never actually saw the shell, only the message.

-target destroyed-

• • •

"Send down the rest of the troop from the *Galtaryax*."

"Yes, captain," replied Kerreslaa, his voice shaky.

"And tell Governor Urdiss to keep his men inside the mine for now. This isn't over."

Vellerik closed in on the enemy shell at half-speed. He saw two alternatives. Either one of the natives had somehow commandeered the vehicle or a Vitaari had lost his mind and turned on his compatriots. Such things did occasionally happen. But when he saw the shell descending slowly with no apparent concern for his approach, he realized the former was far more likely. What he needed to know was whether the pilot had another seeker missile. The auto-evade system only worked half the time and evidently hadn't been enough to save Zarrinda. With no deflector shield, Vellerik was vulnerable.

But so was the enemy pilot. Because he probably didn't know that seeker missiles had a proximity limiter of thirty meters. If Vellerik stayed close, he was safe.

All the displays were now flashing on and off. A small fire had started inside the cockpit but had been rapidly extinguished by some sort of foam. When he saw another enemy shell pop up on the tactical display, Sonus accelerated and headed for the ground. The vehicle was shuddering with every movement. He wasn't sure how long it would stay in the air. He flew toward the fallen shuttle. The smoking wreck offered cover.

Vellerik tried to ignore the traffic coming through coms. It seemed there was also some sort of incident unfolding at Mine Three.

He was now certain the pilot didn't have a missile, which made things a lot easier. And judging by the awkward motion of the shell, he wouldn't need to do much to bring it down.

Vellerik waited until he was close to the optimum firing distance, then activated both cannons.

As the shell neared the shuttle, bullets tore into it.

. . .

Every thump rocked the vehicle. Half of the displays were now black, and Sonus could hear a loud hissing noise in his right ear. He had already tried to engage the auto-pilot, but it wouldn't work.

He threw the shell to the right, and the impacts stopped. Ahead were two columns of smoke rising from the wreck of the shuttle. As he flew through one, the shell suddenly dropped.

-severe damage/multiple systems-
-structural failure-
-auto-eject inoperable-

Another impact, louder this time.

He flew past the wreck, then saw nothing but yellow earth. He tried to check his altitude, but the display was off. He moved his fingers, but the shell wasn't answering. The vehicle dipped again, then rolled over onto its back.

The shell bounced once, then came down hard. Metal screeched. Sonus pulled his arms in just as one of the shell's hands was torn off.

Above him was blue sky.

He saw his mother and father. He saw Karas and Qari.

I did it. I hurt them.

I did it.

Vellerik landed halfway between the *Tarikan* and the downed shell. Once the cockpit was open, he jumped straight out and drew his sidearm. He looked first toward the shell, which was about thirty meters away. Though it was largely intact and had come down on its back, there was no sign of movement.

He selected an all channels broadcast. "This is Captain Vellerik. Can anyone in the *Tarikan* hear me? Is anyone still alive?"

No response.

The front section of the viceroy's ship was so smashed he couldn't make out a single feature, not even a window. The body behind it was basically intact but disfigured by a long, jagged wound. Scattered across the sand were several bodies. It was as if a child's toy had been shaken, releasing dolls from within.

Vellerik first spied the viceroy's guards, bodies covered by dust and blood. Then he saw Triantaa. The loyal lieutenant had landed on his side, both arms twisted and limp. He had been thrown clear with such force that his safety straps had broken—one section of material lay across his chest. Triantaa stared up at the sky, eyes and mouth open. The effect was grotesquely comic, and Vellerik knelt beside him to close them: give him some dignity.

Hearing a weak cough, he hurried over to the next body—the smallest of them all. Viceroy Mennander was lying on his back, blood leaking from ears, nose, and mouth. Only his eyes were moving, and they suddenly fixed on Vellerik, who saw shock and anger and outrage. Mennander's hand moved to the circular imperial clasp over his chest, fingers trembling as he gripped the metal disc. It was the last thing he ever did.

Hearing the groan of metal, Vellerik looked up to see another segment of the fin come away from the hull and hang there, suspended by multicolored cables.

Other than the pilots, who were surely dead, only Talazeer and Marl were not accounted for. As he looked around for some sign of them, Vellerik spied a figure pull itself out of the fallen shell. He raised his gun and ran toward it.

Sonus drank in the fresh air. His back ached, and something sharp had sliced across his thigh—leaving a thin gash—but other than that he seemed to be all right. Narrowing his eyes against the glare, he stepped over the battered arm of the shell, then realized he had forgotten the rifle.

As he turned back to retrieve it, he heard a Vitaari voice.

"Don't move."

Sonus couldn't see much and didn't dare shade his eyes.

The figure advanced. It was the soldier, the older Vitaari officer who had been with Talazeer the day Tanus was killed. In his hand was a small weapon with a triangular barrel. It was aimed directly at Sonus's chest.

"Who are you?" asked the Vitaari, again in his own language.

"My name is Sonus."

"From Mine Fourteen?"

He nodded.

"You have caused a lot of damage—killed four of my men and many others."

"If it matters—only because they got in my way. I came to kill the viceroy."

"It would appear you have succeeded." The Vitaari moved aside and nodded toward one of the bodies. "I do not remember the last time a viceroy was assassinated."

An assassin, thought Sonus as he looked at the lifeless body of the Vitaari leader. *Is that what I am?*

Sonus noticed something move upon the damaged shuttle. Two figures were climbing out of a hatch just below the fin. Even from that distance, one of them was easily recognizable. Sonus knew he could do nothing for the other rebels now, but he did not want to die like Tanus.

"You are Captain Vellerik, correct?"

"I am."

"You once showed mercy to a man like me. I beg you—kill me now."

Vellerik backed away and turned so he could see whatever the rebel had noticed while keeping him in his peripheral vision.

Count Talazeer—the remains of his cloak hanging from his back like a rag—was being helped down the side of the shuttle by Marl.

Vellerik glanced back at the rebel. The man seemed unexceptional: average build, pale and haggard, even for one of the laborers. And yet, there was an undeniable spark in those eyes, something more than anger or determination.

It seemed almost beyond comprehension that he had been able to steal a shell, escape Fourteen, and bring down the shuttle. Vellerik told himself he should hate this man. He should, and yet he did not. He was long past telling himself what he should think.

He was sorry for Triantaa, Zarrinda, and the others; and he wished he'd been killed instead of them. But this man in front of him? He had shown tenacity and courage almost beyond belief.

The truth was, Vellerik admired him.

31

Cerrin was last into the tunnel.

She had no idea how long she had stood guard while the others made their way down. The wait seemed agonizing, but she hadn't dared leave her position. Standing there in the darkness, fingers gripping the spear, she had half-expected the Vitaari to appear at any moment.

Yet it was not difficult to see why they might be occupied. There was clearly plenty of flammable material within the base of the tower because the fire had taken hold. Despite the efforts of the drones dropping water and foam, wreaths of flame were now shooting fifty yards into the air. Every level of the structure was belching smoke. Two separate alarms were blaring across the compound. She had seen more guards running out of the mine but little indication they were concerned about the inhabitants of Block A.

For the briefest moment, she considered going in search of some of the night shift. It was maddening to offer one half of the workers freedom without the other half even knowing, but it was simply too risky. She also thought it possible that if the night shift genuinely knew nothing of the plot, the Vitaari might not take reprisals against them.

Left without a light, she simply kept scrabbling forward until she caught up with someone.

"Cerrin?"

Sadi had her head flashlight on. Lying next to her was the young Palanian boy, Maxis.

"What is it?"

Sadi adopted a tone of voice Cerrin had never heard from her before. "Maxis is a little scared, but he's feeling better now. He'll come along with me in a moment."

"We don't have—"

Cerrin stopped; she had to trust Sadi to handle this.

"I sent his parents and everyone else ahead. Cerrin, some are already across the river."

Thank the gods and ancients.

She placed her hand on the Palanian's arm as she passed her, then crawled on as fast as she could. Once out and down the rope, she found a small group gathered there. Among them were Serras—who was holding a flashlight—plus Kannalin and Maxis's parents.

"What are they doing?" implored his mother.

"They're coming now."

Cerrin took Kannalin's arm and led him away from the others. She looked along the shaft and into the mine. There was no sign of activity. On the other side of the machine, a single light illuminated huddled bodies.

"How many left to go?"

"Around a third."

From above came the boom of another explosion.

"Sounds like they've got some problems up there," said Kannalin with a grin.

"One of them will notice what's going on sooner or later. If they come around from the gate, we can at least try to hold them off while the rest get across."

"I'll go and help Erras."

Just as Kannalin hurried away toward the second tunnel, another—much more powerful—explosion shook the mine. Cerrin staggered and covered her head as dust fell from above. Wiping her face, she heard one of the others cry out.

She arrived in time to see Maxis's father snatch the flashlight from Serras. He ran to the wall and aimed it upward.

The tunnel had collapsed. In fact, it looked almost as if there had never been a tunnel. All that remained was the rope.

"Maxis!" shrieked the mother.

"Keep her quiet," snapped Cerrin as she gripped the rope and hauled herself upward. Where so many people had climbed down, there were indentations in the wall. She kicked her feet in to make more of a hold, held the rope with one hand, and began to scoop away earth.

"Serras, find a trowel if you can. Sadi? Sadi?"

She could hear the mother sobbing as her fingers clawed away. Once again, she lost track of time, ignoring the pain in her feet and hands as she worked. Serras returned and passed up the trowel. Cerrin swapped hands and hacked at the earth. Once she had cleared a couple of feet, she was able to lean into the space and do more.

"Give me the light."

She put the flashlight by her side.

Images of the two lying just yards away, mouths and eye sockets filled with earth came to her. She increased the pace, digging with both the trowel and her spare hand.

"Do you see them?" asked the mother, voice wracked with pain.

Cerrin was about to drive the trowel in again when she noticed something to the left. Two fingers. Sadi's fingers.

She was almost afraid to touch them. But she did. She scrabbled away more earth until she could hold the whole hand. It was cold. Lifeless.

"Do you see them?"

Cerrin felt numb. She let go, then grabbed the hand and shook it, as if she could somehow wake Sadi. But her friend and ally was not asleep. She was dead. The boy too.

May the gods welcome you.

With that, Cerrin put the matter aside. She would mourn them later. She took the flashlight and let herself down the rope. The mother grabbed her by the arm. "Where's my boy?"

"I'm sorry."

The mother gazed into her eyes and saw the truth of it. She let go of her and backed away. The father tried to take her in his arms, but she pushed him off. She was breathing even harder than Cerrin.

"You're bleeding," said Serras. She lifted Cerrin's hands. The nails and fingers of both were streaked with red.

"No." The mother fell to her knees. "No, no, no." With every repetition, the words grew louder until they were almost a scream.

Cerrin knelt in front of the woman and held her by the shoulders. "He's gone. Sadi too. They would want us to live. And that's exactly what you're going to do. Can you be quiet for me?"

The woman's eyes seemed to pass through several different states before she finally nodded and removed Cerrin's hands. Her head dropped. Cerrin brought her husband forward.

"We don't have much time."

He put an arm over his wife's shoulder and led her away.

Cerrin passed the flashlight back to Serras. "Go."

She snatched a last glance at what remained of the tunnel, then followed.

Vellerik watched them. Showing a strength that belied his slender frame, Marl lifted Count Talazeer off the crushed hull and lowered him to the ground.

Talazeer sat there for a few moments. Half of his face was covered with blood and patches of his hair had been burned away. Much of his clothing was blackened and torn, and he appeared to be missing a boot. He looked up, saw the bodies scattered across the sand.

As he struggled to his feet, Marl had to hold him up. The count staggered toward the viceroy's body. Once there, he gazed downward, head lolling, face twitching, as if he could not believe what he saw. Suddenly pushing his bodyguard off, he lurched away, took a few steps and then fell. Marl rushed to him, but the count got to his knees once more. Pointing toward the native, he bellowed something.

The Drellen—whose cloak still covered him—hesitated for a moment, then walked across the sand with that peculiarly smooth gait that always suggested a predator approaching its prey.

"Please—kill me now," said Sonus.

Vellerik pointed at the ground. "Face down, hands behind your head."

"I beg you. Please."

"Do not talk."

The rebel lay down.

Vellerik turned toward Marl. The clawed feet moved quickly, cloak flicking up in the breeze behind him. The Drellen ran his long, clawed fingers over his head as he came to a halt.

"It appears you have failed yet again, captain. The viceroy is dead. That quiet retirement of yours now seems rather unlikely."

"The count?"

"Burning fuel dripped onto his face while he was trapped inside. He'll need a lot of work. But he still has enough strength in him to seek retribution."

Marl reached inside the cloak and pulled out his sword. He walked up to the rebel and placed the square tip of the blade on his head. When the native looked up, Marl gestured at him to rise.

"You'll leave him there," said Vellerik.

The Drellen spoke without turning around. "I don't think the count currently has the presence of mind to be interested in what this rebel knows, captain. He gave me specific instructions to slice him up slowly. Piece by piece."

"Leave him."

This time, Marl did turn. The triangular teeth flashed when he saw the sidearm was now aimed at him. It took Vellerik a moment to realize the narrow white barrel of the Drellen's disruptor was poking out of the sleeve of his cloak.

"I had a feeling you'd do something like this," said Marl, yellow eyes gleaming. "You must know it's over for you now. Shame and humiliation are all that awaits."

Vellerik actually hadn't given it much thought. It all came down to one simple fact: he'd rather see the viceroy, the count, and this skinner piece of shit dead than the rebel. It was the only thing that made sense to him anymore.

"For you, maybe."

Sun glinted off the Drellen's blade, which was still pointing at the ground. "Come now, captain. My disruptor's firing mechanism is far more sensitive than that antique, and a beam travels faster than a bullet. Not to mention the fact that you are an old man."

Vellerik kept his eyes on the Drellen and moved his finger onto the trigger.

Sonus knew his best chance was for them to occupy each other. From the looks of things, the alien creature held an advantage. He decided to try and remove it.

The rebel's kick struck Marl just above his foot.

Vellerik fired as he spun around, hitting his shoulder. The impact slammed the Drellen backwards, but he remained on his feet. Vellerik knew the caliber of the bullets was small, but he'd expected to at least knock him down.

The disruptor barrel twitched, but no beam appeared. Marl's face twisted; he couldn't use the wounded arm. But that didn't stop him from moving the other one.

As Vellerik squeezed the trigger, the Drellen leaped forward and swung the sword. The tip of blade cut across Vellerik's hand and into the weapon. Pain pulsed through him. The sidearm fell.

Marl leaped high into the air, cloak streaming out behind him.

Vellerik tried to follow the arc, half-blinded by the sun.

As the shadow bore down on him, he lashed out with his good hand and hit something hard. He heard a grunt as Marl landed some distance away.

Vellerik's eyes cleared. The Drellen leaped to his feet and advanced, teeth bared, sword out in front of him.

Vellerik looked around for something—anything—to block with. Blood was leaking from his right hand, and one of his fingers seemed to be hanging by no more than a strip of skin. He clenched his fist, tried to shut off the pain.

"What shall I take off first?" hissed Marl, whose own right arm was hanging limply by his side. The disruptor lay on the ground not far from Vellerik's sidearm.

Still retreating, Vellerik tried to turn to the left—back toward the weapons—but Marl cut him off.

"Well, captain? Scalp? Ear? Nose?"

Sonus could have taken the rifle and helped the old soldier, but he could not be sure the Vitaari would let him go. If his compatriots at Mine Three needed him, he had to get there now—while these two were occupied and before reinforcements could arrive.

He crawled away, using the shell for cover, then got to his feet. He scanned the wrecked ship for any sign of another threat but saw nothing. It was difficult to run, but his leg didn't give way until he reached the second vehicle.

Grimacing as he picked himself up, Sonus pulled out the ID and held it against the left hand of the soldier's abandoned shell. For several terrible seconds the sensor did not react, but then came the reassuring beep. He opened the cockpit door.

"You. Who are you?"

Count Talazeer crawled across the sand toward him, one eye open and bright, the other closed and encrusted with blood. His forehead was terribly blistered, and one ear had been burned beyond recognition.

Sonus felt no shame at seeing the Vitaari so injured, only a grim satisfaction at eliminating the viceroy and showing Talazeer what it was to suffer.

"We have met. Not long ago." With his next words, Sonus surprised himself: "I am a free man of Corvos."

With that, he climbed into the cockpit.

The count couldn't move any farther, but he stretched out his hand. He coughed, and watery black blood slid down his chin.

"I will crush you all," raged the Vitaari. "Every last one of you."

Vellerik did not feel strong. Not for the first time that day, he wondered what toll the drugs had taken on his reactions. He was badly injured, but he had been badly injured before.

As the Drellen came on, darting and feinting, Vellerik could barely keep track of the blade. The sand was splattered with thick gouts of his blood. He tightened the fist again, but it felt almost as if his life was draining out of him.

Marl turned to the side, sword still out in front.

Vellerik felt himself stumble.

Marl was not slow to see the opportunity.

As the blade arced toward him, Vellerik threw up his injured hand: it wasn't much use to him now anyway.

The sword sliced through the flesh of his forearm and rang as it struck bone.

Pain splintered through his head, but Vellerik forced himself on. The sword was stuck. He threw himself forward, grabbed a handful of the Drellen's cloak, and hauled him close. Marl was still trying to retrieve his blade, but now Vellerik had gripped his injured arm close to the shoulder. He shifted it up to the bullet hole and squeezed.

He feels the pain. Not me.

Not me.

For all the surprising power he could generate, the Drellen was no match for a large Vitaari at close quarters. Vellerik pressed his fingers down, felt them break through the scaly skin.

Marl's black tongue slithered out from between his teeth. His neck was spasming.

Vellerik felt whatever passed for Drellen blood covering his fingers as he squeezed through the skin and felt bone.

Marl gave up on his sword.

Knowing what was coming, Vellerik let go and swung a punch at him. But the Drellen would always be quicker. Marl's good hand caught him across the throat, claws tearing out skin like a raptor.

Vellerik tottered backwards and almost fell.

Marl gave a brief glance at his crushed arm, then raised his good hand. Two of the green claws were dripping black blood.

"You see, captain, I always keep two of them long—for such occasions."

A dark fog encroached on Vellerik's vision. His throat was now as wet as his hand.

No pain. Fight.

Fight!

Using his left hand, he clutched the handle of the sword and levered it out of his arm. Stars exploded in his eyes, but he somehow stayed on his feet.

Vellerik tried to raise the sword.

Marl walked toward him.

Fight!

Vellerik slashed at him, but the Drellen avoided it easily.

"Death is close, old man. I could make the end easy for you. Then again..."

Marl leapt at him.

Vellerik saw a flash of sky then teeth close to his face.

He felt a claw tear into his cheek, then into his head, then into his throat again. His skin was torn again and again until the pain fused into a single, suffocating wave. Then it just seemed to go away.

He saw Seevarta on the island, waiting for him. He was swimming toward her, but his head kept sinking below the water. With his last glimpse, he saw her waving. He fell into the black depths. He knew there was no way back.

He fell deeper and deeper until there was only darkness around him.

32

Cerrin hauled herself toward the light. Though she was shocked to hear the shouts of the people beyond the wall, the noise from the compound was even louder. There had been two more blasts, each one sending earth down onto her. Twice she had laid there alone, hands over her head, fully expecting to meet the same fate as Sadi. But this section of tunnel was not directly below the compound and had remained intact.

The brightness of the morning was equally shocking. Kannalin took her arm and helped her out. She looked first to the right: if they came, the Vitaari would exit the gate and approach from that direction. She saw only the broad figure of Trantis standing behind a tree, watching for them.

Kannalin shook his head as he gestured down the slope. "We never even thought of it—a lot of the Palanians can't swim."

At least two dozen people were in the water, most using smaller lilies as floats to get them across. Three children were lying on the plants, being pushed across by adults.

From what Cerrin could see, roughly half had crossed to the other side, a quarter were on their way, and another quarter were still on this side of the river. Those on the far bank were barely visible amongst the dense scorra bushes.

"Too slow," she said between gritted teeth.

"Where's Sadi?"

Cerrin told him. Then she spied a prone figure lying in the grass about twenty feet away. Kneeling close by it was young Yarni.

Cerrin ran to them. Serras was on her side, gray hair across her face. She could hardly keep her eyes open.

"It's my heart, girl. You young ones best leave me here."

"No." Yarni grabbed her wrist and tried to pull her up.

Cerrin put out a hand to stop her. "Can you swim?"

Yarni nodded.

"Down to the river. I'll see you on the other side."

The girl was still holding Serras's arm. Cerrin pried her hand away. "I'll bring Serras with me. Go now."

Yarni ran away down the slope.

Cerrin was relieved to see Esteann and her group helping the weaker members across. Torrin was hauling a child up onto the far bank.

Serras put her hand to Cerrin's face. "You are a strong one, girl. I always knew you would…"

Serras said no more. Her hand fell across her chest and her eyes became still.

"Cerrin!"

Kannalin pointed along the wall. A lone Vitaari had appeared and was watching them. At that distance it was difficult to see if it was a guard or an administrator. The figure retreated and disappeared.

Cerrin pulled her spear off her back. "Kannalin, bring those."

He followed her down the slope with a bundle of spears.

Once at the river, she was horrified to find several Palanians— four women and one man—still hesitant about entering the water. She grabbed the man and spun him around. "Unless you wish to die by having your arms and legs torn from your body, you will get yourself in that water."

She pushed him off the bank. As he stumbled into the river, the women followed. About fifteen men had stayed on the near side.

"They'll be here soon," she told them. "We have to make sure they fire at us"—she gestured at the river—"not them." Then she pointed at a small copse of trees halfway between the water and the wall. "We'll use that for cover. Take a spear. If you think you can do some damage, throw it. If not, wait until you're in close."

Without waiting to see who would follow, she raced across the slope toward the trees.

It seemed to take an age to discern the metallic walls of Mine Three from the sprawl of the Great Forest beyond. The apparently endless swath of green gave Sonus great hope: surely anyone who sought refuge there had a chance of escape.

He checked the display again. The shell had been drawing fuel from the reserve tank for a while. From what he could work out, he had less than five minutes' flying time. Forcing himself to ignore the ever-growing pain in his back, he brought up the tactical display. First, he checked—as he had at regular intervals—that nothing was approaching from the rear. Then he focused the scanners on Mine Three and magnified the images.

With the tower and much of the compound ablaze, the scene was not unlike what he had left behind at Fourteen—with one obvious exception. The armory door was open and several shells were marching out. As he closed to within a kilometer, Sonus turned his attention to the assault cannons, which still had more than three quarters of their ammunition left.

primary weapon>select target

Cerrin snatched a glance over her shoulder as they approached the trees. Though grateful for the help, she could not believe how slowly some of the men were moving.

"There!" Trantis was the only one ahead of her.

A squad of six Vitaari guards ran out from behind the wall, every one armed. The rattle of their weapons was not as loud as the impacts. Shards of wood flew past Cerrin as she made for the nearest tree. Trantis was slow to seek cover. The Palanian's big frame saved Cerrin's life.

As bullets tore through him, she rolled under his collapsing body and came to rest behind the tree. Half-expecting the deadly hail of metal to come straight through, she found the trunk was thick enough to protect her.

A cry from her right. She turned in time to see Trantis hit a second time. The bullet blew half his head away and knocked him onto his back. She turned and saw two of the men running back toward the river. The Vitaari cut them down.

She looked left. Those who remained were cowering behind the trees like her: there seemed to be no realistic alternative.

Kannalin got to his feet, darted forward a few steps, and launched his spear at the cluster of Vitaari. By some miracle, he scrambled back into cover unharmed as bullets tore up the grass behind him.

Cerrin peered out and saw one of the Vitaari had picked up the spear. Another, bigger guard snatched it away and broke it across his knee.

Unlike the others, Stripe did not have a helmet on. He threw the two ends of the spear away, then retreated several steps and gestured for the others to lower their weapons. His fingers flicked across the controls, then he raised his rifle and aimed at the copse.

As Cerrin ducked down, a whole section of turf was torn away and the air burned hot. The next thing she knew she was lying on her side, staring at the ruined stump of the tree. The remains of the trunk landed, showering the ground with twigs and berries. That was when she realized she couldn't hear anything.

Her face felt warm. She touched it: it felt tender, like she had strayed too close to a fire.

A hand gripped her arm.

Kannalin helped her to her feet and dragged her behind the fallen tree. Two Palanian men quickly joined them. Kannalin's mouth was moving, but she couldn't hear what he was saying. She looked back. The others were lying on the ground, clothes and skin singed and torn. Only one of them was moving.

Kannalin grabbed her again and pointed in the air above the compound. She was astonished to see he was grinning. Then she saw why.

A combat shell was hovering above the compound, cannons aimed downward. Once the blooms of fire ended, it turned toward the river.

Cerrin had almost forgotten about the mysterious Palanian who planned to steal a shell and turn the Vitaari's weapon against them. *Thank the gods and ancients.*

As their faceless ally came over the top of the wall, the cannons bloomed again; these shots Cerrin could hear. Fire tore up the ground and the Vitaari fled. All except Stripe.

One of his compatriots had been hit: the guard dropped his weapon and flailed around like a man in the dark. As the combat shell kept firing, Stripe darted behind the injured Vitaari and pulled him down on top of him.

Cerrin's hearing was returning. As she, Kannalin, and others got to their feet, she heard the whimpering of a man lying a few yards behind her. His throat was a ragged mess of flesh from which blood was bubbling.

She heard cries from the Vitaari as the shell continued firing. Two more fell, then another.

Kannalin cursed. Cerrin realized he and the other two men were watching the shell. The machine was shuddering as impacts struck its underside and rear. Then she saw Stripe, kneeling beside his dead compatriot, firing at a range of no more than twenty yards.

"Move, man!" yelled Kannalin.

Sparks flew from the shell, then a piece of it fell to the ground. The vehicle swayed one way, then the other, then tipped forward.

The two Palanian men charged, leaping the branches of the fallen tree. They ran across the slope toward Stripe, each holding a spear.

Stripe saw them late, but in time. The first man was blown clean off his feet by a shot to the chest. A puff of blood flew up as the second Palanian was hit in the head. He careened to the ground and slid to a halt only a yard or two from Stripe.

Without a moment's hesitation, the Vitaari turned the gun on the shell once again. More fragments of metal were blown off the vehicle as it veered away, just catching the high branches of the trees on the island. It lurched down again—hovered for a moment while the jets blew into the water—then dropped straight into the river.

Stripe gave a jubilant roar and held his weapon in the air.

Before Cerrin could stop him, Kannalin was already off and running. "No!" Her voice sounded distant and weak.

Stripe turned his weapon on his new target. He fired a brief burst but Kannalin threw himself to one side, then into a neat roll. The Echobe warrior sprang instantly to his feet and kept going. Stripe re-adjusted but did not fire again. He looked down at his gun, then pressed something.

It's empty.

Though she was unarmed, Cerrin ran.

So did Kannalin, bolting straight at the Vitaari. Stripe plucked another magazine from his belt.

Cerrin made sure she ran past the two dead Palanians. She bent down and took a spear from one and a knife from the other. She pulled the blade out and kept running.

Kannalin drew back his spear and charged.

Realizing he was out of time, Stripe dropped the magazine and awaited his foe. Kannalin drove the spear at the Vitaari's neck.

It almost seemed Stripe would not react, but at the last moment he moved with lightning speed. Using the weapon like a club, he swatted Kannalin away, striking him on the shoulder and knocking him into the air. He hit the grass ten feet away.

Cerrin saw the familiar smile.

"Ah, Longlegs. I'm going to enjoy this!"

Cerrin had the knife in her left hand, the spear in the right. At ten feet, she threw.

Stripe used the rifle again and timed his swing to perfection, batting the projectile away.

Cerrin was almost on top of him.

She leaped, moving both hands to the hilt of the knife. Stripe's arms were still across his body from the swing. His smirk faded as he realized he couldn't get them back in time to defend himself.

With her loudest battle cry, Cerrin buried the blade between the Vitaari's eyes. The knife stuck there and she held on, one scrabbling foot lodging itself in Stripe's belt. The black eyes both seemed to turn toward her, then the great frame toppled backwards. As the Vitaari hit the ground, Cerrin rolled away.

Lying on her back, chest heaving up and down, she looked at the hilt sticking up out of the silvery flesh and the black blood rolling down the tattooed cheek.

"Not as much as I will."

She heard a groan behind her. Kannalin was coughing and seemed unable to move.

"Need a hand?" Cerrin looked up and saw Esteann standing over her, together with three of her Palanian friends. Torrin was with them too. All five were soaked.

"Reckoned we couldn't just leave you," said Esteann. "Not after you got us all out."

Cerrin stood. "Help him."

As Torrin and the others hurried over to Kannalin, Esteann pointed down at the river. Only the top and the two hands of the shell could still be seen above the water.

"It's sinking. Looks like he's alive but he can't get out."

Cerrin wrenched the knife out of Stripe's head and wiped it on the grass. Beyond Kannalin, she could see a robed administrator at the gate, watching them. In the compound, at least five separate fires were still alight. The tower had disappeared.

"Collect all the weapons and ammunition you can carry. I'll see you on the other side."

She ran down the slope.

Sonus had never liked water. And having achieved more than he'd ever dared hoped for on this day, he thought he deserved a little more than to drown in here alone.

The shell seemed to be dead. There wasn't a single display on or even a light. And if there was a manual override on the cockpit door, he couldn't find it. Outside, water was now lapping at the window. Inside, it was up to his chest.

He had managed to detach the belts holding him in place, but nothing else really mattered unless he could get the door open. He might have ripped away a piece of metal and tried to pry the lock, but he simply didn't have the strength. The second crash landing had been less unpleasant than the first, but the base of his spine was now nothing more than a ball of pain.

When the water reached his neck, he realized he was actually swimming. He at least had an opportunity to clean the vomit off his overalls, which he did to keep himself occupied if nothing else. Some plant was stuck to the window, which was now fully submerged. Beyond he could see only the sky. It was going to be a nice day.

I don't want to die like this.

A shape landed on the shell with a thud. When he spied arms and legs, he realized the shape was a woman. A dark Echobe woman with long black hair wearing a filthy pair of overalls. Upon her cheek was a thin red scar. Clamped in her teeth was a large knife.

Hands planted on the window, she peered down at him.

Sonus didn't know what to do.

The woman took the knife from her mouth and jabbed it into the side of the door with the lock. Though Sonus appreciated her help, there didn't seem to be a great deal of thought behind her efforts. He heard the blade sliding and stabbing and scraping at the metal, but to no avail.

Sonus suddenly heard a hissing sound and saw one end of a thin hose fly up, liquid shooting from it. The woman slid off the door. Sonus tried to push it up. There was some give in it now, despite the weight of the water. It began to move. He saw the woman's fingers on the edge, and their combined efforts finally did the job: as water poured in, the door sprang open.

Now the shell sank quickly. Sonus let the water take him. He floated up to the surface to find the woman bobbing next to him.

"Can you swim?"

He nodded.

"This way," said the woman, powering away toward the bank, cutting a path through the largest water lilies Sonus had ever seen.

He followed at about a third of her speed and was surprised to find his back actually felt better in the cold water. By the time he reached the far bank, another group had joined the woman, most carrying Vitaari weapons. They were a mix of Echobe and Palanian and had clearly just left the water themselves. One man—a large, muscular fellow—looked rather dazed.

The woman exchanged a look with another, who took the lead and pushed her way through the dense bushes. The others followed.

Sonus glanced back across the river. Several trails of smoke were reaching high into the sky.

When he looked back, the woman had gone. He struggled on through the bushes, catching only glimpses of the others ahead until he finally caught up with them. He straightened and winced as the pain in his back returned.

The woman who'd rescued him tucked her knife into her belt. Only now did he notice how tall she was.

"Thank you," he said.

She scraped her wet hair back over her head and looked him up and down. "What's your name?"

"Sonus."

"You need to move faster, Sonus."

Ehsan and Shakil Ahmad simply love the art of storytelling. It's a passion they've shared since their childhood in New York City, the first-generation American children of immigrants from Pakistan.

Today, the brothers are back in the city of their birth, working for separate tech startup companies while collaborating on novels and screenplays.

Ehsan and his wife welcomed their first child into the world in 2018.

Made in the USA
Middletown, DE
02 May 2019